THE *UH-OH* TO *A-HA* MOMENT

Some people spend their whole lives searching for it. The answer. The truth. The explanation behind that face in the mirror. I found it, and I didn't have to wait until crow's feet and middle age snuck up on me. I guess you could say the answer found *me,* in a place I never thought to look. *Inside.*

Not inside my head, or even my heart, though they were inexplicably involved in my journey of self-discovery. You have been inside this place, too, the beginning of all beginnings, of your beginning. I could never grasp my purpose here until I was on the other end of it, when a spark of life ignited within me.

The Stork Reality

MALENA LOTT

Making it

For Rod Lott.
My co-creator in the true-life
stork reality three times over.

MAKING IT®

June 2006

Published by

Dorchester Publishing Co., Inc.
200 Madison Avenue
New York, NY 10016

ISBN 0-8439-5725-5

The name "Making It" and its logo are trademarks of Dorchester Publishing Co., Inc.

Printed in the United States of America.

ACKNOWLEDGMENTS

I offer tremendous appreciation for the following people who helped in this labor of love:

Natasha Kern, my literary agent, who believed in the book in the early gestation period and stayed with me during the hard labor of many, many revisions.

Leah Hultenschmidt, my editor at Dorchester Publishing, for falling in love with my "baby" enough to bring her to life and show her off to the world.

My treasured girlfriends for listening, sharing baby stories and supporting me: Tina McGarry, Jennifer Schwabe, Tiffany Wilken, Vi Le, Ali Clark, Tina Bouse, Amanda Otsuka and Cynthia Dutton. My mother-in-law, Sheryl, a superstar mom and grandma.

My grandparents Evans and Zola Brown, for raising me and supporting my love of reading and writing at an early age.

My children, Harrison, Audrey and Owen, who fill me up and always give me something to smile about. This book would not have been as authentic without you.

And finally, my husband, Rod Lott, best friend, first editor, amazing father and greatest love of my life. I am eternally thankful for you.

The Stork Reality

MONTH ONE

A Pea in the Pod

CHAPTER 1

It began as a simple worry, one day creeping into the next with no sign of the usual aches and pains that signaled my natural cycle as a vibrant adult woman. On about the third day or so, worry morphed into fear that I had fretted my period clear away, contracted some terrible disease that killed my cycle—or, worse, been knocked up.

A thunderstorm punctuated the drama. Despite the downpour, I forced myself to go where I had never gone before: back to the far corner of the neighborhood drug store, past an assortment of condoms promising more pleasure, more lubrication and more colors; past feminine hygiene products promising to make me "feel fresh again," to the rows of neatly hanging pregnancy tests. Thunder cracked overhead, rain hammered the roof. Flashes of lightning illuminated the store. The smell of plastic and medicine and the blare of cheesy pop music made me dizzy. I reached for the ledge for support, sending boxes of stacked tests tumbling to the ground. The models on the boxes stared up at me from the floor. Four brands, four different models, all with the same expression—not elation, not panic, just solemn wonder. They had each tried to capture that point of not knowing, the moment between singular existence and motherhood. They were all me.

The burly pharmacist, scooping pills onto his metal tray, peered at me with interest but didn't offer assistance. Sure, he was fine with the aisles containing powder for nasty athlete's foot, diapers for incontinence, even creams for jock itch, but all things in aisle G made the man squirm and turn away. He would have nothing to do with me, fumbling with boxes claiming ninety-nine percent accuracy. The pharmacist likewise ignored the pimple-faced teenager staring hopefully at the condoms. Assuredly, the young man snatched one, turned to me with a raised brow, and strutted toward the checkout line. I had neither hope nor confidence about what my purchase would bring.

Still lightheaded, I scanned the back of a box. Urine sample. Results in less than five minutes. One line meant I would continue a chaotic career-driven existence. Two lines meant I would need to reevaluate my place in the universe. Baby on board.

Perspiring profusely, I hastily paid for the test and a pack of Trident and tramped outside into the early spring storm, rain pelting my face like little stinging whips. I sped the next two blocks to our home in Rolling Hills, a new development outside Dallas still full of carpenters and architects finishing houses for the wealthy folks who would reside there.

On the drive home, crazy questions popped into my head like fizzy champagne bubbles: *Who am I? Why is this happening to me? Why do Jake and I have sex so much? How could the Pill fail me? Will I be a good mommy? Do I even want children? Will Jake kill me for this?* Until I bought that test, I had accepted the person I had become, excess baggage and all.

If asked, "Do you work to live or live to work?" I'd concede the latter. Work, sex, travel—in that order. Work and play blended in perfect harmony. First-class travel! Expense account! Pottery Barn–style corner office! I relished my drive home, gazing at the billboards my ad team had designed and spotting slogans and logos we'd dreamt up. I knew it was surprising to actually *like* my job as the creative director at Ace Advertising and not want to be something else, but I enjoyed the macho benefits of the career world. And so did my husband, a prestigious lawyer at a pricey law firm. Jake and I both had an unrelenting drive to succeed.

I punched the garage-door opener and watched the large hunk of steel glide slowly upwards. I screeched into the garage, jammed the gearshift into park, scooped up the brown plastic bag and made a beeline for the master bathroom. I threw off my wet jacket and pulled my hair off my face into a hair clip. Patient I was not, never had been. I chalked it up to one of those only-child traits. Without brothers or sisters, I never had to wait around for anything, take my turn or share, for God's sake. Then again, I was twenty-eight, not six.

I checked my watch. My lunch hour was officially half over. How time flies when you're going zonkers with a pregnancy scare. Really, I didn't know why I was so paranoid. It was probably stress taking its toll on my more feminine side. Well, I really had to pee anyway, so it wouldn't be a problem.

Good thing the box only asked for four drops. That's about all that made it into the supplied cup.

Thunder continued to rumble outside as I dropped my urine onto the test panel and awaited the results. Three minutes tops, it said, earlier if positive. Afraid my stern gaze would screw up the results, I paced the house, picking up as I went along—a half-finished can of Diet Coke (mine), pretzel wrapper (Jake's), boxers and underwear on the living room floor (impromptu romp the night before). I rearranged the towels and put new soap out—the fruity kind my husband hated—and flossed my teeth. In the mirror, I caught sight of the test. It appeared to be ... two lines. I peered closer into the mirror. A little blurry, but ... I turned my head slowly away from the mirror and studied the test. Two distinct cotton candy-pink lines, no doubt about it. "Oh, shit, shit, shit," I mumbled. "Shit, shit, shit."

I stepped out of the room, suddenly lost, unsure where to turn or what to do.

I ran back to the master bathroom where The Test stood mocking my independence. *Could this be true? Could I actually be a mother?*

Something had to be done with The Test. I couldn't have Jake just stumble upon it when he got home. I threw it in my underwear drawer, then took it out and placed it in the medicine cabinet. Then I snagged it and hid it in my walk-in closet on the highest shelf. Then I took it down and set it under my vanity table. Then retrieved it and perched it on the TV. Then snatched it and stuffed it underneath my pillow. Still not satisfied, I looked around the room and saw dependable rag doll Molly on my bedside table.

Molly had been my confidante since I was six, when I begged my mother to let me take her out of her closet so I could play with her. More than fifty years old, Molly had red yarn hair—most of it lost a generation before—and wore a stained blue and red plaid dress with only half of the lace cuff. Molly had just one arm and one eye, a shiny black button, and a red-thread mouth, her expression one stitch short of a smile. I knew the doll was the only gift my mother had ever gotten from her mother. I had never known my Grandma Helen, so Molly meant something sacred to both my mother and me. Molly had been through more tragedy than her stitches could bear. Her cotton held decades of secrets—three generations of secrets. "Hold this for me, Molls." I gave her yet another secret, tucking the pregnancy test in Molly's dress on her lap. I swore I'd tell Jake that night when we were in bed.

Still, I doubted what had really happened. Had I made an error? All those silly commercials with weepy women say mistakes are due to human error. But I followed the damn instructions to a T and that test detected the HCG hormone that made those two lines materialize like magic. Searching for something to discount the results, I suppose, I went to my home office, logged on to the Internet, and did a search for pregnancy. Several hundred sites devoted to pregnancy!

I picked one at random and launched into what could only be described as a different world. Pictures of round women with large bosoms and even larger bellies, smiling and hugging themselves, greeted me. Chubby babies covered the page leading me to various links. My head began to spin again. I told myself I could have the flu. *It was the damn storm, that's all. It couldn't be morning sickness.*

My heart sank as I read that the pregnancy test could be positive even one day after a missed period. Next I clicked on "Week by Week" and typed in "5 weeks." Through teary eyes, I read.

> **Week 5: How your baby's growing:** *The ball of cells dividing in your uterus is now officially an embryo, about the size of a seed. The next five weeks are especially critical to your baby's development. The placenta and umbilical cord, which deliver nourishment and oxygen to the baby, are already functioning.*

What? Already *functioning?* Seeing it right there on my screen made it seem almost *possible.* Not ready to give in, I shuffled through my bathroom wastebasket to find the box and scan for an expiration date. Surely the test had malfunctioned on me. *March,* it read. *March! That's this month! Yippee! It's expired, and I'm safe!*

2010, it said right next to it. Oh.

I want my mommy.

I shoved the box back into the trash and moped to the kitchen in a zombie-like trance. Maybe if I wished hard enough for my period to come, sheer concentration would open the floodgates. During the drive to the office I sent vibes to my loins. A couple of times I thought I felt cramps. That afternoon I escaped to the bathroom five times to check my underwear for a sign from Menses. Each time, nothing. Funny, I had hated my period until I didn't have one.

Chapter 2

My creative meetings that afternoon were a joke. I slumped in the leather chair and half-listened to a know-it-all account executive drone on about a promotion. "They want to show the crispness of their clothes compared to the competitors," Ted explained.

"Ted, they sell polyester pantsuits, for God's sake," I said without thinking.

"They are polyester *blend*," he retorted. "I'll excuse that remark and go on to some bigger news," he said. "Studio Apparel, Inc. will soon have a baby clothes line. Better than anything on the market. And *high quality*, Taylor," he said, sneering in my direction.

For a second, I thought he was staring at me because he *knew*. Like he sensed it or something. We had little time to create a campaign and I, an alien to the smallest of humans, would have to pretend I knew all about babies and mothers. Exaggeration I was used to, that's what advertising is all about; but this just felt *wrong*. I wanted to raise my hand and object, ask for another beer campaign, a boring car dealer campaign even, just not a baby clothes campaign. The next few months I would be absolutely bathed in baby research, baby models, baby products. The timing of the whole thing was eerie.

After the meeting, my associate creative director sauntered into my office. His usual smirk turned into a scowl, his mouth pursed in disgust. "What *happened* to you? You look like shit."

I rolled my eyes. "Thanks a lot. I think I may be coming down with something." I grabbed for a Kleenex and wiped at my non-runny nose. "Am I not *allowed* to have a bad day? To look like hell once in awhile?"

"Settle down, pussycat." He rolled his eyes at my drama. "It's Friday, for God's sake. Besides, you were PMSing last week, so you don't have an excuse."

"I try not to think how creepy it is you know my cycle." I grabbed plain M&Ms from my candy dish and pelted him with them.

"If there's one thing I know, it's women," he said with a wink, trying to catch M&Ms in his mouth. "Besides, your mood is more predictable than the moon's cycle. Week one and two relatively normal. Week three psycho-semantic and week four bloated and neurotic." Allen tossed a piece of candy back at me. "Can't deny it, can you?"

I cupped my hands over my bloated stomach, wishing I'd worn an elastic waistband to work, even though I didn't own any. "Take your perfect hair and your perfect complexion and get back to work. I'm sure you have some runt research you need to be doing."

Allen clasped his hands together. "Oh, this will be a fun one. You *do know* what a baby is, don't you, Tay?"

"Yeah. Yeah. I've seen them on TV. Pampers commercials or something." I popped a few candies in my mouth, then zinged one off Allen's forehead. "I'm surprised you haven't made a few on your many conquests over the years."

"Not that I know of, lady," he said. "Hell, who has time to raise a kid with our shitty hours? I barely make it to the bars before ten P.M."

"How do the ladies wait so long? Poor things." Allen's

womanizing was legendary around the office. After he'd gone through account service (where the cute girls worked), broadcast production (where the loose girls worked) and traffic (where the just-out-of-college girls worked), he'd started preying on the college interns, until the boss deemed them off limits. Still, Allen was so damn charming that even his flings still had a thing for him, which really pissed off all the other men in the office. They hated Allen for being able to get away with treating girls like shit and come off like a prince.

Allen left, but I didn't want the company of my thoughts, either. The storm hadn't let up, and the gray skies only darkened my mood.

That night after the rain subsided, I took a different route home to see a newly lit outdoor board my team had developed for Bowser's Brewery, the hottest after-work hangout for professionals. I'd been at ease with that campaign because it was a part of me—the social scene with friends after work, the life of the party every Thursday evening during happy hour. My creative team excelled at social mingling. My popularity grew with each martini and trip to the karaoke mic. That led me to count the number of times I'd been there while unknowingly pregnant.

Four. That's how many times I'd been semi-drunk to drunk since my last period. Not good. I envisioned Dr. Creighton, my ob-gyn, shaking his head in disapproval. Well, nothing I could do about it but worry for the next eight months.

I tapped my squared red nails on the steering wheel. Jake would probably be tired from a long day in court. As I wheeled into the garage for the second time that day, a conversation we had some months before came back to me. Lorna, his mother, had told him one of his cousins was having her first child and none-too-casually dropped the suggestion that we get started. After all, we'd been married three years, together eight, and it would "stabilize" me to have a child. Lorna believed my parents' dying when I was a teenager had traumatized me to the point of emotional instability, leaving me unable to get close to them as a result. Jake told her we were young and not to worry.

What he said to me later was, "Just what is the point of having children, anyway? It's usually a selfish act on the part of the parents. Carrying on your genes for bragging rights for the next fifty years." Not exactly paternal enthusiasm.

I didn't disagree, but argued anyway. "What if it's just because you want a family?"

"Are you saying a husband and wife aren't a family?" Jake raised his eyebrows; perfect for his profession. He had me cornered.

"Sweetheart," I'd said, grabbing him around his waist. "Of course, we're a family. We don't need kids to complete us." And I meant it.

"Exactly. I will never push you into having children. Our lives are fulfilling enough without them," he said. "Vacations, friends, our jobs, each other."

Most women would be horrified at that. I breathed a sigh of relief. Unlike a lot of married couples, Jake and I never shared fantasies about a white picket fence and kids playing in the front yard. My dream of a perfect family died along with my parents. Perfect families were the stuff of fairy tales, and they ended after the last page was turned.

The phone rang as I entered the house. I rushed to get it, stumbling from my platform heels and lunging over the breakfast bar.

"Hey, Taylor, bad news."

You're not the only one. "Hey, Jackie. Don't tell me you guys can't make it tomorrow," I whined.

"Afraid so," she said, the voice of a child screaming in the background.

"Ashlynn's come down with something. Fever, vomiting—"

"I get the picture. I think I may be getting sick, too."

Maybe the flu *was* going around. I felt my forehead, a little hot perhaps. Jackie droned on about Ashlynn's condition as if I had a clue about childhood illnesses, or *anything* having to do with kids, actually. A few of our friends had children, but not the majority, and those weren't the friends we socialized with most, by happenstance and choice. I liked kids okay (I didn't go gaga), but discussion about the stresses of tantrums and finding a good pre-school left me with a blank stare.

I couldn't relate, never being around kids much growing up, no siblings and only three feisty boy cousins as the standard for comparison. My cousins were such hellions that I didn't start babysitting to earn money in junior high like my girlfriends. I opted instead to deliver newspapers on my bike, a much less demanding job than caring for children. Better exercise, too, wheeling around town in my shocking blue three-speed. As for my mommy friends, they couldn't have cared less about my stories from the office most of the time. Except for the sex gossip, of course.

"I'm telling you, you and Jake are so lucky to have your weekends free," Jackie said.

"Well, Jake's got that marathon in the morning," I started, then decided, *screw it*. Our friends who were parents thought because we didn't have kids, we didn't have lives. We had commitments, jobs, mortgage, and clubs. But then maybe we *did* have it easy.

When I saw young mothers out with their expensive jogger strollers trying to take off that extra baby fat they gained during pregnancy, I felt relieved to be thin and fit, not tied down to anything. Jake didn't tie me down; we had our own free time, did our own thing. I played bridge with my girlfriends once a month, and Jake and I hiked, biked, ran or traveled every weekend.

Not to say I didn't have a twinge of admiration for those women with the jogging strollers and my mommy friends. Juggling schedules and chauffeuring to dance lessons, soccer games and the like. Did their husbands help out? Some of the mommies in our neighborhood had nannies, but what about when the nannies went home? Did these women have lives of their own? Could they still excel at work with so much to do at home? *Could I?*

Each thought sunk me deeper into depression. I couldn't help but think of everything that I would have to give up if I were really pregnant. The happy hours after work. Bridge with the girls—drinking and smoking cigars. The spontaneous vacations Jake surprised me with. The weeklong trips to Jake's parents' beach house. God, Jake loved me in my bikini. No more sex. No, this was definitely not good news. And it was my turn to give Jake a little surprise.

CHAPTER 3

Jake entered the house whistling that evening, a sure sign his day in court had gone well. I didn't know the tune immediately—Jake had never been one to whistle in key—but a few bars later I recognized his efforts as "I'm in the Mood for Love."

Great. He's horny. Winning a lawsuit improved his libido, which didn't need improving to begin with. When he was *really* in the mood, he brought out my sexiest lingerie—he preferred the black sheer Victoria's Secret number—and his silk boxers were off in a flash. That's how I got into this mess in the first place.

That night he threw down his keys on the kitchen counter, loosened his tie, and gave me *the look*. And just in case I hadn't caught on, he flipped the stereo on to romantic lounge music and poured martinis as if he were some bachelor from the 1950s. Jake took a swig of his martini, while I ate the olive.

Like clockwork, Jake spun me around and placed a deep kiss on my mouth, the taste of vodka on his tongue. Not a "Hi-honey-I'm-home-kiss," but a tongue-plunging, take-me-to-bed-or-lose-me-forever kiss. I forgot all my troubles, all about those two lines on the cardboard test.

I barely got out, "So I take it your day went well," before my silk shirt was on the floor, my skirt soon to follow. Thankful I'd worn matching panties and bra that day, I surrendered to Jake as he kissed my neck, lingering especially long on the back just under my hairline, a real weak point for me.

"You can say that, baby," Jake whispered. "I had a fucking *great* day. I won the case *and* I got promoted to junior partner."

"Oh, my God," I said. He got this promotion a year sooner than we'd expected. Apparently we were both on the fast-track.

"Isn't it great?" he moaned. "God, I love your body," he said, dropping to his knees and kissing my flat stomach.

Yes, that kiss reminded me of my troubles, but great sex was worth postponing the news. A few more kisses and that wasn't hard to do. Not only did we have traveling sex that evening (living room couch, his office desk, floor of the master bedroom, and, finally, the shower), but we quite possibly had the best and biggest simultaneous orgasms of our marriage. An accomplishment few and far between. As we lay in bed, still wet from the lukewarm shower, I stared at his chest, the rise and fall of his breath.

"You're amazing." He kissed the small mole on my right shoulder.

"Oh, yeah?" I turned my bare body to face him. "You're not so bad yourself, Mr. Montgomery."

Jake, still naked and glistening, softly rubbed my belly. "Well," he said, propping his head up on his hand. "I just got a twenty thousand-dollar raise today, and I have the most gorgeous wife on the planet."

"In that order?" I teased.

"Of course the money is nice, but you—well, you know how I feel about you."

"Maybe I need reminding," I said. We joined together

again, only we made love slower, sweeter. I wanted to make myself remember that moment in case it wasn't like that again for some time.

The evening had quickly turned into night. We hadn't eaten dinner. Jake didn't bother dressing. He was fond of strolling through the house buck-naked, never mind if the blinds were up and the neighbors could see my well-built husband in all his glory.

From its hiding place under Molly's dress, The Test burned a hole in the back of my head, but I ignored it. I thought if I didn't see it, it didn't exist. Within minutes, Jake returned with a plateful of food—turkey and Swiss sandwiches, pretzels, strawberries and champagne. As we ate, he caught me up on the firm's latest gossip—who was sleeping with whom and who was having extramarital affairs. A part of me rationalized the fact that he discussed the affairs with me was proof he never cheated. In the marble-laden law firm, available and gorgeous girls abounded, girls seeking rich lovers and rich husbands. Some of these women were prettier and smarter than I could hope to be. Often I thought the world was full of women much better suited for Jake than I.

Holding on to him was my greatest challenge.

"Honey, I need to tell you something," I said.

Jake handed me an envelope. "Me first. I've been waiting to give you this all night." With childlike enthusiasm, I tore open the envelope. Two first-class tickets to Hawaii, departing in three weeks.

"Aloha!" Jake said and kissed my forehead.

"Honey, this is great! I've always wanted to go there, but—"

"Ah! Ah! I already spoke to Allen, and he said that week is fine. I know you just got some big baby clothes campaign, but Allen assured me you could take five days for a romantic get-away."

Fine laugh lines framed Jake's piercing gray eyes. I wanted to grow old with him. No matter how much I wanted to tell him I'd rather not leave town—or why—I couldn't say no to that face or spoil that beautiful night.

"Of course I'll go, honey," I said. "And three weeks will give me just enough time to get ready."

"That's more like it, Taylor." He put the tray of food on the floor. "Now, what did you want to tell me?"

My eyes teared up. "That I could really use a vacation."

"That's what I thought," he said, and pulled me down on the bed, pressing his warm body against mine. He kissed me lightly, suckling my skin as his mouth traveled down my chest, stomach, hips and inner thighs.

Ecstasy beat out my sensible side. I was certain that Jake would not make love to me the same way after he knew. I would wait until a better time, any time other than that night to tell him about the baby.

Again I groaned with pleasure and let my worries slip away as Jake took me to that magical place where lovers live.

MONTH TWO

Womb Service

CHAPTER 4

Week 8: Technically your baby is still considered an embryo. He has something of a small tail, which will vanish in the next few weeks. The heart and brain are becoming more complicated, the eyelids are forming, the nose is present, and the arms bend at the elbows.

My period never came. I carried the secret with me into the next month of the pregnancy, never finding the right moment to tell Jake our life together had changed. In a way, keeping it a secret from everyone helped me hide it from myself. Even steeped in baby research, I denied I had any connection to the material, preferring to remain outside the enigma of motherhood. I wanted to be okay with it before anyone else knew.

The April morning breeze blew into my office window, dissipating the fumes of the mounting spray we used for pasting ads on matte board. After an hour of poring over magazine ads of baby clothes on the floor of my office, I gave in.

"Allen, what if your life turns out different than you planned?"

Allen stopped mid-spray and faced me. "Tay, it's too early in the day for existential conversation. I know this isn't your idea of a killer project, but—"

"No, I'm not complaining about the campaign. It's just . . ."

Allen stuck out his bottom lip and baby-talked. "Is Taylor reevaluating her place in the universe? Not feeling like an advertising princess today?"

"I'm serious, Al."

Shuffling past the piles of magazines, Allen sat across from me and took my hands in his. "You're not yourself, are you? Did you switch hair gel and not tell me?"

I began to cry. "No, Al. We still use the same hair product."

"Then what's up?"

"Okay. I think I'm pregnant and I haven't told Jake."

"Holy shit, *mamasita*." Allen looked at me as if I'd told him I'd just grown a third boob. "That's a bigger deal than hair gel."

I hugged Allen as his ultra-stiff, light-socket hair scratched my face.

He leaned back and stared at me with his cool gaze. "What do you mean by 'think' you're pregnant?"

"Two pregnancy tests and three weeks late say that I am," I said. "But I haven't gone to the doctor yet."

"You mean you couldn't squeeze in a doctor's appointment during your eighty-hour work week? Come on, lazy bones."

"Exactly. That and maybe I'm a little afraid to have it officially confirmed." I began chewing a nail when Allen slapped it away from my mouth.

"So you're not exactly maternal material. Doesn't mean you're going to suck at it."

"Oh, now I feel tons better! Why the hell am I talking to you about this? I haven't even told my girlfriends yet."

"Don't play dumb with me, Tay. It's because I can keep a secret, unlike your gossiping gal pals. You obviously aren't ready for the world to know. You're the antithesis of June Cleaver, babe. Nothing wrong with that. Your mommy friends are the golden stroller crowd." Allen leaned back, looking quite proud of himself.

"Since when have you paid so much attention to my girlfriends?"

Allen rolled his eyes. "Your girlfriends are hot, Taylor. Even the mommy ones. Nothing wrong with being a hot mama, either."

I put my hands over my ears. "Okay, I can't talk about this anymore. I think—no, I *know* that I must tell Jake tonight. So what if he didn't want kids for ten more years, if ever? He's going to get one and he's just going to have to deal with it."

"And what about you? Are *you* going to deal with it?"

I grabbed a stack of black and white baby glossies from the floor. "I don't have a choice, do I?"

"Oh, Taylor. Is that a tear? I'm sorry. I didn't mean to upset you."

"It's not you. It's the hormones. Okay, it's you *and* the hormones. See, I suck at being a mother already. I can't even make a proper announcement."

Allen wiped away my tears. "I bet you've been sitting here all day wondering if your baby is going to look like one of these darlings," he said.

"Cuter," I said. "Even cuter."

"That's more like it. Guess you won't be getting smashed with me anymore, huh?"

"How does everything end up being about you?"

"I feel so special being the first to know. You could always tell Jake the big news in Hawaii after he's had a few frozen daiquiris. Big news is always easier to take when inebriated. That's normally how I break up with my girlfriends. But then sometime it backfires and they go hysterical and throw a frozen margarita in my face."

I shook my head. "Not helping, Allen."

"I've spent my reproductive years avoiding making little critters. Thank God condoms haven't failed me yet. I don't know jack about it. But I could can the obnoxious anecdotes that make you feel even worse than you already do."

"Good idea, Allen. Splendid idea in fact."

CHAPTER 5

Three years earlier, Dr. Creighton and three other ob-gyns had built a women's hospital in the suburbs. With its modern architecture and sleek statuettes of naked women and babies, the hospital was a haven for upper-class women throughout the city. When the hospital hosted its grand opening a year earlier—which my pregnant friend Amy had dragged me to—I had stuck my head in the exquisite birthing rooms and only half-listened to the nurse explain the luxuries of childbirth there. At the time, I thought I would only return for my annual physical, not as an expectant mother.

So that day as I walked the granite floors toward the elevators, I peered around the reception desks to the nursery, where, if I squinted, I could see four tiny, wrinkly newborns. The elevator doors swished open and I hesitated, then stepped in, figuring I shouldn't get emotional over those tiny things. I only *thought* I was pregnant. I pressed the button for the third floor, where Dr. Creighton's offices were located. An elevator ride never seemed so long.

When the doors opened to the third floor, my brain sent

a message to my legs to get off, but they didn't listen. An elderly woman, nearing eighty if I had to guess, eyed me with suspicion. Well, what did she have to worry about? *She* wasn't pregnant. At that moment, I would've gladly switched places with her. The elevator door began to close. I grabbed it with my hand and exited. The woman nodded her head at me and gave me a pursed smile.

The room was littered with women of all sorts and yellow and pink gerbera daisies that seemed a tad too happy for my liking. The women flipped through magazines, read the news headlines, and chatted on cell phones. I eyed the refreshment armoire and ached for a cup of coffee, but my stomach hadn't been acting normal, so I opted for water instead. Water and a store-bought sugar cookie. As I munched the bland confection, I overheard the nurses tittering about Dr. Creighton's new cologne. The nurses were as smitten over him as the patients were.

I glanced at my watch every minute or so, thinking much more than a minute had passed each time, until I grew so aggravated that I removed it and stuffed it in my purse. I had a ten o'clock meeting with Studio Apparel I absolutely couldn't miss, but I despised clock-watchers. No one in the room cared that I had a meeting to go to, and no one else seemed to be checking her watch. *Selfish.* There I was, already complaining about how the baby would get in the way of my work. The start of a great mental battle.

"Good morning, Ms. Montgomery," said an elderly nurse named Betty. "Go right on in." She pointed to an exam room.

As frightened as a teenage girl might be in the same situation, I eased back in the cushy chair and took in the decor; the deep eggplant-colored walls were covered with brass picture frames of newborns and exhausted, overjoyed-looking mothers. A stone vase full of fresh flowers sat on the counter next to a rack of sample birth control pills. *You failed me.* The intoxicating charm of the place covered the underlying reality that this was a place where women were poked, prodded, examined, and treated. A pill with a candy coating.

Nurse Betty, with all her grandmotherly good looks, returned, a chart in hand. "Let's weigh you, shall we?"

I exhaled, hoping that would send a few pounds of worry out of my mouth, then stepped on the scale. The nurse fiddled with the scale, inching it further and further right until the bar balanced. *What?* Five more pounds since my annual three months earlier. Was it the muffins Allen brought to work? A wave of nausea coursed through my body with a rush of heat.

"I'm sorry." I ran to the lavatory, where I slammed to the ceramic floor, hugged the bowl and threw up. "Stupid, stupid," I muttered to myself. Stupid for believing it was the flu, stupid for getting pregnant, and stupider still for not telling Jake.

The nurse tapped on the door and hollered, "Go ahead and get a urine sample, dear." I looked up at the clear plastic cups and wept. I didn't want to do any of it, to be there, to feel so alone.

Angry pregnant women with full bladders shot me evil looks when I finally left the bathroom. Betty hustled me back to the exam room. She carried a wicker basket of medical paraphernalia: a syringe, fluffy cotton balls, and several brochures on the first trimester. "Morning sickness got you pretty bad, huh?"

"Not really." The whole week before that I had told myself it was food poisoning, an upset stomach, work stress—anything *but* morning sickness.

"I don't know why they call it morning sickness, 'cause you can be sick any time of the day—or all day. I can get you a seasickness band. Works for a lot of women." Betty grabbed my chart. "When was the first day of your last period?"

"Ah, uh . . . March fourteenth."

"Ooh," Betty said, widening her eyes, "that means a Christmas baby for sure. Or perhaps a New Year's baby. You know, the first New Year's baby here gets more free things than at the very best baby shower. Why, Toys 'R' Us is giving a five hundred-dollar gift certificate and Studio Apparel already called to donate a layette."

That cinched the deal. I mean, what were the chances I would get the baby clothes account the same day that a pregnancy test told me I was expecting, and the nurse was convinced I carried the great symbol of the New Year?

"Hey, there, Taylor," Dr. Creighton said as he entered the room, his cologne as delicious as his nurses claimed. "You're looking as good as ever." (I *knew* he had a crush on me.)

Dr. Creighton reminded me of a Ken doll with a stethoscope. My husband was lawyer-handsome, but Dr. Creighton was doctor-gorgeous, a totally different level. It was almost worth having my cervix poked at each year.

As I sat there looking at the gleaming green eyes and wavy blond hair, I dreamed about Surfer Ken with his tanned plastic muscles and neon green swim shorts, ready to hop into that snazzy red Camaro and pick up Barbie for their romp at the beach. Barbie would of course be Dr. Creighton's wife, Mrs. Tall-Skinny-Ex-Miss America—gorgeous *and* smart. Hated her. When I saw the photo of them with two perfect-looking, blond-haired, blue-eyed children, I was shocked by a wave of envy. A boy and a girl, of course—the son with his father's rugged good looks and the daughter with her mother's ringlets of curls. I wasn't jealous of the fact that they had children as much as that the doctor and his wife were probably wonderful parents, which I doubted I could ever be.

"Hi, doc," I said in as flirtatious a manner as I could muster with a nauseous stomach. "Bet you didn't expect to see me for a while."

"Oh, that's okay, Taylor. We're going to be seeing a lot of each other these next eight months."

Tears sprung to my eyes. "It's true, then?"

"You're having a baby!" he said, and stuck out his hand for me to shake.

I didn't take his hand. I just looked at it, confused. In my mind, being pregnant had been just a notion, but hearing it from the doctor made it real.

"I'm sorry," Dr. Creighton said. "Are you unhappy with the news?"

"Oh, no, just . . . maybe. Wow. Well, uh, thanks for coming to tell me personally." Sweat beaded on my forehead. Dr. Creighton's noggin seemed to enlarge and bob to the right and to the left.

He paused. "Taylor, if you need to talk about options . . ."

"Options?" Again, it took a moment for his words to register. The look in his eyes told me what he meant, and the recognition hit me like a freight train. Not keeping the baby. Getting rid of the baby. That's what he meant by options.

The babies in the pictures on the walls became animated, kicking their legs, waving their arms. In front of Compassionate Ken, with his large hand comforting me and holding the hair out of my face, I threw up in the pink plastic trash can.

When I gained composure, I blabbed incoherently, "I've never thought of myself in that way. But now that it's me, and we weren't planning on a family anytime soon . . ."

Dr. Creighton put his hand on mine. "I can refer you to someone who can help you. Or if you just want to talk to someone."

"I don't think so. I just feel like a schoolgirl who forgot to use protection. I mean I'm on the Pill."

"Well, did you forget to take them?"

"Not once."

"Mixed it with other medication?"

I thought back. "I just take multivitamins, but I was sick a couple months ago."

"Did you take antibiotics?"

"Yeah. Sinus infection. Took them for a week or so."

The doctor cocked his head. "You know, antibiotics can decrease the effectiveness of birth control pills."

"Oh." I hung my head, the air stifling, and the eggplant walls closing in around me. His wife *was* smarter than I was. She would've known about those wicked antibiotics. "We never talked about raising a family. I just can't imagine—"

"Being a mother? Lots of first-time moms feel that way. You're not alone. It's normal to be scared."

Normal. I laughed, but choked on my tears. *If only.*

"I'm here to help in any way. I recommend you bring your husband in for the next appointment. You can hear the baby's heartbeat for the first time. That usually excites even the most hesitant parents."

With that, and the date of December 27 buzzing in my head, I left those plush offices with a free diaper bag full of samples and pregnancy information. I passed by the swollen-bellied women whose ranks I had suddenly joined. A drafted soldier, fresh-faced and wide-eyed with wonder and fear. My mission had only just begun. Eight months on a tour of duty into the complete unknown, and I was ill-prepared. Hell, I was ill, period. I had to throw up again in the restroom next to the elevator, and when I returned to go forth and conquer, a fellow soldier, further along than I, upon seeing my bag of maternal goodies, said, "Congratulations." I could not say thank you, for the words got stuck in the back of my throat where the fear had blocked my speech. I forced a smile.

The Christmas I had known all my life would be no more. The holly and decorations and fake Santas and parties and Salvation Army bell ringers and buying toys for less fortunate children and baking fudge would be the same, but I would be different. I would be about more than the fancy party dress and bringing the best wine and wrapping elegant gifts.

As if I were a part of a covert operation, I walked lightly, tiptoed almost, to the nursery and stood in amazement at the object of my mission—the little beings behind the glass, who were kicking, crying, new to the world. I put my hand on my stomach and felt a connection, a knowing that though I looked like just another pretty woman, inside me was a life . . . and I would be a mother.

CHAPTER 6

"Aloha!" Jake sang. He kissed me full on the mouth, then descended the steps of the plane. A postcard-pretty Hawaiian stewardess greeted us on the ground and placed a lei around Jake's neck. She smiled bashfully, and I wanted to hit her. Not because she flirted with my husband so much as for her tiny waist and bronzed skin and carefree life. I assumed because she lived on a magical island and stood in the sunshine greeting visitors all day, she had it easy. That day I barely made it through the ten-hour flight, the rough ride tossing my own carry-on passenger to and fro. Even with three trips to the loo to hurl, Jake was none the wiser.

He squeezed my hand, breathed in the hibiscus and salty breeze. "God, I can't wait to hit the beach, can you, honey?"

I nodded, trying to hold my own. The bed. A big, comfortable bathroom for puke space. *That's* what I was looking forward to.

There we were on the breathtaking island of Kauai for a five-day getaway full of biking and hiking and surfing and a whole bunch of other things I wouldn't be able to do. I had never felt so exhausted in my life. I read that during the first trimester, even if you were just sitting, your body was doing the equivalent of a long hike. Due to fatigue, I'd given up my morning runs two weeks earlier, but I still got up and got dressed in my jogging suit to carry off my deception. Eyes half-opened, I walked all the way to the kitchen to make myself some hot chocolate and click on the TV to a barely audible volume for twenty minutes until I could return to the bedroom, where Jake would be on the floor, huffing through his hundred sit-ups. I had actually come to enjoy the new ritual—watching my husband sculpt his body while mine became limp.

The absence of exercise began to show at the airport, as I slugged along behind my eager husband, too athletic for my liking at that point. "I can almost taste those piña coladas," he said.

"Uh-huh," I said, breathing heavily. A nice tall glass of orange juice, fortified with calcium, of course, was all I craved. That and a bag of Fritos. Jake could get sloshed on piña coladas and then I would tell him he'd be a daddy.

"You okay, honey?" Jake asked as I plopped on a chair in the baggage claim. "You look a little peakish."

"Hmmm." I'd never heard him use that word before to describe me. What he really meant was *fat*. I had noticed a certain roundness to my face appear, thanks to all those cinnamon rolls Allen brought me in the mornings and the cheese and peanut butter crackers that settled my stomach throughout the workday. The peanut butter had made a home on my ass, the cheese on my thighs.

"Just tired from the flight. Isn't that our bag?" It wasn't, but Jake was staring at me, studying me, so I had to throw him off. I wasn't the radiant wife he'd had just two months before. I was a plumping, basting, baby-making mortal.

The baggage finally appeared on the whirring belt, and I widened my eyes as if glue had been placed on my lids to hide the tiredness that plagued them. I wanted to become the vacationing sexpot wife my husband longed for.

"Do you like piña coladas?" Jake cheerily sang, as he wheeled our luggage to the rental car station where Jake had reserved a silver convertible. *Next time, it'll be a minivan.*

Ahhh. Buzzing around the island with the top down, sipping frozen, sappy drinks as the ocean tickled our toes was Jake's idea of vacation. It had *always* been that way. Sex and drinking, drinking and sex were the haphazard staple for our getaways. And all I needed was a sinus infection and an unceremonious quickie to get preggers and change Jake's idea of a vacation forever after. *Let him enjoy the convertible. Give him one last day as he had imagined.*

It hadn't been easy to keep "my condition" a secret. Missing out on happy hour two weeks in a row would have been a dead giveaway if it weren't for Allen making excuses for me, and for the pressures of the Studio Baby campaign. Truthfully, I lounged at home watching *Oprah* and crunching saltines, too tired to keep my eyes open, let alone write a decent slogan. Fortunately, Jake had been working so late he hadn't noticed how plum lazy I'd become.

As much as I wanted to confide in my coworkers, I also wanted to go on living the life I'd been leading. No woman at Ace Advertising had remained after she had a child. Ace employees joked that they lived at the agency, but to a mom, that much work isn't funny—and let's face it, not conducive to being a good mommy. Most women left while they were pregnant, because they were ostracized by the child-free, party crowd that dominated the agency. (Me being past president of said club.)

As for my closest friends, the eight bridge girls, would drown me with their baby advice and mommy talk my ears and heart weren't ready for. Never a great liar, I couldn't fake my way through. I'd have to come up with some way to avoid my favorite night of the month, at least until the truth revealed itself.

When Jennifer had called the week before to remind me of shrimp and white wine bridge night, I felt boorish declining. "May I ask why?" she inquired. After all, her excuses had to do with the calamities of her precocious one-year-old. What did I, motherless and free, possibly have more important than our girls' night?

"Work," I said dryly. "Got a big presentation the next morning and I'm just not prepared." I knew Jen was thinking, *And how is this different than the other dozen times you've had a presentation the next morning and still got wasted and had us pasting matte boards at 2 A.M.?* But she didn't. Maybe she sensed a mommy vibe from me and wanted to keep my little secret. "More shrimp for me," she said, before launching into minutia over Max's grand accomplishment of the day. Ah, someday I would bore another friend with anecdotes of my own spawn.

While Jake swam power laps in the Olympic-sized pool, I enjoyed a quick power nap in a king-sized bed with the sound of the ocean outside the terrace door. I told him I was getting a massage, but I swore to myself it was the last fib before the big news.

Mother's Day the week before had provided the perfect (and appropriate) occasion to tell him. I nearly broke down. Okay, I *did* break down, right there in the card aisle at Target. For twelve years I had avoided the card section before Mother's Day and Father's Day, leaving the card-buying for my in-laws to Jake. The day before we left for Houston to spend Mother's Day with Lorna, I had gone shopping for a quick pick-me-up. New lipstick had never failed me. As I decided between Passion Plum and Marvelous Mango, the brightly colored sign screaming REMINDER! MOTHER'S DAY IS TOMORROW caught my eye. It may as well have read: REMINDER! TELL YOUR HUSBAND YOU'RE GONNA BE A MOTHER! It was an appropriate occasion to be sure.

So I tossed both lipsticks in my basket and sauntered cautiously to the cards, two hundred or more to choose from, and started reading, and weeping. How I'd missed picking out cards for my mother! She loved cards, the funny ones, the fancy ones, the handmade ones, and kept them in a blue box in her bedroom. I still had them. Finally, I selected one for her and placed it in my basket. I would put it in the memory box in my closet when I got home.

Could she see me in Heaven purchasing a card for her?

I'd heard about people still talking to their relatives after they had passed on, but I wouldn't even know where to begin. Perhaps I'd ease into it with a card. As I wheeled toward the center aisle, a small grouping of cards meant for expectant mothers seemed to shout for me to pick them up. I hurriedly wheeled away, telling myself I needed to buy Jake a six-pack of a sports drink.

Mother's Day had gone on, as it did every year, with Lorna in the spotlight.

Mentally recharged, I met Jake on the white sand beach where he'd already pitched an umbrella. "Hi, honey." I greeted him with a kiss. "Swim good?"

"Great! How was your massage?"

"Ah, put me right to sleep. How many drinks have I missed out on?"

"Three for me. You know I can hold my liquor. Come take a dip with me. Let me show everyone what a babe I have."

Nice choice of words. I could tell he was tipsy, feeling good. I could sober him up with two little words. "Sweetie, I really need to work on my tan here. I hoped we could talk, actually." I took off my wrap and Jake gasped.

"My God, your breasts! That a new bikini?"

He liked the gift from the fertility fairy. "Yeah, it's one of those push-ups," I lied.

Jake groaned and kissed me. "Can we talk later? The waves are really calling to me, babe." He strutted off, his feet flipping through the hot sand as pairs of eyes all over the beach watched him. Two women even followed him into the ocean, but I was used to dealing with voracious flirting. My heart raced at the thought of telling him. Jake didn't like children. He thought they were noisy and precocious. When we got together with our friends with kids, Jake never offered to hold the babies or play with the toddlers. But I hadn't married him with that quality in mind, so I couldn't complain. I thought it only fair that I marry someone that had as little desire for having children as I did. I couldn't think of anything harder or more heartbreaking than having a child. Why would I put myself through that on purpose?

The sun quickly coaxed me into a warm slumber, where I dreamed of floating in the pool with a naked baby on my chest. The raft shook back and forth from the choppy water, and I leaned up enough to see sharks circling. I tried to scream, but nothing came out. Tightening my grip on the sleeping baby, I frantically looked around the pool for Jake to come to the rescue. The sharks darted closer, tipped the raft. Again, I tried to scream. Not even a puff of air escaped my throat. Any moment we would go under, but then I saw him, standing just inside the sliding glass door of the house, smiling at me. He turned away, leaving us in peril.

I awoke to cold drops of water falling on my stomach from a young girl standing over me with a huge, gummy smile on her face. A woman snatched the girl away. "I'm so sorry, ma'am. Savannah is quite curious. She loves to make new friends."

"Oh, that's okay. I was having a bad dream, anyway." I touched my chest where the sleeping baby had lain. I was safe on land, the sharks hundreds of feet away in the ocean. Jake splashed in the surf, acting like a kid himself.

Savannah stuck her hand out. "I'm Savannah Williams. I'm four years old. I live in L.A. Someday I'm gonna be a movie star." The little blonde tossed her curly locks and shook my hand vigorously.

"I bet you are, Savannah. My name's Taylor Montgomery."

"What do you do?" Savannah asked.

"I'm a creative director in an advertising agency." Sensing her confusion, I tried again. "I write commercials and stuff."

"Oh," the little girl said. "I was in an Oscar Mayer wiener commercial last year." She cleared her throat and flashed an even bigger smile as she did just what I feared she'd do. "Oh, I wish I were an Oscar Mayer wiener. That is what I'd truly like to be . . ."

Savannah continued to sing as her mother yelled at a young boy playing in the sand. "Matthew! How many times have I told you not to feed sand to your cousin? Stop it now, or you're grounded for the rest of the day!" The woman plunked down as if exhausted. "I'm sorry. Geez, these kids are a handful. My sister's getting lunch, so I'm in charge of the troop. I'm Marcia, by the way. I'm my kids' mom. Two kids actually, with one on the way."

"Wow," I said, instantly looking at her flat stomach. "You aren't showing."

Marcia lowered her voice to a whisper. "I'm nearly full-term. It's this new pill that lets you stay skinny while you're pregnant."

I raised my brows. Marcia cackled and slapped her thigh. "Hell, I wish. Really I'm twelve weeks along," she said, patting her small tummy. "In the next week, I'll just balloon. I go from size six to full maternity clothes like *that*." She snapped her fingers. "I wanted to take this vacation before I get mistaken for a beached whale."

Savannah had finished the jingle and took a deep low bow as her mother and I clapped. The little star quickly exited to join her brother and cousins.

Marcia looked out at the waves. "Is that your husband?" she said, pointing to Jake.

"Last time I checked."

"Lucky you. Who needs to boogie board when you've got that to play with in Hawaii?" Marcia slapped my thigh and snorted through her nose.

"I'm lucky, all right."

"Got kids?"

I shook my head, unable to lie through my teeth.

"Well, I was going to say I bet your children will be beautiful. Savannah got her looks from her aunt. I was the smart one. Top of my class in law school. But then I got pregnant, and you can imagine what happened next."

Actually, I couldn't. "People started treating you differently?"

Marcia's head sprung like a jack-in-the-box. "I was the only female partner in the firm. The men couldn't help looking at me differently. I was big as a house. I was tired, cranky, working ridiculous hours. And I thought I could conquer the world, bottle in one hand and briefcase in the other. But it's too much. You know? Too damn much. One look at that wailing, adorable baby of mine and I knew I couldn't handle the workload and the diaper load. Gosh, that seems like ages ago. Don't think I don't miss it. Hell, I get so jealous hearing my husband talk about his work sometimes, but a woman's got to be smart enough to know she can't do it all without sacrificing something." Marcia removed her sunglasses. "Look at me, talking your ear off. Probably boring you to tears. Anyway, don't listen to me. If that ever happens to you, you've got to make your own decision, that's for sure."

Just as I was about to object and thank her for telling the truth, her sister, a blonde bombshell with a perfect hourglass figure and a pierced navel, arrived with a plateful of cheese fries, hamburgers, chips, and guacamole. Marcia and I both looked her up and down. "I know. Isn't she disgusting? She has two kids and her boobs are still perky, the bitch."

"Are you talking about my breasts again, sis?" The blonde looked at me. "Hi, I'm Tina."

Tina sat next to us in the sand and set the plate of food on a beach towel. I hoped they would leave before Jake got back, because he would definitely be attracted to her. Who wouldn't? The kids stormed the food, gobbled it down in front of our eyes. I felt a craving like I'd never experienced before, for crispy, greasy onion rings. I *hated* onion rings.

"She's the one with the hunk," Marcia said.

"I *completely* hate you. You probably even have a great job, right?"

"She's a creative director in advertising," Marcia said.

"Well, I'll still be friends," Tina winked. "Our kids may drive you nuts in five minutes flat, though."

Even screaming children couldn't keep my thoughts off of hot, crunchy onion rings. Excusing myself, I made a beeline for the food court, where I got a large order (keeping my eyes on Tina, whose eyes were on my man) and smothered them with ketchup and mustard.

An elderly couple seated under a canopy watched me in amusement. "Excuse me, dear," the woman said. "It's none of my business, but are you pregnant?"

I licked my finger, realizing what a sight I must be, standing there in the middle of the courtyard stuffing my face. "Why do you ask?"

"When I had my first child forty years ago, I always ordered onion rings with ketchup and mustard."

"Yes, I am," I said, which pleased the woman and felt freeing to admit.

Soon, Jake and I returned to our room to shower and change for dinner. He pulled me into the shower with him. I kissed his chest, thinking he tasted like a hot-from-the-oven salty pretzel. He moved his hands over my body, from my neck to my pelvis, then retraced his moves with his tongue, stopping at my navel. "I think you should get a navel ring," he said.

I immediately thought of the ring puncturing the balloon inside of me. "I knew she would turn you on," I said, my mind on the other rings that were still stuck in my teeth. I traced my tongue over them to savor any lasting flavor.

I knew if I voiced my indecisiveness over steak versus shrimp for dinner, he might catch on that something was wrong. After all, I rarely talked about food, especially while being pleasured. Before I got pregnant, eating was just something that I did two or three times a day. After I got pregnant, food became a calling, a passion, and the thought of food and the act of eating it consumed me.

He moved back up to my ample bosoms, kissing them, and the ache felt pleasing enough for me to get turned on by something other than food. A few minutes later, as he slid into me, I made up my mind on a nice, juicy steak.

Dressed in a white tuxedo, my husband had transformed into a cover boy from *GQ*. I slinked into a tiny black dress that thankfully still zipped up in the back. While Jake shaved, I tore into the minibar and, out of his line of sight, ate Snickers and peanut butter crackers. The more I ate, the hungrier I got. I wondered if my hunger was partly due to nerves at the upcoming Summit of Spilling the Beans. Or if it was just the preggo thing.

Just as I had hoped, the evening, the weather, the view, the dress—everything idyllic. I became excited to share the news with Jake, mostly because finally *I* was excited about the news. Still scared as hell, but excited. I'd grown attached to the thing attached to me. I thought about it more and more, and instead of feeling anxious, I felt calm. Calm is good. This would be a night we would always look back on. Oceanside at the garden restaurant, the waiter finally seated us at our table.

"Have I told you how beautiful you look tonight?" Jake said, leaning his freshly tanned face in closer to mine.

"Thank you. Keep that up and you just might get lucky again."

Jake weaved his fingers through mine. "Oh, I plan on getting *very* lucky. All I've been able to think about since we got here was being with you."

"That's strange, I thought it was *you* I was with in the shower an hour ago."

Jake rested his head on his hand. "Yeah, but I was just getting warmed up."

"I thought you were pretty hot, Mr. Montgomery," I said, rubbing my leg against his. I could be a sexy flirt and a mother, too.

The buttoned-up waiter returned, interrupting our dirty talk. Jake ordered champagne, and I didn't object. *A few sips wouldn't hurt.*

"I thought Tina and Marcia and Tom were nice folks," Jake said.

"I know you liked Ms. Belly Ring. Kids were nice, too, didn't you think?"

"Didn't really notice," he said. "Not too obnoxious, I suppose. I wouldn't want to bring kids on a vacation like this, though."

"Why is that?" I took a long swig of ice water. My nerves

and the Hawaiian sun had risen my temperature one thousand degrees.

"Honey, it should be a romantic getaway, making love any time, any place, without kids around. But we don't need to worry about that for a long time. Hey, did I tell you Thomas's wife Gracie is pregnant? And she just turned forty-one."

My stomach knotted. "Good for them. I know they've been trying for several years. In vitro?"

"Yeah, I think so. Did I tell you that Thomas asked me for my sperm last year?"

"Jacob Montgomery, that's not even funny."

"I'm not kidding. The docs thought it was a problem with him, so they told him to consider donor sperm."

I put the white napkin in my lap. "What did you say?"

"Well, their embryo isn't mine, if that's what you mean."

"Jake!"

"What do you *think* I told him, Taylor? I told him you thought it was unethical."

"That *I* think it's unethical?"

"Yeah, remember when they did that story on *Dateline*—"

"Jacob, I remember the story, but don't *you* think it's unethical, too?"

Jake shook his head. "I don't feel one way or another. I know that legally, if I sell the sperm, I can't try to reclaim the baby later. Men don't have parental rights like mothers in those cases."

"*Legally?* Do you *hear* yourself, Jake? We're talking about human *life* here, your flesh and blood. It wouldn't bother you to have a son or daughter somewhere that you know nothing about?" I huffed, slamming my fork on the table.

"Whoa! Whoa! Settle down. I would never do that and you know how I feel about bringing kids into the world at the right time and the right place to the right parents."

I took another drink of water, wishing instead I could pour it over my head. Or his. I couldn't help but wonder if Jake thought he and I would fit the description of the "right parents."

"But, hey, if you can still have kids when you're forty-one, then we've got a ways to go," he said, taking another swill of the champagne. "Let's just enjoy life while we're young."

I knew the conversation was over, and I didn't have the heart or the energy to continue it, anyway. I thought the restaurant was the perfect place to announce the news of our child, but I was wrong. There wasn't such a thing as the right place when Jake thought it was the wrong time. I buried my disappointment in my meal, which came to an appetizer, salad, steak, rolls, baked potato, and a big slice of key lime pie, thank you very much.

That night, under the moonlit skies of Kauai, Jake and I lay naked on our comforter on the terrace floor. The smell of the salty sea and a honeyed aroma filled the air, as a palm tree scratched against the railing. Jake hummed "Somewhere My Love" in my ear. My anger with him over spoiling our dinner diminished with every whisper of the cool breeze.

As hard as I tried, I couldn't stretch out that glorious moment or hold it until I was ready to let it go. Like so much in my life, it would slip away before I could record it in its entirety. The sight, the smell, the feel of my husband's body pressed up against me, his hand lying on my belly and the secret that lay beneath would soon slip away. Under that soft, bronzed skin was our child, an embryo with a beating heart.

I shuddered and Jake was quick to respond. "Are you cold? Can I get you a blanket? Here, let's cover you up or maybe go in and watch a movie. I could order up some popcorn."

I nodded as a silent tear ran down my cheek. If only I knew he would be the same man, love me as sweetly, hold me as warmly, I would have told him that instant, but fear kept me mute. In my mind, I put our marriage on pause. When I released the button, a different tune would play.

CHAPTER 7

I awoke to the sounds of the ocean lapping against the shore as Jake stood at the terrace door dressed in a white Hilton robe, a cup of coffee in one hand, looking out at the scenic morning. He turned and saw me watching him.

"Good morning, sunshine," he said, lifting his cup to me. "How did you sleep?"

"Mmm," I stretched and yawned. "Couldn't have been better. This was a great idea, honey."

Jake sat the cup down, sauntered over and flopped on the bed. "We haven't made love in the morning in months." He brushed away the strap of my gown.

"You're voracious." I touched the dark stubble on his face and pulled him on top of me, feeling slight pressure as he laid his full body on mine. With the sounds of paradise around us, we welcomed the morning as one.

Some time later, as we lazily readied for the day, Jake dressed in biking clothes while I studied my naked profile in the bathroom mirror. My breasts had swelled almost a full cup size in just a month, but considering I didn't have large breasts to begin with, I was pleased with the enlargement. Besides our tropical surroundings, I was sure their size had something to do with my husband's increased libido. From the side, my lower abdomen had also swelled, similar to my PMS days, but Jake hadn't seemed to notice. According to the hotel scales, I'd gained a few more pounds, my heaviest since I'd gained the freshman fifteen in college.

With each passing day, I felt the intricacies of my new state of being, the changes and the shared body. As I moved, a weight amassed that told me I was not alone. My mind, too, had shifted from self-interest to concerns for the welfare of the baby. True, I had indulged in a few sips of champagne, but without consciously realizing it, I had been making decisions based on the baby for three weeks. I had stopped partying. *Major coup.* I cut out caffeine and drank more juice. I stopped running. Besides being dog-tired and lazy, I chose not to run because when I had attempted it, I got cramps and worried it jiggled the baby too much. And in Hawaii, I skipped the eco-challenge activities my husband was fond of, as well as the frozen-liquored treats. Perhaps I had accepted the little schmoo and didn't *want* to lose it. Dare I say I was falling in love with it?

"The concierge said there's a great rocky trail for experienced bikers just down the road. I was hoping you'd join me."

"I'm sorry, babe, but I think I'm just going to grab a bagel and start in on a new novel. Care to join me for breakfast?"

"Nah, I'd better get started before it gets too hot. Why don't we meet up for lunch? Then maybe a luau tonight and have some drinks in the hot tub?"

"Sure, sounds great." Damn. I had to find a way to get out of the fetus-endangering hot tub that night or better yet, *tell him*, which is what I decided to do. Jake would just have to get used to the idea of sharing his youth with a little youth of his own. I scurried to the restaurant, where I ordered scrambled eggs, bacon, toast, and cereal. While stuffing my face, I waved to Marcia, who frantically seated her exuberant children and nephews, her hot babe of a sister nowhere in sight. Probably eco-challenging my husband's fidelity.

* * *

The opulent pools greeted me as I plunked my tote full of research and the novel next to a large, cushioned chair. With a bare face and lip gloss, I slipped on my black Gucci sunglasses and enjoyed the serenity of the island. For a moment, I tried to imagine my baby, right then, its little eyes, nose, and ears already formed. The hands already a tiny replica of those that would squeeze mine for years to come. That little heart was beating, beating quickly as I nourished it within me.

Within minutes, I was fast asleep and dreaming again, this time of a babe suckling at my breast as I awkwardly held the infant, unsure if I was nursing correctly. It looked up into my eyes. I lay the baby on the floor, marveling at her beauty, and the baby flipped over on her belly and began to crawl. As I reached down for her, she transformed into a lizard, its tongue slithering in and out of its tiny mouth, and she quickly scurried away.

I woke abruptly, obviously freaked by my dream. I looked around, half-expecting a lizard to be staring up at me with its shocking pink tongue. Instead, I found a bronzed hunk lying in the chair next to me. If the dream wasn't bad enough, I had a slight burn on my chest and shoulders. I didn't know how long I'd slept. As if reading my mind, the hunk said, "It's 10:30 A.M. You had quite a nap."

Adjusting my bikini top, I noticed my nipples were extremely erect and appeared to be much larger than they had that morning. My mammary glands were already in overdrive preparing for suckling eight months later. My boobs were the reason the man sat next to *me* instead of the twelve empty chairs around the pool that morning.

My company was Dave, a thirty-five-year-old architect from New Hampshire, in Hawaii for a convention. Sans his wife and two children, I might add, and apparently enjoying the morning with me.

"I was just getting ready to order a margarita," he said. "Can I get you one?"

"Uh, a virgin daiquiri, please." I turned over onto my stomach to sun my backside. My butt was hanging out, but

I didn't bother with it. I figured I may as well give it as much attention as possible before it got any bigger.

In typical tropical flirting fashion, Dave asked to put lotion on my back, but I kindly declined the offer. In a couple of months, I didn't expect that too many men would be offering such favors.

Not that I didn't fantasize about Dave rubbing lotion all over my body. Sexual fantasies were another gift from the gestational gods. Dave's hands were large, appeared soft and strong, and I imagined them at his drafting boards, designing incredible hotels and complexes. Then he was drafting on me as I lay on his table, and you can guess where my fantasy went from there.

"What's a beautiful woman like you doing all alone out here?" Dave asked.

"My husband's biking and I'm pregnant," I said flatly. Who did he think I was, a sexy flirt? I was going to be a mother, for goodness sake!

"Oh."

Dzzzzzz. I almost heard his hard-on deflate.

Then, as if he realized he was being a putz, he said, "Congratulations," then excused himself. *No adulterous lay here.* For me, that was a practice run, making the announcement, albeit to the wrong man. Just as I had expected, the word "pregnant" turned me from a cute chick in a bikini to a turn-off in two seconds flat.

A few minutes later, my husband appeared in front of me, peeling off his shirt, exposing the sweaty, toned body beneath it.

"Hey, sexy. Damn, it's hot." He quickly looked around the pool, then dropped his shorts and dove in, wearing nothing but his mischievous smile.

Jake rose to the surface and splashed me. "Take off your clothes and jump in," he said.

"Honey, do you see all those windows up there? People can *see* you," I said, perturbed.

"You're not exactly Ms. Modest. They don't know us from Adam. C'mon, babe. I need some company."

I rolled my eyes and took off my top. "This is as far as I'm going." I dove into the pool beside him.

"You're irresistible," he said, ogling my breasts floating in the pool. He pulled me into him, and I wrapped my legs around his body as we started kissing. His manliness pressed up against me, and he started to remove my bikini bottom.

"Not here," I said. We climbed out of the pool, naked bodies glistening under the sun, and walked to an empty cabana room, enclosed but open to the sky, and made love on the cotton mattress with linen sheets meant for another. Afterwards, I lay there, taking in the last bit of afternoon rays, nearly drifting into sleep but for the pangs of hunger. I poured myself a glass of iced tea and gulped it down, then ate the peanuts that were set out on a ceramic tray. I covered my sleeping husband with a towel and wrapped one around me. An elderly couple entered the cabana and gasped in surprise.

The man looked at his key. "This *is* number four, isn't it, Harriet?"

His wife looked at Jake admiringly and smiled shyly. "Let's not wake him."

"Is this *four*? I thought it was five," I said apologetically. "We'll get right out of your way then. I'll send a maid to clean up, and I'll order you another pitcher of tea."

"Don't bother," Harriet said. "Fred and I were young once. There's nothing like young love."

Fred patted his wife's hand. "Or old love!"

I practically shook Jake out of bed, and the first thing he did was take off the towel, causing Fred and Harriet to gasp again. Fred covered Harriet's eyes, though she didn't bother to close them. Jake noticed our company and covered up again.

"Sorry. Sorry," he said, as we left the couple. We giggled all the way back to our room.

The beach was particularly breathtaking that evening, with the sand a warm beige, the ocean a brilliant aqua blue. The rich, vibrant color of the night invigorated me, and I melted in its majesty, a hopeless romantic to its lure. Jake and I walked hand in hand for what seemed like miles along the shoreline. A large rock served as our perch, and I dangled my feet in the waves. The cool water licked my toes, and I was in love with love, with that moment and that place, and most of all, with my husband.

I squeezed Jake's hand, and his head was turned just enough so that I could admire the curve of his jaw and the adoration in his gray eyes. "It's so beautiful here," I said, more to myself than for conversation's sake. "I couldn't dream up a better setting to tell you."

"Tell me?"

"I've been such a chicken about this. I know I'm just being crazy, but I've waited long enough. It's just really hard."

Jake looked at me full on, a slight twinge of curiosity in his brow. "Go on. What is it?"

It was then that the tears welled up and my throat tightened. "I know how you feel about kids, Jake. And I feel the same way. We never talked about having kids, and last night at dinner you said we had time for that." I started crying, which quickly turned into sobs.

Jake looked concerned. I wasn't a crier. I usually kept my emotions inside, where I could control them. My crying seemed to frighten him.

"Are you okay, Taylor?"

I shook my head. "I don't know if I'm okay. But I do know that I'm pregnant."

"What?" He seemed confused, as if I'd told him something from across the room and he didn't quite catch it.

I looked him square in the eye. "We're having a baby, Jake." My sobs turned to laughter. I didn't think it was funny. Jake sure as hell didn't think it was funny. But my inability to properly express emotions got the best of me. Laughter felt better than trying to drown myself.

Obviously it registered that time, as he jumped off the

rock into the knee-deep water, his back to me. For a moment, I just looked at his backside, hoping that when he turned around I would see joy.

He pivoted, and his face was red, hardened. Then the color just left him.

"Are you okay, honey?" I asked him, seriously believing he could faint right there in the ocean.

"How did this happen?"

"It may have been when I had that bad cold and I was taking antibiotics," I said.

"Your *cold?*" He put his hand on his head, thinking back. "My God, Taylor, that was two months ago."

"Almost."

"So, you're two months pregnant and *just now* telling me?"

"Jake, honey, I wanted to, but it was just never a good time. You had your big case, then I was really busy at work and coming home late and I just . . . I'm telling you now." I paused. "I'm sorry."

"So what are we going to do?"

"*Do?* I'm due just after Christmas, if that's what you mean."

Jake sat back on the rock, but farther away from me. "So I guess I have no say in this, then."

His words stung. I jumped into the water, nearly falling over. Jake grabbed my arm to steady me, but I pulled away. "I knew you'd be unhappy."

"Do you want me to be happy?"

"Is that too much to ask?"

Jake crossed his arms. "You've had weeks with the news. I've had one minute. *Of course* I'm surprised. This changes everything."

I walked to the shore, my legs splashing through the water, in a hurry to be away from him.

"Taylor, wait!" he yelled after me. "We need to discuss this!"

Crying, shaking, I spun around to face him. "Don't you understand, Jake? You say it will change everything as if it's a bad thing. That's my worst fear. But I wanted you to want this baby."

Jake didn't even try to come after me. Even in his profession, Jake wasn't good at feigning sensitivity. He wore his emotions on his face, in those large gray eyes, in his square jaw, his dark brows. I felt like an idiot for believing that a beautiful setting would make a difference.

I slept alone that night in that big, fluffy bed for two. Listening to the waves slapping against the shore was torture. My entire trip was defined by the moment Jake abandoned me. He was my rock, my support, my reason for being. Besides work, my entire adult existence was built around being loved by Jake Montgomery, successful lawyer, lover, and friend. All cried out, I eventually fell asleep around 2 A.M., but woke an hour later from a nightmare.

I dreamt I'd had the baby and it emerged as a long, slithering snake. I thought no one would love my baby, least of all me. The horror of it kept me from falling asleep again. With nowhere to turn, I called Allen back home.

"Allen Lawry," he said, chipper as usual.

"Allen, it's Taylor," I said in a muffled voice.

"My God, girl, what's the matter with you? Are you still in Hawaii? Gotten lei'd yet?"

"Please, Allen. Jake and I had a fight. He hasn't come back to the room."

"You and Jake? A fight? What the hell do you lovebirds have to fight about? Who gets to be on top?"

"I told him."

"And *what*? The bastard should be thrilled his gene machine is working!"

"I think he's mad I waited so long to tell him."

"Tell him to grow up and take it like a man."

"Is that what you would do?"

"Hell, no. I'd go get drunk at a bar and hook up with a two-bit sleaze."

"Shit. That's what I thought. You two are more alike than you know."

"Don't even go there."

"I mean besides your better taste in clothes and food and wine and music."

"Thank you. So what do you want me to say, Taylor? That he's a bastard or that he's a wonderful husband and you should forgive him for leaving you all alone?"

"Both. Neither. I'm a mess. I don't know what I'll do if he leaves me," I said. Clouds covered the half moon out my window.

"Leaves you? Hey, if there's one big difference in Jake and me, it's that I'm the leaving kind, not Jake. He's one of those guys you hear about in old wives' tales, all committed and gushy in love with their college sweetheart after a jillion years together."

"You really think so? I'm not so sure. Why am I not sure? Shouldn't I be sure after eight years together? What's wrong with us? I should know him better than this. If I felt better about our relationship I would have told him before I told you."

Allen sighed. "I can't argue with you there."

"How did this happen? It's me, isn't it? I'm emotionally distant; I like routine and avoid conflict. I paid all that money to the shrink you referred me to and it didn't do me a damn bit of good. In one ear and out the other. Just like my mom used to say."

"Again, I'm not arguing. Taylor, just tell Jake what you're telling me. He'll understand. Listen, you know I'm there for you, but Susan is up my ass about this Studio Baby campaign. I'm not even going to go into it, because you've got enough to worry about. You take it easy, okay? Call me tomorrow."

As I hung up the phone, a slow cramp made its way through my lower abdomen. The cramping had increased substantially through the week, but a pregnancy book I kept hidden in my desk at home assured me it was just growing pains, the uterus stretching for the first time. I cried again, not so much at the pain, but that I didn't have Jake there to rub my belly and make me feel protected, as he did when I felt sick.

A deep, pounding ache filled my heart and brought back memories of my mother. I was eight years old and bedridden with the flu. She sat on the edge of my bed, holding my hand while the mercury in the thermometer slowly rose. She didn't speak, only looked reassuringly into my eyes. I was drowsy, ill beyond belief, but her gaze put me into a kind of hypnotic state. In her blue eyes, which I had inherited, I saw the worry she had for me.

That night I mourned all things lost to me, most of all my parents. The memories were always there, just beneath the surface, waiting for moments of weakness that allowed me to conjure them up. I rarely thought of them when my life was sound and stable. Times when my brain was tired, my body sick, my soul crushed—those were the times I let the pain of missing them creep into my head, and there the memory of my parents' faces could mix with my agony, make me yearn for them, and wish I could let go of the past altogether. In my mind's eye, I saw my mom's dark, curly hair, sophisticated when she pulled it up, and so carefree when she let it down in curls about her shoulders. Her ballerina posture so graceful as she glided across the room with her head held high. Her brilliant eyes glistening, opening wide as she smiled, like you were her audience and she sought adoration. I missed the way she flirted with my dad, as if they were still courting and she was trying to win his heart all over again.

My chest tightened. My father's square but gentle face appeared. The slight wrinkles of his eyes turned up as he smiled at me. It was my first dance recital and he made it back to town just in time to watch me twirl clumsily in my pink tutu. He picked me up and spun me around, laughing. "That's my girl. My little pink flamingo."

As it usually went when I started thinking of them, the memories of their death weren't far behind. A numb, hot wave passed through me. My Aunt Barb, my mother's younger sister, had driven me to the hospital. Her face pale and rigid, her hands gripped the steering wheel as if glued. White streaks covered her cheeks where the tears wore through her makeup. She opened her mouth, but didn't speak, didn't even look at me. I burst into tears, threw my books at my feet and screamed so loud I knew those outside could hear me. I knew they were gone.

Just as the bars were closing down on the island and my husband was wandering who-knows-where alone, or even with someone else, I drifted back to sleep, too exhausted from my body's wondrous works to fight sleep any longer. Alone. Just me and my baby.

I woke to the stroke of flesh on my arm. Jake lay beside me, his thumb on my forearm, caressing me as if we'd just made love. The bed creaked as I turned over to face him. Dark stubble covered his jawline. Dark circles hung like hammocks under his eyes. The smell of toothpaste and deodorant hid the effects of a hard liquor night.

"Your husband is a jerk," he began.

"Your wife is sorry."

"The jerk is sorrier." Jake ruffled my hair and kissed me.

I couldn't help but smile. "The jerk keeps late hours."

We sat up in bed, looking out at our last morning in Hawaii. "I came in around two-thirty, then woke up at six to run on the beach. I wanted to wake you, but figured you might need the rest."

I wrapped my arm around Jake's. "I started this thing off badly. I should've told you the day I found out. It was the day you got the promotion."

"Well, you were right to think it would've put a damper on my day. Quite a coincidence, though. Junior partner and Jake Jr. on the same day."

"Did you drink away your sorrow?"

"Sorrow?"

"My pregnancy. Is it okay now?" My breaths shortened.

"I'm not upset. Just surprised. I need a little time is all."

I placed his hand on my breast and moved in to kiss him. "We've got some time."

Jake removed his hand and patted me on the thigh. "I'm starving. What do you say we go get some breakfast?"

I lay back on the pillow, rejected. I couldn't believe Jake was actually putting food before make-up sex. That was *my* role! What I didn't know was I'd gotten lei'd for the last time in Hawaii.

CHAPTER 8

The plane ride back to California was hot, almost stifling, and passengers kept their window shades down, darkening the cabin to attempt sleep. Despite a few dirty glares, I kept my window shade up and stared at the vast sky, the pillows of clouds in our path. All I could think about was what came next when we stepped back into our normal lives at home. I contemplated who we should share the news with first. His parents would be ecstatic; my Aunt Barb would cry; my girlfriends would faint from shock—the bridge girls thought I would be the last of our crew to bring a child into the world. Work. Well, work would be interesting. Ace had never had a pregnant creative director. First time for everything, right?

Jake didn't seem to mind the endless flight. He kept his nose buried in a crime book, clearing his throat and smacking his lips after each sip of water. Either I'd never noticed such annoying habits before, or I had developed superhuman senses. I resisted asking if he hot-tubbed with Tina while "celebrating" the news of his impending fatherhood.

Midway through the trip, he put on his headphones,

then grinded his teeth in his sleep. To block out the noise, I put headphones on as well, but didn't bother plugging them in. I pulled out a journal I had picked up on the island at a small bookstore owned by an elderly native. After sorting through a large box of old books, the owner had removed a thick journal of burgundy leather that smelled fresh and woodsy.

"I can tell you have many things to write about," he had said as he handed it to me.

Journals of all shapes and sizes filled my drawers back home. They contained my fears and aspirations, sketches, slogans, advertising copy, poems, whatever I was going through at the time. For a long while after my parents' death, I tried to write letters to my mother. I wanted to share my most intimate feelings about life and love and family and memories from my childhood. But I couldn't muster a single legible sentence. A person would have to read between the lines to learn about my life before the age of eighteen. If someone stumbled upon my journal, the reader wouldn't even know I had parents, let alone a childhood. I had paid a shrink one hundred dollars an hour to tell me I had to let it out. Let it go. Move on. But I couldn't.

I wasn't ready to write about the past, but I could write about the future. That stately journal with crisp white paper would contain letters to the stranger within.

May 20

Dearest Baby,

As my pen hits the paper, my hands are shaking. I'm nervous writing my first words to you because I want to get it right. I want this journal to be your keepsake, a gift to you from your mother. I want so many things, many of which I haven't figured out yet. But I do know that while you are just nine weeks along inside me, I am starting to accept you. I can't feel you moving, but I know you're there.

I've always wanted to stumble upon a diary of my

mother's. I thought it might help me make sense of things.
Of why she was the way she was. This way, you'll have
something to know more about me, no matter what hap-
pens. Unlike friends, you have no choice in who you get
for a mother, just as I had no choice about mine. Mother-
ing has not been a strong suit in my family. I may never
get a World's Greatest Mom coffee mug, but I promise to
do my best. Long life would be progress. Maybe you'll go
easy on me?

Sincerely,
Taylor Montgomery

I closed the journal and put it back in my bag. Jake removed his headphones long enough to say, "Hey, Taylor.
This is the one time I can tell you your head's in the
clouds and it's not a metaphor." He laughed hysterically
at himself.

I hoped our child would get my sense of humor.

I watched as we sliced through the air, speeding closer
to home. The farce was over. The Taylor returning was in
for more than I ever dreamed. And so was my unfunny
husband.

MONTH THREE

That's Not a Gut. Really.

CHAPTER 9

Week 13: Nearly 3 inches long and weighing in at four ounces, your baby's still small enough to fit in the palm of your hand. But soon he will be able to see light. And you may even feel your baby shake with a case of the hiccups.

The next month was the worst yet. Just as morning sickness weaned itself out of my life, work stress latched on with a vengeance. My junior partner-husband was all but a ghost in our house. We hadn't had a meal together in weeks, and the sex (the one thing we did really well together), was strangely absent, also.

With the remarkable engineering of elastic waistband pants, something I swore I wouldn't wear until I hit at least seventy, I kept the baby under wraps a wee bit longer. The only person I'd told besides Jake and Allen was Aunt Barb, who had promptly sent me a baby basket that barely fit through my front door. She showed more enthusiasm about my pregnancy than the rest of us combined. Because I didn't have my mother to coddle me, I appreciated Aunt Barb's support, even if she went overboard at times. As for the bridge girls, I decided to wait until our next bridge night so I could tell them all at once and in person.

At the agency, I didn't play the ruse of Taylor-the-Workaholic, I *was* Taylor-the-Workaholic, more so than before I had become pregnant. That month I only had to lie once, calling a prenatal checkup a dentist's appointment, but Allen was in on it.

"I expect to see dazzling bicuspids," Allen said as I left the building. "No cavities, young lady!"

With so many women at the ad agency, I figured I would run into one at the doctor's office, but that was just paranoia. The waiting room was full of strangers, just as I liked it.

Nearly dozing off in an overstuffed floral chair, I shared the company of three other pregnant women, clearly showing. One of them was a Hispanic woman with a toddler boy in tow; she read Dr. Seuss's *Oh! The Places You'll Go!* to her son while they waited. Another woman, probably in her later thirties, flipped through a baby name book. She seemed inquisitive, thrilled with the prospect of naming her child. I named things for a living—new companies, products, and events, but a *baby?* I was frightened by the idea. Companies can be sold, products expire, but the baby would be stuck with its name forever! The third woman was pretty and young, wearing a sharp pinstriped suit, talking on a cell phone about office drivel. She looked to be about my age, in her third trimester if I had to guess. All very fitting mothers, from the looks of it.

In that room of baby-makers, I was the only one who looked out of place. Shifting uncomfortably, I couldn't even decide what I should *do.* Pick up the *Parents* magazine and flip to the "expecting" articles? Pick up the baby magazine with the chubby, red-headed baby on the cover and start learning how to be a good mom? Or just watch *Days of Our Lives*, which I hadn't seen since I was in college? Within fifteen minutes, I had caught up on the storyline.

One by one, the other pregnant women left me for their checkups. I hesitantly picked up the baby magazine and scanned the article. "Breast-feeding Basics," "How to Care for the Umbilical Cord," "Saving for Baby's College" and "The Best Name for Your Baby." All of them scared the hell out of me. *What was I doing?* Maybe Jake had reason to be freaked out. Neither of us had the slightest clue what to do with a baby, so I made a mental note to stop by the bookstore to buy an armful of intelligence. As the mother, I would be expected to know a thing or two more than Jake. Besides, the little thing would be entering the world through *me*, a gynecological journey I didn't care to dwell on.

Finally, the nurse called me. "Taylor Montgomery. How are you feeling today?"

"Good, thanks." Well, at least that was the easy response.

She led me to an even more floral room, this time lime green and red, where I sat on a sheet of thin white paper draped over the examining table. The nurse took my blood pressure. "Morning sickness over with?"

"I still feel woozy in the afternoons a bit, but I'm much better than I was a few weeks ago," I told her.

"Well, since you couldn't make your last appointment, this will be the first time to hear the baby's heartbeat."

"I'm ready," I said, settling back on the exam table.

"Will your husband be meeting you here?"

I scrunched up my forehead. I'd forgotten to ask Jake if he could come. He hadn't mentioned the baby since we'd been home. "Next time," I told her.

"Good," Betty said, kindly.

Minutes later, Dr. Creighton bound into the room. "Hi, Taylor," he said, sporting a fresh tan. "How did the Aloha State treat you?"

"Great. God, I *really* needed the vacation. Looks like you got some sun yourself."

"Just a weekend at the lake house. I can't help it. I'm still a sun god," he said, pulling up my shirt a few inches and pulling down my pants to the top of my pubic bone. He took the wand of the Doppler machine, placed a clear gel on the tip and rubbed it on my lower abdomen.

"Sorry, it's cold. The baby's still really low, so it's hard to find them immediately."

"Oh, don't say 'them,' doctor," I said. "I'm scared enough with the prospect of one."

"Just one," he said. "Super heartbeat, too."

A tear sprung to my eye. The noise sounded like a train rolling down a track. There really was a person in there!

"One hundred sixty beats a minute. That's very good," he said, wiping away the goo with a tissue and helping me sit upright. "At your twenty-week visit, we'll do the ultrasound. Ready to find out if it's a he or she?"

I raised my eyebrows. "This is all going so fast for me."

"And your husband? How's he doing?"

My eyes watered. "Let's just say he's not overjoyed. Which is why I waited so long to tell him in the first place." Crybaby. First the handsome doc had to watch me puke in his trash can, then I slobbered all over his lab coat.

Dr. Creighton put his hand on his chin. "Sometimes it takes spouses a while to get used to the idea of being a father. They don't live with it inside them twenty-four hours a day like mothers do. The only thing I can suggest is education and communication. Share with Jake the book I gave you. Try to make him feel a part of the pregnancy. And in another ten weeks or so, start taking the childbirth classes. You'll meet other couples going through the same things as you are. I hope he'll come to the ultrasound. That usually makes it all real for dads."

How would he know? He had to love kids more than most men, watching them come into the world each day. He was probably a super soccer dad, too. Bet *he* didn't need Daddy Boot Camp. "I'll see if he can make it."

"Take good care of yourself. Your emotional well-being is very important right now."

You mean being a basket case is bad for the baby? Caffeine, alcohol, and now I had to give up going nuts, too?

The door clicked behind him, and I stared at it for a solid minute. Six weeks from then, we would know the sex of the child, and Jake and I still hadn't had a serious conversation about the impact on our lives, let alone have prepared for it.

I had the lightbulb moment, right there in the doctor's office. *Reality check, Taylor. Most mommies would've spread the news of their baby halfway around the globe by now. What's wrong with you?*

CHAPTER 10

"Very impressive. I can tell you've done a lot of research, Taylor," Susan said, plopping the four-inch Studio Baby Clothes notebook on the granite conference room table, surrounded by the agency's executives.

Susan Hawk, the forty-five-year-old president of Ace Advertising, definitely looked good for her age, but then money *always* helped the aging process. Susan was thrice-divorced and seeing gorgeous men ten years her junior. That day she was dressed sharp as usual, in a baby blue satin shirt and a short black skirt to show off her runner's legs. It was no wonder I was leery of telling her, a woman who deemed travel and sex the best parts of her life (sound familiar?), that I was in a state of womanhood she had never known. She had a strict policy of separating work from personal life, and the only reason she even knew my husband's name was because she had once sidled up beside him at an office Christmas party.

"You look great in your darker shade. Hawaii did wonders for you," Susan said, in her usual I'm-better-than-you tone.

"Thanks. We still have a lot of work to do on Studio Baby, but we're right on track."

Susan put on her four hundred-dollar glasses, the black oval-rimmed ones she saved for when she wanted to be taken extra seriously. "Looks like Taylor is the only thing looking good lately. Billing is down, people. Clients are cutting back on advertising expenses, which means we have no room to screw up. Taylor, everything that comes from your department has to be the best damn creative the client has ever seen. And you'll need to do it two people short. Have their names on my desk by morning. Account executives, we have to make compelling cases for the clients to let go of their death grip on their ad dollars. And I want a hundred grand in new billings from you by the end of the week, or you will also turn in two names to me. Is our situation clear to everyone? From here on, I'm watching you like a hawk. If I see anyone slacking in your departments, they're gone."

The VPs nodded. It was never a good idea to be the first one to say anything after Susan gave us a verbal spanking. She preferred to have her bitter words sink in. Everyone left the room except Allen, who sat across the room staring at me, holding in a laugh. As soon as Susan was far from hearing distance, he burst. "Hawk said she's going to watch us 'like a hawk!'"

"I caught that. We're so lucky to have a motivating leader."

"Guess I'll have to cut back on Tetris, huh?"

I swiveled, kicked off my heels and put my feet on the leather chair next to me. "How are you so sure you won't be on the chopping block?"

Allen turned serious. "Who you gonna let go?"

I banged my head on the table. "God, I hate this. If I let our oldest employees go, then it's ageism. If I let our youngest employees go, it's reverse ageism. If I let our newest employees go, we'd be losing our two best designers."

"Sucks to be the big dog, don't it?" Allen asked.

"I'll do the only fair and intelligent thing."

"Draw straws?"

"Yep. Short straws lose. Shit, I'll just think about it overnight and see who wants out the most. I'll squeeze the shrew for a decent severance for the lucky bastards," I said.

Allen kicked the conference door shut with his foot. "Honestly, Taylor. You're working yourself to death. Despite what Susan said, you need to ease up. For you and the baby's sake."

I got out of my chair and lay flat on the red-carpeted floor, which felt strangely comfortable. "You're right. If I worked any harder, my brain would be fried. I can smell the smoke of my impending burn out."

"That brain of yours is a bottomless well of good ideas," Allen said. His voice lowered to a whisper. "Unless you've already got preggo brain."

I sat up and leaned in closer to him. "Have you been holding out on me?"

"Well, my friend Nancy—"

"The one you go antiquing with?"

"Yep. She's got a baby now, and for months during her pregnancy she was like a zombie. She called it preggo brain. Memory just disappeared altogether."

"Crap, Allen. Do you think I need to be hearing this?" I slammed my fist on the chair. "That wasn't in the book the doctor gave me. It makes sense, though. I'm so tired I can't think. And with the Hawkster staying late to check in on us, I won't be able to sneak out early."

Allen got down on the floor behind me to give me a much-needed neck massage. "We look really concerned for our jobs, don't we?"

I laughed. "Hey, there are two of us. Why don't I just turn in our names in the morning? Get the hell out of Dodge."

"This hellhole needs us," Allen said. "Don't worry. Allen will take care of you. He always does." The neck muscles must have been attached to my tear ducts, because as soon as he squeezed my neck, I began crying.

Allen peered around at my face. "Hey, tough girl. You letting that spiky-heeled wench get to you?"

I grabbed Allen's arm and used his sleeve as a tissue. "I'd never give her the satisfaction. It's Jake. He hasn't made love to me in four weeks, which is *forever* in our marriage. He barely says two words to me when he gets home; he spends as much time as possible with his buddies. To make matters worse, my in-laws are coming into town soon."

Allen turned me around to face him. "Let's break this down."

"And you're qualified to help me with this *how*? Your idea to break the news in Hawaii didn't exactly go well."

"No, this is something I know a lot about. S-e-x."

"Ugh. I'm not in the mood for your sexploitations right now."

"Trust me. You need to attack him," Allen said.

"How did I know you'd suggest such a subtle tactic?"

"Talking is highly overrated."

I got up to leave.

"No. No. Sit. I'm going somewhere with this," he said. "As expert as I am, I think what you need to do is talk to a mommy friend. She'll make you feel better about your pregnancy and you can spend some time around a little tyke. As much as I pride myself on knowing the wiles of women, pregnancy is as foreign to me as commitment. Although I still stand by my recommendation to attack him."

"Of course you do. Thanks for being a friend."

Allen mussed my hair and got up to leave. "I'll make sure you have the meeting notes by this afternoon."

"Because you're going to flirt with Monica so she'll give you hers?"

"You know me frighteningly well."

CHAPTER 11

My closest bridge girl was Amy Meyers, my best friend in college. She had seen me through all the tough times in college (Mom's Day with no mom, Dad's Day with no dad, Cancun with no fake ID) and never took any credit for it.

Like me, Amy got married right after graduation to the man of her dreams. Your typical football player/cheerleader match made in Party Pic heaven. They dated for a year before tying the knot in an elaborate wedding in Dallas.

Despite her good grades, Amy never quite decided what she wanted to do with her life. She never aspired to be a career woman, and having fun and throwing parties were the two things she truly did the best. So when she got married, joined the local Junior League and stayed home, I wasn't too surprised. That way she had time to work out every day at the gym, keep an active social life, and shop, which she was famously good at. She seemed to love her role as mommy, too. Not to mention, she had a bit of money—a chunk more than Jake and I brought in. Amy would be in the upper echelon of the Golden Stroller crowd, as Allen called it.

Although we weren't as close as we had been in college, we still saw each other often, including at bridge night every month, when she wasn't pregnant or nursing a baby. When Allen suggested I speak to a friend who had kids, she came to mind first. I decided to tell her before our bridge night and make her swear not to leak the news to the others before I could. We'd been joined at the hip until she got pregnant with her first child, McKenzie. Watching Amy get bigger and her interests changing from sprints to Vegas for the weekend to nursery décor, I simply slipped away. Every time she spoke of burping techniques and baby contraptions, I thought she was speaking a foreign language. Amy had never even especially liked children. *Who was this person she had become?* I had thought. I didn't recognize her anymore and I thought she thought less of me because I couldn't relate to what she was going through.

I attended her baby shower, a mega-party the likes of which I'd never seen. Pregnant women seemed to crawl out of the woodwork. But they were *rich* pregnant women dressed in designer maternity clothing, all speaking the same lingo about the best cribs and breast pumps and birthing centers. Along with several of my sorority sisters who had yet to experience such things, I politely nodded my head and listened and watched package after package being opened, revealing tiny clothing and educational toys.

When I visited Amy in the hospital and set my eyes on the fresh, pink human who was her daughter, and glimpsed the most passionate look of love in Amy's eyes, I *almost* understood how she had transformed. Amy had matured in a way I didn't think I ever would. Her concerns were no longer self-centered. She had given her entire being to another. I felt ashamed I had been so envious of her unborn child. I may have lost the friend I knew, but the person she had become was obviously a better one. I was simply not there yet.

Now that Amy also had a second child, a son named Austin, our communication became limited to a pleasant monthly e-mail, and I visited their family Web site to see pictures of their growing clan when I could. *Welcome to friendship in the new millennium.*

Unsure why, I twisted my ring nervously when Amy opened the door of their three-story mansion in the gated community Jake wanted to move into as soon as he made senior partner.

"Taylor!" Amy squealed grabbing me by the shoulders and wrapping me in one of her tight, perfumed hugs. "Gosh, you look great as ever! Come in!"

"It's good to see you, too," I said, stepping into her large marble foyer. The scent of lemongrass filled the hall. In the distance, I saw McKenzie, wearing a casual dress with a blue bow in her blond hair and watching *Sesame Street* on a big screen. Spotting me, she got up and bounced my way.

McKenzie tugged at my leg. "Hi, Taylor. I made some cookies for you."

Instinctively, I knelt down and gave her a hug. "I love cookies. You've gotten so big since I last saw you!"

A small cry from the family room sent us all after Austin, who seemed upset his sister had left him alone. Austin was a pudgy-faced six-month-old wearing a Nike jumpsuit. Truth be told, he looked more like his fragile mother than his rugged, six-foot-two father.

"Amy, he's just adorable!" I said, picking him up from his navy-blue bouncy seat. I hadn't seen him in months. Gooier than I remembered. Drool covered his dimpled chin and the rolls of his neck, as well as his bib and onesie. He gave me a gummy smile and grabbed my hair and yanked.

"Ow!" I said, removing my tangled hair from his wet fist.

"No, Austin!" Amy said. "He's into the hair stage now."

"Shows what I know. I didn't think there was such a thing."

After a short tour of the house, we proceeded to the spacious gourmet kitchen, where McKenzie flung open the stainless steel fridge door to offer me a glass of milk.

"Taylor doesn't drink milk, honey," Amy told her. "Coffee?"

"Water's fine." Amy knew milk had been off-limits since my parents' accident. I couldn't stand to look at it, to taste it.

Nestled around the kitchen table, we caught up while Austin played with a colorful butterfly toy on the tiled floor. McKenzie served us oatmeal chocolate chip cookies, which immediately went into my mouth; then she went back to her dolls lined up in front of Elmo singing on TV.

Amy beamed, still the ever-excited sorority girl. "Tell me *everything*. God, we haven't talked in *ages*! I wanted you to see the kids, but we really should spend the afternoon together sometime. Just you and me."

"I'd love that."

"How was Hawaii?"

"Good," I said, not too convincingly. "Gorgeous."

"Well, tell me all about it. And the bridge girls. I'm so behind."

"Everyone's great. Gretchen and Tara have new boyfriends, Shannon and Dave are going to London next month, and Jen and Jackie are still full of cute kiddo stories."

"See, you're probably glad I haven't been coming to fill your ears with mine. But I am going to come next week. Jackie said you had a surprise for us. She guessed a stripper."

"Stripper, huh? Well, that's a good idea, but that's not what it is, actually." I ate another cookie, careful not to cram the whole thing in my mouth, *à la* the Cookie Monster. If I didn't eat every hour, I *did* feel like a monster. I longed for a chocolate chip tooth to be installed in my mouth so I could get my chocolate fix any time of the day. "No, Ames. Everyone misses you. I actually missed the last two months, though, too."

"*You?* I thought nothing could keep you away from bridge," Amy said, astonished.

"Well, almost nothing," I hinted.

Amy's face dropped. "You're *not* getting a divorce!"

"No, no. Nothing like that." I paused. "My surprise is . . . I'm pregnant."

Amy's mouth fell open. "Get *out!* Ohmigod! I'm so happy for you!" She jumped out of her chair and gave me another tight squeeze. "Great news! When are you due?"

"Right after Christmas," I said.

"You're three months! I thought your jeans looked tighter than last time I saw you," she said, looking me up and down.

"I knew if anyone could tell I was changing, it would be you," I said, starting to tear up.

"So how does Gorgeous feel about it?" she asked more seriously.

"Says he needs to get used to the idea. So far, that means avoiding it altogether. He's gone this weekend on a biking trip, and next weekend he's going sailing with some guys at the firm. It's like he's purposely tying up every weekend so he doesn't have to be with me."

Amy thought it over. "I'm sure he's freaked out about the idea of being a father more than the idea of *you* changing. He's probably also a little jealous someone else will horn in on this marriage of yours. Let's face it—you two aren't really settled down. You work like crazy, but you spend all of your free time traveling and partying. You're like a couple of big kids yourselves. He knows that'll change once the baby comes. Maybe he's trying to cram in as much as he can now."

"So what should I do? I don't want to lose him."

"Just plan a romantic dinner and make him feel safe. Show him he's still the love of your life. When he's had time to adjust, I'm sure he'll be happy about the baby."

"I thought everything was fine between us, but maybe not. I mean, what is fine, really?"

Photos of Amy's family decorated the fridge. Tim and Amy in Vail. Tim and Austin in the pool. Amy and McKenzie in Easter dresses. Jake and I didn't have photos on our fridge. I didn't even have a photo of him at my office, which was strange not only because he was so damn good-looking, but because I loved him. Was I just photophobic, or something else?

"Amy, why would you think Jake and I would be getting a divorce?"

She paused, squinting. "You know I don't think before I say things. But I'm going to be honest. You guys love each other so much, but you've never been big communicators. When your lives just sort of coexist without mental check-ups, how can you know where you stand?"

I exhaled. "God, you're right—as usual. I'll be one of those pathetic women on a daytime talk show who complains that she never knew her husband was cheating. Gets slapped with divorce papers out of the blue." I held my stomach. "It makes me sick to think about."

Amy patted my arm. "I don't want to see that happen to you. You've got a good thing with Jake."

I wiped at the cold beads of water on the crystal glass. "I think he's revolted at the idea of having sex with me right now."

"It can be a little intimidating going in there the first time. Just reassure him that he's not going to hurt you, and most of all, you want it. Come on, this is coming from a woman who married the biggest walking batch of testosterone on the planet. Tim really got into the round belly after awhile. But it's not just about the sex. It's about being a couple. Really get to know each other, *before* the baby comes."

"I've really missed you," I said.

"Come on. I'll give you some of my baby books and stuff. I'd love to go shopping with you *anytime*. Nurseries are my passion, you know."

I accepted a bag full of books and headed on my way, feeling slightly more confident than when I had arrived. Since I'd been feeling sorry for myself, I hadn't made a concerted effort to re-connect with Jake, who, I had to admit, had a right to feelings, too. I avoided conflict as much as he did. But the last thing I wanted was to push him into the arms of another woman.

As I tried to cram a much-too-large load of laundry into the washer, the phone began to ring. I hurriedly shoved the rest of the whites into the machine, clicked the start button and ran for the phone in the kitchen.

"Hello?" I answered.

"Con-grat-u-la-tions, sweetheart!" my mother-in-law sang into my ear. "We are so happy for you two!" she said with her usual Texas-drawl enthusiasm.

"Oh, thanks. I'm sorry I haven't called you back. Work's been crazy." I was conveniently busy or napping when Lorna had called the last few weeks.

"Yes, of course, hon. You know that son of mine can't keep a secret from his mama. Now tell me all about it. Are you feeling all right? I remember when I was pregnant with Jake, I was just sick as a dog for the first four months, day in, day out. Couldn't keep a thing down."

"Well, I'm actually feeling pretty good. I was sick at first, but now I'm getting some energy back." I swung open the fridge door to find a snack. Calories were energy, right? The fridge was bare of all no-nos, so I grabbed a wrapped cheese slice instead. Dairy *good*.

"Well, I don't blame you two for waiting to tell everyone. You know I miscarried before I got pregnant with Jake, and of course I'd already blabbed to everyone."

I swallowed the last bit of cheese, suddenly feeling guilty for eating while on the phone. Lorna was trying to *bond*, after all. "Actually, I didn't know that," I said. "Jake never mentioned it."

An exasperated whimpering filled my ear. "That's because I never had the heart to tell him."

Guess the secret sharing didn't go both ways.

"Jake's father and I could never get pregnant again after Jake, and I always felt so bad we didn't give him a brother or sister. You know how that is," she said.

I did. Being an only child was not for everyone, especially after the loss of my whole family unit. "I'm sorry, Lorna," I said. "That's nice of you to share with me. And thanks for understanding why I waited to tell the news."

"And don't you worry about Jacob, either. He'll be the best father that child could ever want. I *guarantee* it."

I shifted on the barstool in an effort to wake up my right leg, which had fallen sleep. "Did Jake say anything? You know, about his feelings about the baby?"

A gutteral laugh shot out of the earpiece and bounced off the kitchen walls. "Jake's my son, but he's still a *man*, sweetheart. He told me the news with about as much enthusiasm as his father has reading the newspaper headlines every morning. Believe me, he gets his laid-back style from his daddy. It's nothing personal."

She was right. Jake only got excited about winning a case, winning a bike race or winning, period. Birthday and Christmas gifts were received with the same regard as his morning cup of coffee. If he had won the baby in a cross-country race, maybe then he would've shown some genuine glee.

"Now I don't want to step on toes, but we'd love to come down and go shopping with you for a crib and the nursery set. Would you be a dear and let me have that one little joy?"

I cringed at the thought of a pink teddy bear and lace room frilled to Lone Star State proportions. Typical Lorna, but her heart was in the right place. "Why don't we do that next month? I have a convention in New York, and then I'll be here most every weekend," I said. Maybe even Jake would be home. For his mother, if anything.

"Wonderful!" she squealed. "What fun we'll have! I did Jake's room in Raggedy Ann and Andy and it was just precious. You pick out a weekend and give me a call. And take care of yourself and my grandbaby."

"Will do," I said, and rested my forehead on the cold granite countertop. Ah, this baby now belonged to the world—or at least the great state of Texas.

CHAPTER 12

Furiously I shook chocolate martinis in my stainless steel shaker, fighting the temptation to lick the spillover on my hands. Only Amy knew I wouldn't be drinking martinis that evening. With a hankering for red meat, I'd ordered ribs and chopped brisket and a gallon of high-calorie potato salad from a nearby barbecue joint. I know, I know. Barbecue and chocolate martinis don't seem to go together, but you'd have to know the bridge girls. With chocolate martinis, you get two sins in one. Twice the pleasure, all at once. They were thrilled with my selection.

"I hope you bought an extra bottle of Absolut. I've had an Absolut-ly shitty day," Gretchen said, throwing her red hair into a ponytail and kicking off her heels.

Shannon handed Gretchen a martini glass. "Trouble in paradise so soon?"

"I thought he was the one," Jennifer said, taking a seat at the bar.

Gretchen downed the first martini. "Another one who bites the dust, you mean. Men suck. Who's with me here?"

Tara shook her head. "Sorry, still reeling over last night's tantric sex session with Grant."

Jackie rolled her eyes and put hamburger buns on china, another rule we had for bridge night: no matter the meal, we had to dig out the china. "Please. You're having tantric sex and all I get are tantrums. Just wait until you have kids."

Gretchen held up her martini glass. "I said men suck. Can I hear a 'hell, yeah?'"

"Hell, yeah!" Jennifer said as she entered the room and plopped her red leather Coach purse on the kitchen counter.

"You don't mean that," I told her with a hug. "Unless you're joining Gretchen's pity party over another lost boy."

"Oh. Well, if Gretchen says men suck I think as her best friends we should all agree," Jennifer said. "We can always take it back when she's not around."

Gretchen dished out brisket on plates. "Fine. I'm sure all of your men are perfect, with your tantric sex and your surprise trips to Hawaii and London and all. Maybe someday I'll get that lucky."

"Hey, there's a big difference between perfect and sucks," Jackie said. "These days Mark taking out poopy diapers is romantic."

"Taking thirty minutes away from watching baseball to help me fold laundry," Shannon added.

"Taking Max to the park while I take a nap," Jennifer said. "I hadn't loved him so much in months."

"Basically, enjoy the sex while you can," Jackie said in Gretchen and Tara's direction. "Once you get married and have kids, sex becomes more obligatory. Do I get a second on that, Jen?"

"It's guilt sex. Thinking, has it really been a month since we've made love? I sure as hell don't feel like it, but I know Mark wants it every day. Why should he have to sacrifice because I'm not feeling frisky?" Jennifer asked.

"Then I'm in for it," I piped up.

Gretchen laughed. "Oh, no, you don't. You've told us you and Jake have sex five or six nights a week."

"Spill it, Montgomery," Jackie said.

"Did I miss it?" Amy's voice came from the front door. "I'm here! Wait for me!"

"Chill, Ames. It's just barbecue," Shannon yelled back.

Amy bound into the kitchen and gave me a knowing hug. "Good, I'm glad I'm not too late. For the gossip. Ooh, and before Gretchen drinks all the chocolate martinis."

"How'd you know?" Gretchen asked.

"A little birdie," Amy said. "I'm sorry, sweetheart. Men suck."

The group cheered.

"Damn straight," Gretchen said. "Now, our gracious host was about to tell us why she and stud muffin don't have sex every night anymore."

The girls looked at me, waiting impatiently, thumping their martini glasses and holding barbecue on their forks in midair. "We haven't had sex in weeks," I blurted.

The group gasped.

"Is it broken?" Tara asked, seriously.

"His penis or their marriage?" Jennifer asked.

"Well, it worked fine in Hawaii," I said.

Amy tapped her foot. "It's okay, Tay."

My eyes welled up with tears. "I'm pregnant."

The group was silent. Each girl looked at the next until everyone had exchanged glances and then rushed me with hugs and congratulations, and proceeded to jump up and down like a basketball team after a big win.

"More martinis for me!" Gretchen yelled.

"Forget what I said about obligatory sex," Jackie said.

"Mommies are in the majority now, gals," Jennifer told them. "Guess it's your turn next, Shannon."

"Hey, let's take this one conception at a time," Shannon said.

The girls treated me like a queen the rest of the night, switching my role from gracious hostess to pampered preggo. My pregnancy enthralled them. Pregnancy does that. Each one is unique, has its own splendid story. Jackie had tried for a year before successfully conceiving. Jennifer had two miscarriages before carrying a baby full term. Amy had not one, but two picture-perfect pregnancies. And my unplanned one was coming out of the closet, into the light where it deserved to be. Only then did I know that my feelings were natural.

Scared.

Anxious.

Confused.

But that didn't mean it was going to be any easier to overcome them. My friends had had their mothers to lean on, maternal grandparents to share in their blessing. For me, it was another joyous occasion I kept my parents from experiencing when I refused to run an errand. My mommy issues ran deeper than that—three generations, in fact. I would need help sorting through them.

My friends were there for me, Aunt Barb was there for me, and Jake would be there for me, too. He had to be. Didn't he?

CHAPTER 13

Pacing back and forth in front of her office window with a view of the Dallas skyline, Susan spoke sternly into her phone headset. "I don't give a shit about budget constraints, Marcus! They knew going into this it would be a million dollars, so don't give me that! Their stock is up fifteen points and we made those bastards a helluva lot of money last year! It's not the money; it's the strategy! Do whatever you have to do to make the media plan work for them, and I want it signed on the dotted line and on my desk in the morning, is that understood?"

Susan glanced at me with a cold look I was sure was meant for Marcus Williams, a vice president of account services in our Denver office.

"Marcus, if you make me go clean this up, you're fired! I don't need to do your job in addition to mine." Then her voice calmed. "You know you're one of my best, Marcus. I trust you can straighten this all out."

She pulled off her headset and threw it on the desk. Grabbing two Tylenol from her front drawer, she downed them without water, then leaned into her desk, giving me her full attention. "Tell me about Studio, and it better be good."

I laid the matte boards of the TV and print campaign on her desk for review. "Studio is very pleased with the concept, wants only one change in an actor selection," I said, pointing to a chubby redheaded baby. "They want another ethnic baby in the mix."

"Fine," Susan said, tilting back in her executive chair. "They want the fucking United Colors of Baby Benetton, let 'em have it," she said. "When and where are we shooting?"

"Studio wants Shelton to direct, so Atlanta. All of these babies are from a talent agency there," I said. "In four weeks."

Susan grabbed a bottled and took a swig. "Hoffman won't show. He'll make me look like an asshole to Shelton like he always does."

I sat in the Gucci-upholstered chair across from her, wishing I'd gone to the bathroom before our meeting. Half a cup of decaf coffee, two bottled waters and hot honey lemon tea. I could tell from her expression, I wouldn't be excused.

Susan sat on the corner of her desk. "Good job, Montgomery. I can always count on you to deliver killer creative. But I'm going to need more of your time to come up with three positively *brilliant* campaigns by month's end or we're going to have to let more staffers go."

"If we keep letting creative go, then who will do the work?" I bit my bottom lip.

Susan threw up her hands. "I guess our new creative director."

"I'll do whatever needs to be done. I've been getting six hours of sleep each night. Let's see if I can live on four."

"What's with the fucking lip, Montgomery? Who needs sleep when you've got Starbucks? Listen to me, and listen good. Revenues are down. I've been working to get us on six national account reviews. I want you on the team pitching the accounts, so it's going to mean more travel. You'll have to start doing great work on airplanes."

I looked at Susan's wall, plastered with advertising medals from the past three decades. New. More. Bigger.

Revenues were down because the economy sucked. It would take bigger accounts than we'd ever had to make up for the losses. It would take pitching against larger agencies.

"I'm not Ace's strongest salesperson," I told her.

"Of course not. *I am.* You'd go because you're top creative dog. You represent our commitment to their account. And you'll be presenting the spec work."

"Spec creative? Then let me hire back the two creatives you had me fire last month."

She eyed me evenly. "I'll let them freelance, but only until you're caught up."

"Fine. But there's something else I wanted to tell you. Of a personal nature."

Susan got up and sat next to me on the couch, something she did when she wanted to appear that she gave a damn about what you were saying. "Divorce doesn't hurt as much as you think it would," she said seriously. "I should know. I've been through three."

"Why does everyone assume I'm talking about divorce?" I shook my head. "Jake and I are fine. We're having a baby."

Susan looked at her Andy Warhol on the wall, out the window, then back at me. "You?" she said. "Not to sound derogatory, Taylor, but I didn't think you even *liked* kids."

"Well," I said cautiously, feeling heat rise up my neck. "I'm an only child, as is my husband, so we weren't really around kids much. I guess I haven't really been exposed to them, but yes, of *course* I like them. Why am I explaining this to you? Of course I'll like *mine.* I'm due at the end of December."

Looking me up and down as if she didn't quite believe me, Susan crossed her arms. "Well, if that's what you want, then of course I'll be supportive. I just can't see you with a baby, Taylor. Apologies if that sounds harsh."

"I know I've always been a workhorse and independent. It took me a while to get used to the idea, but I think I'm ready for it."

"You'll be a pregnant workhorse, then. But then you'll want some time off, won't you?" She got up and paced the floor again.

No, I was thinking about coming straight to Ace from the hospital. Better yet, we could wheel a delivery table into your office. It's big enough. "I'll take some maternity leave, sure. I plan to continue to work right up until my due date."

"It does put a kink in the plans," Susan said. "We can't have a pregnant creative director pitching new accounts. They'll sit there and wonder whether or not you'll come back after the baby."

"I assure you—"

"Don't. You'll regret it later. I'll just have to get someone else." She dialed her assistant as if to excuse me. "Nancy, get Johnson in New York on the phone," she barked.

My cue to leave, I took my boards and whispered to myself, "Congratulations, Taylor, I'm so happy for you."

With meetings and photo shoots and radio productions and new client pitches, Father's Day snuck up on me. While the un-orphaned world planned for cookouts and family celebrations, Jake and I normally did what we did every Sunday: ordered pizza and watched the latest movie from Netflix. Because we traveled to Houston for Mother's Day, all Jake's dad got was a short phone call and a card, if Jake remembered. Jake and his father were pleasant to one another but distant, a common theme for us. Jake talked more about his parents than I did, but then his were still living. He had shared that he didn't feel close to his dad because his father had traveled all the time when Jake was a kid. So had mine, but Jake's dad was negotiating million dollar deals, while mine was selling cheap insurance just to put food on our table. But gone is gone all the same.

The Sunday circular was full of last-minute efforts to lure customers to their stores for Father's Day gifts. After the tenth ad for grills, I decided a big, fat, juicy hamburger would be great for dinner. Besides, Jake was going to be a father, so why not celebrate early? I hadn't eaten this much beef in my life. Did my craving for red meat mean I had a little cowboy in there?

While Jake mowed the lawn, I picked out a cute maternity halter top and low-rise shorts from a bag of clothes Amy had given me when I told her I hadn't shopped for maternity clothes yet.

"They've come a long way," Amy said. "Pregnant women can almost be as stylish as the skinny chicks these days. Just be sure to give them back when I get pregnant again."

"Again?" I'd said, astonished. "You going for some kind of baby-making world record?"

"Oh, hush. I just see you and miss that feeling of being pregnant." Amy clasped her hands. "And that newborn skin! And nursing! God, they grow up so quickly."

"Okay, crazy woman. Are you sure you're talking about the same thing that I'm going through? 'Cause I'm still waiting for the angels-to-start-singing feeling."

"It'll come. I know not everyone has an easy pregnancy like I did, but just wait."

Not everyone has an army to help take care of the kids and house, either. Amy had been right about the clothes. They were cute, and didn't really look like maternity at all, just loose where required. But when I told Jake I was leaving for the store, he did a double take. "Cute," he said, before putting his iPod ear buds back in his ears.

After I bought all the fixings for the perfect big-mouth burger, I decided they needed to be cooked on a brand-spanking new stainless steel grill. If my father were alive, that's what I would buy him, and Jake loved to cook out, especially since I rarely cooked in. I'd start the baby/father relationship off right. An employee took the grill to the front for me, and I headed toward the checkout lane when I saw a young mother and two toddlers at the dreaded card aisle. I parked the cart next to them, feeling a little giddy that one day I'd be standing there with our little one as the child selected one based on the picture on the front of the card.

"I want the kitty one," the girl said.

"No! The monkey one," her brother argued.

The mother eyed me and shrugged. "Let's get both, okay. Daddy deserves it."

I scanned the selection for the expectant father cards and picked one hesitantly, then the cards started looking fuzzy and I felt as if I'd stepped into the Mojave Desert. I began to sweat and could feel my legs turn rubbery, when I caught the basket on the way down.

"Are you all right?" The other mother asked me as she took my arm and helped me to the ground, where I sat on the cold hard floor perspiring.

"Now I know what shop 'til you drop means." I fanned myself with a stack of Father's Day cards I pulled from the rack.

The mother leaned down to eye level. "I always got faint with these two." She rummaged through her oversized mama-purse with a black and white photo of her kiddos adorning the front. She handed me a cherry LifeSaver. "Keep these with you at all times. When your blood sugar is low and you feel like you're going to faint, these will do the trick."

"Really? I didn't read about that in my baby book."

"Oh, there's lots of stuff they don't put in those things."

I opened the LifeSaver and sucked on it. The kind mother and her little helpers fanned me. After a minute the desert heat passed, and I was just a silly-looking woman sitting on the floor of Target. "Wow. These *are* a lifesaver. And so are you. Can I take you home with me in case any further pregnancy phenomena occur?" The kids giggled. The woman helped me stand and I pondered what Amy could've possibly meant about missing being pregnant. Did she not have the pleasure of puking and passing out like the rest of us?

None of the expectant cards seemed to fit my hesitant father-to-be husband, and telling him he could forget life as he knows it for dirty diapers and lullabies wasn't about to make him feel any better. I settled on a "can't wait to meet you" card from Baby. Next I got my dad a card to add to the blue box back home, a weepy, sentimental card that I knew would make him cry if he were alive. "You're the best daughter in the whole wide world," he used to say every Father's Day when he'd read my handmade card of construction paper. "How did I ever get so lucky to get a girl like you?"

I wheeled to the front of the store hoping Jake would be as good a father as mine had been. What if he wasn't? But what if he surprised me?

While Jake cycled on nearby trails, I decided to get a head start on dinner by forming the patties. It wasn't much of a Father's Day gift if I made him do all the work. I'd placed the grill on the back patio with a large red bow on it, the card setting on the grill inside. Today, I was determined to be a typical "good wife." Laundry done. Jake's boxers in their proper drawer instead of just thrown on his side of the bed as usual.

As soon as I dug my hand in the cold beef, my stomach turned. *Get a hold of yourself.* I picked up a chunk of the beef and began rolling it into a ball and started gagging. I turned my head away from the unsightly pink mass, closed my eyes and held my breath. When I inhaled a minute later the smell of raw meat filled my nose and I gagged again, tossing the beef back in the tray and running to the sink to throw up. So much for the good wife idea.

Shopping and getting sick made me tired. What didn't make me tired? I rested my eyes while lying on the couch, which turned into a two-hour nap. When I awoke I heard the sliding glass door to the patio slam shut. *My surprise!*

I bounced up to catch him before he saw the grill and stubbed my toe on the corner of the couch. "Shit! Honey!" I yelled. I hobbled into the backyard to find Jake standing in front of the grill, reading the card. The sun hung behind him, like a halo around his head. He turned to face me. I squinted to see his expression. Was that a tear I saw in his eye?

"What was that noise?"

I looked down at my red, throbbing big toe. "Oh, nothing."

He waved the card. "Thanks for the grill. I think it's the best gift you've ever given me."

I limped towards him, swelling with joy. "Really? You like it?" *I am a good wife!* Now if he'd just lean down and kiss my belly and thank the baby it would be the perfect moment we would look back on for years to come.

He rubbed his eyes, tearing up. "Damn allergies. That mowing really got to me today."

Oh. Allergies. Of course. When had I ever seen Jake cry? Never, that's when. As he swept by me to get the half-finished patties from the fridge, he *ruffled my hair*, leaving the card from our baby on the patio table. What did I expect? That he'd take it to work and display it on his desk?

"Happy Father's Day," I said in a whisper.

CHAPTER 14

Eating for two is no joke. I ate two burgers that night, and was now usually having seconds at every meal. The women you see who look like they're carrying a round basketball up front and stay skinny everywhere else? Not me. I wasn't eating junk food most of the time, I just ate a lot of whatever it was. I even ate two servings of broccoli! (With cheese on top.)

Still determined to make Jake a romantic dinner, the next night I put on a face mask Jake usually wore for mowing and made a pot roast. Deep in the recesses of the hall closet I found candles I'd bought eons ago, and set the table with the delicate blue and silver china we'd picked out together eight years before. How many times had we used it since we'd been married? For the bridge girls when it was my turn to host . . . That's about all. Tonight I would go all out. I would be sexy and funny and flirty. Jake would look at me the way he had before I got pregnant.

I'd been waiting for him for nearly an hour, pacing the floor of the formal living room, peeking out the blinds, sitting on the front porch. I wrung my hands in worry, imagining Jake's SUV lying on its side on the highway, Jake pinned under the wheel, bleeding profusely. Dark thoughts were the leftovers from my parents' death. I'd finally weaned myself off anxiety medication my senior year in college. Jake and I were engaged and I ignorantly thought I'd never have another worry in my life. Soon I was throwing up and biting my nails and having nightmares about Jake's demise. I'd imagined every possible way for Jake to die. He'd been shot by an angry defendant, burned to death in a house fire, drowned when he went skiing, fell off of a mountain hiking, eaten by a bear in the woods and, of course, killed in a car accident at least a hundred times. I didn't share my dark thoughts with Jake, but he knew that I couldn't stand for him to be late. My worry expressed itself in anger. He still didn't know most of our fights were based on fear.

Once I got back on the antianxiety meds, my fear had calmed, but I could still feel it itching every time Jake left the house. After a few years I got fed up relying on the drugs again and dropped them cold turkey. When a black thought entered my head, I gave the imagined scene a positive ending. Jake running out of the burning building unscathed, surfacing from near drowning, and walking away from his crashed car. It worked most of the time. But combine high levels of pregnancy hormones with my innate anxiety and I was back at the edge of the cliff. Jake wasn't helping matters. I'd called his cell phone a dozen times. I'd turned on the news to make sure he wasn't the breaking story.

When I saw his Range Rover pull into the drive, and I could see the shadowed outline of his body behind the wheel, I relaxed my posture and muttered, "Son of a bitch," when inside I meant, *Thank God he's still alive.* Just as I headed for the garage to greet him, his car reversed and sped away again down the street. My heart sank. What the hell was going on? Moments later, the phone rang. I let it ring. Once, twice. It was in a tight grip in my hands. I held it to my ear.

"Hello?" I answered, trying to restrain my anger.

"Hi, honey. Listen, I'm going to be late tonight. I just re-membered I forgot to finish up some papers for a deposi-tion in the morning. It'll be a tough one and I want to be prepared," he said from his cell phone, which miracu-lously had survived being broken into a thousand pieces on the turnpike as I'd imagined.

"Oh," I said, disappointed. I cleared my throat, my voice strained. "I just saw you, Jake. I've been waiting for you. For a fucking hour!" Careful. I sounded desperate. I *was* desperate. I'd cooked for God's sake! And I'd made myself a widow in my head. Right now I was so mad, I was considering buying him the cheapest casket the funeral home sold.

"Sorry, honey." He didn't sound sorry at all.

"Well, I don't feel like working tonight, so maybe I can bring you dinner at the office?" Perhaps an office seduc-tion would do the trick. I'd planned a romantic evening and by God I was going to get it one way or another.

"No, I don't want to trouble you, honey. You probably need the rest. Just watch TV and relax. See you later to-night, okay?"

Tears streamed down my face as I mustered the word, "Fine," before hanging up.

The pot roast and mashed potatoes would turn cold. Frank Sinatra would spin on the CD changer to an empty room. The candles would burn their romantic glow for no one. The baby and I would spend another night alone with my desolate thoughts. Why did I fear he was lying to avoid being home with me? We both knew he could damn well work at home.

Feeling out of control again, I wept on the bed. What had happened to the strong woman I'd become? I had cried more in the last three months than in my entire life, save for when my parents died. I told myself it was just the hormones, the anxiety, but I knew it was more than the baby and my body's state of flux. When Jake and I had been dating he couldn't wait to spend time with me. I was up for any adventure with him, and he told me over and over again how I wasn't like other girls. I didn't suffocate him, or act jealous. I gave him his freedom and now it was coming back to bite me. Not being like other girls wasn't a compliment. I hadn't wanted to get too close to Jake and I hadn't wanted to bring a child into the world because I was afraid, but for the first time, I wanted to make it right. Feel like a normal woman acting like a normal wife and a normal mother. I didn't have a clue how, though.

Determined to make the best of a lost evening, I dressed in a jogging suit, grabbed my headphones and listened to the Dixie Chicks. No matter my mood, the Chicks had enough spunk and men-be-damned lyrics to lift my spirits.

Crickets chirped and dogs barked as I walked the streets of our neighborhood, watching families arrive home and kids play in the summer evening air on their bikes and in their front yards. I still couldn't imagine a child on a bike in my driveway. *My* child. As usual, everyone seemed happier than I did. Mom knew how to get a laugh out of me even when I was maddest at the world. Instinctively I knew Mom would've been better at being a grandma. Less worry, zero blame for how the child turned out. I sometimes wished I could skip to being a grandma, too.

As the Chicks jammed, I pumped my arms and legs faster, trying to walk away my gloomy mood. My waist had thickened and my gut was pronounced, but I still fit into my lycra jogging suit. For pregnant, I didn't look half bad. Better yet, I didn't really care. Six blocks later, I got up the nerve to get in my car and move forward with Operation Attack Hot Attorney.

I pulled into Jake's law firm parking lot eight minutes later, still unsure of what I would say when I got in. Maybe I wouldn't need to speak at all. I was wearing red lingerie underneath my jogging suit. Hell, I was his *wife*; what excuse did I need?

Punching in the combination to the keypad, I marched into the building and heard sounds of laughter coming from his office. Unfamiliar laughter, one distinctly Jake's. The other, an unknown female's.

I crept down the long dark hallway and stood in the shadows where I could see into his office. From my vantage point, I saw his legs in his Italian slacks, propped up on the coffee table, and two bare legs next to his. She wore a brick red skirt, what little there was of it, her black high heels kicked off under the table, which left her barefoot with hot pink toenails. I didn't recognize her feet; it wasn't what most wives looked at when they visited their lawyer husbands with the school of model-pretty office staff swarming around them. Leggy, they were all leggy, every sparkling-toothed one of them.

I didn't recognize her voice, either, deep and flirting with a sigh at the end that seemed to show impatience to get on with whatever they were going to get on. They all had smooth, lilting voices. They raised their voices an octave when the lawyers entered the room, and rolled their shoulders back to give their breasts full attention. They were smitten and husband-hungry; at the least, they were lovelorn and didn't mind being kept in an apartment rented especially for them, or spending their evenings at faux depositions at the office. I'd heard all of that before, straight from Jake's mouth, when he talked of a partner who had slipped up, got caught with a pair of pantyhose in his couch or didn't hide the receipts from the expensive dinners for two. I'd taken his gossip sharing as a sign that he thought adultery was wrong, though he never said it. I assumed he thought his partners were stupid for cheating, but stupid for getting caught seemed to make more sense.

My mind raced as to what to do next. Did I want to wait there for something to happen? What did I think would happen, anyway? Would he really cheat on me? I realized I'd locked my knees, and they were about to give in and send me falling into the doorway. As I bent them, my right knee cracked. I held my breath and moved an inch to the right, enough so that I could see the rest of the scene. The blonde vixen made her move. She stood and stepped over Jake's legs, obviously to give him a better show of her, and he responded by patting her on the behind. My mouth dropped, I squeezed my eyes shut. I remembered that feeling of being on the outside, looking in horror into a room, wishing my eyes were deceiving me, that it was all a terrible dream.

At the funeral home the day after my parents had died, after they had been readied for viewing, Aunt Barb wanted me to go in first, as if it were a privilege instead of a curse. I stood in the doorway to the small, well-lit room where their handsome caskets lay. From my post, I could see all that I needed to: that they were really dead, too cold to be sleeping, too posed to be alive. I didn't cry then either; I felt as frozen as they looked.

I witnessed just the hint of her small frame, her thin arms, the profile of her porcelain face, the curly hair against the satin pillow. I had picked out the outfit earlier that afternoon, her favorite cashmere sweater, the pink one I'd bought for her the Christmas before. She had eyed it in the department store for a month and I used all of my saved allowance to get it for her. In life, it had complimented her, softened her tough persona. In death, it represented all she would never be again. The sight revolted me, the pink against my pale, dead mother, the matching lipstick she only wore on special dates with my father. But he was there, too.

I couldn't move my body, but if I cranked my head to the left, I saw my father there, his broad shoulders lifted slightly, leaning as if to get up. I stared at his chest a long while, too afraid to look at his face. I had picked out the clothes I remembered him best in, the navy blue suit with the navy tie with red triangles. He wore it every week on trips selling insurance. He bounded out of the house in the suit on Tuesday mornings, muffin crumbs on the tie, and returned with it on Thursday, no worse for the wear, perhaps a coffee stain on the crumpled white shirt. I would run up and hug him upon his return, pressing my face against the tie, taking in the smell of sweat, coffee, and cologne. Finally, I looked at his face, imagining it was a wax figure on display like a movie legend in a museum.

That way I could admire the face, the likeness this figure had to my father, though caked with makeup and void of expression.

That was all I needed. A visitor in a museum—not allowed to walk past the imaginary red rope that kept me from getting too close to the displays. I did not want to belong there, to share the space with the bodies that were my family, the three of us together again for the last time. Two passed on to another life, one left to figure out this life on her own. I would have no part of it. I turned and ran then, past my Aunt Barb, who was gibbering to other relatives, past my cousins who had pity in their eyes, past girlfriends who wept more for themselves at the thought of losing their own parents than they wept for me.

Twelve years later, I was frozen in place, detached, unsure if I should turn and run. *I was about to lose him, too.*

"Can I get you a drink?" the woman said, walking over to his minibar.

"Yeah. Grab me a beer, would you?"

The woman brought back two bottled longnecks. She took a swig, set the beer on the coffee table and stood in front of Jake. She took off her top, revealing a silver see-through bra. Victoria's Secret spring collection. I had the same one at home. Surely Jake would recognize it. "I could think of better ways to spend the next half hour." She straddled Jake and sat on his lap.

Jake laughed nervously. My heart pounded through my chest. The woman bent down to kiss Jake, but as their lips touched, he pushed her away and off of him. She landed with a thud on the couch.

Jake stood. "I'm sorry, Kate, but I can't do this."

I let out a sigh of relief.

"What do you mean? You've been coming on to me for weeks. Don't tell me I was getting the wrong signal!" she hissed.

Pacing the room, Jake ran his fingers through his hair, as he often did in uncomfortable situations. "No. I've defi-

nothing we can do to stop it. I'm not ready to start a family, because I've realized I don't even know who you are. You put a wall up. You've always kept your feelings inside. Not telling me about the baby from the beginning is a perfect example. I didn't think you *wanted* children, but that didn't stop me from marrying you. I think your girlfriends and Allen know more about you than I do."

I opened my mouth to argue, but he was right. I probably hadn't shared with him the way a wife should share with her husband.

"You've never talked to me about your parents, either."

I flinched. "There's nothing to talk about."

"Sure there is. What were they like? How did you feel about them? How did you deal with their death? You don't even have pictures of them around the house. I don't know the Taylor who existed before she was nineteen. It's as if you were born the day I met you, as if you had no past."

"I was reborn the day I met you, Jake. You saved me from my past, and it doesn't have a place in my life now."

"Being a mystery when we were dating was one thing. But it's not fun anymore trying to figure you out. I want a marriage with real intimacy."

I put my sweaty palms against the wall, pushed myself up and retreated to the corner of his office, as far away from him as the space would allow. I sat at his swivel desk chair and stared at the photo of us in college, after he'd given me his fraternity pin. I was nearly the same woman today as the one in the picture. Our time together filled albums, but I'd kept him on a circular track around my heart. "You've got a funny way of showing it." I paused. "I love you. Isn't that enough?"

"Not when we're going to bring a child into the world. I want to make sure we're going to be good parents and do this thing right."

I swore after my parents died, I would never love anyone again that deeply. My self was intertwined with his, and I felt like half a person without him, despite my efforts at independence. "I made you dinner tonight." He knew that was a miracle in itself—I, Queen of the Drive-Thru, actually using the stove.

"I can't remember the last time you made me dinner," he said. He moved in closer to me.

"If you think pot roast is something, wait until you see what I have under here." I removed my T-shirt, revealing the first red lace bra Jake had bought for me in college. I happened to be fifteen pounds heavier then, so it was perfect for my more voluptuous pregnant form.

Jake reached out and touched my bra. "This I do remember. I'm sorry, Taylor. I'm a heartless bastard."

For once, I didn't argue. Why did I feel like all I could do was screw everything up? We embraced, and I felt alive. His tears united with mine on my flushed cheeks. We shut the door to his office and locked it and made love on his leather couch. What he wanted was not so simple; he wanted to be inside me like never before.

CHAPTER 15

As much as we tried to be together, our busy lives interfered. We kissed more often, smiled more, left each other sweet voice mail messages. Beyond that, I worried about not being good enough, not being able to achieve the kind of intimacy Jake longed for.

One night while I lay on our bed and waited for Jake to come home, I grabbed the pregnancy test from Molly's skirt and pitched it in the trash can.

I recalled how Amy had wrapped up her first positive pregnancy test in a small box and gave it to her husband as an early Christmas present. He'd told her it was the best gift he'd ever been given. *Better than a grill.*

I could've done the same thing—wrapped up the test in bright blue wrapping paper with a tiny silver bow and surprised Jake. He might have nearly passed out as he'd done in the waters off Hawaii, but I would never know because I was too afraid. It would have been a lie—a sweet lie, no doubt—but a lie nonetheless, because at the time I could not see my baby as a gift.

Molly abetted my secret, but she understood my motive, my fears. She'd been around for three generations and saw how love was not the white knight the fairy tales claimed. Love came with an entourage of other emotions—jealousy, dependence and most of all, pain.

In my family, the children suffered the most from love's byproducts. It was safe to assume my child would be no different; that as hard as I tried otherwise, I would cause irreparable harm. If I opened the decrepit doors of my past, Jake would see that I came from a long line of unfit mothers. He would see that to raise a child properly, he would need another woman, another wife entirely. That the baby within me was poisoned simply by being in my womb.

Molly lay tucked in my arms, a place she was familiar with, as I cried on my down pillow. She was there when I didn't have the strength to clean out my bedroom after my parents died. I hadn't wanted to leave the small space I'd had since I was born, the room where my crib had stood, my Barbie house had taken residence, and where dreams of young love filled my head. The house had sold within a week of the accident. Seven days of lying in bed all day, too sick and numb to care about the time of day or what day of the week it was. I heard Aunt Barb whispering outside the room as I slipped in and out of tearful fits of troubled sleep. Then I was kicked out of my cocoon so the new family could move in, a family whole and alive—two adults, two children, and a dog. Molly was all I had left.

The last moments with my parents alive plagued me, a video loop of it replayed in my mind ad nauseam. I picked it apart, one minute at a time, like a defeated player analyzing a loss after a big game. I had said the wrong thing, done the wrong thing, and I could never take it back. I could not leave my bed because I didn't want the truth to come out. *That I did it.* I caused my parents' death. How could I ever look at myself in the mirror? The loathsome creature that caused such an atrocity. Over and over all this played.

My mother, back from a PTA meeting, had rummaged through the fridge, contemplating our dinner choices.

"Honey," she said, turning toward me. I was seated at the table finishing an algebra assignment, still not speaking to my mother since the day before when she'd grounded me. I didn't respond.

"Taylor, we're almost out of milk. Think you could run down to the store and pick some up?"

I continued with my homework, ignoring her.

My father, just home from a business trip, walked into the kitchen and wrapped his arms around my mother. "Hey, pumpkin," he said to me.

"Hi, Dad," I said, not looking up.

Out of the corner of my eye, I saw my mother place her hand on her hip. She let out an exasperated sigh. "Yesterday you hated me, today you won't talk to me? Taylor, you're always begging to take the car. What's the big deal?" my mother said, more irritated with me.

"Dad, please tell Mother if she wants some milk, she can go get it herself."

Mom sighed again, tired of trying, I presumed. Dad just shook his head, knowing well enough not to get in the middle of one of our fights. "Come on, hon," he said to Mom. "I'll go with you. It's a beautiful day out. Maybe we'll even pick up Ms. Grump some of her favorite chocolate chip ice cream."

"Whatever," I said, as they headed out the door, the last time I would see them alive.

If I had done as my mother wished, ran her errand, would I have taken the same route to meet the drunk driver? Had I driven faster or slower, perhaps I could have avoided the same tragedy. In the days after they died, I longed to trade places. Or at least I wished my dad had coaxed me into taking that fatal drive with them.

Twelve years later, the guilt still lived within me, pushed deep inside but there, nonetheless. It had risen once more and I wanted to hide from it, take refuge in my bed.

My body, my baby, needed nutrition. I had to eat. My job needed me there, so I went about my schedule in a mum-

mified state. I don't know if the paranoia was because of
the pregnancy hormones or because of my newly surfaced
grief or just a powerful mix of anxiety from impending
motherhood, my marriage, and work. But, all of a sudden,
I was worried about everything.

Did men divorce their pregnant wives? Maybe I was
just a bad wife, pregnant or not. After all, I didn't like to
do the traditional wifey things. On a good day, I didn't
burn dinner, and as for housekeeping, we hired a maid to
do that. I was a good lover, but I'd learned that wasn't
enough.

I was not naïve. Every so often on bridge night, I'd hear
the tale of a friend of a friend who'd been served with divorce papers, women who had no idea their husbands were
unhappy. Thin, gorgeous, nice women. Women more apt at
being good wives than I was. So, yes, I was worried sick.

What would become of me if Jake left? A workaholic
with a baby, too tired to socialize, no time for anything
but diapers and takeout. The bridge girls would try desperately to set me up on dates, but I would always cancel
at the last minute or find a million reasons not to like the
men they set me up with. After all, they wouldn't be Jake.

Then there would be the shared custody. Jake would decide he loved our baby, maybe too much. He wouldn't be
satisfied with weekend visitation, so he'd sue for custody,
right after he married the woman his mother had wished
he'd married in the first place. He would unveil the secrets
of my mother and grandmother, convince the jury that a
woman that came from my heritage couldn't be a good
mother.

Whoa, was this out-of-control paranoia, or what?

Eating my fourth slice of supreme pizza, I called Allen,
needing a voice of reason before Jake's plane arrived a few
hours later.

" 'Lo?" Allen answered breathlessly on the other end.

"Either I caught you on the treadmill or in the middle of
a romp. Which is it?"

"I'm planning on my own fireworks after the fireworks," Allen answered. "What's up? Jake not back yet?"

"No. And I'm too tired to pack for New York. I wish you could go without me. I really don't think Jake and I should be apart any more than we already are."

"Hey, at least you're back on track in the sack. That's all I promised."

"I think the problem is that I'm a little bit too much like you."

Allen shut off the treadmill. "What's that supposed to mean?"

"I mean you're an emotionally distant swinging single and I'm an emotionally distant pregnant wife. Only you can get away with it because you haven't committed to anyone, and I can't get away with it because I vowed to give everything to this man for the rest of my life."

"Well, you're giving him a baby."

"That's physical. Yes, that's *huge*, but I haven't completely given him my heart."

Allen paused. "Because you're in love with me?"

"No, asshole. Because I haven't shared my past with him. I haven't really opened up to him."

"You know how I told you talking was overrated?"

"Yes."

"Forget that. You've got to tell him everything. I know you're still broken up about losing your parents, but time is never going to heal it. Jake seems like a damn good guy. Coming from an asshole like me, that's saying something."

"I know. I know. I'll do it when we get back from New York."

"So you're going to go, anyway?"

"Susan threatened two more heads on the chopping block if we don't come up with three amazing campaigns while we're gone."

"Great. I thought we'd get some downtime in the Big Apple. We've been working like slaves as it is."

"Hey, that's what cocktail napkins are for, right? We can

combine work *and* play. Maybe NYC will inspire us. Was that your doorbell?"

Allen sighed. "Looks like my fireworks arrived earlier than expected."

"Eww. Good-bye."

"Ta-ta."

After I got dressed in my red, white, and blue, I headed to the hall closet, where a photo box sat underneath the spare blankets and pillows. I inhaled deeply and removed the lid for the first time in ten years. I took out a photo of my parents that I had taken at my Aunt Barb's Fourth of July picnic the year they died. My dad had his arm wrapped around my mother, her hand resting on his wrist. Cheek-to-cheek, they smiled and I smiled back at them. *I've missed you.* I placed the photo on Jake's pillow. Why had I told him I didn't have any photos of them? He'd seen pictures of them at Aunt Barb's. It didn't pain her to display them.

Sitting against the headboard, I pulled my baby's journal out from the drawer in my bedside table and propped it on my knees. I hadn't written in it since Hawaii. So much had happened since then. I contemplated giving the laundry list—told my bitchy boss, put girlfriends in shock, considered shopping for maternity clothes, but chickened out at the last minute and bought new shoes instead. But if I were to open up to Jake, to have a real relationship with my family, I had to speak from the heart.

Dear Baby,

You've made your presence known and my world is suddenly turned upside down. It's been the craziest four months of my life. I don't think I've ever known anyone more afraid of being parents than your father and I. If I were better equipped at this mommy stuff, then I think I could pull your daddy around sooner. But you know what? This—you—are the best thing that ever happened to us, because otherwise I can see your father and I living together the rest of our lives without ever growing any closer. Can you believe you're the size of a lime and have the power to do that? I've always heard children can either bring parents together or pull them apart. I'm going to make sure it's the former. Hang in there, little guy (or girl). Your mother's going to figure all this out.

Love,
Taylor

Kids were splashing in the pool in their father's arms when I arrived at Amy and Tim's patriotic party, making me miss Jake. I imagined he'd be a good pool dad. And soccer. Golf. Riding bikes. The list in my head grew longer with each passing day.

A band played rock and roll in the far corner of their immaculate backyard, landscaped with red and white roses. Four misters kept guests cool. Already sweating, I considered standing under one all night, soaked or not. A dozen guests sipped frozen drinks around the pool.

McKenzie rushed up to me with a handful of small U.S. flags. She wore a red, white, and blue striped dress with silver-star ponytails in her hair, bouncing as she spoke. "Here you go," she said sweetly, pushing the flag into my hand. She reached out with her empty hand and placed it on my belly. "How's your baby today?"

I put my hand over hers. "The baby's fine. Thank you for asking."

"Does your baby like cupcakes? 'Cause I made cupcakes."

I fingered her soft ponytail. "I think so. Especially if you made them."

Jennifer and Jackie eyed me and strolled over. "How's our little mama?" Jennifer said, air-kissing my cheek.

Jackie gave me a squeeze. "You're finally starting to look pregnant. I think I was already in maternity clothes in the second month. And here it's been 18 months and I'm still not back in my pre-baby clothes."

"Unlike some people," Jennifer said, referring to Amy,

who looked hot in a teeny-weeny stars-and-stripes bikini.

"Just know she's an anomaly. Don't hate yourself if you can't get into one of those seven months after delivery," Jackie said. "I guess having a hot personal trainer might motivate me, too."

"My ears are burning," Amy yelled, approaching us. She put her arm around my waist and led us to a table shaded with an umbrella. She motioned to a waiter dressed like Uncle Sam, albeit shirtless. "Virgin margarita, please."

"Where's Romeo?" Amy asked, sitting next to me.

"Flight delayed. Says he'll meet me here."

"Things okay there?" Jennifer asked hesitantly. I'd told them about Kate. Like good friends should, they didn't know whether or not they should trust Jake. Especially away on a business trip.

"When he's in town, things are better. He's not avoiding me at least."

My friends looked at me pitifully. Their husbands had all been ecstatic about having a baby. Well, maybe not ecstatic, but they didn't consider office trysts, either.

A crying baby noise came from Amy's hip, but there was no baby. Amy pulled a tiny receiver the size of a lipstick tube from the side of her bikini. "Wireless baby monitor. Don't you love technology?"

"Hey there, little guy," a man's voice said through the receiver.

The girls exchanged curious glances. Tim was in the pool with McKenzie.

Austin stopped crying and started cooing. "You want to go party?" The voice spoke again.

"Is that who I think it is?" Jackie asked.

"No way," Jennifer said in dismay.

A moment later, Jake emerged with Austin in his arms and my heart leaped. The bridge girls stared at him. He'd never volunteered to pick up a crying baby before. "What?" he said, walking toward us.

"Nice party accessory," I told him.

"You look pretty comfortable there," Amy told him.

"Oh, this?" He shook Austin, who giggled and drooled on Jake's forearm. "Piece of cake."

Maybe there was hope after all.

MONTH FOUR

Hot Mama

CHAPTER 16

*Week 19: You've almost made it to the halfway mark—
way to go! Your baby measures six inches and weighs
eight ounces. This is a crucial time for sensory development. The brain is developing specialized areas for smell,
taste, hearing, vision, and touch.*

The rush of New York City was a welcome reprieve from
being chained to my desk at work. Allen and I hailed a cab
at the airport and headed for the Paramount Hotel. As
usual, the cabbie drove like a bat out of hell. "Jesus, man,
she's with *child*," Allen said repeatedly, as if that would
make a difference.

"Congratulations," the driver said dryly around the un-
lit cigarette between his lips. "You two must be very
happy."

Contorting his face in zealous glee, Allen put his arms
around me and kissed me on the cheek. "Oh, we're both
just *peachy*," he said, playing along.

Once we screeched into the ritzy entranceway to the hotel, I felt relieved just to be alive. The concierge took our
bags and we checked in like giddy tourists. Traveling with

Allen was never a bore; he was always thankful to be traveling *anywhere*, especially on the company dime. Because the Big Apple had great *Cosmo* gals and cosmo drinks, he usually wore a stud grin on his face the entire trip. What he liked most, I believed, was the fact he could have a one-night stand and not have the woman look him up afterwards. Convention sex was far freer than any local liaison. Five minutes in the hotel and he had already eyed a good-looking sophisticate at the front desk, another at the bar.

"Down, Fido," I teased, placing my credit card on the counter.

Allen cocked an eyebrow and whimpered like an injured puppy.

"Behave. I think I'll just check out my room and meet you down here in an hour to go to dinner," I said. "Remember, we've got enormous brainstorming as an appetizer."

"Can't waste a minute," Allen said, already moving away from me, like a magnet being pulled to the Yankee babes.

"Calm down, Al. You decide where we should eat tonight. I'm exhausted."

"Okay, Mama Bear," Allen said, wrinkling up his face. "I'll just have a martini or two and be right over there next to that gorgeous little thing in the corner."

"Great," I said, and turned to see my old college nemesis, Nikki Parsons, walking through the hotel doors. We were fiercely competitive in school, vying for the top awards at all the state and regional Addy's, as well as in competing sororities. She, the leggy blonde; me, the duller brunette. If I had to give her any credit, it would be that she was a slightly better artist than I was, just as I was a slightly better copywriter than she was. Together we'd make the perfect ad team. But damned if I'd let that happen. When we graduated, we both ended up at Ace Advertising, where our rivalry continued with fervor, each trying to outpitch the other and come up with the "big idea" that would hoist us up the rungs of the advertising ladder. Nikki left a year later to start her own ad agency with two associates. All three were young, hip, and hot. They had no problems getting clients who wanted a "fresh" approach and quick turnaround.

Shortly thereafter, I got promoted to senior copywriter, then assistant creative director and finally, creative director and vice president. Nikki's small firm had big billings for a ten-person operation, but a part of me still wanted to compete with her instead of rejoice at her success. Most of all, I was pleased she'd gained about twenty pounds since college. She was now more Amazon than supermodel. As she surveyed the room, she spotted me. I couldn't duck in time.

"Taylor, you haven't changed a bit," Nikki said with an overly friendly hug. I knew she she was probably taking in my rounder face and new belly and secretly doing a happy dance. In college, I'd always been thinner than she was.

"How are you? Can you believe we're billing five million this year?" she said, ever eager to prove herself.

"Good for you," I said, noticing her jewelry—gold and diamonds dripping from every patch of exposed skin. She had ruined the moment for me. Nikki was an entrepreneur, a smart businesswoman and obviously well-to-do. I was a hanger-on, clinging to the only company I'd ever worked for, following procedure instead of instigating change. She was in charge. I was a Dilbert.

"Are you expecting?" she said.

"Expecting what?"

"Expecting a *baby*, silly."

I looked down at my protruding tummy, not at all hidden by the cotton shirt that hugged it. "Due December twenty-seven. What about you—got kids?"

Amazon nodded, flashing her still perfect smile, probably recently whitened. "Two. One of each. Carly's three and Carter is one," she said, wasting no time whipping out pictures. Damn, they were cute.

"Good for you." Hadn't I already said that? Why did I sound like such a dimwit around her?

"I haven't even been gone half a day and I miss them like crazy. You'll see. Motherhood changes you. Must be tough being pregnant at Ace. I remember what the hours are like."

"They're being supportive," I lied. "I'm managing okay."

Nikki shook her head. "Yeah, right. The only support Susan knows about is bras and pantyhose. Just remember Ace isn't the only game in town. Or the country for that matter. At my firm, we're very family friendly. Four days in the office and one at home," Nikki said. "I converted one of our offices into a day care room."

This didn't sound like the same Nikki I'd worked with until the wee hours of the morning one too many times to count. The Nikki who was paranoid what clients would think of her. The Nikki who sacrificed love affairs and friendships for work until she finally met someone who stopped her in her tracks. The former advertising diva was diva no more.

"And the clients are okay with that?" I managed to say. I tried to imagine Nikki pitching a new client while a child wailed in the background.

"Oh, sure. If they aren't, then it wasn't meant to be in the first place," she said assuredly. "Besides, we sound-proofed the day care room."

"Wow. You seem so . . . *happy*."

Nikki appeared to have tears in her eyes, but Nikki never cried. Not even when Susan had raked her over the coals in front of everyone. "You have no idea," she said. "But you will, Taylor. You will. Now promise me we can go to lunch when we get back to Dallas."

Do lunch? An alien had surely body-snatched her. It made more sense than just popping out a couple of kids. Nikki Parsons, my future play date buddy? Could it be?

I was a little miffed that my nemesis had given me an awfully good idea. Ace had plenty of room for day care. Why hadn't I thought of that first?

Still puzzled by my surreal reunion, I headed for the eleva-tor and stepped back to the right corner, as was my custom, and a handsome man in a beige suit with dark shades stepped in, tilted his head, and smiled.

"Five, please," I told the handsome stranger, who looked slightly familiar.

The man hit the button with his knuckle and the elevator ascended. "What a coincidence. I'm also on five," he said in a voice like a radio announcer, smooth and low. Pivoting on his heel, he turned to me and removed his sunglasses, revealing dark chocolate eyes. "I'm Jude Waters," he said, placing his large palm out for me to take.

Mmmm. I shook his hand. I knew I'd seen him recently—on the cover of *Advertising Age.* "Hi, Jude. I'm Taylor."

"In town for business?"

I nodded. "The advertising convention down the street."

"Me, too," he said. "I own Titan Advertising in Chicago."

I knew all about Titan, but didn't want to sound too impressed, even though they were five times larger than our agency. "Creative director in Dallas," I said. "Ace Advertising."

"Ace, huh? I know Susan. She's a bright woman."

"Bright, indeed." That was *one* word for her.

The elevator stopped and the doors opened onto our floor.

"Well, I'm looking forward to seeing more of you at the convention," he said, and turned down the long hallway. I paused a moment just to watch him walk. He had the rich-man swagger down, but he didn't seem as arrogant as I'd expected. Knowing that he ran Titan Advertising, however, his reputation preceded him. Word through the ad-biz grapevine was that Jude was quite the ladies' man. Voted Most Eligible Bachelor in Chicago. He had to be a bachelor for a reason.

I unlocked my hotel room door to the cool rush of air and the clean, big bed just waiting for my long-awaited afternoon nap. The harder I tried to sleep, though, the more it eluded me.

After tossing and turning, I decided to call my Aunt

Barb in Austin, who sent weekly motivational e-mails about pregnancy and God and other cyber-esteem that she hoped would make me feel better, but her digital good tidings could not compare with hearing her voice. She had a laugh much like Mom's, which made me cry instantly.

"Honey, it's so good to hear from you. How are you feeling?"

"Oh, good," I said. "Physically, good. A little exhausted."

Her voice lightened. "You sound a little depressed."

Bingo. Damn, that woman was good. "I'm not sure I'm cut out for the motherhood stuff. I just ran into Nikki Parsons. You remember her from college?"

"How could I forget? You two were always the top of your class."

"Well, she has two kids already and she seems to have it so together, and I just feel like a mess, mess, mess."

Aunt Barb sighed. "You're going to be a *great mother*, Taylor."

"You think so?"

"I *know* so. Just take all the negative thoughts you're having and toss them out," she told me, as if my worries were physical manifestations I could throw away like garbage. If only it were that simple.

"I'm trying," I said, my voice cracking a little, but I wanted to be as strong as she was, the woman who never crumbled when faced with adversity.

"I recall having this same conversation twenty-eight years ago, and I told her what I'm telling you now. History does not have to repeat itself. You make your own destiny."

"I know—you're right. When are you not right? But I didn't think I'd be going through so much emotion."

Aunt Barb was patient on the other end. She had to be patient with me, her sister's only child, little girl lost. The wall of confidence I'd built from my career was a façade, and she knew the real person beneath the freshly pressed suit.

"This should be the happiest time of your life."

There it was again. That word, *happy*. Jake had said we couldn't be the "old" happy, the one that I was comfortable with, the happy that allowed us to live in the same house and exist together without sharing our most intimate selves. The happy that didn't mean opening up my soul to him to reveal the wounds and heal them once and for all.

"I'm going to tell him everything after I get back from New York."

"Why do you still blame yourself, sweet girl?"

"Because! Because I have to. Because Mom and Dad should be alive. She almost got through raising me and she and dad could have gone on the long vacations they talked about. They could be grandparents. It's because of me that they died so young."

"I know it hurts. I miss them, too. But our spirits live on, Taylor. We're going to be reunited with them one day."

"I'm sorry, Aunt Barb. That doesn't make me feel any better." Taking advice from her would be wise. Aunt Barb played David in the Goliath story of her life. She had suffered and survived. I'd never known anyone quite like her. Never had a bad word to say about anybody, no matter the circumstances. Perhaps it was her birth order that caused it; being the middle child of three girls, Aunt Barb was always the mediator trying to fix whatever her siblings seemed to get into.

"If you survived your childhood, I should be able to survive mine," I told her. At least I was older when it happened, didn't watch my mother die, as my mother and aunts had done.

"It's not up to you anymore," Aunt Barb told me. "It's not about you wanting to be a mother. God has made that decision for you. And as for fearing you won't be a good mother, that's just rubbish."

Deep within me, a seed of caution had been planted that I should not get so close to anyone again. When Jake and I were dating, I couldn't talk about my parents or death with him, for fear it would scare him off. Inside I was a basket case.

"I'd like to go back in time and see who placed a hex on

our family. I feel like the only card our family is dealt is the death card." With Aunt Barb I could get away with feeling sorry for myself, but I could only take it so far.

"Superstition is only for people who don't believe in God," she said, her voice strained.

We'd worn out this conversation long ago. She preferred to think I didn't believe in God, when in fact, I just believed he wasn't the good God she did. Who else dealt us the death card?

"You lost your mother and your sister. You and I know better than anyone that kids and family come with pain and heartache. Why would I want to subject myself and Jake and our child to that? I don't think I can go through it again." I grabbed a tissue off the bedside table and wiped at the mascara running down my face.

"You're only looking at a piece of the puzzle, sweetheart. Death is inevitable, but it's only one piece. Some of us get more than our share of it, but the rest of the puzzle is the good stuff. The rest makes life worth living."

I blew my nose. I didn't know how Aunt Barb always found the silver lining. Nothing seemed to rattle her cage. She had a calm faith that I could not know unless I surrendered to it, and after all those years, I wasn't sure I could.

"I know it's hard not having your mom here with you now," she said. "For most women, a first pregnancy bonds them to their mothers. Moms suddenly make sense when you become one."

I sobbed into the phone. "I thought I was over it. I *want* to be over it."

"You never completely get over a loved one's death. I still miss my mom after forty years, and I don't even have that many memories of her. It hurts a little less over time, but there are triggers. Holidays, birthdays, having a baby. It makes the pain as harsh as the day it happened."

"So I'm not crazy then." I opened up my suitcase where Molly lay between my black pants and pajamas. I took her out and leaned her against the bedside lamp.

"Mourning is a lifelong process. Dealing with it makes it easier, though. Sharing your grief with Jake would make it better. You could have a relationship stronger than you ever imagined."

How many people would I need to hear it from to make it sink in? To cause me to act, do what needed to be done for my marriage's sake? "Aunt Barb, you remember that doll I have of Mom's? The one that Grandma Helen gave to her?"

"Of course I do! How is Molly these days?"

I smiled. "She's still the best doll a girl could have. I never asked you how she lost her eye and her arm."

Aunt Barb's voice softened. "Your mom did that after our mother died. She let out her rage on poor Molly, and threw her in the trash. I dug her out and put her back on your mom's bed after the funeral."

My mother had been filled with more grief than I realized. She'd let her grief guide her life, and the pain kept her from showing her love completely. I did no better. Molly had been my mourning doll, too. I'd shared everything with her instead of a real live person. From that moment, I decided she would stand for something else, something good like hope and love. A symbol of family joy. It was possible.

I heard Aunt Barb's oven squeaking open.

"Mmm-mmm," Aunt Barb said, sniffing into the phone. "Snickerdoodle cookies, your favorite. I must've had an intuition you'd call," she said. "I'll eat two just for you, then stick a batch in the mail. Comfort food."

I could nearly taste the hot cookie in my mouth. "I miss you, Aunt Barb."

"I miss you, too, honey. But you're not going to miss me for long. I've got some big news for you," she said. "We're moving to Dallas."

"You *are*?" A tear streaked down my face and I twisted the phone cord with my fingers.

"Yes, Timmy is being relocated there with his accounting company, and he and Jamie and Sam will be moving next week. Mike and I just figured, why not be close to two of our kids?"

Her kid. I was still like a daughter to her.

"Thank you, Aunt Barb. This couldn't be happening at a better time." I needed her. I could admit that to myself.

"I'm thrilled, honey. I don't want to be a nuisance, but I'll be there for you whenever you need me."

Although I only lived with them two and half years in high school and on summer breaks during college, Aunt Barb had become a mother figure to me and I the daughter she had always wanted. She visited me during parents' weekends in college, sent me goodie boxes every month at school, and called me every week.

I longed to see her again. I hadn't had to tell Aunt Barb that the demons of my past had revisited me. We were sisters in the bond of motherless daughters, even though she had been a young girl when it happened to her, not the stubborn, ungrateful teen I had been. Hardly an accessory to her mother's death.

After we said our good-byes, my mind calmed. I fluffed the pillows and thought how nice it felt to love someone with no strings attached, to let the love rise to the top. I suppose it was my family's destiny to suffer and experience loss, to have a few darker puzzle pieces than the rest.

My mother didn't tell me the fate that befell her parents until I was twelve, old enough for the grisly tale that she herself didn't fully understand in adulthood. All I had known was that I only had one set of grandparents and got half the number of Christmas and birthday presents that my friends did. I hadn't told Jake the whole truth. I was still ashamed, two generations later.

CHAPTER 17

Aunt Barb had told me their family had been dirt poor. The girls were born in the country in a makeshift house with two bedrooms, one for the parents, one for the sisters, who slept in one double bed. Their father, my Grandfather Albert, was a mechanic and farmer who died at the age of twenty-nine from heat stroke during harvest. My mother, Mary, was eight when it happened, Aunt Barb seven, and Little Annie only three. She didn't recall any of the tragedy that became of their parents.

My Grandmother Helen stayed at home with her husband, her sweetheart since she was thirteen, and her three girls. When Albert died, my grandmother went insane with grief, or so my mother had told me. It wasn't a surprise to the townsfolk when my grandmother, a petite and pleasant country girl—still a girl at the age of twenty-four—went crazy; she'd always been a weak girl in mind and spirit.

Grandma Helen was so stricken with sorrow after Albert's death she couldn't get out of bed each morning. Instead, she hid under the covers alone with her tears while my mother poured cereal, assuming there was any, for herself and her younger sisters. Around lunch, Mary would check on Helen (to see if she was still alive) and leave a cup of coffee on the floor next to her bed. Before sunset, the coffee was usually half-drank and Mary would take it and wash it out with water and a bar of soap and put it back on the counter for the same routine the next day.

Sometimes in the evening, the girls would hear their mother crying out, "Why, God? Why my Al? Take me, Lord, please take me!" *Take me where?* Barb had thought, but Mary knew her mommy wanted to be with her daddy, and she had a feeling she would get her way.

Weeks had gone by, and the cupboards were empty. Helen's mother, who lived a few hours away, visited one hot afternoon because she'd been unable to reach her daughter by phone, which had been turned off because of an unpaid bill. Grandma Bertha discovered the girls filthy, hungry, and sickly. Helen's mom Bertha lived up to her name—big and mighty, round and fierce.

Bertha didn't even check on her daughter until after she cared for her granddaughters and put them down for a nap.

Mary awoke to the sounds of her mother screaming.

"Hush up!" Bertha yelled, as she picked up her daughter and headed for the bathroom. "Albert is gone and he's not coming back! You have three girls to think of now, Helen. If Mary weren't so bright, they'd all be dead by now. Is that what you want?"

Bertha fed and cared for Helen like a child. Within a week, Helen's prettiness had returned to her face and she had gained some weight back. She smiled when the girls entered the room, didn't cry all the time. Satisfied her daughter was well enough to be left alone, Bertha squeezed the girls good-bye and pulled away in her Chevy, never to see her daughter again.

Mary didn't buy her mother's return to the world. While she smiled on the outside, Helen was crying on the inside, and Mary knew it. Overnight her mother was *too* happy. She talked and acted as if she had somewhere to go and couldn't wait to get there.

It was a blustery June day when it happened. The wind had been strong that morning, blowing tumbleweeds across the field and leaves off the scattering of trees. The windows rattled and the unstable house shook, as lightning sporadically lit the sky and thunder rolled through the land. Annie grabbed her mother's skirt in fright, but Helen was overjoyed by the storm, dancing around the room with Barb and asking Mary to turn up the radio.

The song ended, and an urgent-sounding man said the area was under a tornado warning and for listeners to take cover.

"Mommy," Mary said. "He said *tornado!*"

Barb started crying as a roaring sound filled the air.

"We'll be fine!" Helen said again, twirling Annie in her arms.

Mary looked out the small window, and in the distance saw a great circle of wind kicking up dirt and debris. "It's a tornado!" Mary screamed.

Helen watched the whirring storm dance closer and closer, and smiled and said, "Thank you, Lord."

Mary grabbed her sisters and headed outside towards the cellar. They had ventured there many times over the years, though she had never actually seen a twister. The fierce wind blew little Annie off of her feet as they scrambled the twenty feet to the cellar door. Mary held Annie tightly with one hand, Barb with the other. Annie held on to Molly, which she called her baby. When Mary reached the underground, she asked Barb to lie on the ground on top of Annie so she wouldn't blow away. Small Mary, with her fifty-pound frame, couldn't open the heavy wood and steel door. Each time she lifted it a couple of inches, it slammed down again.

Mary felt the tornado at her back, the roar deafening. Less than a hundred yards away, it lifted a tree out of the ground as easily as Mary had picked a berry the day before.

"*Mommy!*" Mary cried again, tugging at the door. Helen had followed the girls outside and stood in the yard, her arms up at her sides, allowing the wind to flap them as if she were a bird. She stood transfixed, staring at the tornado, a smile still on her face, waiting for it as she had waited for Albert to return from his work in the fields.

Finally, an angel, or so Mary supposed, caught the door as she attempted to open it, and it swung open, slamming to the earth on the other side. She grabbed her sisters and pushed them onto the stairs, where they hobbled down themselves. Watching her mother watch the tornado, Mary cried out, "Mama, *come!* Mama! *Mama!*" but Helen could not—or *would* not—hear her.

As Mary started down the stairs, the tornado licking the ground of their gravel driveway, she looked back to see her mother looking at her for just a second, at peace once again.

Unable to shut the cellar door, Mary huddled in the corner behind the twin mattress, holding on to her sisters for dear life, as their mother and the only home they had ever known swept away like flowers being plucked from the earth.

That's the way my mom liked to remember her mother: a gentle flower being plucked from the earth. She said she didn't feel bitterness toward her mother for wanting to die, for not helping her children to safety, for not caring enough about them to live. Mary felt only a sadness that would stay with her. It was simply a part of who she was, and she could never quite get past it, even when the man she would marry spent his life trying to free Mary of her sadness.

My mother came right out and told me it was why she had never wanted to bear a child of her own. Although I wasn't sure how to take it when she first told me this, I am now certain that a mother should not tell her only child she never wanted children. She never tried to convince me it was a wonderful mistake, either.

The day after Annie's high school graduation, my mother fled to New York, where she fulfilled her dream of becoming a ballet dancer, lived on her own, cared only for herself for the first time in her life. She danced for four years, in plays on and off-Broadway, wherever she could find work. Finally, she was recognized for being Mary the beautiful dancer, and not poor Mary, the daughter of Crazy Helen.

She met Vince, my father, in a small coffee shop where she worked the morning shift. Vince was a traveling salesman, lanky and quick, at the time selling Hoover vacuums door-to-door, and as my mother put it, she just "knew" she was meant to be with him.

They lived together for a year, Dad traveling borough to borough while my mother continued to dance. He gave her the independence she needed to not feel tied down to him or as dependent on him as her mother had been on her father. She told herself if anything happened to Vince, she would survive it. After much coaxing, she agreed to marry him and a few years later, I was born.

That was all I really knew of my mother: the ill-fated childhood, her hesitance to motherhood, and the emotional distance I felt growing up. I could not change my past, but I recognized its influence on the woman I had become. I would do whatever it took to heal and start a new legacy for my family's future generations, starting with the first in line.

As I drifted into sleep, I dreamed of a black tornado whipping through a sunny day, heading closer to the baby in my arms. *My baby*. Fear consumed me, but was quickly overcome with a resolve to save my child. "It's going to be okay. Mama's here."

CHAPTER 18

When I awoke a half-hour later, I'd nearly forgotten where I was, and realizing I was a thousand miles from Jake, my heart hurt. I grabbed my cell phone and rang his.

"I was hoping you'd call before your night out on the town," he answered.

"It's not going to be like the good ole days."

"I take it you mean doing shots until you're dancing on the bar? I think some new good ole days are in order."

"I'd like that. Not that I've gotten to see you much since you became junior partner. We're like strangers bumping in the night."

"We'll make time when you get home. Well, for two days before I have to go to California, anyway. How do you feel?"

"I feel like a whale. And I'm having the strangest dreams. I dreamt about a tornado coming after our baby. I talked to Aunt Barb and it made me think about how my grandma died."

"Yeah, in a tornado, right?"

"Only I didn't tell you everything. My Grandma Helen

wanted the tornado to take her away." I could feel my heart beating faster.

"Suicide by tornado?"

I held Molly to my chest. *You were there, weren't you? In Annie's arms when it happened.*

Jake sounded like an attorney, all logic. "The wind was probably really strong and it kept her from making it to the cellar in time."

"Well, that's not what my mother believed. She said her mother killed herself to be with her father in heaven, only it wasn't *really* a suicide if it was a natural disaster. She said Helen was praising God for bringing the tornado. I know it sounds crazy, but she *was* a little crazy. Love makes you crazy. And it kinda screwed up my mother about relationships from then on."

By now Jake knew I was serious, and he couldn't change my mind. "It must've been hard on your mother to see that."

"Well, whatever happened, it changed things. My mother lived the rest of her life in fear, right up until the moment that the car crashed into her. I'm sure of it. She *never* relaxed. Never trusted in anyone. And that's why she never went to church after she moved out of her grandma's house. That's why I've never gone to church. They say you turn into your mother, and I have. I'm living my life the same way she did hers. I know it sounds crazy, Jake, but I believe there's some sort of curse on my family. I fear I'll die young. Or I'll lose you."

Jake was silent on the other end. He hadn't pressured me to become a pretty couple attending church in our finest clothes every Sunday like his partners' families did. I'd never told him I was angry at God. I had no childhood memories of Christmas Mass or Easter Sunday or church picnics like Jake did. Another big difference in our upbringing.

"I had no idea. I wish I could hug you right now, Tay. Consider this a hug, okay?"

I couldn't help but start crying again. I wanted to tell him everything. About what an awful teenager I'd been. About those fights with my mom—especially the one that led to their death. "Thanks for listening."

"I don't believe in curses, Taylor. I believe in changing things for the better. If you think it's a curse, then I'll break it. I'll do whatever I have to do."

"So you don't think I'll be an unfit mother?"

"Hell no. I think you're going to be a better mom than you realize."

He doesn't think I'll be an unfit mother? Well, that made one of us for now. "So you're coming around then?"

"I sent out a companywide e-mail."

"You didn't!"

"I've got the Cuban cigars to prove it. The partners are meeting at the country club for drinks after work to celebrate. Now go do what you have to do on the town and hurry home to me, okay?"

Hanging up and feeling quite high on my husband, I was ready to enjoy myself. I checked my watch, realizing I was thirty minutes too late to look fabulous and would have to settle for acceptable. Allen was probably already smashed downstairs, too busy flirting to check into his room and change into a better suit until the last minute, when vanity would beat out his libido and he would still manage to look better than me.

The nap was sufficient for an energy boost, though I could've slept all night and been satisfied with a meal of Cheese Nips from the mini bar. Instead of showering, I decided to cocoon in a hot bath with the freebie shi-shi bath salts before I took on NYC.

The water rushed into the tub. I was careful not to get it *too* hot, as I'd read that was bad for the baby. Instead, I scrutinized my naked body, halfway through the pregnancy, in the full-length mirror.

My belly was definitely a round, firm presence. Dare I say, it was *cute*. At the least, it was a mighty important-looking belly. Why would I even want to cover up such an adorable thing? I could prance around New York in those midriff maternity shirts the stars wore. *Hey, look at me!* Hell, I could be sexy with a big baby belly, too. Except for *those*, those jiggly creviced pockets on my thighs. Oh, and those jelly floppers on the back of my arms.

I leaned in closer to the mirror. What had happened to my cheekbones? I poked at them. Yes, they were there, underneath quite a bit of extra skin. And my big blue eyes were all but sunken underneath puffy eyelids. I looked myself over. I was a practical goddess from the knees down. Great calves, thin ankles and slender feet. I had a good month before my legs would succumb to pregnancy's metamorphosis. Damned if I wouldn't wear high heels and short skirts while I could.

Smelling of lavender, dressed in a sharp black suit, I met Allen just where I left him, though he had changed into an expensive gray suit and had applied some bronzing powder to his skin. The bombshell blonde was gone, but beside Allen sat a very dashing Jude Waters.

"I knew it was fate we would meet again," Jude said, standing to greet me. "I hope you don't mind, Allen has asked me to join you both for dinner. My associates won't be arriving until the morning."

"I don't mind at all," I said, intrigued at the prospect of getting to know him better.

Allen stood and stepped back, obviously feeling the weight of the liquor he had drunk the prior two hours. "You know *I* can manage it," Allen said, as if reading my mind. "I always do."

We dined in style at Sardi's. It was my first trip to New York without expensive liquor and cigars, and I didn't miss them one bit. Out of respect, Allen and Jude declined the stogies, but they drank to their hearts' content.

A graduate of Harvard, Jude had lived in almost every big city in the U.S. before settling in Chicago to start an ad agency. "A couple of Harvard buddies and I didn't want to run our father's businesses, and advertising was the only thing we could think of that married celebrity with creativity and business, besides Hollywood, of course."

"And what's wrong with Hollywood?" I inquired.

"What *isn't* wrong with Hollywood?" Jude said with a crooked smile. "Don't take this the wrong way, I have my share of friends out there, but they are *never* satisfied. The bastards have appetites for success and power and fame like you wouldn't believe. Living in gated communities in multimillion dollar homes, and all they can do at the dinner table is talk about the next renovation they hope to do, to make their home better than so-and-so's."

"So money hasn't spoiled you," I said cautiously.

"Money has afforded me the wisdom to know it's not everything," Jude said, taking another sip of his wine.

Allen shook his head. "Don't rich people always say that though?"

"Fair enough. But most rich people are still looking for what's *next*, and it always comes with a price tag. I believe you have to live in the here and now. Appreciate each day as it comes. Enjoy friends and family. That's the true key to happiness," Jude said.

"Then may I ask why you're not married?" I asked.

Jude's expression changed, a cloud passing across his eyes. "Well, I was married for two years," he said, lowering his glass. "She died in a plane crash three years ago."

I put my hand over his. "I'm sorry. I was rude to have asked."

"No," Jude said. "I don't mind talking about it. I like telling people about Margot. She was the light of my life. Tall and beautiful. She was kind and loving and made you feel as though you were the only person on earth when she spoke to you."

Allen raised his glass. "To Margot, God rest her soul."

I raised my water glass. "To Margot." And the Most Eligible Widower in Chicago. That gave him sympathy votes.

I'd gotten him all wrong. He was at the top of his game and all he wanted was what I had, a marriage, a baby on the way, loving friends and family. What was I doing in

New York when I wanted to be home with Jake? I'd be home in two days and then Jake had his next trip. Couldn't I think of great campaign ideas at home, curled next to him in bed instead of being miserable so far away?

"I'm sorry, gentleman," I said, getting up. "I think I need to go home."

"To the hotel?" Allen asked, helping me stand.

"No. I mean *real* home."

"Are you not feeling well?" Jude asked.

"Actually, I'm feeling better than I have in a long time."

On the late night flight back to Dallas, I plucked my baby's journal from my carry-on, and turned to a blank page.

July 15

Sweet Baby,
   I'm flying back to your father. What a fool I've been! Thinking I could snap my fingers and we would become this idealized 1950s family. I told you I was going to figure this parenthood thing out and finally I'm making some progress. Nothing in life is easy, least of all relationships. I'm not crazy enough to believe when you pop out I'll have all the answers, but I do have one—your daddy and I must be together to be affectionate. Sounds simple, but when you have two people who love their work, it feels like you're married to your job more than your mate. Which is why I took the red-eye from New York to be with your daddy back home.
   My mother wasn't very affectionate with me so I have a backlog of hugs coming your way. I will wrap you in my hugs every hour of the day. I will kiss you good morning and kiss you good night. I want to tuck you in and wish you sweet dreams. I don't want to look back on my years with you and feel any regret.
   Wow! Next week I'll learn if you're a boy or a girl. My predictions? A boy. Must be all the meat I'm eating. But I don't have a preference, really. I think if you are a boy it

might be easier for Jake to bond with you, but you know what they say about daddy's girls, too. I know. I was one. I can't wait to meet you. I hope you're doing okay in there. Cozy? I skipped the coffee so as not to give you the jitters on our flight home. Let's sleep now, shall we?

Mom

The cabin was dark except for a few reading lights. The whir of the engine and the plane soaring through midnight air lulled me into a relaxed state where my mind was free of concern.

It was then I felt a soft whirring motion within my abdomen. I snapped open my eyes and peered into the darkness, concentrating on the movement. *There!* It happened again. As if little bubbles were popping, my baby stirred inside of me. In the blackness, I smiled and put my hands over my tummy.

"Hello there, little Montgomery," I said, rubbing my lower tummy.

My seat neighbor, an Asian businessman, was asleep next to me, but I was tempted to wake him to share the news with someone, anyone.

The next morning I awoke to the smell of bacon and eggs and slightly burnt toast. "Time to rise and shine," Jake said, setting the breakfast tray next to me.

He hadn't made breakfast for me—ever. I raised my head, which felt like a bowling ball, a couple of inches before slamming it into the pillow again. "What time is it?"

"Ten-thirty," he said. "I wish you would've called me last night. Let me pick you up from the airport."

Pulling myself up, I apologized. "I forget sometimes. That it's okay to ask you to help sometimes." I put the tray over my lap, a tight squeeze to say the least.

"Well, I'm glad you're home. And I don't know if you noticed, but I happen to have come down with the flu this morning." He grabbed my hand and put it on his forehead.

"Raging fever," I said, playing along. "We haven't played hooky together in ages."

"That's too long," Jake said. "I thought I could take you sailing. The open air will be good for our maladies."

"I'd love that," I said. "It means a lot you'd do this for me."

Jake took a slice of my bacon. "I know work gets in the way of our marriage, Taylor, but I want you to know that's not the way I want it to be. I really do want us to come first."

"Me, too. But unfortunately we'll have a third wheel with us today. My handy dandy notebook to come up with big ideas to keep my job."

"Good thing I happen to be the most creative lawyer I know," Jake said.

CHAPTER 19

The hot July sun beat down on the little outdoor café where Amy and I lunched the next week. My petite friend, whose babies were with the nanny for the afternoon, dined on a Caesar salad with a Cabernet. I enjoyed a large club sandwich, chips, and a tall cream soda.

Wearing sunglasses and a black cotton knee-length mini-dress, I felt feminine and confident. Because I was showing and people could tell it was a baby and not just a double cheeseburger overdose, I actually *strutted* my new form.

Being pregnant definitely had its fringe benefits. The maitre d' seated us promptly, although three businessmen were clearly in line before us. People on the street smiled at me, and women, obviously mothers themselves, nodded and gave me a look that seemed to say, "Welcome to our world. You're one of us now." Men who used to push by in a hurry took the time to open doors for me. If only the world were that polite *all* the time.

"Just wait until you're a little further along," Amy said, sipping her wine. "Women and the elderly see your pregnancy as an open invitation to comment on their kids, grandkids, labor stories. You name it."

"I don't think I'll mind so much," I said, stuffing a crisp piece of bacon in my mouth.

Amy rolled her eyes. "Just wait. After the tenth story about how so-and-so's baby turned out to be a boy after the ultrasound showed it was a girl and the baby boy had to go home from the hospital in a pink outfit, you'll wish you had a magic potion to make yourself invisible."

"You have a point," I said with a laugh. I put my hand on my abdomen. I hadn't felt the baby move since the airplane.

Amy leaned into the table and looked me squarely in the eye. "You're awfully chipper today. You've obviously gotten *lucky* recently."

"Amy! How about a little louder next time! But, the answer is yes, thank you very much. Jake and I are good to go in that department. But it's not just that. Jake is gentle with me. I'm seeing a different side to him now. He's sweet, if you can believe that."

"I told you so. Pregnant is sexy. And babies turn the most macho men into little softies. Enjoy the sex now. Your hormones are raging totally out of control. Second trimester is when all the great sex and sex dreams happen. It's God's little gift before you start waddling and swelling," Amy said, pushing away her half-eaten salad.

"Is that how you stay so thin? Drink two glasses of wine and eat half a salad?" I asked, looking at my empty plate.

"Oh, I'll go home and eat a half dozen Keebler chocolate chip cookies during *Oprah*, don't worry," she said with a wink.

"Thank you for everything you've done for me, Amy. You and Jen and Jackie have already been so much help. I still don't know what I'm doing half the time."

"I don't want to be annoying, so stop me if I go overboard. Besides, with your in-laws coming to town this weekend, you'll get an earful, I'm sure. You're so lucky to have Aunt Barb moving to town. Now you'll have the rich

grandma who buys your kids things and the Betty
Crocker grandma with fresh-baked cookies."

"I'm not sure how I'm going to take having all this family back in my life," I said, sucking the last bit of cream
soda from my glass. "I feel like I've been an outsider for so
long."

Amy reached across the table and squeezed my hand.
"Do you know how long I've wanted this for you? Sure, relationships change when a baby comes along. But it can be
for the better," Amy said. "Besides, you'll need free
babysitting, believe me."

"I'm taking it one day at a time."

"Like coming out at work? How'd that bitch of a boss
take the news?"

"She treated it more like a disease," I told her. "She
raged for an hour about my coming home from the conference early. She's searching for my replacement as we
speak, I'm sure."

"She's got too much testosterone in those Prada heels,"
Amy said. "If she doesn't relate, then screw her. You're
the best creative director in Dallas. Everyone knows
that."

I shook my head. "She'll hire big. From a larger agency.
She said she can't see me as a mother, can you believe that?
Even if she *thinks* that, did she have to *say* it? I have enough
of a complex about it as it is."

"Don't let her get to you. Just be your ultracreative self
and your work will prove you are still committed to your
job," Amy said. "Unless you're going to join the league of
the happily home-employed."

"Allen calls it the Golden Stroller crowd. I'm not sure I
can be a stay-at-home mommy, wealthy or not. Hell, I
don't even know how to change a diaper. I'm not sure I'd
be good at it full time. But even thinking it makes me insanely guilty. How can I know before I know?"

"The great mommy question of the ages," Amy said.
"Will you work and give your child abandonment issues or

will you stay home and shrivel up your soul because you'd rather work with adults?"

I sat on the edge of my seat. "And?"

"And what? You're going to piss people off, either way," Amy said. "See, the thing about the mommy question is that there *is* no right answer. You just have to find what makes *you* happy."

"Happy is currently under investigation." I looked at my watch. "God, I've got to get back to the office." I started to get up.

"Oh, no you don't," Amy said. "Pregnant women get long lunches. It's an unwritten rule."

That afternoon I sat at my desk at the agency, staring out the window at the sprinkler shooting back and forth over the manicured lawn, doing nothing but digesting my supersized lunch and daydreaming. A stack of job jackets awaited my attention, but I left them for the moment that inspiration struck. Another unwritten rule about pregnancy? You'll get to it when you damn well feel like it. Suddenly, inspiration struck. Just not for radio copy. I opened my drawer and pulled my journal from my purse.

My little babe,

Gestation: 19 weeks. You look like a miniature person now. With your daddy's genes, I'm sure you are a very handsome/beautiful little person, too. Hope you're enjoying your first summer. You're mother's been sweating like a pig—I'm sure you've heard me complaining. I'm trying to lay off the curse words. Don't want your first word to be dammit, but I've never been hotter in my life. Honestly, I didn't know you could have sweat rings under your breasts! My thighs stick together when I walk. Damn Texas humidity. (I'll start a curse jar.) I took to wearing only mascara and lip gloss as the rest just makes me break out and look like I'm sixteen again.

Did you hear my boss ask me if work was too much of a

bother? Why didn't I say yes and be done with it? She's not very nice, baby. Don't ever work for someone like her! I guess I need to follow my own advice.

I wonder what you think of my life, listening in as you do. You must've heard your father tell me how beautiful I was last night—and that was without any makeup on! Well, he may be crazy for loving me, but somebody's got to do it. I've started thinking you're going to be pretty lucky after all. I've thought of a few traits that might be handy to pass down. Or else just keep you entertained.

Jake (Daddy)

—Always has a joke—usually toddler I.Q.

—Nice hairline. But I heard babies get their mother's ancestors hairlines, so if that's the case, then you're screwed.

—Has a weird fascination with bugs and creepy-crawlies. He tells me he had a huge frog collection when he was a kid. I'm afraid that will have to be a bonding experience I won't participate in.

—Loves kid food—especially mac and cheese, french fries and Froot Loops. Oh, and chocolate ice cream with hot fudge. Better hope you inherit his metabolism, too.

Taylor (Mommy)

—Can touch my nose with my tongue. All the babies I know love this trick. Your mommy has talent after all!

—I'm a famously bad cook, so you can eat more of daddy's favorite kid food.

—I grew up poor, so my family usually went camping for vacations. I can put up a tent, start a fire and use a compass to find my way around.

So, that's a start right? Will add more later.

Love,
your mother

P.S. Are you a girl or a boy? Amy did the needle over my wrist trick and it went round and round and back and forth. No big deal. I'll love you just the same.

I stretched my lazy arms over my head and took in a deep breath, feeling the urge to do preggo pilates. Just a few simple stretches to get the blood flowing. I began spinning my arms around and around, walking around the room, trying not to look at the deadline board our traffic coordinator Roxy kept updated. The dry-erase wallpaper covered the entire wall, and due to Susan's manic tour for new clients, the board was full, and my creative well was dry.

Roxy used color-coded systems—blue for radio, red for TV, green for print, black for direct mail, purple for logos and taglines. The colorful wall seemed to scream at me. *Work on us! Get me done! What are you stretching your jiggly legs for when you could be bringing us to life?*

"Oh, shut up," I said to the board.

You'll never get caught up, the taglines sneered at me.

You've got twenty-one weeks before your baby and thirty-two weeks worth of work up here, the TV column said.

"Oh, yeah?" I marched to the board, grabbed Roxy's precious eraser and expunged each project from the board, from left to right, top to bottom. I bobbed my head and smiled as the projects wailed in protest. I sang, "Good-bye to you!"

When I was done and the board was a beautiful sparkling white wall, I felt at peace. I sat on the floor, crossed my legs into the lotus pose, and inhaled. I'd found the path to enlightenment. The power to erase my stress was within my grasp all along.

Some time later, what I thought was an earthquake was actually Allen shaking me to consciousness. I wiped at my mouth, noticing the pool of drool on the rug.

"What in damnation has happened to you, Taylor?" Allen helped me to a sitting position. "If you weren't pregnant, I'd think you got into the holiday party liquor cabinet."

I looked at him dreamily. "I just had sex with Brad Pitt in the elevator."

Allen raised an eyebrow.

"Only I wasn't pregnant. God, Amy was right about the sex dreams. God's little gift, she told me."

Allen stared at my squeaky-clean wall, his mouth agape.

"Isn't it just the prettiest thing you've ever seen?" I said, hugging myself. "They always say allow for lots of white space in creative, you know."

Allen grabbed my arm and we stood staring at the board. "I have a sneaking suspicion you didn't finish all those projects."

I rolled my neck, cracking and popping. I wondered if padded carpet was too much to ask. "Think Susan would let me bring a sleeping bag up here? And maybe a pillow? Ooh, I know! A chaise lounge! That nap did me a world of good."

Where had my work buddy gone? Why didn't Allen think this was as humorous as I did? He picked the stack of manila job jackets off my desk and looked at me in desperation. "You've finally done it," he said, without a smile.

"Yes! You told me to stop stressing out and I've done it. Yea, Taylor!"

Allen shook his head. "No, princess. You've lost your mind. You've got preggo brain so bad you've lost all sense of reality. You've worked yourself to the brink of psychosis. Just because you erase the jobs doesn't mean they *really* disappeared. You know that, right?" He put his well-manicured hand on my shoulder.

I felt a tear tug at my duct, swelling to break free. "So Roxy has to put them back on the board? All those mean, ugly projects yelling at me—I can't have it, Allen. Please." I held his hand and he walked me to my chair.

"Allen will take care of everything," he said. "You just sit here in case Susan walks by. I'll get started on these. We'll give the easy ones to the interns. I'll come get you at six to take you home, okay?"

I nodded and reached into my top drawer. Having sex with Brad Pitt had worked up an appetite. I pulled out a Whatchamacallit candy bar—zero nutritional value, extraordinary crunch. After the chocolate had woken up my tired brain, I felt slightly guilty for erasing Roxy's handiwork and for eating junk food. Junk food, junk brain. I'd buy a mini-fridge over the weekend and stock it with grapes and orange juice. I'd bring my little blender and make smoothies every afternoon.

By no means would I put the projects back on the board, but the sugar did give me the slightest creative buzz. When I was a kid I'd wanted to be a teacher just so I could write on the board. (It was not wanting to work with children that changed my mind.) Why did Roxy get to have all the fun?

I reviewed the marker selection and picked a neon orange one and started at the top of the board, standing on my tip-toes.

<u>Ten Rules for Preggos</u>
1. For nine months, chocolate goes to the base of the Food Pyramid.
2. Her bite is as big as her bark.
3. Housecleaning goes on hiatus.
4. Do not wake from a nap unless house (or office) is on fire.
5. Gets automatic cuts in bathroom line. See #2.
6. Hard work and sex are optional.
7. Foot massages are mandatory.
8. As your mind goes, so does your bladder control.
9. Gas is a right of *passage*.
10. Moody is as moody does.

Feeling justified that I'd worked my brain for the day, I laid back down on the floor, hoping I could feel Peanut move. I'd taken to calling the baby Peanut in my head, though I hadn't said it aloud to anyone. *Pea* stood for small. *Nut* stood for *you must be a nut to choose me as a mother.*

I half-expected the Hawkster to walk in on me while I reenergized, but I didn't care. I had to start taking better care of myself. I'd already come down off the chocolate bar high. I would eat more whole-grain foods and yogurt, milk, and cheese. Calcium. Vitamin D. I would replace my

M&Ms with raisins. Only I'd never liked raisins. They looked like shriveled up little bugs to me. Well, maybe the M&Ms would be for emergency use only.

Finally, my waiting paid off. He moved! Or she moved! A short but powerful whirring motion inside of me. Baby mine. "There you are, Peanut," I cooed affectionately, not recognizing my own voice. Satisfied, I got up and felt a surge of energy to conquer the world—or at least my stack of job jackets, which Allen had absconded with. Confidence filled my body. I would write the greatest furniture TV commercial the world had ever seen! I would create a billboard that would stop traffic, congesting the highway, only no one would be angry because they would be so in awe of that billboard. I would inspire my creative team with wondrous works and my raw enthusiasm.

Where had this energy come from? I marched down to Allen's office, where the art directors and Ted, the account executive, were brainstorming for the Studio Baby campaign. What did a bunch of young, hip single guys know about babies?

"Well, if it isn't our living, breathing target market," Allen said. "All bright-eyed and bushy-tailed."

I waved him off. Pantone color chips were strewn across the worktable. They had selected a bright color palette of red, blue and yellow. I shook my head. "Guys, this isn't kindergarten. Where's the warm fuzzy?" I picked up the Pantone book and pulled out soft hues in powder blue, vanilla, pastel pink and mint green. "You've got to get the 'awww'. No 'awww,' no sale."

They looked at me as if I'd been body-snatched. I was the least warm and fuzzy person they knew, but they kept their traps shut. I was the boss, after all. Allen handed me the boards with mock-ups of the Studio Baby logo. I studied them, six type treatments with various baby icons. All strong, dominant treatments more appropriate for a powerful corporation. Ryan, the youngest art director, took the boards from me. "I know. I know. No 'awww'. I may go watch a baby drool for inspiration."

"You seem pretty sure of yourself," Allen said as the group dispersed, forgoing reminding me it was my idea to go with a powerful palette and strong icon back when I was in baby-making fear mode. Everything had softened in four months—my thighs, my brain, and my heart.

"I may be starting to get the hang of this baby thing," I told him, patting by belly. "Professionally and otherwise."

CHAPTER 20

My ultrasound and twenty-week checkup was scheduled for ten A.M. on a Friday morning, when most of my clients were playing golf or taking a long weekend. Even though I had checked with Jake's schedule first, a last-minute court date meant he might not make it. So much for putting us first. He seemed genuinely upset that he could miss finding out the sex of our baby, but I couldn't wait another second. "Don't you want me to be there?" he'd asked that morning, wrinkling his forehead.

I'd wrapped my arms around his barrel chest and tucked my chin in his soft cotton shirt. "I want you to see him, Jake. Or her. I read that most men want a son. Is that what you want?"

Jake held me close. "I want a healthy baby. A boy would be nice, but a girl? A girl would be great, too. The way I see it, either way we're in for a wild ride."

"If it's a girl, will you take her fishing like my daddy did me? And teach her how to dance? And put her hair in pigtails?" I could feel my heart quicken.

"I'll even coach her T-ball team," he said. "I love blowing the whistles."

All morning my mind raced with thoughts of Barbie dolls and dump trucks. That day would determine so much about my future. The sex of our child would determine so many things about my life from then until the day I died. Would I buy dresses or overalls? Play with dolls or Hot Wheels? Spend my Saturday afternoons tossing the baseball in the backyard or at a dance rehearsal? Naturally, I was stereotyping, but Amy told me no matter what she introduced to her kids, her daughter preferred the stuffed animals and tea parties, while her baby boy preferred cars and sports. Would I help my daughter plan the most perfect wedding or see my son enter the army, as my father had done before he went to college?

Girls required more stuff—accessories, for instance. The cost of hair accessories was astonishing. Girl clothes were cuter—my Studio Baby research had taught me that. McKenzie and Ashlynn were both mini drama queens. Boys loved their mamas. Teen girls fought with them. History showed me that. Yes, a son would be easier for me. Mothering a son would be tough enough. Mothering a daughter might be impossible.

Aunt Barb had moved to town just in time and insisted on taking me to the appointment when she heard Jake couldn't come. She claimed I would be too nervous to drive, but I knew it had more to do with her excitement. She had sons; she was closer to me than her daughters-in-law. Being a part of my pregnancy was as special to her as it was for me. I was relieved not to be alone. For months I'd watched women and their exuberant mothers come in for the ultrasounds together. I knew my mother would be glad her sister was there with me.

Seated in the comfortable chairs in the waiting area, Aunt Barb couldn't contain her glee. "Honey, I'm going to be the best grandma to your baby, if that's okay with you," she said.

"Of course it is, Aunt Barb," I said. "I'm just happy you *want* to be."

Aunt Barb nestled in the chair, and I noticed all the

physical traits she shared with my mother. The high cheekbones, slightly upturned nose, and wavy dark hair, now sprinkled with gray. Perhaps my baby would get one of my parent's traits, something I didn't have, and it would remind me of them every time I looked at my baby. My mother's long torso or my father's dimple in his chin. Would I be able to tell from the ultrasound?

"They sure have come a long way in maternity care, I'll tell you that," Aunt Barb said. "Back when I was birthing babies, we sat in sterile straight-back chairs in a hospital lobby with the sick and dying walking by, contaminating us! Now you've got gourmet coffee and miniature cookies and a big-screen TV," she said, shaking her head. "And don't even get me started on the hospital rooms we had to share with two other women in labor! The other women's screams nearly scared the baby out of you. Nowadays, you get a huge room with a wooden floor, your own bathroom, and designer towels! You're just lucky, that's all I've got to say."

Nurse Betty, as spirited as ever, swung open the door to the waiting area. "Today's the day!" she announced, as if to the whole room.

I appreciated her enthusiasm, but looked at the door for Jake. "Let's do it."

Aunt Barb gathered her purse, always stuffed too full with who knows what, and followed me.

After my usual urine sample and weigh-in (seventeen pounds gained), I waited in a smaller waiting area, which I thought was an ingenious trick on the part of the practice. Just by moving from one area to another, you felt like your wait was shorter, although I usually sat in the second room at least another fifteen minutes before the nurse took me back to an examining room. That day they couldn't be fast enough or slow enough for me. I was anxious to know. I just wished Jake would tell the judge he had a more important ruling.

Peggy, a pretty blond ultrasound technician, took us back right away to a room with the ultrasound machine, a rather dull-looking gray machine with computer paper hanging from it, as if sticking its tongue out at me. The technician clicked on the monitor. I held my breath, in awe of the machine. It was a technical sage, revealing the mystery within me.

The woman looked at my wedding ring, probably to confirm that I was married before she spoke. "Will your husband be able to make it?"

I sat up on the table and shrugged my shoulders, feeling a bit foolish. "He was going to try. He had a court appearance. . . . Oh, not for *him*. I mean, he's a lawyer." I knew that look. Peggy probably thought we were upper-class snobs who didn't appreciate the miracle of a baby. And the fact that my husband couldn't break away from the courtroom for what could be the most amazing thirty minutes of his life *did* seem shallow.

Peggy smiled politely, her lipstick glossy pink. "Well, shall we get started? Maybe he'll come in soon. I have a good half hour before the next patient," she said.

I lay back on the table, turning my head to the right side to see the monitor. Peggy spread the thick, cool gel on my abdomen and placed the scope on it. Goosebumps covered my body. On the ultrasound screen, my baby immediately appeared. The gray and white image of this little body with a bobbing head and a perfect spine jerked on the screen. It was lying facedown and moving its arm, a backwards wave to its mama. My goose bumps got goose bumps.

As Peggy took measurements, Aunt Barb squeezed my hand. "A perfect baby!" she beamed proudly, jumping up and down.

My eyes widened in amazement. Warmth spread from my chest to the top of my head and to the bottom of my feet, and I could only imagine it was the ache of love. Yes, I loved it with every ounce of me, and I didn't stop the feeling or push it back down inside. I wanted to love it, unashamedly, boy or girl, even if the love could hurt me later. At the moment, the risk—for love was an awful big risk—seemed worth the taking. After just feeling the baby move for the first time the week before, I couldn't believe it was so active inside of me. Ten little fingers and ten little toes. Everything was there.

As the scope made its journey across my abdomen, we saw different parts of my baby's body, an outstretched arm, legs tucked underneath it. Then, responding to a deeper jab of the scope, the baby turned its head and looked straight at me, its alien eyes wide.

"Hi, baby!" I said, my eyes moistening. "Did we wake you up?"

"They look a little strange through ultrasound, but we are seeing everything we need to," Peggy said, pointing to the screen. "Here's the heart."

The heart beat rapidly at 158 beats a minute.

"And here are the kidneys," she pointed out. "And the brain," she said, moving up and measuring the head.

"This will be a smart baby all right," Aunt Barb said.

"Wow. *Wow*," I said over and over, too dumbfounded to come up with another word.

The baby turned over again, displaying its front side, but kept its legs tucked in.

"Do we want to know the sex?" Peggy asked.

The door swung open, and Jake, dressed in a conservative navy suit, burst into the room.

"We certainly do," Jake said with a smile and a wink to me.

"Hi, honey," I said, relieved he had made it.

Jake stared at the screen in amazement. "That's our baby, huh?" he asked, taking my hand.

With a wiggle of the scope, Peggy attempted to get our baby to uncross its legs so we could get a view of its goods. The baby kicked in response and turned over again.

"Stubborn like mama," Jake said.

Stubborn or not, the baby gave in, figured the intrusion wouldn't stop until full cooperation. The baby turned again, revealing its underside to us.

Peggy laughed. She typed on the screen, *"It's a . . ."* She paused. "Are you ready?"

"Yes," the three of us said together. I held my breath.

She clicked the keys—*G-I-R-L.*

Aunt Barb squealed. Jake squeezed my hand and kissed me on the forehead again. I let out a little yelp. "A girl," I whispered. A girl, a girl, a girl.

"She'll just be *gorgeous*," Aunt Barb gushed, clasping her hands together.

Peggy saved the image and printed it out. On the screen, she showed us how she could tell the gender. "See those two little lines there?" she said, pointing at what were two very small vertical lines. "That's the girl parts. If it were a boy, it would look more like an apple with a stem on it. Girls resemble hot dog buns. This is actually a very good picture."

"Wow," I said again, the only word I could muster. Even for a wordsmith, my vocabulary was mush.

A few more measurements and Peggy was finished. She clicked off the machine. I said a silent good-bye to my baby girl. I would see her again in four and a half months. I felt privileged to carry her around with me everywhere I went.

We received thin paper printouts of her face, body, spine, and gender to show our relatives, and keep in her memory book. I realized they were the first of hundreds of pictures I would have of our little girl through the years.

Misty-eyed, I stared at the image of my girl. Our baby was more real to me than ever. I wondered if Jake felt the same, but couldn't bring myself to ask.

Aunt Barb talked nonstop on the way to the elevator and out to the car, and Jake held my hand in silence. At the car, Jake kissed me. "I'm glad I came. A baby *girl*," he said, shaking his head. "We've got a lot to do for our little princess." As I leaned in for a hug I noticed wetness in his eye, the first good cry our daughter would cause him. The ultrasound had worked to win him over. *Little princess.* Just the kind of thing a nice daddy would say.

As Aunt Barb started my car and chatted on about girl names, I watched a young couple put their new baby in the backseat of their SUV. The father stuffed pink balloons and flowers in the trunk. The mother looked tired, but confident.

I witnessed their new chapter, page one. Adults plus completely dependent baby who would rely on them for at least the next eighteen years. They looked ready for the journey.

That's when it hit me that Jake and I had a huge say in how this would turn out. A blank slate. I'd gotten so hung up on the genetic history of my family, that I hadn't thought about what I could do to make things different, better. Positive thinking was the first step. We had four months to prepare, mentally, physically and emotionally. In all respects, I was halfway there.

August 1

Dear Baby Girl,

Today we found out you're a girl! As I'm writing this my hands are shaking, I'm so nervous. Now I can prepare for having a daughter and all that goes with raising a little girl.

Of course, being an only child, I didn't have a sibling to care for, let alone a sister. My cousins were all boys, so I've never been around girls, except for my girlfriends. But what I can provide is my experience as a female, a girl who felt awkward through junior high with long legs and braces and unruly hair. And then I came into my own, "blossoming" as my mother called it, when I was 14. I don't think she liked my growing up. That made her nervous as hell. That I would get too boy-crazy. My mom's advice about boys was to stay away, but when that didn't work, she said, "Don't let them be more important to you than yourself." But the longer I've been with your father, I've realized its okay for people to be important to you. I need to tell him that more often.

Girls still have a "hard row to hoe," as my mother used to say, but we've come a long way, baby. Girls can do anything boys can do—sometimes better. Girls also run the economy. We are the gatherers, the household decisionmakers, and I believe by the time you are all grown up, girl power will be stronger than ever! I've thought of a few more great reasons to be a girl, so we can build your self-esteem in the womb. It's never too early!

1. *Multi-tasking. Studies have shown guys can't get as many things done at once. I keep reminding myself of this so I can work and raise a baby at the same time.*

2. *Emotion. Girls in general are empathetic, something I think the world needs more of. We take care of each other. Thanks to you, I'm getting more sentimental every day.*

3. *Underdog syndrome. Because people will underestimate what you can get done, it is easy to impress.*

4. *Girly stuff. Just because we can scale mountains and visit space and hold office and run companies doesn't mean we don't enjoy the fun stuff, too. Clothes, makeup, pedicures, clearance sales, shoes, smelling good, cooking and baking delicious meals (I'm still growing into that one). And of course, the one thing men will never be able to do—the most precious thing God gave us—is the ability to bear children. As much as I bellyache, pregnancy is a miracle and guys just don't know what they're missing.*

So there it is. The first thing we have in common. Think I'll go do some "gathering" of my own. It's time to buy bigger maternity clothes, and I'll pick up a few things for you, too. I figure I have a few years to dress you as I wish before you hate everything I pick out.

Love,
Mom

Closing the journal, I wondered what I could do for Jake to show him how much I loved him. We'd been dating so long, having a real marriage felt new and challenging. Coming back early from New York City was just the beginning. With our busy lives, what could I do to let him know he was priority one?

MONTH FIVE

Ben & Jerry Thighs

CHAPTER 21

> *Week 23: Your baby now looks like a miniature newborn. She is eight inches long and weighs about a pound. Her lips are becoming more distinct and her eyes are developed, though the iris still lacks pigment. Eyebrows and eyelids are in place. The first signs of teeth appear as buds beneath the gum line.*

A happier hippo you would not find. That was the state of my fifth month, pleasantly plump and not giving a damn. August in Dallas is unbearable; even with sleeveless tank tops and loose cotton tees and breezy skirts. My big belly radiated heat on its own. My feet had swelled a half size so most of my shoes no longer fit, or else they bunched up over the top like Cinderella's stepsisters trying to fit into the glass slipper. So I wore flip-flops when Susan was out of town and went barefoot at the agency as often as I could get away with.

I bought Peanut—scratch that—*Princess* Peanut two sundresses for her first summer—orange and pink floral dresses with little bows and matching sticky bows for her head. Amy had promised me McKenzie's baby wardrobe, so my child would be set in designer baby duds. I'd never seen McKenzie wear the same outfit twice. Shopping for my baby girl was more rewarding than shopping for myself. Mommy shopping is instant gratification because we don't have to try it on, but we can take credit for how cute it is.

Because of my mother, I'd always compared my body to lithe ballerinas, and I always came up short—legs too stocky, chest too big, waist too thick.

Five months pregnant, I could not compare myself to the ballerinas. Whoever saw a pregnant ballerina, anyway? Instead, I compared myself to the other pregnant women I passed on the street, and it wasn't so much comparing as admiring the way in which we carried our babies, some high, some low. The short women seemed to be loaded down with baby, the taller women looked to have perfectly round basketballs protruding from their hips. Then there were the ones in the middle, like myself, who were not too short and not too tall, and looked not so pregnant from the backside, but pregnant everywhere from the front.

For that month alone, I didn't even care that beautiful women with gorgeous bodies could steal away my fit husband. Being in the "sexy second trimester," we made up for the sex we didn't have the first trimester.

Jake started asking me how his girls were doing, which made me melt, and he told me how cute he thought our daughter would look in the clothes I'd bought her. Okay, so he grunted it when he said it, but at least he'd looked away from *Sports Illustrated* when I showed him. Things were finally gelling, and I thought nothing, not even a visit from my in-laws, could spoil it. I was wrong.

"Hel-looo!" Lorna squealed as she grabbed me for a Texas-sized bear hug upon entering our house. She smelled of Chanel No. 5—her signature scent—with a bit of hairspray, which went directly up my nose as her big bottle-blond hairdo stuck in my face.

"Hi, Lorna," I said, as cheerily as I could muster.

"Let me see that grandbaby of mine," she said, sticking her palm directly on my abdomen.

I flinched, but allowed her to feel my stomach. "She's getting there."

"Well, you don't look like you've gained much *yet*," Lorna said. "I gained twenty pounds with Jacob, but for my little frame that was quite a bit!" she said moving on to her son for hugs and kisses.

While I wondered what "little frame" she was referring to, Frank hugged me, which was completely out of character for him. He typically nodded hello, his hands still in his pockets and granted me a small close-mouthed smile. A hug was ultra-affectionate for Frank, who hadn't even hugged me on my wedding day. What my father-in-law did next truly surprised me. He hugged Jake.

"Congratulations," Frank said to Jake. "I'm really happy you two are starting a family."

"Why thanks, Dad," Jake said, visibly moved by his father's gesture.

Lorna clapped her hands together and looked around the house—the inspection, I called it—which was followed by a barrage of questions. Which room had we picked for the nursery? Did we have the dimensions? Should we take digitals with us to the furniture store?

Fortunately, Jake could settle her down. He knew I simply couldn't deal with her hyper nature by myself all day. I had threatened Jake with his life if he and his father ditched us at the baby store to go play golf. No, I needed Jake's support *all day long*.

Not that I minded hearing about the Houston society, but I could only take so much information about the Junior League, Feed the Children, PTA, Christian Women's League, Houston Symphony, Chamber of Commerce, and so on. Every significant event required Lorna's stamp of approval. Loudmouthed and beautiful, with a knack for fundraising, Lorna Montgomery was the first person to see if one needed to connect with the "right people." I was not a part of that crowd. Distant and somewhat detached, Frank was more like me.

Frank, steady breadwinner, and Lorna, enthusiastic socialite, had thirty-two years of solid marriage. It wasn't that I didn't get along with them, but I felt as if they wanted to know me, to own more of my life, and I was unwilling to give it to them. At least thus far.

Perhaps it started off badly when in my junior year in college, Jake picked going with me to Cancun for spring break over going to Paris with his family. He told me it was the first time he'd ever turned down his parents' request. Mrs. Society had selected a roomful of young ladies who were surely better suited for her dashing attorney-to-be son. Jake had shared a dozen stories of arranged dates he reluctantly accepted to keep his mother happy. He couldn't go home for any break without being set up with the "most charming" girl from "a good family."

And it didn't end there. After the initial shock wore off that Lorna's angel would marry "beneath" him, she had wanted to plan every single aspect of the glorious wedding. Because she knew I didn't come from a wealthy family, or was—how had she put it?—"an orphaned girl with no help on the most important day of her life," she offered to pay for the entire wedding. She didn't know of the significant insurance settlement I had received from my parents' accident or the hefty life insurance my father had secured should something happen to them. Nonetheless, in an effort to become friends with my future mother-in-law, I conceded and allowed Lorna to play an active role in our wedding.

If a one-day event like a wedding could cause so much stress and discord, what would a grandchild do? That was the question I was asking myself as I swiped my finger over the end tables to make sure the cleaning lady hadn't missed a spot of dust. Shopping for our baby girl's nursery could be either my worst in-law experience to date or the blessed start of a new bond. Yes, I, Taylor Moore Montgomery, was the vessel carrying on the great Montgomery genes. One might think that fact, above any other act of God, would cause Lorna to cherish me and accept me for who I was.

Then again . . .

Lorna didn't think we had picked the right room for the nursery. Even though it was directly next to ours, she felt it was limiting compared to the larger guest room down the hall. *Better yet, wouldn't Jake's corner office be the best choice since it was quieter and more spacious?*

Neither idea worked for us, but I let Jake explain that one to her. *And when,* she inquired, *could we move into the bigger house in Amy's neighborhood? A junior partner could afford it. Before the baby, perhaps?*

After what already seemed an exhausting period at home, we piled into Jake's SUV and headed for Baby Furniture Plus, a large store with everything under the sun for babies.

The smell of cedar and spring flowers greeted us as the automatic doors slid open. A pretty redheaded woman wearing a monogrammed denim Baby Furniture Plus maternity shirt welcomed us with a wide smile. "Hi, I'm Becky. May I help you all today?"

"No, we're just—" I started to say.

"Yes, we definitely need some help!" Lorna said pulling out a long list she had failed to show me at the house. "We need a little bit of everything," she said. "This will be our first grandbaby, and this is our treat to prepare her nursery," she said proudly. "I'm hoping we can have more than one, anyway," she said in my direction. Was the woman going to force me to procreate?

"Oh, isn't that nice!" Becky said. "Well, I'll take your list, then, and we can get started."

I had the feeling they were getting ready to spend more in one day than I had spent my entire freshman year of college. Jake looked at me as if to apologize, and he took my hand as we traipsed behind Lorna and Frank and the slightly waddling Becky. *Don't mind me, I thought. I'm just the vessel.*

"It's usually best to start with the nursery bedding, then we'll coordinate the furniture with that," Becky said. "You're having a girl, right?"

"Yes, we are!" Lorna said.

"Super!" Becky said enthusiastically. "Let's look at some bedding!"

"We just have no idea what we want," Lorna exclaimed, which did not include me in the "we." I did work with color and design for a living.

The next twenty minutes were spent walking through narrow aisles from one crib to the next, admiring the wide selection of crib bedding to choose from: bears, florals, plaids, in every color and price range.

"Classic Winnie the Pooh and Beatrix Potter are always favorites," Becky informed us.

With no preconceived idea of what I thought the perfect baby girl bedding would be, I was surprised I was drawn to the simple floral and plaid selections, in soft, muted colors. The idea hit me to propose a bedding line to Studio Baby. Hey, Ralph Lauren did it. Why not my account?

But, of course, Lorna had her favorites.

"Ooh! Look at this one," Lorna exclaimed, leaning over a mahogany crib with a pink, frilly crib set inside. "It's angelic!"

"Perhaps a bit too much lace," I said. Understatement of the trimester.

Next Lorna suggested an expensive white percale set with embroidered pink roses.

"Looks old, Mom," Jake said. "Besides, a few burp stains and it's ruined."

"What do you know about burp stains?" I asked.

Jake shrugged his shoulders. "I've heard they project things from all ends."

"You've been reading those books I bought, haven't you?" I teased.

"They actually make pretty good bathroom reading." He grinned.

Tired from standing, I headed for the glider rockers, an

excuse to sit down and put my feet up. I also needed a bit of space between my opinionated mum-in-law and me. I began feeling faint, so I pulled out a cherry LifeSaver and popped it in my mouth, breathing deeply, and gliding. I had half a notion to climb into one of those king-sized cribs and nap like a baby myself.

Jake sat down in the glider next to me. "These *are* comfortable," he said. "We'll have to get one of these."

"You don't look so good," I said, noticing his pale complexion and the perspiration on his brow.

He shook his head. "I'll be fine. It's just a little suffocating in here."

I looked around at twenty thousand square feet of baby stuff. Amazing how a man could be suffocated in such a large place. But I knew what he was feeling. Having cribs and gliders in our home just didn't seem *natural*. Not yet.

Lorna and Frank were quick to catch up. "Oh, you just pick the glider you want, Jake, and we'll add it to the list."

"You pick, because you'll be doing all the rocking," I said with sarcasm.

Lorna continued, "Becky said we could get a matching glider cover once you've decided which bedding you want." She looked at me, the much too hesitant decision-making vessel. "Come on, Frank, let's go look at dressers to get a head start," she said, grabbing his arm and taking off, her bracelets jingling on her arm.

"This is a race," I said, putting my head on Jake's shoulder. "It's a race and you didn't tell me."

Jake sighed and took my hand. "You're being a real pal about this."

"Does she really think we're going to pick out *everything* in one day?"

Jake nodded. "Of course she does. She was the one who had our entire wedding planned in a week, remember?"

"Don't remind me."

Standing near us was a couple around our age, the woman at least seven months pregnant, the man a kind-looking fellow carrying a toddler.

"Down! Down!" the girl said, squirming in her father's arms.

"You keep running through the store," her father said sternly. "If I put you down, you have to promise to stay with Mommy and Daddy."

"Okay," the little girl said sweetly. And as the father set her down, she turned around and pointed at me. "Look, Mommy, that lady is having a baby, too."

The woman smiled at me. "Yes, she is."

"I'm having a baby brother," the toddler told us.

"That's nice," I said. "What's your name?"

"Madison," she said, her fingers in her mouth. "I'm two." She stuck two fingers out. She waved good-bye at me and ran down the aisle, her father in hot pursuit.

"That's a pretty name," Jake said.

I nodded. "Madison Montgomery. Yeah, I like it."

"I've actually marked a few names in one of those baby books by the toilet."

"You *have* been doing a lot of bathroom reading," I said. "I'm impressed."

"Peanut's gotta have a name," he said, getting up from the rocker and pulling the ticket. "And I've *gotta* have this rocker. If I'm going to be rocking and feeding the baby, I might as well be comfy."

Surprised he would say such a thing, I leaned over and kissed him. He looked nauseated, but somewhere within him, he was accepting fatherhood.

Some two hours later, our nursery set was complete. I had selected an English country garden print with floral and stripes in wine, ecru, and taupe in a six-piece crib set that included the sheet, bumper pad, headboard, comforter, blanket, and pillow. Logically, we had to get the matching balloon valance, diaper stacker, and glider cover, not to mention balloon wall decorations. Next, we purchased a mahogany crib with ornate designs on each end and a matching dresser and changing table. Then there was the taupe wicker hamper and wastebasket. Everything we could possibly need for a nursery, I thought.

But, alas, we didn't stop there. We moved on to our own credit card, which we used to buy a wall clock, several picture frames and a side table.

"That should about do it," Becky said as she gleefully rang up Frank's $3,000-plus charge.

"You can just add that to your little one's college fund," Frank said with a wink.

With delivery scheduled for later that afternoon, we treated ourselves to a large meal (mine larger than most) at a local Mexican restaurant. Lorna was still in shopping mode, hoping to stop by a baby clothes store to purchase a few things.

"You've done enough for one day, Mom," Jake said, scooping up cheese dip with a large tortilla chip. "We still have four months to go. Can't you spread your enthusiasm?"

"Oh, I know," Lorna said, adding sugar to her tea. "I just like Taylor's opinion, that's all."

If I hadn't just swallowed a bite of corn tortilla, I'm sure I would've choked on it. Since when did Lorna ask my opinion on anything? Who was she kidding?

"Well, you do have that baby clothes campaign at work now, don't you?" she asked. "How's that going?"

"Great, actually," I said. "The TV shoot is in two weeks in Atlanta."

"Such an exciting career you have," Lorna said. "Big companies. Traveling to New York and Atlanta and all over the place. It would be hard to give that up, wouldn't it?"

"Have baby, will travel," Jake said, coming to my defense. Jake and I exchanged looks. Lorna had just been buttering me up to find out if I was staying home with the baby.

"I do love advertising," I said, feeling guilt with each word. Despite how much Allen and I loved complaining about it, I did enjoy my career.

Frank also took the cue. "I'm sure you two will find the best option for your family."

"Of course, Frank," Lorna said. "I'm sure they've already started interviewing nannies. It takes a while to find a good one, that's for certain. We had such a good nanny for Jake. Maria was a godsend."

Jake and I looked at each other again. "We're working on it," Jake said.

With the excitement of finding out the sex of the baby, and shopping for her, I had put off the issue of day care. No doubt I would worry about it until we had settled on what to do. Was I already failing our baby? Should I have been interviewing nannies? Or day care centers? Or home day care? What had I read about all that?

Heartburn set in quickly, but the tacos may not have been to blame. Seventeen weeks to go, and I didn't have a *clue* as to who would take care of our baby while Jake and I worked. I was going to work, wasn't I? My friends were all stay at home mommies. Were they so different from me? They said they admired me for having a career. Did they pity me behind my back?

Shopping, heartburn, and anxiety made a nice sleep concoction so I was all too happy to excuse myself to our bedroom with a glass of water to nap while Jake entertained his parents. When I awoke, the furniture had been delivered to the nursery. I hadn't decided what color to paint the walls. Lorna suggested lavender with white trim. I absolutely agreed, especially if I didn't have to paint it.

CHAPTER 22

Atlanta welcomed us with a cool September shower that lasted the two days of our Studio Baby commercial shoot. I soon found out that babies didn't particularly like the rain.

"Why are they crying like that?" I said, stepping into the soundproof studio to find six babies crying their lungs out. Despite their hot pink faces from screaming, they lived up to their glossy headshots.

"Babies *do* that, Tay," Allen said, as if I should know better.

"But at the same *time*? Is it contagious?" I grabbed my script and Shelton's director notes.

"Tsk-tsk," Allen said. "Someone got up on the wrong side of the Hyatt bed this morning. Have a latté and a bagel and you'll feel better."

I looked at the craft services table spread with bagels, donuts, croissants, and a young man to fix me anything my heart desired on his griddle. "I'll have an omelet with bacon," I told him.

"Sassy girl," Allen scolded. "You told me you don't want to gain more than thirty pounds, remember?"

"Thanks, Richard Simmons. I'll keep that in mind while

I'm enjoying my protein and you fill up on those sugary carbs and caffeine."

Allen shrugged his shoulders. "You being the recovered Carb Caffeine Queen, right? Don't you want to go play with the babies?"

I looked over at the group of babies sitting or lying in their mommy's arms. The wailing had stopped for the most part since their mouths were plugged with bottles, breasts, or pacifiers. They were cute. They'd better be. I'd hired them. They had squishy legs and tiny feet and round cheeks and wispy soft hair. Watching them made me daydream about my baby girl. I longed to rush over to the babies to smell their freshly shampooed heads and feel their fresh skin. "I better stay back behind the camera with the director," I said, fearful of causing the squirming sirens to start up again at the sight of a stranger.

The TV concept was Studio Baby clothes for every age and stage of babyhood. Since Studio had made the wise decision to stay away from polyester based on focus groups, the entire line was cotton and fleece, nothing but complete comfort and softness.

To demonstrate those qualities in the commercial, we set up an elaborate stage that looked like a baby's heaven on earth, with large, soft stuffed animals, pillows, and a white crib the size of a small house with a giant mobile hanging over it playing "Rock-a-Bye Baby" as it rotated above the babies' heads.

The first shot was of the newborn, an Asian baby just six weeks old, who thankfully was asleep, as scripted.

"I can't put him on *that*," the mother protested about the fluffy pillow her baby was supposed to be asleep on.

I rushed over.

"Newborns aren't supposed to be near pillows or blankets," she said hotly. "Don't you know they can suffocate?"

All eyes were on me, the obviously pregnant creative director who hadn't caught such a safety blunder. Of course we couldn't put the baby on the pillow and have millions of Americans watch the commercial and do the same thing. *What a moron.*

"You're absolutely right," I told her, and motioned to the prop coordinator to get me one of the hand-sewn quilts to spread out and lay him on instead. Satisfied, the mother placed her son on the quilt.

"Rolling," the director said, and he captured the peaceful sleeping baby on film.

"Thomas was perfect," he said to the crew as the baby's mother quickly grabbed up her son. "Let's hope the rest of the day can go this well. What do you think, Taylor?"

"I liked it. Barring no more safety issues." The mother of a baby wearing a pink onesie and matching socks and cap placed her four-month-old daughter in an oversized bouncy seat. The scene called for little Jillian to eye the large objects in front of her with wide-eyed wonder and grab for them. Jillian was so excited by the toys, she waved her arms around and batted at them vigorously until the lamb swung back and smacked her in the head. Jillian shrieked.

"Cut," the director said, perturbed, looking at me to fix it.

"Okay," I said running to the baby's aid. Mother shot me an it's-your-fault look. "I'm sorry. Is she okay? The lamb's soft, so it probably just scared her."

"Are you okay, sweetie?" I asked Jillian. I smiled and made a funny face. Immediately, Jillian laughed and was ready to be placed back in the bouncy seat. Four more takes and we had it.

On to the six-month-olds, a girl and boy playing together in the crib. The scene called for the babies to do something cute, though I wasn't sure what that was. *Weren't babies always supposed to be cute?*

Inside the crib sat soft rattle balls, which I hoped they might toss to each other. One mom informed me this was too much of a feat for a six-month-old. My lack of baby development knowledge was shining through. Fortunately, the boy grabbed the ball and the girl grabbed the stuffed kitten and gave it a tight squeeze, which seemed to look much better in soft focus than it did in person.

The Studio CEO arrived on his private jet, stayed just long enough to view the stage and tell me how fabulously he thought the shoot was going.

"You know what they say. Never work with animals or kids," I responded.

"Well, I can tell your pregnancy has been beneficial to the campaign," Hoffman said. "You know, you're the only reason we're still with Ace. Someone who doesn't understand the miracle of children could never come up with a spot this beautiful."

I didn't tell him it was called *imagination*. Nor did I share with him the near-mishaps from earlier in the day. But thankfully someone could see that pregnancy did not erase my abilities to create, and perhaps could even enhance it. It was rare for a client to back slap. Now if he'd only share that with Susan, who I was sure would can me when I went into labor.

Hoffman seemed impressed when I told him about my ideas for his bedding line. I handed him a bound report Allen had helped me with. We hadn't mentioned it to Susan. I liked to pull a rabbit out of my hat every now and then. If Studio loved it, Susan would have to keep me and give me a fat raise.

Finally time to break for lunch, the crew swooped in on the craft service table, where Chicago-style pizza and pasta was served. Tummy grumbling, I first had to appease my pregnant bladder and made a beeline to the bathroom.

On my way I heard rock music blaring from another sound stage. Standing inside the doorway was Jude Winters, wearing a pinstriped suit and looking as handsome as I remembered. As if he felt my stare, he spun around and shot me a wide grin and rushed out to greet me. I tried my best not to waddle toward him.

Jude kissed my cheek and gave me a quick squeeze. "You look fabulous, Taylor," he said, which my pregnant ear translated to *fat*ulous. "I can't believe we're running into each other like this!"

"Small world," I said. "What are you shooting?"

"Oh, an MTV-like spot for a skateboard company. As if the punks with the orange hair didn't give it away," he said, referring to the teen boys chugging energy drinks at a table nearby. "What about you?"

"Oh, the Studio Baby clothes launch."

"How appropriate." He glanced down at the maternity twin-set I was wearing, which was filled out with my nice-sized midsection.

"You could say that." The happy hippo felt more hippo than happy at that moment. With the rain, my hair looked a mess, and my cheese omelet from breakfast had settled on my rear. I looked like a fat, drenched cat.

"I'd hoped we'd see each other again. You took off so quickly in New York," he said. "Would you care to do dinner tonight?"

Bladder pulsing, I shifting nervously from one swollen leg to the other. "That probably wouldn't be a good idea," I said. "But I appreciate the offer."

Jude just smiled. "I've got some business in Dallas this fall." He lowered his voice. "Maybe we can get together again," he said, and kissed me on the cheek again. We didn't kiss all the time in business in Dallas. Except for Allen.

Getting back to my shoot, I realized I hadn't considered any option but to work at Ace Advertising after the baby. If I didn't stay at home with the baby, there *were* other options, as Nikki had mentioned in New York. Other agencies. Was there such a thing as a nice boss? A nice work environment? Could I downsize and work for someone like Nikki, a former competitor?

The last scene of the shoot called for two one-year-olds to sit in an oversized rocker and "read" the popular children's book *Goodnight Moon*. The darlings wore "Goodnight Jammies" and began rocking and turning the pages of the book. The boy, excited and giggling, began rocking vigorously, sending the pint-sized twosome sliding out of the big chair. The boy landed on his feet. The girl, unfortunately, did not, and the crew and her worried mother rushed to help her. My fear was substantiated. Kids hurt themselves every chance they got.

Shelton slid his glasses down and glared at me. "Shall we add a disclaimer that the Goodnight Jammies are slippery when rocked?"

I dragged myself to the accident scene, where yet another monstrous prop had hurt one of our actors. In theory, my large playland had been a great idea. After the promise of a cracker from the crafts services table if Ellie dried her eyes and did the scene again, we were back in business. A few shots later, we called it a wrap. The only thing left to do was shoot some stills for the print campaign the following morning, when Jude would be safely pursuing pregnant women on another coast.

After eight hours with the babies, they'd grown on me. Despite the crying, they were fascinating little people.

Too pooped to party, I retired to my hotel room after a stuffy gourmet dinner with the client. I fondly remembered the days when Allen and I would find the coolest dance club around and party until two A.M. despite a seven A.M. call time the next morning.

After the baby shoot, I was lucky to get through dinner without dozing off. As I slipped off my boots and got undressed, Jude popped into my mind, but I quickly shooed him out. I couldn't handle the job I had. Wouldn't moving to another agency be even more stressful? Wasn't that what I wanted less of in my life?

Chapter 23

Eight expecting couples converged in a small classroom in the basement of Glory Women's Center waiting for the childbirth instructor to arrive. Jake completed our paperwork, an informational sheet on our lives, lifestyle, and my pregnancy facts while I engrossed myself in eating plump green grapes. Nearly everything gave me instant heartburn that month, so I ate my snacks in two-bite bursts every hour or so. I wrapped up the cookie to save it, a habit I'd gotten from Aunt Barb. A quick trip through her purse revealed half-eaten candy bars, half-full bags of peanuts and loose sticks of gum. I popped a Rolaids, hoping I could swallow it before I felt the burn in my chest.

I'd been home from Atlanta for three days. A handmade greeting card from Jake was on the kitchen counter when I returned. He'd drawn a heart with a red pen, and in black, wrote:

Missed you, babe. Be home around 7.

Love, Jake.

He had started leaving notes around the house, voice mail messages at work. Told me where he was going, when he'd be back. I started to do the same. It wasn't that we didn't care to know before, but it felt right to do it now.

I started looking for ways to do special things for Jake. His cycling shoes were worn out, so I bought some he had earmarked in a cycling magazine. I took his favorite Italian food to the office when he worked late, and he was always alone (no buxom blonde on the couch). I picked up a new CD of his favorite group the day it was released and put it in the CD player in his car. Playing nice worked. He reciprocated with thoughtful gifts and romantic gestures. I fell in love with him all over again.

Unfortunately, Susan had started leaving me notes, too. On her rampage to win big accounts and grow the agency, she was more "hands on" than ever. Her notes were short, but not sweet.

> *Benson Tires. Need print concept tomorrow A.M. Vintage Wines concept is crap. Hailey Auto says they want a monkey in their TV spot. Don't make it cheesy.*

Those kind of love notes.

"How much do you weigh?" Jake asked.

"It doesn't ask that!" I grabbed at the sheet to check nonetheless. "I suppose you'd rather be at home watching ESPN."

Jake shook his head. "This *is* Superdads one-oh-one, isn't it?"

"Preparing for Baby" was a prerequisite to the childbirth classes, covering how to get ready for the big event, including learning safety tips and newborn care information as well as the material things necessary for baby's arrival.

Studying the other expectant parents, I was intrigued at the wide range of couples represented in the class. Jake and I were overdressed, wearing our business clothes from the workday. Getting to a class at seven was practically impossible. I'd worked through lunch, as had my entire staff.

Jake sped through Wendy's drive-thru, where I ordered a salad and baked potato, my plan for healthier eating, and scarfed them down before class.

Most of the other couples had dressed in jeans and sweaters, appropriate for the cool September weather. My pajamas sounded best of all. I wanted to kick off my shoes, as a couple of brave women had done, but I was afraid my feet were more swollen than theirs. Allen promised he would get me a box to put up my feet in my office.

The couple directly opposite of us was a nice-looking Spanish couple holding hands and speaking to each other in their native tongue. Next to them sat a short, homely woman wearing a homemade flowery maternity shirt. Her husband, tall and lanky, wore a flannel shirt and a cap that read GONE HUNTING and blue jeans with a hole in one knee. The man crossed his arms as if he would much rather be in the woods facing off with a bear.

Next to the hunter sat a forty-something woman and her pregnant daughter, who looked all of sixteen. While her mother filled out her paperwork, the girl flipped through a *Seventeen* magazine.

The next couple was a pregnant midget and her chuckling husband, who I guessed was about five-foot-eight. The little person, sitting in the straight-backed chair with her feet barely dangling off the end, shifted uncomfortably. Her miniature hands rested on her large belly and she kept fidgeting until she hopped off the chair and headed for the bathroom. The sight was surreal.

Sitting to my right was a grossly overweight, greasy man who smelled like pizza; he made me hungry and nauseous at the same time. I was afraid his smell alone would bring on the heartburn. He passed time making fun of the agenda: "Baby safety tips. What, like don't put their fingers in the light socket?" Then he laughed at himself hysterically as his plain-looking wife, who wore large round glasses, punched him in the arm. "This is serious, Dick," she said. "Ignore my husband," she said to me.

I smiled and nodded while Dick gave me his sweaty

palm to shake. "Dick Halloway," he said. "This here's my wife Paula. I'm the manager of the Pizza Hut up there on Sixth street," he told me proudly.

"I'm Taylor, and this is my husband Jake." Jake shook the couple's hands, then continued reading his *Business Week*, leaving me to deal with our newfound buddies.

"What do you folks do?" Dick asked.

"I'm in advertising and Jake's an attorney."

"Figured something like that," Dick said. "Gotta have people to sell us stuff and help us sue people, that's what I always say."

Paula punched him again. "He's not always saying that."

I dove back into the *Adweek* I had brought from work, hoping for some inspiration for my not-cheesy-monkey-in-a-car commercial. I had a roomful of potential car and truck buyers, a captured focus group. I had to have an idea by eight the next morning. I turned to Dick. "If you had to put a monkey in a car commercial, what would you do, Dick?"

Dick sat up a little straighter, honored I asked his opinion. "A monkey, huh? Seems I've seen that before. Sure you wanna go that route?"

"Actually I don't, Dick. In fact, I think all local car commercials are pretty awful, but the client is demanding that we use a monkey, and the boss doesn't want to lose the business."

"I hear what you're saying. I hate to put pineapples on pizza. Think it goes against everything that's good about pizza. But when a customer wants pineapple, by God, I give 'em pineapple."

"You got it."

Dick scratched his brow, licked his lips and tucked his hands under his thighs, rocking forward. "I once had a friend that owned a pet monkey. Pretty hard thing to control. You ever worked with a monkey?"

"No, but I just did a commercial with babies," I offered.

"Okay, then. What I suggest is a monkey in a toy car. You know, have him all dressed up and driving around the parking lot in a toy car. Won't seem as silly as having him in a real car. They can't reach the pedals, you know."

I kicked off my shoes and cracked my toes. I liked Dick. Dick was my friend. Dick had just saved me from a night of insipid monkey concepts. "I like it, Dick." I slapped his back. "I think it's a winner."

Dick beamed, and his wife clapped politely. "That one will cost you," Dick said. "Promise you'll come to the Pizza Hut on Sixth Street next time you're hankering for a pie."

"We'll order it this weekend," I promised. You never had to twist my arm to buy pizza.

Jake looked up from his magazine. "You're going to go far in the ad business, honey. Monkeys today, Nike tomorrow."

Dick resumed counting ways not to harm baby. "Don't let them play with plastic bags!" he shouted.

"Good one, honey," Paula said.

I cursed the damned instructor for being late, prayed the fruit wouldn't give me gas during class. Flatulence had overtaken my life, and I had no control of it. It just *happened*, as if the baby was sitting on the cannon, firing at will. The bridge girls had warned me of Preggo-Gas, but I didn't fully comprehend its power until that month. Holding it in just wasn't possible, so I surrendered, usually just farting away, pretending it wasn't me or that I just didn't give a damn. Fortunately, I had escaped embarrassment, but I was racking up near misses at the office right and left. Even though I was in a room with my kind in the class, I hoped not to be the first to fart aloud, even if I were the leader type.

Eventually our instructor bounded into the room, wearing nursing scrubs and carrying a stack full of papers. "Sorry I'm late, class," she said, plopping a large mysterious bag on the desk at the front of the room. "I'm Anita, and I'll be teaching your class this evening," she yelled, as if on the sideline of a football game. "I'm an RN here at Glory and I'm also a lactation specialist, so for any of you who will be taking the breast-feeding class, which I hope is *all* of you, I'll be teaching that also."

Jake listened to her intently, which I figured had more to do with how cute she was than what she was saying. "We'll definitely have to take that class," he whispered to me.

It figured that he'd find someone to flirt with in a birthing class.

"So, I'll gather up your papers and let's introduce ourselves," she said, nearly skipping around the room gathering our sheets. "Why don't we start here," she said, standing in front of Jake. "Tell us your name, your occupation, when you're due, if you know the sex of the baby, and what quality your partner has that you hope passes on to your baby," she said, never losing eye contact with him. Yep, I hated her.

"I'm Jake Montgomery, and this is my wife Taylor. I'm an attorney and Taylor is a creative director in advertising. We're due December twenty-seventh, and it's a girl. I hope our baby has Taylor's eyes and creativity," he said.

I groaned. "I hope our baby has Jake's sense of logic, appetite for adventure, and his smile," I said, cheesier than Dick's double-stuffed pizza.

Pizza Boy was up. "Gosh, I just hope our baby has Paula's purty face!" he gushed. "And just so you know, at the end of our childbirth classes, I'm gonna throw us a pizza party on the house!" Everyone clapped, his status sharply elevated. Dangling pizza in front of eight pregnant women was more precious than diamonds.

"I like Canadian bacon and sausage," the hunter said.

"You got it, buddy," Dick responded with a wink.

In our circle was also a handsome realtor with slicked-back hair, and his wife, who sold Mary Kay cosmetics. I made a mental note to ask her what she was doing for her skin. Chloasma—"the mask of pregnancy"—had exploded with red splotches on the right side of my face, taking over my usually good complexion. Allen had informed me three inches of cover up was a little much.

The little person and her husband turned out to be attorneys and they were expecting a normal-sized boy. Ouch.

"Three lawyers in our class," Anita exclaimed. "I'll

make sure and watch my p's and q's. All the information we'll cover in the next three hours is basic newborn care and tips to help you get ready for your new bundle of joy."

The checklist of items to buy for the baby, we aced. The only items we hadn't yet purchased were the car seat and a breast pump for nursing mom's returning to the workforce.

Jake admired the drawing of a woman with enormous breasts and long nipples getting ready to feed the wide-mouthed baby.

"Excuse me? What exactly are you doing?" I asked him.

"It's a picture," he whispered. "Quite an alarming picture. Did you see it, Taylor? Your breasts don't look like that. Did you see the *size* of those nipples?"

"Should I have signed you up for the Maturity one-oh-one class?"

Meanwhile, Dick couldn't stop yukking it up with the jokes, while Anita dug in her large Mary Poppins-like bag and pulled out an assortment of home safety devices. First were plastic plugs for outlets.

"It's a good idea to go ahead and put these everywhere in your house before the baby comes," Anita said. "You'll be tired after the baby gets here, and before you know it, your child will be crawling around and trying to stick things in the outlets."

"Don't want no crispy critter," Dick offered.

Anita ignored him and showed her next item, corner bumpers for sharp tables and furniture. "They come in a variety of colors at most baby stores so you can match your furniture," she said. Then she pulled out a fold-up safety gate for fireplaces, contraptions for covering the faucet in the bathtub, locks for cabinets and so on. By the time she had finished, I had a dozen items on the sheet circled that we needed to buy to make our home a baby fortress. Hell, why not cover everything in bubble wrap just to be safe?

During our break for fruit and water, I ordered an ungodly amount of cosmetics from my new, convincing Mary Kay lady. She was *good*. At this point, I was willing to try anything to look and feel better. Class resumed to the how-to portion of the evening with newborn baby dolls at diaper-changing tables. Most of the couples laughed at such a ridiculous task, but Jake and I had never changed a diaper in our lives. Seriously.

Anita encouraged everyone to get the sex-appropriate dolls, so we selected a girl doll with all the right girl parts. Dick held up his naked boy doll with a small penis and large scrotum and exclaimed, "You won't find *these* at Toys 'R' Us!"

I opted to go first, taking directions from Anita, who walked around the room watching us. "First, strap the baby in," she said. "We don't want any falling off the changing table, which can happen."

Strapping our plastic baby, I practiced wiping the baby's bottom in downward strokes with a baby wipe and unfolded a tiny newborn diaper. "It's the size of a Kleenex," I said. Wouldn't all of the poop fall out of such a small diaper? Taking the doll's feet with both hands, I placed the diaper underneath the baby's bottom only to notice I had it backwards. After turning it around, I folded the top of the diaper down—so as not to touch the healing umbilical cord stump—then stuck the tabbed sides into the diaper to close it.

"Good job," Jake said. "That wasn't so bad, was it?"

"Can you believe women used to use safety pins? I can barely diaper a fake baby, and real babies squirm like hell," I said. "I saw it live in Atlanta. It wasn't pretty."

The baby bath followed. We filled our little tubs with real water and placed our baby in it.

"No, watch the head," Anita said to Jake, who was handling the baby like a football. She demonstrated the proper way to put the baby in the tub, holding one hand under the head to support the neck and head, the other hand on the bottom, supporting the back and trunk. The perky instructor tested each of us, and we failed on all accounts. Our water was too deep, too hot. We weren't supporting the baby from slipping. Tina also informed us we had started rinsing the baby with the clean water before we let out the dirty bath water, which again made it too deep for the baby.

"Can't we just take her outside and spray her down with a hose?" Tim, the hunter, asked with a chortle. It didn't sound like a half-bad idea.

Finally, we learned how to swaddle the baby in a receiving blanket, which was a tight wrap around the baby. After several stressful attempts, we got it right. I wasn't about to deny our child proper swaddling.

"We *so* suck at this," I told Jake, exasperated.

"We're much better at our day jobs," he agreed.

Anita suggested that we might want to babysit for friends or family to get more practice. Figuring out how to take care of a baby would require some hands-on, real life experience. The big question was which bridge girl would trust her kid to a novice like me?

MONTH SIX

The Poop Affair

CHAPTER 24

Week 26: Your baby is beginning to make some breathing movements, but there's no air in the lungs yet. If you shine a light on your abdomen, your baby will turn her head.

As I discovered in the sixth month of my pregnancy, all the irrational fears I thought I had under control had only been dormant, waiting to rise again. I was happy with my bloated body and my new campaign and then *bam!* The extreme importance of my impending motherhood shook me.

Figuring knowledge conquered fear, I read three baby books back to back, all written by doctors and child development specialists. I kept manic to-do lists and began following the pregnancy guidelines to the T. I drank sixty-four ounces of water a day, plus two glasses of orange juice with calcium. I gave up chocolate and nixed fried foods. Green vegetables and strange fruits took the fridge hostage. The sodas hid in the back corner died a fizzless death. If it weren't fresh, it got trashed. The freezer, former home to bland, quick-fix meals, was a frozen wasteland where ice cubes and a gallon of fat free vanilla bean yogurt lived alone.

I had all seventy-five pages of the pregnancy disorders chapters memorized. Every disease seemed a possibility, though I had no genetic disposition to any of them. The only ailment our child could expect with any certainty was nearsightedness, but in any given hour of the day, our little girl was going to be deaf, blind, mute, disabled, or the carrier of a rare disease. What if her brain didn't form correctly? What if her lungs were underdeveloped? What if she was born premature, the precursor to a number of developmental challenges?

By the time my next doctor's appointment rolled around, I was more worked up than ever, with a list of questions a mile long. Dr. Creighton had seen me cry, puke, and that month, rant and rave. He arrived in the examining room, glanced at my chart, then measured me, as was usual. I feared he'd mention my weight gain, which was topping twenty-five pounds, placed fairly evenly over my frame. If I squished my calf down, I could even see dimples of fat there, too. I didn't even wait for him to ask me.

"Something's wrong with the baby. Or me. Or it's the world. Yes, the world is not a safe place to bring this baby. Germs are everywhere. Did you know most people don't even wash their hands after they use the bathroom? And you should've seen me change a diaper on a doll. It was atrocious. This baby deserves to at least have a respectable diaper."

His blue eyes, mesmerizing and sincere, watched me finish my tirade. "Taylor, you've been spending too much time online," he said after I was finished. "If you weren't so far along in your pregnancy, I'd send you to Hawaii again!"

My body relaxed. I let out a small giggle, then a bigger one until I was in a full-on laugh. "I need a vacation from my mind."

"Yes, you do. What have we said about stress?"

"Stress, *bad*." I laughed some more.

"Everything you've done is fine, Taylor. You can have one cup of coffee and one soda each day if you wish. You can have a small dessert. Walking is great, but if you feel too tired, don't push yourself. Try to stay away from fatty foods, but an occasional slip won't hurt you or the baby."

I looked at him. He was a smart man with a degree. He was a doctor, but he wasn't me. He wasn't a mother, would never be one. He was there to take care of me, but I was the one ultimately responsible for taking care of my baby.

I put my hand on my belly. "And what about all those diseases?"

"Your ultrasound looked good. You opted not to have the amnio, but there's only a tiny chance you'd have anything wrong. Your blood pressure has been great, and your weight gain is normal. May I suggest just *enjoying* the rest of your pregnancy?"

"I'll consider it," I said.

"Worrying is normal. We all do it. But it doesn't help. Think of all the precious time you're wasting."

I was going through the motions, doing everything I thought was expected to be a good mother, a good wife. I was opening up, learning, willing to change. What I hadn't done was to let go of the fear. I was still hesitant to turn my life over to fate, but I was only mortal. I couldn't control the world, couldn't control drivers on the road or natural disasters. I couldn't control the actions of other people, but I could influence some of them. My daughter among them. I didn't want her mother to be as paranoid as mine had been.

I promised myself I'd address what I could control and turn the rest over. To ease some anxiety, I tried not to be so hard on myself. I treated myself to a chocolate frozen yogurt instead of a chocolate sundae on my drive home just to prove it. I called Aunt Barb on my cell phone, despite my fear of brain cancer, but used my earpiece just to be safe, and updated her on the baby's progress.

For the baby's brain development, I listened to Mozart, and turned it up loudly, the calm but pulsing rhythm invigorating. When I got home, I rocked in the new glider, imagining Peanut swishing comfortably inside, while reading from our new Dr. Seuss collection, a gift from Aunt Barb. Amy suggested I meditate and I vowed to try.

The evenings we didn't work late were ours. Jake had compromised on some of the athletic activities we did together. Instead of running, we speed-walked until I was breathless, and he circled me until I could continue. Instead of hiking, we walked through the woods hand in hand, pausing at nature's wonders we had previously sped by—a squirrel sitting by a tree pecking at a nut watching us watch him; a group of butterflies flitting in the air in an open clearing; the rich, wet bark on an old oak tree.

Our neighborhood readied for Halloween with its plastic ghosts hanging from the trees and the freaky-faced pumpkins lining porches. I told Jake what Dr. Creighton had said about worrying, about the rare chance there was anything wrong with our baby. Jake seemed surprised; the thought that anything may have been wrong with the baby never even crossed his mind. He hadn't noticed I'd been worried. He furrowed his brow. I'd blown it. I vowed the next time I would share with him first.

One evening, we almost made love outside, even got down on the sweet smelling earth, using our jackets as a blanket. An elderly couple whizzed by us and kindly pretended they didn't see us just beyond the tree. Nonetheless, I couldn't go through with it. With my ballooning body and new state of grace, having sex in the wild didn't have the appeal it had in our former days.

We saved our lovemaking for later that night in a more comfortable place: our bed at home, which hadn't been the love nest that it used to be. Due to the orb protruding from my abdomen, I couldn't lie flat on Jake or even kiss him, but if I leaned down just slightly, looked over my big, bouncing boobs, I could see him smiling. Lovemaking was physically awkward, but I cherished it more than I had in the past. It was making love for *love* and not just the physical gratification.

Afterwards, we lay cuddled together and Jake placed his hand on our baby, whom I felt moving beneath his hand.

"Feel that?" I asked

Jake pressed his hand more firmly on my abdomen. "Kick Daddy, Peanut."

The baby kicked again. "There's my little angel," Jake exclaimed, then kissed the spot where he'd felt the movement. "We really need a name. Though I've grown quite fond of Peanut Montgomery."

I leaned over the side of the bed and grabbed one of the baby name books we'd been making notes in of possible names. We used sticky notes to mark the pages, and I flipped to the first one.

"Margaret," I read.

"Too old-fashioned," Jake said.

"Elizabeth?"

"I like it," he said. "You?"

"Maybe," I said. "But it would be a nice middle name. You know my mother's middle name was Elisabeth." I'd never told him that before.

"Okay. It's settled then. Now comes the hard part." Jake took the book from me and quickly listed off the rest of the names we had marked. Emily, Faith, Georgia, Hallie, Haley, Hayden, Madison, Regan, Sadie, Victoria. Most of them went well with Elisabeth.

I'd named dozens of companies and products, but naming a baby, my own baby, was the hardest thing I'd ever done. I'd asked the bridge girls for ideas, and they'd all made additions to the list. Then Jake took the list and promptly marked most of them out. For someone who hadn't wanted much to do with the pregnancy, he was a tough client when it came to our daughter's name.

Jake looked at my round stomach intensely. "I'll know it when I hear it," he said, as did all of my difficult clients.

"I wonder what she wants to be called. She'll be stuck with whatever we give her for life."

Jake crossed his arms behind his head and looked up at the ceiling. "Maybe you'll dream her name. Unless your dreams are still all about getting busy in the elevator." Jake turned away from me to sleep, clicking off his lamp.

Unfortunately, the sex dreams had passed, replaced by

fear dreams—getting to work only to realize I'd left the baby asleep at home. Having the baby prematurely and watching it shrink before my eyes until it was small enough to fit into my hand. Going about my day as usual until I shrieked with the realization that I hadn't fed the baby all day, and she was probably starving. Jackie told me the pregnancy dreams, even the bad ones, are our bodies way of preparing to be the best mother we can be. If so, I would be a blue-ribbon mama.

Dreaming of my baby's name didn't seem out of the question. Maybe if I wrote to her she would reveal her name as I slept.

Baby girl,

Your Grandma Montgomery and your honorary Grandma Barb are begging me for your name, claiming it's to get gifts embroidered. Can't anything be a surprise these days? (Kidding, of course.) I'm ready to call you by your given name, too, only it's me who needs to give it to you. I've looked up exactly 45,000 baby names. Everyone I know has offered suggestions. I've even called a linguistic specialist at a local college claiming I was doing research for work.

My brain is on information overload. I've taken to carrying a small notebook in my purse so when I meet someone with an interesting name I can write it down. I'm prolific, but not very productive. What good is a long list of names if I can't make a decision?

Here's what the linguist told me: "A" names typically are more successful than any other names. A is at the first of the alphabet, a very leadership letter. M's are maternal, soft. Most girl names end with the e sound for the same reason. Like Sophia, Brittany, etc. The new trend is girls getting traditional boy names. Logan, Ellory, Kendall, et al. A unisex name came in handy for me growing up, but perhaps I'm more old-fashioned than I thought I was. Nineteenth century names are popular again, too. Mary, Sara, Ashlynn, Ava. So, which is it, baby? Are you

*a modern woman with a hip name like Felicity or a quiet
girl preferring to go by Charlotte?*

The linguist said it's the old chicken and egg thing.
Does a child become the name she is given? Could a name
have the power to impact your destiny?

My coworkers think because I am in the creative field
that you need a creative name. But this is Dallas, not Hollywood. When Gwyneth named her daughter Apple, even
fruits became a possibility! Allen suggested Pear, but I've
always preferred Kiwi. I imagine a girl named Kiwi to be
carefree and energetic. And unusual, I imagine, which
may not be a bad thing.

Besides the power of the sound and imagery, you have
the definition to consider. When you ask me what your
name means I'd like to have some deep answer that makes
you proud to carry the moniker. Irene was the Greek goddess of peace. But Irene? Then there's Dionne, the mother
of Aphrodite, the goddess of love. But I'm sure there's a
football player or two named Deon or Dijon or something
to that effect.

You can see my dilemma. I want your name to give you
the flexibility to be who you want to be, without the extra
baggage of the word following "I am . . ." So if you have
any ideas, just let me know. Perhaps my next lightbulb
moment will be a message from you.

                                    I am . . . ever your loving mother.

CHAPTER 25

Gagging and tearful, I tried unsuccessfully to hold Austin's ankles so I could wipe his dirty bottom. Kicking his legs and flailing his arms, the nine-month-old turned and almost leapt from the changing table. So that's what the straps were for. The diaper was loaded with dark green poop carrying a smell I could only describe as rotten eggs. He thrashed again, this time landing hard on his poopy diaper, causing it to fly everywhere—on the door, my arm, my new white maternity shirt. Now the green doo-doo was all over Austin's thick little legs and on his feet.

"Ma-*ma!*" he squealed.

"Mama's not here right now, Austin, but you're not the only one who wishes she were!" I reached for his hands before they got in the mess, but he was too fast, and into the pea-colored poop they went, then right on my arm, leaving a perfect little poop print.

"Oh, God!"

"Ga-ga-ga!" The baby was fast becoming impatient with me.

Completely nauseous, I eyed the nursery trash can and grabbed it with my foot, because my hands were more than occupied, and got it within safe puking distance. The sound and sight of my vomiting entertained Austin. He stopped squawling to watch me.

"Hello?" Jake's voice called up the stairs.

"Up here!" I yelled back. Thank God I'd asked Jake to help me.

McKenzie bound up the stairs with Jake. *"Pee-yew!"* McKenzie said, pinching her nose.

Jake made gagging reflexes. "Holy toxic poo-poo, Batman! What have you been feeding that boy, green eggs and ham?"

Twenty wipes later, I was finished wiping Austin's bottom. "Mommy never uses that many," McKenzie told us.

"Are you two going to help, or stand there making fun of me?"

Jake pointed to his chin. "You've got a little something there. *Ewww!* You threw up, didn't you?"

"Take Austin and I'll go clean myself up." I figured out how to use the diaper-eater-thingie. "Did McKenzie let you in?"

"Um, no. The door was unlocked," Jake said.

"God, you could've been an axe murderer for all I know. You could've kidnapped McKenzie! What was I thinking, not locking the door?" I turned to the toddler. "You should've screamed when you saw a strange man come into the house, McKenzie."

McKenzie shrugged her shoulders. "I remembered him from the firecracker party. He tolded me he's your husband," she said.

"And you *believed* him? If today was worth a mommy grade, I'd get a big fat F," I told Jake.

"Hey, don't be so hard on yourself. Look, you've changed a very shitty diaper. Doesn't that count for something?"

"Language, Jake!" I wrapped Austin in a towel and carried him to the bathroom. Jake went with McKenzie to her play room, where she showed him her Barbies. I found a baby tub under the sink and filled it with warm water. I remembered to get the washcloth, baby shampoo, and fresh towel in place so I wouldn't have to leave Austin's side. I set him in the lukewarm water, and he gave the water a karate chop, splashing me in the face. He giggled, then urinated on my shirt. I placed my hand over his privates until he was finished, then quickly scooped out the yellow urine from the tub. "I hear urine is actually very pure."

Jake appeared at the bathroom door, his nose held. "You need a case of Febreeze in here, hon."

"Thanks for being a sport and playing with McKenzie."

"Actually it was kind of fun. Like looking into the future. It's like being on a different planet when you're around kids. Here, let me do that."

Impressed, I handed Austin over to Jake, who rinsed Austin's hair and wrapped him in a hooded towel with a frog head. Amazingly, Jake didn't look awkward at all.

"You have to sing him 'Twinkle, Twinkle, Little Star,'" McKenzie instructed. It seemed as if the toddler were baby-sitting us instead of the other way around.

"I don't know, McKenzie. I've heard her karaoke and she's not easy on the ears," Jake said, making his exit.

"Not *her*. You," McKenzie said, pointing to Jake. We went back to Austin's nursery, diapered him and plopped in the glider, exhausted. I watched from the doorway. Jake started to sing, "Twinkle, twinkle . . ."

"Wait. How about after you make me a milkshake?" McKenzie asked.

"You're cute, but no," I said. "Your mom said no ice cream this afternoon."

McKenzie slumped her shoulders and left in defeat with her Barbies hanging upside down at her side. That was too easy.

As Jake sang the first and only verse he knew, Austin's large brown eyes drooped to a close, and he went limp in his arms. We shared a quiet look of achievement. Jake took him to his crib to lie him down. His eyes shot open and he screamed. I stifled a giggle. Deflated, Jake returned to the rocker, where he resumed the routine again and again until finally Austin did not stir as he put him in his crib, and he slept. I'd never been so proud of something so simple before.

Grinning at my husband's daddy-sized feet, I heard a high-pitched scream from downstairs. I raced down the spiral staircase followed by Jake and saw McKenzie screaming in the kitchen.

What I saw made me freeze in place.

"Taylor? Taylor!" Jake tried to get my attention.

"What?" I said, coming out of it.

"Are you okay? You're white as a ghost. What's the matter?"

My shoulders shook and I let go of the tears. "It just reminds me . . . ," I said leaning against the wall, my eyes fixed on the ice cream and the carton of milk.

"It's a puddle!" McKenzie laughed. "I'm a duck splashing in the puddle," she said, beating her chubby hands in the spilled milk. The carton lay empty at her feet, the container of chocolate chip ice cream toppled on its side, melting onto the ceramic floor.

A worried look passed over Jake's face. "Tell me."

How innocent he seemed at that moment, trying to make a go of learning the parenthood thing. All he wanted was a piece of my past, something to understand more about the woman he'd married. Jake knew my parents were killed in a car accident, but I'd never told him the details.

"I ran all the way from my house to the accident. I pushed through the crowd, people everywhere. I don't know where they all came from, but they were staring at something, and I had to see it. I had a feeling, and . . . it was there. My dad's car. Like a crumpled piece of paper. I could see the groceries in the back seat, the milk pouring out, covering the leather seat. The chocolate chip ice cream that was meant for me, melting and dripping onto the asphalt."

"God, Taylor. I'm sorry," Jake said, taking my hand. Jake's gaze locked on mine, and he teared up. For my parents' wreck, maybe. For my huge loss. Or maybe just because I had let him in. "Look, I'll clean up this mess. You go and rest."

"I'm fine." I took McKenzie's wet hand as Jake mopped the floor. McKenzie, dripping in milk, had rescued me from one of my worst memories.

"What exactly were you doing, McKenzie?"

"Well, I was trying to make us a milkshake." She licked her sticky fingers.

"I told you your mom said you couldn't *have* any ice cream."

"I'm sorry I made you cry," she said, rocking back and forth.

"It's okay, honey." I needed it. "I'm going to give you a bath now. You smell like a milk factory."

"Goodie! A bath!" McKenzie squealed, jumping up and down, then slipped in the milk and fell on her bottom. She cried hysterically.

I scooped McKenzie up, covering myself in the milk and ice cream from her wet clothes, and headed back upstairs.

The bath proved to be a good move on my part, as McKenzie seemed happier than she had been all day. Covered in suds, McKenzie squealed in delight, splashing and giggling. We made words on the tile with her letter sponges. She spelled *mom*, then *dad*, then *cat*. I took the letters, and, without realizing it, spelled *Emily*. My baby kicked. I stared at the word on the tile. Emily was my great-great grandmother's name, Bertha's mother. I had only two pictures of her—one on her wedding day in 1870 and one holding my mother on her knee in 1954. Emily had lived a long, happy life as I recalled, living well into her nineties with a sweet disposition like my Aunt Barb.

Soon after, Jake appeared in the doorway. "We may not suck at this after all," he said. "Getting the hang of this marriage thing, after all these years? Maybe we could even be good at it, along with parenting."

I squeezed his hand. "We may just surprise ourselves."

Jake sniffed at the air. "That cologne you're wearing—"

"It's called Scent of a Mother. Poop, urine, milk, and ice cream. You watch McKenzie. I'll go raid Amy's closet for a T-shirt."

Jake stared at the tile. "Is that our baby's name?"

I shrugged. "What do you think? You like it?"

"I do. She could be a poet or a surgeon with a name like that."

She could live to a ripe old age, I thought. Only later did I look up the meaning:

Emily (Latin): flatterer
(German): industrious

So she would be a hardworking flirt. It could be worse. Emily Elisabeth it was. And if she got rebellious as a teen and insisted on a derivative, she had plenty to choose from.

Amy returned home from shopping, her arms full of packages from all the best stores, full of things she didn't need and would probably only wear once. She didn't seem to notice that the bathroom floor was sopping wet or that Jake had used up a whole roll of paper towels cleaning up the milk or that the play room looked like an Oklahoma twister hit it.

What a pal.

The Studio Baby Collection readied for launch with more than three hundred department stores carrying the line. The twenty million-dollar multimedia campaign was about to hit nationally. I was pleased with the media schedule, which had our spots playing on all the women's cable channels, as well as during national morning news and daytime soap operas and talk shows. The magazine schedule was just as impressive, and our online strategy had sweeping banner ads on all the parenting sites.

Not to brag, but I knew we'd hit a home run. I'd proved I had what it took to nail a damn good campaign, pregnant or not. Although the bitchmeister hadn't said it, my boss was proud of me. The client was pleased; therefore, Susan was pleased. I expected her to pull out the sparkling grape juice when she called me into her office later that afternoon.

The air smelled of thick cologne, but I was too excited to dwell on the offending odor. I'd recently smelled worse. Kudos were hard to come by with my shark of a boss. I had to revel in it.

Tossing her black leather Daytimer on her desk with a plunk, she coolly sat down on her contemporary leather couch and motioned for me to join her. I sat back and smiled, ready for my ass to be kissed for once.

"Fucking good job on Studio, Taylor," Susan said matter-of-factly. "The media hasn't broken and I can already see pregnant moms and weeping grandmas clamoring for those overpriced clothes."

"Thank you, Susan," I said, trying not to swell with pride.

"But I called you in here to let you be the first to know about an important ad exec who will be joining our team next week. Just between you and me, he'll be a consultant behind the scenes with strategy and creative to see how we all mesh. I've done everything in my power to try to grow this agency without resorting to a merger, but this may be the only way. Anyway, he's done some mind-boggling work with Chrysler and Coke and some of the dot-com companies. I'm expecting some big things from him for some of our new clients," Susan said.

This couldn't be happening to me. "Who is he?"

"Jude Winters."

My throat tightened. "Jude Winters? From Chicago?"

"Yeah, from Titan Advertising," she said, surprised. "You've heard of him?"

"I met him at the convention in New York," I said. "Then I saw him when we were shooting the Studio campaign in Atlanta."

"So you know how *wonderful* he is then."

Where exactly was the ass-kissing I so deserved? "So, you're basically saying Jude's going to hold the creative reins from now on and I should expect more of my team to be laid off in a merger?" I could be sassy after six years working for Susan. It never fazed her.

Susan nodded her head. "Titan and Ace are in different markets. We both go after national accounts, but they are so much larger than us that we've never truly been competitors."

"Great. So I get to fight for my job now?"

"Aren't you always?" Okay, that was straight-shooting enough. "Jude can bring big accounts with him. Sometimes it takes an outsider to shake things up."

"Admit it. I have ten weeks before I take off for maternity leave. Why couldn't you even ask your senior team before making this decision?"

Getting up from the sofa, Susan paced behind her desk as she often did when arguing with employees or clients. "You are a stakeholder in the company, but I still own the majority, so ultimately it's my decision." Susan raised her voice. "My life is this business, and I have to protect its interests. If that means I have to add to our brain trust and hurt one of my employee's feelings, so be it."

The rest of the day I drifted from appointment to appointment, half-listening to my department's creative concepts and project status, all the while thinking about what my baby's entry into my life would really do to me. That was exactly what Susan expected, that my mind would be drifting more and more to my impending birthing and paying less attention to my work. Perhaps Susan was right preparing for the worst-case scenario.

Returning to work after Emily was born seemed natural. Work was all I knew. Besides Jake, it was the greatest high. And I thought of my mother, the ballerina who always regretted that she'd never become a star.

CHAPTER 26

Another win under his belt, Jake hummed as he entered the house and threw his arms around my rock-hard belly. He gave Emily a quick rub, then spun me around and kissed me squarely on the mouth.

"Junior partner on the way to becoming the youngest senior partner in the firm," Jake beamed. "I'm four-and-oh for the year. Old man Dickson is the only one with that good of a trial streak." He opened the fridge and pulled out a long-necked Bud.

"Good for you, honey," I said, not at all convincingly.

He didn't seem to notice. "Smells delicious," he said, looking into the skillet where the chicken, rice, and spices simmered. "Special occasion?"

"Every night's a special occasion, right?" I said dryly. "To tell you the truth, Susan has a big creative poking his nose around to see if he wants to merge our companies. Needless to say, I'm no longer top dog."

"I don't see the problem. Bigger company could mean more money," he said.

"Is that all you care about? I don't want bigger. He could be worse than Susan, if that's even possible. Or I could get fired, Jake."

Jake pulled me in for a hug. "Everything will work out."

"You sound so sure."

Jake grabbed a lighter from the kitchen drawer and lit the candles on the table. "I don't know what I can say or do to make you feel better about the future. We've come a long way in the last few months."

I wanted to be the kind of wife who supported her husband, relished in his success, and planned joyous celebrations around his achievements. But I also wanted to be just as successful as he was. Jake would become a bigwig attorney. I envisioned myself spiraling down the ladder of success I'd so valiantly climbed. Somehow it seemed mothers weren't supposed to desire success beyond raising healthy and successful children.

If I gave up my career but told my daughter she could be anything she wanted to be, would I be lying? Does it mean a woman can be anything she wants to be until she has a baby? Why was this a struggle in the twenty-first century? Hadn't we progressed beyond this kind of debate? Of course I knew it wasn't the government that said I couldn't do it, or even my boss. The struggle was within me.

I placed the meal on the table, and Jake dug in. "Good stuff," he said.

I tasted it, then nearly spit it back onto the plate. The chicken tasted like hell, rubbery and dry. The only reason Jake liked it was because of his win. "I'm happy for you, Jake—how fast you're moving up in the firm. But you've already had to travel more since you were promoted to junior partner. What will happen when you're senior partner?"

"I can tell Aunt Barb has given you some recipes. This is delicious, hon." He wiped his mouth with a cloth napkin. "Long hours? I wouldn't think I'd be home past seven or eight o'clock except for big trials," he said. "Our firm's been getting a lot of press lately, so we could see more and more clients pouring into the office, which just means more for me," he said with a wink. "For us. Maybe we can get that bigger home you wanted in Amy's neighborhood."

"And the travel? With more international cases, you could be gone for a week or more at a time."

Jake's enthusiasm began to fade. "I don't see that happening very often."

I set down my fork. "Jake, I'm going to start looking for a day care or a nanny, but I just want to know that you plan on doing your share with Emily. That might mean cutting back on stuff."

That got his full attention.

"Of course I plan on taking care of Emily," he said, sounding almost hurt. "Why do you think I've been going to the child care and birthing classes with you? I realize it's my responsibility, too. But I don't think we'll have to cut out everything else in our life."

"Cutting out, no. Cutting down, yes. If you're not home until seven or eight o'clock each evening, which is usually when I get home, who'll pick Emily up from day care at six o'clock? And if we have a nanny, unless she's a live-in, she'll want the same kind of hours."

Jake looked at me blankly. "What do you want me to say, Taylor?"

I threw my napkin on my plate and got up from the table. "I want your advice, your opinion, your perspective on this. I didn't think I'd have to be making all these decisions myself!"

Jake shifted back. "Since you seem to think I'm so complacent, let me make it clear that I *do* care who takes care of our daughter. But since you brought up our hours, may I remind you that this is why I didn't think now was a great time to have a child in the first place."

"Oh, that's great, Jake! It's my fault again for getting pregnant, right? I thought we were beyond this. The baby will be here in less than three months. I can't raise Emily alone."

Jake threw down his fork on the plate. "So are we supposed to stop climbing the corporate ladder, is that what you're saying? Tell my boss, 'Sorry, can't stay late to finish working on the case, sir. The wife says I have to go home and do my share of diaper duty.'"

I threw up my hands and stomped out of the kitchen. "Yes, dammit!" I slammed the door behind me. I wasn't sure where I was headed, but I knew I had to get out of there. Yearning for my mother, I went to the closest thing I had, my Aunt Barb.

I drove through the crisp October evening with the windows down to cool my temper. The sweet smell of an oncoming rain filled the air. The trees were turning a golden yellow and a slight wind rustled the row of trees lining the highway. A part of me wanted to run away through the trees and get so lost no one could find me. But what I was running away from was a part of me that I still couldn't comprehend.

My soul ached with what the challenge of being a parent would bring. Chat rooms and articles on being a working mom did little to ease my anxiety. That was *their* lives. Maybe they could find a way to job share or cut back hours at the office or work four-day weeks, but none of that clicked with me yet. I liked how I had risen through the ranks in the advertising world. Could I enjoy the solitary life of a freelance-working mom who worked a few hours a day at a home computer while the baby slept? After all, I'd never been good at being alone. I panicked at the thought of being alone with the baby, wondering when Jake would be there to help me.

Jack-o-lanterns lined the winding driveway leading up to Aunt Barb's suburban home just like when I was growing up. The crazy Halloween parties, the costumes she made my cousins, she seemed to have more fun dressing up and acting like a kid than her sons did. Before I even rang the doorbell, Aunt Barb threw open the door and welcomed me with a bear hug that smelled like cinnamon.

"Perfect timing," she said. "Brownies are just coming out of the oven. You know how your uncle likes brownies in the fall. And as I recollect, so do you." Aunt Barb led me into her sunshine yellow kitchen. Life was one fresh-baked goodie after another for Aunt Barb.

I waved to my uncle, who was curled up in his Lazy Boy watching CNN and drinking a large cup of coffee out of his Dallas Cowboys mug. Although a bit grayer and a few pounds heavier, he hadn't really changed much in the last twenty years. I liked it that way.

"I like what you've done with your house," I said, admiring my aunt's homespun décor.

"Well, it's not contemporary like you like," she said. She pulled out a chair in the kitchen for me. "But it's comfortable."

"I think you could make any house comfortable."

Aunt Barb set two brownies and a tall glass of milk in front of me, and I started to sob.

"I know it's not easy, sweetie," she said. "What's going on?"

My shoulders shook. "I don't know what we're doing. I thought Jake was happy about the baby now, but we don't know what to do about day care. Jake doesn't seem to want to cut back any hours at the office, and to be honest, I don't know if I *can* without losing my job. I'm too depressed to even start looking for a sitter because I also don't want anyone else watching my child!"

Aunt Barb produced tissues for me. "You blow, and I'll talk. I don't really want to give you any advice, because what you decide will be the best decision for your family. All mothers go through this. Even thirty years ago, when I was pregnant with Timmy, I wasn't sure I wanted to give up teaching. Sure, I got the summer off, but being away from your child for any amount of time can be painful. But lots of other women find day care and keep their jobs and do very well balancing work and family. You love your work, so don't let guilt make you decide to stay home if you're going to be miserable later."

"That's just it," I said, blowing my nose again. "I don't know *what* to expect. I just wish someone could make this decision for me. Jake's obviously no help."

"Most men are nervous to suggest one thing or another. If he said he wants you to stay home with the baby, then he looks old-fashioned. If he says he wants you to continue bringing home a paycheck, then it appears he can't take care of his family himself."

"You're right. Maybe I'm expecting too much of him. I know how demanding his work is, how much he loves it. But no less than I love my job! At least I thought I did. Don't you think Mom regretted giving up her career in ballet?"

She shook her head. "Lordy, no! Is that what you think, Tay? Goodness, the best thing she ever did was marry your father and have you. She was sickly skinny until she got pregnant with you. First time in her life she weighed anything. She even ate three meals a day and splurged on brownie sundaes!"

"I don't think I ever saw Mom eat a piece of chocolate."

"Well, a ballerina has cravings like everyone else. Honey, don't feel guilty about your mom giving up her ballet. Your mother was a strong woman—if she had wanted to continue to work she would have. Besides, she really gave up her career when she married your father. She didn't like to show it, but she was afraid he would find someone else while she was traveling. She always underestimated the love your father had for her."

"I may have inherited that from her, too."

Aunt Barb walked to the china cabinet and removed a frame with a black and white picture of my mother and aunt, holding babies in their arms. "Tell me what you see."

"It's you and mom and Timmy and me." A chubby baby, I looked big against my mother's thin arms. My face was scrunched up into a wide-mouthed smile. Her face was relaxed, not at all like I remembered. Young, but self-assured. Aunt Barb had a large, open smile, and her Timmy gazed shyly into the camera. Two sisters, as different as night and day. Back then I wanted Mom to be more like Aunt Barb, but when Mom died I wanted Aunt Barb to be more like her.

"What you see is two mothers, plain and simple. Mothers are just people, honey. Some are serious, like your mom, and some are silly, like me. But what we all have in common is that we'd do anything for our children. We don't know it starting out, but that power is within us, and it starts when we are pregnant and it grows as our children grow. *That* you can be sure of."

I thought of our childbirth class, the eight expecting couples so unique from each other. Just as their personalities varied, so would their parenting styles. Who started out knowing what to do? How to act? What to say? Not say?

"I want to know the secret to being a good parent," I told her.

Aunt Barb reared her head back and laughed. "You find that one out, be sure and tell me, will you? There is no magic formula. As far as I know, you just have to keep on loving your kids and when you think you've loved them enough, love them some more. Be there for them. For life. Set a good example. Be a good partner to your spouse so they'll see what it takes to have a strong marriage. You'll make your share of wrong decisions, but it doesn't mean you're a bad parent. We usually get it down pat by the time we're grandparents." Aunt Barb stood on her tiptoes and kissed my head.

I looked at my mother's picture again. That she loved me in her own way was little consolation. I snuggled against Aunt Barb's large shoulder. "Is it bad to want what I never had?"

Aunt Barb put the picture back in its place and closed the china cabinet door. "All we know is how we were raised. We fear we'll eventually turn into our mothers. You know I was more optimistic than your mother, but I feared it, too. That I wasn't geared for motherhood. But I thought it for a split second. I replaced it with a desire to be better."

"Nurture over nature."

"We're born with some things in place, but those around us shape the rest. That's reason enough to be hopeful." Aunt Barb took the pot of coffee to my uncle and filled his mug. After thirty years of marriage, they had a pattern, but they were open to change. They'd moved to a brand new city, adapted to a new environment. Adapting was letting go a piece at a time, replacing the old with a shiny new coat.

One of us had always been running, missing each other in the dark. Before my pregnancy, we hadn't had much to fight about. Not putting the toilet paper on the roll. Leaving crumpled paper towels on the kitchen counter. Smelly running clothes at the foot of the bed. Little stuff, annoying, but minute compared to this. Fighting over the big stuff, the big decisions, was new territory. Avoiding the situation was the easy out, but in this case, the situation wouldn't go away. It was growing bigger, coming closer, the conclusion unavoidable. If we kept running in circles, our marriage would never get to the finish line. Our child would suffer. We both knew that.

Jake sat in the family room on the couch, drinking a flavored tea that was supposed to help you relax. He'd switched from a liquor nightcap to tea three months earlier since I couldn't drink alcohol. A second full cup sat on the coffee table.

"For me?" I joined him on the couch and kicked off my shoes.

Jake nodded. "Aunt Barb called. She told me you were on your way home."

I patted his knee. "I'm sorry if you were worried. God, I used to run out on my mom like that when we fought. I never stuck around to finish it off. We'd get into new fights before the last fight was resolved. She died that way, midfight." I grabbed the cup and took a drink.

"But not anymore," he said. "I mean, with your mom. You're not still in a fight with her, are you?"

I tightened my grip on the cup, the heat burning my palm. It sounded so ridiculous to be in a fight with a dead person, but as foolish as it sounded, I was. She wasn't around to bring any closure. "I guess so. I've been so mad at both of them for dying. But I'm trying to let go of that. I'm tired of fighting. Ready to move on."

Jake scooted closer to me. "So we need a fighting philosophy. I mean a 'disagreement philosophy.'"

"You're on," I said. "I'm pregnant, though. Gotta go easy on me."

"We're not so much arguing as resolving," he said.

"That's a very lawyerly way to put it." I lay my head on his chest. He wrapped his arms around me and rubbed my belly.

"Well, I have to admit, you running out did mean more chicken and rice for me," he said.

"Ugh! You can't be serious about liking that stuff."

"I ate the whole skillet. Go see for yourself. I even cleaned the kitchen," he said.

Jake began massaging my shoulders. I relaxed. "You clean, you massage. This kind of fighting, I could definitely get used to."

An old photo box peeked from under the coffee table. I'd gotten it out of the hall closet earlier that day, on a whim, a moment of found courage. I was ready to share the rest. "Promise me you won't laugh at what a stocky kid I was."

He rubbed his hands together eagerly. "I promise."

Lifting the lid on remnants of my past, captured moments in time fell to the table. They were snapshots of my once-upon-a-time family. We spent the rest of the evening sorting through them, sometimes laughing, sometimes crying. At the bottom of the heap were the photos of my beginning breaths, my body curled up on my mother's chest, her radiant face smiling into the camera. My father wore a screaming orange jumpsuit as he tossed me into the air some months later.

"They were a handsome couple, seventies duds and all," Jake said. "They look happy."

"Sometimes they were," I said. I held the pictures of our family vacation at the Grand Canyon, just two weeks before the accident. I'd wanted to stay back with my friends instead of spending a whole week alone with my parents. But I didn't look miserable in the photos, pitching the tent with my dad and hiking down the canyon on a hot afternoon. So strong my mother looked. In charge of her life. Her family. The vacation was her idea. To get away and be together, just the three of us. Maybe my mother was tentative with me. Didn't tell me she loved me every night. But every now and then she said it, and when she did, she meant it.

Looking at the photos, something Aunt Barb said came back to me. *Take the good and leave the rest behind.* I set aside a few of my favorites and boxed the rest up.

The final ten weeks were upon us. We were seventy-five percent there all around. But the last quarter would be the toughest round yet.

MONTH SEVEN

In Search of Poppins

CHAPTER 27

Week 30: Your baby now weighs about three pounds and is about seventeen inches long from head to toe. The brain is growing rapidly, and the head is getting longer to accommodate it.

A bitter October wind blew the morning I had scheduled three nanny interviews. Jake canceled a weekend hiking trip to stay home and help. The tile was cold when I'd stepped into the bathroom. Barefoot weather was officially gone. Jake clicked the thermometer setting to heat.

I pulled on a beige cashmere sweater and maternity jeans. While I went over questions to ask the nannies, Jake brewed French vanilla decaf coffee. "I don't know anything about nannies," I said, nibbling on a blueberry muffin. "If it weren't for that Web site with these questions I'd be clueless."

"We'll know if she's the right one. I'm not so sure we even need a nanny, though," he said.

I nearly choked on my muffin. Had he dreamt I'd suddenly turned into the perfect mother? He of all people should have known I was going to need all the help I could get. "Really? I figured since you had a nanny, you'd be all for it."

Jake sat across from me at the table. "It's just that. *Raised by a nanny*. I completely lucked out with Maria, don't get me wrong. She was the best surrogate mom a kid could ask for. But why have a surrogate when your parents are more than able to care for you?"

"So, I'm not the only one with mother issues. Did you ever tell your mom how you felt?"

Jake shook his head. "It wouldn't have mattered. Half the kids on our block had nannies. I might feel different if she'd worked. She was around, but not with me. If I had a game or somewhere to be, she'd say, 'Maria can take you.' After a while, I just stopped telling her. Maria took me everywhere. Doctor's appointments, soccer practice, piano lessons."

"But you and your mom are so close now," I said.

"I think you're mistaking nosiness for closeness. Sure, she loves me, but looking back on it, she wasn't really there for me."

We were raised so differently, I'd never dreamed Jake wasn't happy with his upbringing. We had even more in common than I imagined. "What about your dad then?"

Jake looked out the window, watched the leaves fall from the trees. "When I think about my dad, I see him in a business suit with his tie loosened, a tired look on his face. He never seemed to come home in a good mood. Or I saw him on his way out the door with his suitcase. He seemed stressed out and in a hurry all the time. Even when we had time together, we were always on the clock. Even vacations seemed rushed. And that was even before cell phones. Then there were the black-tie affairs. I thought, 'They must be important people to get so dressed up all the time.'"

I put my hand on the back of his neck, rubbed my thumb along his hairline. "I know how you feel. My dad was gone at least three days out of the week. I think my mom liked it because she didn't want to be too dependent on him. Think she liked the chance to miss him. But I hated it. Dad was the only one who really listened to me. Mom usually made us dinner or we'd go out for burgers or something when he was gone, but I felt like nothing I said was right. She criticized my friends, my boyfriends. She cursed at the TV news every night. Talked back to the newspapers. I started not telling her my problems because she blew everything out of proportion."

The buzzer to the dryer went off. Jake went to the laundry room and opened the dryer door. I followed him to fold the towels. I put the towel to my face, the warmth on my cheek. Suddenly I felt a weight had been lifted. Jake was back in the parenting saddle with me again, at galloping speed. Jake's childhood wasn't as perfect as Lorna led me to believe. Being rich did not afford him the luxury of more love. We knew what we wanted for our child more than we realized.

After the last towel was folded and stacked, the doorbell rang. I shrugged my shoulders. "Who knows," I said.

Jake shrugged. "I'm going to need another pot of coffee. Caffeinated."

Nancy Beckett was a wiry woman in her early forties, wearing dark-rimmed glasses and dressed head to toe in gray. She looked like a nun, minus the habit, except for the light peach lipstick that didn't do much for her pale complexion. Her bony hands met mine for an abrupt handshake.

"Nice to meet you," Nancy said crisply, surveying the room with a 180-degree swoop. No nonsense and straight to the point. Someone Jake could relate to, I thought. I peered down, expecting to see an oversized Poppins bag with endless room for stuffed teddy bears and the complete Dr. Suess collection. I was a little disappointed to find she carried a brown attaché case. All business.

"Can I get you some coffee?" I asked, sitting next to Jake on the couch.

She shook her head and sat across from us on the chair, her back straight as a board. "Coffee gives me the jitters," she said, revealing a hefty notebook that put my tiny notepad to shame.

"Let's get started then," Jake said.

"Yes, let's," Nancy jumped in, flipping her page and looking at us squarely. "Let's delve right into the details, shall we? I do feedings every four hours, and use a Microsoft Project Management Chart for wets and dirties. If we're not seeing good output and you'll be breast-feeding, we'll need to discuss your diet."

Jake's mouth hung open. For a litigator, he was strangely speechless. He looked at me, and I realized my mouth was also agape. I suddenly wished I'd checked out *Nannies for Dummies*.

"Well, I'm sure we'd appreciate a chart," I said, patting Jake on the knee. "We'll just have to see how the breast-feeding goes." I straightened my spine to match her posture. I didn't want her to think I was a slouch. I looked down at my blank page. "Back to the questions then," I started.

"Certainly," she said, handing me a worksheet. "I'll need you to complete this questionnaire and return it to me before I can assess whether we'll be a good fit." I looked at the list—a pseudo-psychological profile and criminal background check all in one. I began to wonder if she had a tiny spy camera in her ugly briefcase. Was Jake trying to play some twisted joke on me? Or was it Lorna, trying to frighten me into staying home with the baby?

Jake looked at me, bewildered. No, he wasn't crafty enough to pull off a practical joke like this. I opened my mouth to protest, trying to shove the worksheet back in her hands, but she was spry and was already halfway up the stairs.

"Let's check out the nursery," she said, writing down notes as she went along.

"Look, I don't think—"

"Oh, my," Nancy said upon entering the nursery. She shook her head furiously, scribbling again. "You can't put the crib there by the window. Too much natural light, and you'll get a draft this winter," she said.

She began opening drawers, fingering the tiny socks.

and clothing. "I've got a checklist for the layette," she said, thumbing through her gigantic book again.

Furious, I struggled to maintain my temper. "I don't think we'll need your checklists or your charts."

Nancy slit her eyes and leaned forward. "I'm the most highly referred nanny in Dallas," she said. "I have babies still warm in their father's loins waiting for me to take care of them in ten years. If you want to hire the best in the business, you'll have to meet some conditions." This time she pulled out a long stapled document that appeared to be an official contract.

Jake put his hands on my shoulders, not for comfort, but to keep me from lunging at her. If I didn't have a baby between us I'd pounce on her like a cougar and scratch her beady little eyes out.

"Why don't we just go back downstairs and we can review your contract," Jake said in a business tone.

"Jake," I hissed. "A word."

As Nancy descended the stairs, I pulled him into our bedroom. "We're not hiring the nanny from hell, I don't care how many sperm are on her waiting list."

"Calm down," Jake said.

"Calm down? No, I will not calm down. She's been here ten minutes and she already wants control of my diet, my baby's bowel movements, and our entire household. She's supposed to work for *us*, not the other way around."

Jake nodded. "I know, honey. But she *was* voted Top American Nanny by *Child Magazine* three years in a row. She obviously knows what she's doing."

I grabbed Jake's arms and shook him. "Are you listening to yourself? I won't have some trophied, lunatic nanny running our lives and telling us how to raise our child. Yes, we need help, and a lot of it. But I still want to be the boss."

Jake leaned down and kissed me on the forehead. "Of course you do. And there's only room for one lunatic boss in this house." He tossed the contract in the trash can.

"Thank you," I said. "Now go tell her she can scare the crap out of some other expecting couple."

As Jake left to tell Nancy to get back on her broomstick, I felt a kick. I took it as a high-five from within. Emily hadn't liked her, either.

Upon hearing the front door slam, I began to panic. What if all the good nannies belonged to some union and Nancy had us blacklisted? I'd be all over the message boards by nightfall.

"There'll be lots of other highly qualified nannies," Jake assured me later. "No one could be as bad as her."

Next up was Andrea Simmons, whom Jackie assured me was the best babysitter she had ever hired. Because Jackie was one of my best friends, I took her word for it. Andrea arrived on time, dressed in an embroidered Alpha Chi Omega sweatshirt and designer jeans. A studded cell phone hung from a metallic belt clip, which rang a rap song I didn't recognize, but she wisely let it go to voice mail.

"Sorry about that," she said, sticking out her hand, which I thought I was supposed to shake, but instead she plopped it right on my belly. "This must be Emily," she squealed, raising her shoulders and rocking them back and forth. "I can tell I'll like her already."

Jake entered the room and none-too-discreetly looked the pretty sorority girl up and down. He liked her already. "Jake Montgomery," he said offering his hand, which she shook for a beat too long.

"Shall we?" I said, pulling Jake away. I was determined to take charge. "So, Andrea, Jackie tells me you have lots of experience with children."

"Love kids," Andrea said. "I feel like I've spent like my whole life babysitting."

"That's great. I don't know what your plans are, but we're really looking for a long-term commitment," I said.

"Oh, I plan on babysitting 'til I die," she said. "Or at least until I have kids of my own."

Jake crossed his legs. "You have a boyfriend?"

That wasn't on the list. "You don't have to answer that," I said.

"No, it's okay. I do have a boyfriend. Longest one yet. Four-week anniversary is next week. So my Friday nights need to be free."

I made a note. "Well, we probably won't get out much anymore on the weekends, anyway. We'd need you here by seven thirty A.M., though."

Andrea fluttered her glittery eyelids. "Wow. I'm not much of a morning person. My roommate has to literally shove me out of bed just to get me to chem lab on time. I could come, say, around nine, though."

I bristled, feeling my neck catch fire and spread to my face. "Nine? I wish I had that luxury, but my boss is a bit of a stickler for her eight A.M. meetings, so we'd need you here by seven-thirty."

Jake cleared his throat. "What about staying late? Sometimes we're both working on projects until seven or so."

Andrea thought it over, rolling her tongue over her icy pink lip gloss and looking into the air as if her schedule appeared there. "Great, except I have drama class on Tuesday nights. I want to be an actress. Did Jackie tell you that? Like the next Charlize Theron. Only probably more like Sandra Bullock. Do you ever wonder what happened to her? So, no, probably more like Charlize." She snapped her fingers. "Oh, and we have our fraternity mixers on Thursday nights, so as long as I'm outtie by six-thirty on those nights, we'll be fine. My boyfriend gets jealous, but hey, I don't see a ring on my finger, you know?"

I set down the paper and placed my palms in the air, stopping her. "Andrea, you do know that we are looking for a full-time nanny, right? That our baby is coming this Christmas, and that we can't rearrange our busy careers and put our baby on hold to meet your social calendar or big-screen ambitions?"

Andrea's phone began to ring again. Beyonce. I recognized it from my karaoke past. She glanced at the number.

"Ooh. It's Jack. Hey, babe. I'll call you back." She clicked it shut and looked at us. "He gets jealous if I don't answer. I'm sorry, Mr. and Mrs. Montgomery. Jackie told me you were looking for a babysitter. I had no idea this was like a real live job. When I graduate I'm going to be a—"

"We know," I said. "A big-time star."

The third woman called just moments before her interview and said her eldest son couldn't get a ride home from school and she would have to go get him. Could we reschedule? Afraid not.

So we moved on to the next alternative, which was an in-home day care at a licensed provider's house. I told Jake I would handle a few of those on my own, and if I found one I liked, I could take him to meet her. After twenty phone calls to sitters who didn't have newborn openings, I stumbled across a lead that would have an opening after the New Year. Perfect.

Dottie's Darlings was referred to me by Jackie, who knew someone who knew someone who had a child there. So much for "connections." The location worked—just a mile from our house in a nice middle-class neighborhood.

As I stepped into the modest three-bedroom home on a cul-de-sac, I noticed it smelled of vanilla. The street was quiet—no afternoon traffic, which I found to be a plus. Dottie had her graying hair in a loose bun and wore a flowing floral dress more appropriate for warmer weather. Well, I wasn't looking for a fashion plate.

It was nap time, and her five day care kids lay about the house in afternoon slumber. Three toddlers curled in sleeping bags in the formal living room and the two babies slept in bassinets in her guest room. One wicker bassinet sat in the corner empty. Is that where my baby girl would be sleeping?

"As you can see, every child has his or her own space," she said. "And I'm very strict with nap time schedules. All the kids go down at one P.M. and I don't let them sleep longer than two hours. Of course, the babies sleep longer than that at times, but I do put them down sleepy. I don't believe in rocking a child to sleep or letting them fall asleep on the bottle. That will save you headaches at night," she said proudly.

"What if one of the babies is screaming? You just let them cry it out?"

Dottie nodded. "Tough love, but it works after a while. Maybe your baby will already be able to fall asleep on her own before you start bringing her here."

"I hadn't thought about that. But doesn't the crying wake the other babies?"

"If I have a problem baby, I can always move her to one of the other bedrooms," Dottie said, showing me the master bedroom and a room that looked to belong to a high school boy and smelled like a locker room. Sports pictures of her son adorned the walls—basketball, football, baseball.

"That's my Matthew," she said, smiling genuinely for the first time. "He's quite an athlete. He'll get a scholarship to somewhere next fall. I'm sure not looking forward to an empty nest, though."

"It won't quite be empty with your day care, will it?"

Dottie looked at me evenly. "Well, of course not, but it's just different when they are your own," she said, then realized how that sounded. "I love kids, or I wouldn't have done this for the last seven years."

After a brief interview in her cramped kitchen and a glass of lukewarm tea, I excused myself. Dottie was perfectly pleasant, kept a nice home, and obviously could care for a gaggle of kids at one time, a feat I was sure I could never master. But one thought kept creeping into my head: Would she love Emily? Would her heart melt when their eyes met? Would she hug my baby close just for the sheer joy of it?

This nanny thing was so much more than ABCs and smiles and diaper counts. Above all else, I wanted a woman to fall in love with my baby and have my baby love her almost (but not quite) as much as she loved me.

Dottie's words echoed in my head. *Problem baby? Cry it out? Different when they're not your own?* And she seemed like a perfectly nice lady, really.

I received a call the next day from a woman who heard I was looking for a sitter. She would have an opening around Christmas for a newborn, so I interviewed her over the phone, keeping hope at bay. She currently specialized in babies, meaning she only kept five babies under the age of one. The reason being, her own child was six months old, and she wanted her day care to have the same age range so her daughter could have kids to play with as she grew. Sounded logical to me. Mandy seemed like a nice fit over the phone—nonsmoking, Christian, married to a fireman for four years. Hugging and cuddling were very important to her and she didn't believe in a lot of TV time—less than an hour of *Sesame Street*, she told me. Better still, she didn't mention "cry it out" once. Satisfied, I set up a meeting for the next morning to visit her home.

When I arrived and rang the doorbell, I heard two babies crying inside. As I waited on the porch, I noticed the gargoyles she had in her flowerbeds watching me. *Don't let that creep you out. Keep an open mind.* Moments later, the door swung open and Mandy appeared with a baby in one arm. Two babies continued to cry in the background.

I stepped in and saw that although it was just eight-thirty in the morning, her living room was a virtual playroom. Toys, bouncy seats, and a swing littered the room.

"Can I get you some coffee?" Mandy offered, as she swooped down and picked up a pacifier off the floor and stuck it in the crying baby boy's mouth. He began sucking vigorously and closed his eyes.

"No, I'm fine." A smaller baby girl cried big tears and looked up at me questioningly. *Would you help me?* she seemed to ask.

"It's okay, Samantha," Mandy said, flicking the switch that started the vibration on the bouncy seat the girl sat in. Samantha calmed for a moment, her lip still quivering, then started whimpering.

"Time for breakfast," Mandy said, bounding for the kitchen. I followed. "Ethan already ate. Samantha's next. She's a breast-fed baby—her mom sends me her frozen

milk each week. Then this is Brittany, my six-month-old,"
she said, holding out the sleeping baby in her arms. "Also
breast-fed, so she feeds every three hours like clockwork.
And baby Grayson there is my eight-week-old. This is his
first week, but his mama is going to stay home after Christmas, so I'll only have him for a couple of months. Too bad,
because I know I'll get attached." She laid Brittany down
on a U-shaped pillow. "So, will you be breast-feeding?"

"I'm not sure," I said. "I'm going to take a class next
month."

"Well, breast is best, as they say," Mandy said with a
wink, and grabbed a bag out of the freezer labeled *Samantha* and proceeded to thaw it in a cup of hot water while
she prepared the liner in a bottle. All *without washing her
hands*. I'd turned into a germ Nazi.

I watched Mandy with amazement. I'd never seen
frozen breast milk before. Frozen, it looked more yellow
than cow's milk. Would my freezer be full of breast milk?
As soon as the milk was thawed and warmed and poured
in the liner, Mandy scooped up Samantha and plunked
down in a glider rocker and began feeding her. "So, what
questions do you have?"

I sat on the plaid couch opposite her and tried to catch
my bearings. Seeing the babies made me giddy, nervous.
"So, I guess you stay in this room most of the day then?"
The room was small, but modern and comfortable.

Mandy nodded. "But I rotate the kids a few times a day
so that they each get their turns on the swing and bouncy
seat and some tummy time to build up their muscles. I
also play classical music in the background part of the
day. They say it stimulates their brains. I also sing a bit
each day, though I don't have the greatest voice," she said
bashfully.

"I'm sure they don't mind," I said. "So tell me about
your family."

Mandy spoke lovingly about her husband, two sisters,
and her parents, who had been together for forty years. I
kept waiting for her to say something really stupid.

"What about you?" Mandy asked. "Brothers and sisters? Do your folks live around here?"

Squirming in my seat, I twisted my wedding ring. "I'm an only child and my parents died when I was in high school."

Mandy's face cringed in horror. "That's awful! And with your baby coming! That must be hard."

I cleared my throat. The last thing I wanted to do in an interview was cry. I left Mandy's home with the feeling that she was an option—perhaps not the answer, but an option. What the right answer was, I still didn't know. How mothers were supposed to make such a difficult decision was beyond me. It was harder than hiring an employee. It was more than credentials and experience and environment and parenting style. My expectations were probably too high. All I knew about nannies and babysitters was from watching *Mary Poppins*. But then we weren't just looking for a warm body to care for our child.

The next Monday I finally caught Susan in her office. Her jet-setting days were, on one hand, a relief from her looming presence, but on the other hand, I needed to present a brilliant piece of work: Little Aces, which carefully avoided using the words "day care." I knew the word would send her into cardiac arrest. Sometimes cute and clever worked for winning her over.

An on-site day care was my last resort. I couldn't know exactly how I'd feel when Emily came, but I knew the closer she was to me, the better. Besides a nanny at the house, this would be the most convenient option. I usually worked through lunches anyway, so I rationalized I could see my baby more if she came to work with me.

I sat across from Susan, wringing my hands and feeling Emily flip inside of me while Susan flipped through the slim presentation, which included line drawings of how we could convert the large storage room and spare kitchen into a fully functional and soundproof day care and two pages worth of benefits to productivity and staff morale.

Two more Ace women had become pregnant after me, so there would be three babies and several after-school children who would benefit. After barely skimming through the booklet, she tossed it back at me. "No."

Before I could stop myself, I shot her a devilish look. "What do you mean *no?* It won't even cost you—"

Susan tilted her head, which she did to make you feel insanely stupid. "It's not a cost issue, Taylor. It's a style issue. I don't want that sort of reputation."

Crazed look still on my face, I shot back, "A *family friendly* reputation? A *great place for working women* reputation?"

"Basically. Just not in the cards, Taylor." She began to pick up the phone to place a call so I would leave, but I stood up and covered her hand with mine.

"I really thought you cared about your employees more than this, Susan." I left her office, the building, and the parking lot before I broke down in tears on my way to Amy's house for a shoulder to cry on. I didn't care if she fired me at that point. There should be a law against emotional cruelty to pregnant women.

CHAPTER 28

"Nah, man. Can't do it," Jake said into the receiver at the ungodly hour of seven A.M. on a Saturday. "Gonna paint Emily's room today. You'll survive without me. Have fun."

I tossed and tried to go back to sleep while Jake got up and showered. Like a little girl dreaming of her perfect wedding day, I had a similar fantasy of a ponytailed mom-to-be dressed in denim maternity overalls looking on as her radiant husband painted the nursery in pink or blue. (Probably from a TV movie or something.) Nothing in my pregnancy had gone as I'd imagined it would, so I shouldn't have expected decorating the nursery to be any different.

Jake had put off painting the nursery for a month, deciding instead to run in a breast cancer marathon one weekend, work at the office the next, go camping the third, then conveniently get sick with a cold. Finally tackling the chore, Jake rattled around the garage finding the lavender paint I bought and all the tools he would need.

Seven months pregnant, I didn't do anything quickly, least of all get out of bed on the weekend. Especially after the royally shitty day I'd had at the office with Susan the day before. Normally I didn't take things she said personally or I'd have cracked a long time ago, but when it came to stomping my greatest wish for having my daughter close to me while I worked just yards away, I couldn't help it.

I heard Jake singing, which was unusual since he hadn't been looking forward to the chore. He wasn't exactly Bob Vila around the house. The crib Lorna bought us still sat in its box unopened, the pretty comforter still stashed in the nursery closet. Jake may have gotten used to the idea of having a child in our home, but making a space for Emily was surreal.

Huffing, I rolled on my left side and closed my eyes again. Jake's singing grew progressively louder. "Oh, I wish that I had Jessie's girl! Why can't I find a woman like that?"

I put the pillow over my head and Emily started kicking. "Oh, you like eighties rock, huh?" I said, putting my hand over the movements on my belly. "Well, if you're not going to let me sleep in . . ." I threw my legs over the edge of the bed and noticed slight swelling in my ankles. *Not yet*, I thought. *I still have ten weeks to go!*

I was debating going shoe-shopping for bigger shoes, when I remembered a box of my mother's favorite shoes. Since we weren't wealthy, she didn't have many, but I'd refused to let Aunt Barb sell them in a garage sale. *Someday I'll grow into these*, I had told myself in my grief. As it turned out, I'd just swelled into the right size.

I threw on a robe, padded past Jake, and pulled down the ladder to the attic. In my quest for my mother's shoes I'd forgotten that pregnancy throws off your balance, but I carefully climbed the ladder and felt for the old stereo box tucked behind our Christmas tree box. Dust flew in my face, causing me to cough.

I threw the box to the floor below. It landed on its side, sending the shoes spilling out. I cried at the sight of them and cradled her pink ballet slippers in my hands. She had worn them on the weekends, stretching and dancing across the living room floor to stay in shape. I opened the box. Her beige bunny slippers, complete with whiskers and ears, that my father had bought her on our last Easter together. I rubbed the soft fur, longing to put them on. Her black dress shoes, conservative pumps she wore on dates with my father. And lastly, her red Keds, which I had told her time and again were too young for her.

I tossed the shoes in the dryer to remove the dust while I drank hot chocolate and ate a bowl of oatmeal. When I made it back upstairs, Jake had moved on to Guns N' Roses cover of "Every Rose Has Its Thorn." Emily continued her somersaults as I stepped under the hot, pelting shower. My back ached from the weight of the baby and my enlarged bosom. With more weight everywhere, I couldn't see over my belly to study my legs. I avoided the full-length mirror at all costs.

Wearing Jake's Hike & Spike T-shirt and my mom's bunny slippers, I checked on Jake's progress. Two walls were covered in the soft lavender paint, which had made its way onto Jake's bare skin. Dressed only in raggedy khaki shorts, flip-flops and a cap, Jake was covered in little specs of paint.

"That's a nice color on you," I said, standing at the doorway.

Jake smiled. "You shouldn't be in here, honey. Fumes are bad."

"They may have already gotten to *you*. I heard your eighties medley."

Jake continued to paint in long strokes with the roller. "I've been thinking about high school a lot lately."

"I try to forget my eighties hair as much as possible. You have rocker bangs?"

"You'll never find any proof. I've hidden any and all records. It's just I've never been satisfied with where I was. In high school, all I could think about was going to college. In college all I could think about was going to law school. In law school all I could think about was joining a practice. And so on."

"So you're junior partner and you can't wait to be senior partner."

"Exactly. What's that all about?" he asked seriously.

"I'm no psychologist, but I'd say it had something to do with not living in the moment." I sat down against a wall that Jake hadn't painted yet.

Jake put the roller back in the pan and sat across from me. "Yeah. *Carpe diem*. There was this kid Jeremy in our neighborhood. I loved to go play at his house. When his dad was home, we'd play catch, or wrestle or work in the shop on a birdhouse or mailbox or something. I have more memories with Jeremy's dad than my own."

"God, Jake. That's just *sad*." I put my hand over his paint-streaked cheek.

"So if I have a choice, I want to be like Jeremy's dad. I want you to be like Maria."

I rubbed the spots of purple on his skin. "Well, I'll have to brush up on my Spanish." I leaned in for a kiss.

"I just don't want to wake up one day and our daughter is grown and I'll look at my beautiful gray-haired wife and wonder where the years went."

"Who says I'm going to go gray? I plan on being brunette all my life, thank you very much. Emily will have the youngest-looking mom on the block. But I appreciate the thought."

Jake stood and helped me up, nearly toppling both of us. "You were right the other night. We want the same things. Not to come home late every night too tired to give our child the few hours a day we have for her. And for us not to travel all the time like our fathers both did. So we're going to figure this out. Together," Jake said.

"I didn't have the nerve to tell you yesterday, but Susan said no to Little Aces."

Jake's face fell. He couldn't hide his disappointment. "No surprise, I guess. She doesn't have a Little Ace of her own."

"We'll figure something out. There's still some time left." I cracked a smile. "And you should know, I'm a master at birdhouses."

"A carpenter, eh? What else has Ms. Montgomery been keeping from me besides her handy skills and a secret stash of animal slippers?"

I grabbed the roller and handed it to Jake. "I happen to be a great painter, too, but . . ." I pointed to my stomach. "I'm afraid you'll have to see that for yourself another day."

Jake touched the roller to my nose. "I think my office would look great in red," he said.

"Don't hold your breath. Bagel's calling my name. Back to your one-hit wonders, Mr. Springfield."

The pre-preggo Taylor had used Saturday mornings for long runs and shopping when Jake and I were in town. The third-trimester Taylor had slipped into a much more comfortable Saturday morning ritual. After a short (okay, *very* short) morning walk, I watched cartoons—just to see what Emily had in store for her, *really*. The pregnancy books said that Emily could hear by that point, so all in all, the cartoons were for her enjoyment.

Things had changed a lot since I watched cartoons as a kid. Major network cartoons were practically a thing of the past. These days kids could watch cartoons twenty-four hours a day on several networks. And how they'd changed! Strange shows about deep sea sponges and clay bath toys. Bizarre Japanese cartoons and crime-fighting little girls. Okay, I was slightly addicted. Now I had something to talk about with my friends' kids, though. I'd be the coolest mom-to-be on the playground.

After shaking bagel crumbs off of my belly and hoisting myself from the couch, I usually took a stab at some copy for work. My PowerBook no longer fit on my lap, so I piled pillows in my home office chair for my aching back and put my feet up on a stack of encyclopedias. With Jude's help, Ace had won three new accounts, the biggest in our history. I told myself it was his charm and experience and good looks that got him the new accounts, not his creativity.

But I hated to admit he wasn't awful to work with. He gushed over my ideas and thanked me for long hours. Unreal in the ad business. Most of our communication was via e-mail or phone; he was too busy scouring the country with Susan. Fine by me. The wins were too easy in my opinion, but I got to work on more interesting creative than car-driving monkeys. Susan hadn't let me hire more employees to help with the load, though, which meant working weekends. Allen sometimes came over to brainstorm and share a can of potato soup and bacon bits. On one visit, he found a stack of photos of my last bridge night.

"Who's the hottie?" he had asked.

I, not really knowing who was hot and who was not in Allen's book, didn't even attempt a guess. Sometimes he went for the plastic fake-boob women, sometimes he went for the au-natural granola type and sometimes the girl next door. "Which one?"

"Which one? The redhead. You know I dig redheads," he said.

"You dig redheads once a month, Allen. Not exactly a reason to hook you up with one of my dearest friends."

"She looks like she works out. Is she married?"

"I'm not telling you anything about her. Not even her name."

Allen looked hurt, so I stared at my computer screen and tried to switch the topic back to nasal spray, which was supposed to be the reason for his visit. "We stopped at 'clear from ear to ear,'" I reminded him. He would have none of it.

"Taylor, I can't believe you would try to get in the way of fate," Allen said.

"If fate is you and every redheaded woman in America, then by all means, let me step aside."

Allen put his hands behind his head and rested on the couch. "I think I'm ready to settle down. Watching your transformation these past few months has put things into perspective for me."

I felt myself soften for a moment, but then I remembered whom I was dealing with. "Wait a minute. Didn't you say that back in the mid-nineties—when you were depressed because all your friends were getting married—that all the good girls would be all used up? And that was, what, like a hundred girlfriends ago?"

"So I'm a hundred girls closer to finding my soul mate, and I feel a strong connection to the glamour-puss in the picture."

"The fact you would use 'soul mate' and 'glamour-puss' in the same sentence tells me you haven't changed enough to let you loose on Gretchen."

Allen sat up. "Gretchen, huh? God, that's a beautiful name. If you give me her number I'll write this entire nasal spray ad myself this weekend."

Gretchen was a dear friend. As if I would sell her out for a measly television spot! Allen was adorable, his face crinkled up in man-boy glee at the prospect of a hot date. The whole weekend lay before me like a big long nap devoid of any deep thought. "It's 621.5524," I told him.

Scratching it on his notepad, Allen leaped up and already had her digits dialed into his cell before he was out the door. I was halfway asleep before any guilt set in over my barter. Then, poof, I was a goner.

This particular Saturday, though, Allen was antiquing, and I, uninvited, sat alone at my desk, listening to the *swoosh* of the roller as Jake finished Emily's room. The laptop screen remained a snowy white. The client wanted "fresh" creative, but there was a finite number of words to describe laundry detergent. If they'd change the damn scent, no problem. New! Berry Linens. New! Winter Woods. New! Lemon Fresh. Nah, lemon was so nineties. I opened the box of detergent I'd brought for inspiration and took a sniff. The powder went up my nose, causing me to sneeze. I typed on the screen: *Smells like soap.*

I laughed. Would I dare submit it? Hey, it was as honest as anything on the shelves. I saved my infamous line and clicked off my computer and returned to my unmade bed, making it easy for me to slip back in the covers. Emily had probably gone back to sleep. She'd enjoyed the bagel and the Powerpuff Girls saving the day and was taking a mid-morning nap. Smart girl.

"They say to do this now before time slips away from us," I said, down on all fours on the Berber carpet in the living room later that afternoon.

"And why like this?" Jake said, doing a belly crawl across the floor.

"To see the room from the perspective of the baby." I inserted a plastic outlet cover in one of the two dozen outlets in the house. He'd been so smitten with the cute lactation-consultant, Anita, that he'd forgotten all of her instructions.

"Oh," Jake said. "Hey, I found a quarter! Sure is dusty down here."

I scowled. "Wanda will be here tomorrow."

"Let me see *you* do the belly crawl."

"Very funny. This feels pretty good on all fours, though," I said. "She's like a little hammock under me. No pressure."

Jake placed the corners on all the end tables and protectors on the brick fireplace. Meanwhile, I tied up the blind cords and put away all choking hazards, small trinkets on the tables, pennies in the couch, paper clips on the office floor. After turning down the water heater, putting safety latches on all the lower cabinets and drawers in the house, and sweeping under every bed, we lay exhausted on the living room couch.

Taking my feet in his lap, Jake pulled off my socks and gave me a massage, which I still had written on my dry-erase board as a preggo rule. "That feels great," I moaned. "You haven't done that in awhile."

"That's not the only thing we haven't done in awhile," Jake said with a raised brow.

I laughed heartily. "God, Jake. I'm such a cow I didn't think you'd be interested. I'm nearly eight months pregnant!"

"I know," he said. "Eight months sexier than before you got pregnant."

"You're on then," I said, getting up and straddling him, laughing all the while at the awkwardness of it. I could barely lean in to kiss him. We ended up having sex on the bed, lying side by side, Jake behind me, the first time we'd tried that position. I suppose in that position, without being able to see him, I could imagine he was anybody. But I wanted him to be Jake.

The house was in order. Jake and I were in good working order, too. I hadn't found my Mary Poppins dream sitter, but I was getting closer. I could feel the pieces clicking together for the first time in my pregnancy. If I could just survive the holidays and the Titan merger, we'd be home free with a baby on the other end of it.

MONTH EIGHT

Home Stretch and Stretch Marks

CHAPTER 29

Week 34: Continuing her growth spurt, by the end of this week your baby weighs about five pounds and is approximately nineteen and a half inches long. By now, she's probably head-down in your uterus, although she may continue to change positions. Her skull bones are still pliable and aren't completely joined, to help her exit from the birth canal.

Balloons of pink and white flitted in the wind from their perch on the mailbox. Luxury cars lined the long winding driveway in the opulent neighborhood. Amy had promised the most grandiose shower of all time, and from the looks of it, she had succeeded. Amy adored excess and reigned as supreme party queen. Put the two together, and watch out.

I weaved my SUV into the driveway and parked behind a black Mercedes. I couldn't recall ever seeing a Mercedes that *wasn't* black. I judged them as if they weren't my friends, my sorority sisters, my colleagues. Two generations before, the baby shower would've been held in a rickety old shack.

Her home was immaculate as always. I complimented

the housekeeper as I handed her the black maternity coat Amy had let me borrow. My lineage kept me from spending four hundred dollars on a coat I would only wear for two months.

"She's here!" I heard Amy squeal as she pounced in the foyer wearing a well-tailored suit with shiny hose and four-inch heels, a knockout as usual.

"God, you're a gorgeous preggo!" Amy said, kissing both of my cheeks and wrapping her arms around me as much as my body allowed. "All the bridge girls are here."

"Amy, I have to say you've outdone yourself," I gushed, admiring the enormous bouquet of pink and white roses on the foyer table.

Gretchen came out to greet me. "Hey, you. I've been meaning to call you all week."

"I bet you have," I said. "To kill me, I'm sure."

"I've never met a more persistent man in my life. I told him it was a conflict of interest to date someone who works with my friend. But after two dozen roses, I'm willing to reconsider my policy."

"Gretchen, just remember—"

"He's a male slut, I know. And he cheats. And he can charm the pants off of anyone. Believe me, I remember every bad thing you've said about him," Gretchen said, leading me into the roomful of guests.

"But there's lots of good stuff," I told her before being surrounded by mother hens wanting to pet my belly.

Several pastel floral arrangements filled the formal living room. Above the mantel was a wreath of more white and pink roses, scattered with baby's breath and tied with a long pink ribbon.

Old friends and new warmly greeted me. Thirty-some women had gathered to celebrate the coming of Emily, and I was overjoyed. Among the gleeful ladies was my Aunt Barb, dressed sharply in a green sweater that matched her eyes; my mother-in-law Lorna, who couldn't stop gabbing over the glorious home that was "just her taste"; Maria, crying at the sight of me; and several sorority sisters I hadn't seen since college. A few coworkers and neighbors rounded out the group. And no party was complete without my bridge girls. As for my boss, whom Amy insisted on inviting, she was not surprisingly absent, in Florida on business, scouting locations for an upcoming photo shoot. Shooting in Florida was not my idea, since I couldn't travel, but she assured me Jude would fill in for me. My work life seemed remote from that day, the first day I was celebrated for my near-becoming.

Strawberries, pastries, mousse and gourmet coffees filled the elegant china and silver on the dining room table. Raspberry ginger ale colored the crystal goblets. A two-layered chocolate cream cake topped with fresh flowers adorned the middle of the table. And in the corner sat the gifts, piled high in pretty pastel papers and wrapped in fancy bows. *When I unwrapped them, would I feel more like a mother?*

The afternoon went by in a whirlwind of food and laughter and guessing games and advice. I got one of everything. There were a few gifts whose purpose eluded me, but the mommies gasped and *oohed* and *aahed* at each one, so they must have been something important. God knows I wasn't going to make a fool of myself by actually asking.

For the first time, I thought my mother-in-law had been right: we should've given the baby the larger room for the nursery. Where in the world were we going to put all this stuff? Would our house become one big Romper Room?

"This is too much," I said when the last gift had been opened. "Thank you all so much. And thank you, Amy, for the best party a mommy-to-be could ask for."

The party scattered into its gossip huddles and Jackie cornered me with a wild, wet look in her eye. "I'm pregnant," she said, in a whisper so faint I had to read her lips.

"Congratulations," I said, unsure of the secrecy. "Or . . ."

"No, I'm happy," she said. "It's just that Ashlynn's growing up so fast, and Mark and I have been getting along so well lately."

"Which is how this happened."

"Yeah! Well, babies take a heckuva lot of energy. We have to get it in when we can."

"Thank you! I feel like you're the first person to be honest with me about it."

"Oh, everyone knows it's a huge responsibility and a lot of work, but no one wants to spoil the baby fantasy, either," Jackie said.

"The baby fantasy. All coos and cute clothes?"

"And adoring fathers and helpful relatives."

"So I should just tell you what everyone's been telling me? That everything will work itself out and you'll be a great mom again?" I hugged her and Emily kicked her.

"I felt that!" Jackie said. "I just don't know how much more of me can go around and still have some of me for myself. I don't know if I'm ready to go through it all again."

"Oh, you're ready. Or you will be. It's amazing what happens in nine months! And Ashlynn will be so excited about being a big sister."

"Gosh, Taylor. You don't even sound like yourself! Where did all this wisdom come from all of a sudden?"

"Somewhere," I said, unconsciously rubbing my belly. I anointed myself a mommy advisor before my official inauguration.

"How's the hunt for a sitter coming?"

I bit my lower lip. "It's coming. We're doing background checks on three women. Picking out her crib was hard enough. One wrong move with the sitter and she could be scarred for life. No pressure there. Hey, you never told me how you decided to stay home with Ashlynn."

We walked to the back patio, enjoying the view of the immaculate pool and the fall landscaping. "I never told anyone this, but I had a terrible time after Ashlynn came," Jackie said. "I got mastitis twice and when I went back to work, I was stressed out all the time. The doctor ended up diagnosing me with post-partum depression."

"You've just said two things I've never heard of. Mast-what-is? And you were depressed? Why didn't you tell us?"

Jackie shrugged. "It's embarrassing. Like mothering should come so easily. But even though it's the greatest joy, it can be hard, too. So I got on some medication and after awhile I didn't need it anymore, but I realized I couldn't do it all. So I stayed home, and I've felt much better since. Not that I don't get jealous when I hear your work stories. I crave dealing with adults sometimes."

I exhaled. "So I'm not an idiot for being a little scared, then. But I would be the one who would be insanely jealous if a friend watched Emily. I'm not sure about anyone watching her at this point."

"Well, the mommy bridge girls were wondering if we could start having a play date every month instead of our night thing. With you on the mommy side, we're now the majority. And we can lunch once a month without kids with Gretchen and Tara and Shannon. We don't want them to feel left out. What do you think?"

"I think it's a fabulous idea. I've missed you guys like crazy, anyway. And it's time to say good-bye to my old party days."

That's what baby showers used to feel like to me, a sad good-bye. The showers were the final gatherings for the ladies before the mother went into hibernation with her young for months, only to come out for the occasional holiday or grand party, wearing her finest wrappings from the dust-ridden party closet. *Good-bye, skinny clothes! Good-bye, social functions! Good-bye spontaneity! See you at mother's day out! See you at the park! See you grocery shopping, filling your cart with boxes and bags of food you don't have the energy to cook.* At the very least, baby showers were the bar mitzvahs of baby-makers. See how big we've gotten! See how I've stretched in places not thought humanly possible! Watch everyone lie and tell you how wonderful you look in that lavender-colored tarp you bought in the gloomy maternity section of the department store.

But that day, I wanted to celebrate the coming of Emily. I just had to be there, so they could revolve around me, stare at me, and love on me. I was on cloud nine. It felt better than winning an account. It felt better than launching a campaign. It felt better than getting a promotion.

That afternoon I was schooled in a new business with the CEOs of Family who accepted overtime with a tired smile. Their winning pitches were pleasant bedtime rituals and their achievements were not framed awards on a wall, but Crayola artwork on the fridge. Their annual reviews were first days of school and they didn't get vacations. They were 24/7 employees in the mommy task force, not so much bosses of the children, but attendants and teachers and trainers and coaches and nutritionists and healers and spiritual guides.

I caught a glimpse of the elders' wisdom. It seemed that mothers never had to be pried for advice.

On inducing labor:

—"A glass of red wine and then sex doggie-style. I was in labor thirty minutes later."

—"A quick walk around the block and then sex."

—"Mexican food and two glasses of wine."

—"I'd just let nature take its course. Why rush the inevitable?"

On getting the baby to stop crying:

—"In the car seat on the dryer."

—"A drive through the neighborhood."

—"Bouncing up and down while standing."

—"Just sing to her. It'll pass."

Or hand her to Jake.

The most enjoyable part of the shower was getting to know Maria better, the ever-chipper woman whose voice lilted in excitement as she spoke of Jake. Since Jake proclaimed he hoped I'd be as good a mother as Maria was, I wished for some of her baby magic to rub off on me.

"Thank you for inviting me," Maria said. "I'm so thrilled for you and Jake. Are you feeling okay?"

"Tired, but otherwise, fine," I said. "Your gift is my favorite." It was a photo album of black-and-white photos of Jake, all pictures she had taken in their years together, starting with pictures in his crib at just a few days old. We looked through the book together.

"It was a joy for me to put it together. Just as it was a joy to watch him grow into such a fine man," she said. She traced her finger along the photos. "Jake's father got me a camera when they brought him home from the hospital, and he said, 'Take as many photos as you like.' So, I did! Every day! He was so photogenic. I'd always wished I'd taken more pictures of my girls. I even learned to develop the film. We turned a spare room into a darkroom."

"They are beautiful, Maria. We'll cherish this." Jake taking his first steps, jumping in the swimming pool, getting licked by a puppy. She'd seen it all.

Maria wiped away tears. "I miss my boy," she said. "Some of the best years of my life were caring for him."

"You did a fine job," I said. Jake playing T-ball. Jake wearing braces. Jake going to his first school dance.

"I was the lucky one," Maria said.

"He wouldn't be the Jake we know now if it hadn't been for you."

It came to me then that our past shapes us, that it was okay to accept the ugliness along with the joy. In that room was my mother power. I had more than my own mother to search for the answers to my past and the resolution for my future. It was all around me, life's lessons, the aunt that loved me as her own, the grandmothers to my unborn child, the friends who'd always been there.

I didn't know everything, but I had the source to aid my way, and my own mother power was growing every day.

The baby gifts were piled high in the nursery waiting for Jake to put them together or for me to put them into their proper place. There were clothes to be washed, linens to be folded, and sheets to be fitted on the crib. If everything else were done, then I would only have Emily to wait for, so I prolonged putting order to the chaos until I felt stricken with it.

Jake was out of town working on a case, so I had the house to myself for three days. I'd gotten lazier by the minute, preferring to drink hot chocolate and stare out the window, watching fall turn into a mild winter. The leaves on the large maple trees fell in haste, as if glad to be returning to the earth or drifting away from their confinement on the tree. One evening I almost had the energy to go outside and rake the burnt orange leaves into a big pile and nap in the rustling bed until dark fell. Turned out, the thought was enough of a pleasure, and I moved on to my second bowl of sugar-free ice cream and flicked on *Entertainment Tonight*.

I pulled up a memory from the year before when Jake and I had zipped up our light jackets and bounded outside for a brisk jog in the November air. Afterward, we raked up the leaves in the backyard, then made love in the pile, nestling down until we were almost covered entirely by them. The smell of crisp leaves and Jake's cologne. The contrast of Jake's warm kisses and the cold air on my cheek lingered still. Such spontaneity seemed so long ago, like another life. Another marriage.

Wrapped warmly in a fleece throw, I dreamt of Emily and ached for Jake. *This is what it would be like if he left.* The pain was there, but the hopelessness had faded. I wasn't as worried about abandonment anymore, but if he did leave, I would survive. I would be alone, but I could make it because my heart had been bruised before and had healed. The fear had lessened because I drew him closer to me, loved him without restraint.

Emily turned inside of me, and I lifted my shirt to see her—what appeared to be her bottom move from my sternum to my side. A jab hit me in the lower back.

"You're stretching, huh, Em? Not much room in there?" I patted what I thought was her bottom, and she rolled, and a sharp pain shot into my cervix.

"Ooh." I shifted, then stood, elongating my space. Emily

took up the whole middle part of me, and my body was just as much hers at that point as it was mine. My body wasn't the only thing she had controlling stock in. My mind, or what was left of it. My heart, which had grown in size over the last eight months. My soul, which I had come to believe was a real thing. As for my other organs, she used them as a punching bag at her will and leisure.

Jackie canceled shopping plans due to morning sickness.

Amy canceled what was to be our final bridge night due to Austin's cold.

Aunt Barb had to grade papers.

Allen was on a third date with Gretchen, which killed two birds with one stone.

My circle forced me to spend too much quality time with myself, talking to my tummy. I walked into Emily's room, finally put together into a place for a little girl to grow up. It was dainty and comfortable. The crib ready to be slept on. The changing table ready for a wet baby. The dresser filled with tiny clothes and socks no bigger than my thumb. Something was missing, something familiar. I went to my room and grabbed Molly from my nightstand. I placed her in the crib. "You watch over things in here," I said. "It's almost time to be tossed around in a baby stroller and sit at tea parties again. The cycle of life continues."

I opened a yellow and pink plaid memory box Amy had given me at my shower. It contained a memory book, a scrapbook to keep Emily's photos and record our memories. Her ultrasound was tucked neatly on page one. I read the well wishes from my friends at the baby shower, jotted down the facts I already knew. Her doctor's name, the hospital, her family history. I neatly penned my parents' and grandparents' names without so much as a catch in my throat. I owned my history. I thought of how I might tell Emily some day about the grandparents I didn't know about and the grandparents she wouldn't know. I could be matter of fact. I could be romantic. I would not be tragic. What I knew for sure was that I would share stories; she would know where she came from.

CHAPTER 30

The next day I lunched with Allen at a nearby deli, hoping for some comic relief and to catch up on the party world to which I used to belong. Allen was my only source for office gossip since I didn't do after hours anymore.

"You haven't told me what you think of handsome Jude joining the firm," Allen mused. "I thought you'd be pissed as a cat in the bath."

"I'm not *delighted* about it, but I have other things to worry about," I told him. Partially true, anyway. "Better him than me traveling the country with the Hawk, that's for sure."

"I saw you two in New York. You had a whole vibe thing going on."

I rolled my eyes. "Can I help it if I'm ravishing? I just wish he'd get on with announcing the merger so they can fire us or let us hire some new people. The not-knowing is killing me. I only have one more single friend to barter off, so I don't have to do all the work myself."

"That won't be necessary," Allen said, raising his right brow.

I knew the brow. It was a sex brow. I put my hand up. "Not sure I can take any mental pictures of the two of you—"

"I'm in love," Allen gushed. "I know she doesn't want to believe it yet because of all the horrid things my former best friend told her about me, but it's true."

My macho friend had never uttered those words to me before. He loved a Dead Sea–salt facial. He loved a sale at Barney's. He loved Super Bowl tickets on the forty-yard line. But a girl? Girls kept the right side of his bed warm. Girls hung on his arm (among other parts) as party trophies. Girls were friends and sex partners, but never lovers with emphasis on l-o-v-e. Allen was the man who told me love was a four-letter word. Until now. "Not in lust or infatuation or kinda-like?"

Allen shook his head. "I love Gretchen, Taylor. She's just like you, only without the paranoia, the papoose, and the wedding ring. What's not to love?"

"I'm not sure whether that's a compliment, but if you last past my due date, then I'll believe you," I said. We dug into our chef salads. I instantly wished I'd asked for real ranch instead of low-cal. Allen seemed to sense my distaste and traded with me.

"You guys going to Amy's Halloween party?" Allen asked.

I set down my fork. "I nearly forgot. Things have been so crazy with work and getting the nursery ready. I haven't had time to buy a costume."

"Ooh, I'd love the challenge of dressing a big preggo like you. The possibilities are endless."

"Geez, thanks a lot. But I've been so stressed I'll take you up on that. Just don't make me look like an idiot."

"Trust me," Allen said. "Oh, and speaking of a witch, I've got scoop on your old college chum Nikki."

"Really? That's weird. She left me a message earlier."

"So she told you?"

"I didn't call her back because I thought she just wanted to go to lunch to rub in how much better her life is than mine. Why? Has her company gone public? Got the Mc-Donald's account? What?"

Allen shook his head vigorously. "Guess again."

"Last guess—she's going out of business!"

Allen leaned in and whispered so loudly he wasn't really whispering. "Her creative director quit."

"C.D.s quit all the time. Why, was he sleeping with her?"

"This isn't *As the Agency Turns*," he said. "He's done such great work he was offered a job in L.A."

I put down my fork. "You're not trying to beat around the bush and tell me you're going to be her new creative director, are you?"

Allen scowled. "You really suck at this game, Tay. Why—think she would hire me?"

"I don't know. She's kinda picky."

"Heard she's gone through every Dallas and Houston creative director, and can't find anyone she likes," he said.

"Then you're S.O.L., buddy," I said with a wink. "Besides, you couldn't leave me even if you wanted to."

Allen threw down his napkin. "Think of all the pregnancy whining I'd be missing out on! And, oh, let's not forget the poop stories I'm going to have to hear from now through potty training! God, just thinking about it . . . I deserve a raise."

"I'll have to talk it over with the big new consultant," I said.

Allen shook his head at me. "Don't you get it, Taylor? She's obviously calling to beg *you* to come work for her."

A pile of job jackets awaited me when I returned to the office. They were like weeds. I picked them, but they just grew back again.

Hell, who really cared about Mr. Beef's Jerky slogan, anyway? In the old days, I would've racked my brain and used up pages and pages of my idea notebook before settling on the perfect copy. Now I scribbled my approval without reading it and left the rest of the pile untouched. The only campaign I was passionate about was the Studio

Baby summer line, and I had until my due date to get all the pieces in order.

To work off my larger-than-necessary lunch, I took the stairs to the media conference room, where I could escape from the madness for a moment before the swarm began again.

The sound of soft patters of raindrops filled the quiet of the media conference room on the third floor. The lazy afternoon had lulled me into an almost hypnotic state, unable to think about the tough video conference call with our Kansas City office and one of our biggest clients, Sunco Computer Systems, that was threatening an agency review.

Jude arrived first for the meeting. Swinging the large conference door open, he spotted me and paused, as if he were considering whether or not to be alone with me. He risked it.

"Afternoon," he said.

"Hi, Jude," I turned slightly in my chair to face him. "Settled into Dallas?"

"I like it here," he said, taking a chair on the other end of the table. "Nothing like two homes to call your own."

"You and Susan have been racking up the frequent-flier miles. I appreciate you throwing me a bone on some of the new accounts. Not that I haven't noticed most of the juicier accounts have been going to Titan's creative department," I said. If I could confront Susan, Jude was a piece of cake.

Jude shifted uncomfortably. "Well, you're a little short-handed at Ace," he said.

I looked him in the eye. "That's normally what happens before a merger. You whittle down the staff so you don't have as many messy layoffs when you make the announcement."

Jude smiled. I was on to him. Hell, the whole industry knew something was up. Agencies don't pitch together unless there's something in it for both parties.

"Truthfully, I almost told you about it in New York, but if Susan knew I had talked, she would've backed out of the deal. I didn't know if I could trust you."

The merger would be the perfect time to let me go, or at the least demote me. This new company wouldn't need two creative chiefs. And yet I almost felt relieved by the possibility. Someone would be making my decision for me. The thought of being fired made my stomach flip until I realized it was Emily telling me everything would be okay.

The videoconference screen clicked on and Phil, a vice president in our Denver office, appeared. "Hey there, Dallas," Phil said. "Hi, Jude. Welcome aboard."

"Hi, Phil," Jude said. "Sunco ready?"

"Yeah, I'll send them in now," Phil said, and with the push of a button, the Sunco president and marketing director appeared on a smaller screen as Susan and two other account executives entered our room.

Susan set her Evian water bottle on the marble table and flashed a quick smile. "Let's get down to business then."

Perky Anita had perky little breasts, unlike the dozen pregnant women with large mammaries who gathered to learn what we were to do with them. And how was the pert-bosomed Anita who'd never milked her own qualified to do this? She told us she was a lactation specialist, emphasizing the word *specialist*. This apparently meant she spent hours and hours researching and studying the ways of the hungry infant child latching onto its meal.

We congregated in a cement-walled room in the basement of the hospital with a gray sign that read PRE/POST NATAL EDUCATION, far less homey than the one we'd been in for the child care education. The teenage girl, the little person, and the Mary Kay lady from my childbirth class were there. No comfy chairs and pretty wallpaper, but it would do. I sat in the stiff-backed metal chair and stared at the ugly wall with posters of nursing positions, wondering how learning how to breast-feed could possibly take four hours on a Saturday.

The posters looked rather self-explanatory. Exposed boob, open-mouthed babe, suckling child. One, two, three, right?

"It's not as easy as it looks," Ms. Know-It-All said, grabbing a diapered doll from her stash in the closet.

"Let's kick back for a video. Three volunteers allowed us to videotape them so that you can see what it's really like," Anita said, clicking off the bright lights.

The real point of the video seemed to be that anyone could breast-feed, no matter the size of their breasts. You don't have to be built like Mae West to nurse a baby. You don't have to have nipples the length of a baby bottle nipple to feed. Glad that was cleared up. Perhaps it was worth my twenty-five bucks after all.

When the lights came up, the women quickly brushed cookie crumbs off their large bellies. Time to learn how to nurse our plastic babies. We all chose dolls, and Anita demonstrated different nursing positions.

Looking at the other moms-to-be, I was pleased to see they looked just as uncomfortable as I did holding the dolls against their breasts and maneuvering their real babies in utero. I didn't relish the thought of sharing my breasts with anyone. They had their purpose in shaping my clothes, and Jake got some enjoyment from them, but actually to sustain a baby's life? Seemed like an awfully big job for a pair of boobs.

I knew breast-feeding a live baby would be much harder than handling the doll, but I wasn't about to borrow a baby to practice.

"How many of you are planning to return to work after the baby?" Anita asked.

A young woman in the front row raised her hand, and I raised mine halfway, noticing we were the lonely minority. The other women looked at us with pity in their eyes. I slowly lowered my hand as Anita dragged out some cone-shaped contraptions from behind her old wooden desk.

"These are breast pumps," she said. "They're great for pumping while you're at work. But stay-at-home moms can use them, too, if they need to get out for a romantic evening with their husband."

The women chuckled. Was that such an outrageous idea?

Anita continued. "This small one is a manual pump, but it takes quite a while compared to this one, the double electric breast pump. This is what I'd recommend. It's expensive, but well worth it. Still a lot cheaper than buying formula. It has a storage compartment to keep your milk cold all day. You can also buy a battery if you don't have access to an electrical outlet, and you can even get a cigarette lighter adapter to pump in your car."

Pumping at work? What—between my staff barging in my office or being stuck in a meeting with clients? On my lunch break? That was a joke—I was lucky if I had time to wolf down the sandwiches Allen brought me each day. Or on location: "Excuse me, can you hold that shot while I take my large battery-operated black bag and pump for fifteen minutes?" I didn't have fifteen minutes. I didn't even have *five* minutes most days. What would I do, stick a note on my door that read, *Milking in Progress*?

Sensing my worry, Anita chirped, "Any questions, Taylor?"

The mommies looked at me. "No," I said, feigning a smile. "That all sounds great."

CHAPTER 31

"I'm not sure this is such a good idea," I said as Jake rubbed orange costume paint on my naked belly.

Jake looked up at me and hissed through his Dracula teeth, "It's the Great Pumpkin, Charlie Brown."

I pouted and pulled at my ponytail. Allen had thought it would be hilarious if I went as Lucy, who had stolen the Great Pumpkin. Allen had rented Jake a Charlie Brown costume, but as usual, Jake wouldn't play against type. He had to be the big guy, the monster, the Donald Trump, the werewolf—every year another macho character.

"It doesn't make sense unless you're Charlie Brown," I complained. "I look like a pregnant teenager—how's that setting an example for the little kids?"

Jake lunged for my neck. "I vant to suck your blood!" He kissed my neck, getting red lipstick on it in the process.

"Ugh," I said, pushing him off. "Where's a stake when you need it?"

"You're no fun, Lucy," he said. "This is our third favorite holiday behind Christmas and Fourth of July, remember?"

I cracked a smile. I imagined our little family dressing up together every year, trick-or-treating until Jake's large candy bag was full. If I knew him, he'd have our baby out next year, even though Emily wouldn't even be able to speak yet. Usually a health nut, Jake allowed himself all the candy he wanted for the week of Halloween, and then he made me take it all to work, where I munched on it until it was gone. I hadn't told him I'd already eaten his favorites, Kit Kats, out of this year's black cat dish.

"I'm sorry, Jake. I just feel a little pooped today. You sure you want to go to Amy's costume party? We can stay here and see all the cute kiddos."

Jake slicked back his hair with my hair gel. "No can do. Best costume gets a trip to the Bahamas."

I studied my orange belly with the mean pumpkin face in the mirror. "You seem to forget it's a *couple* prize. Best couple's costume wins. I'm afraid teen girl, the unborn, and the undead aren't exactly prize material."

Jake gave in. "Just remember I'm only being a dork for you, babe. Right after I get some use out of this costume."

The doorbell rang, followed by the sound of children's chatter. Jake's eyes widened. He got a kick out of scaring little children, which hadn't really bothered me until we were bringing one into the world. Well, at least he only scared them on Halloween.

Jake went overboard at Halloween, buying the creepy music and the fake webs with large spiders and scarecrows and electronic flying bats. Each year our collection grew. This year he'd even made a graveyard in our front yard with fake hands reaching out from the earth. He marked the gravestones with his partners' names.

Jake's cape flew up as he ran to the front door, swung it open, and cackled an evil laugh. "Who dares steal my candy?"

Instead of running scared, the little football player, ninja, and ladybug stared up at Jake with blank looks on their faces, and then as if on cue, said in chorus, "Trick or treat!" Had I always loved the sweet sound of tiny voices? Or was that new, too?

The ladybug, four years old, I guessed, thanked us

while her brothers ran off. Then she pointed to my belly. "I like your baby pumpkin," she said. And for that, she got an extra lollipop.

When Jake and I arrived at Amy's party, it was already in full swing, with nearly a hundred guests and a live band. The house was dark and noisy, with a smoke machine in the corner of the living room. Feeling faint, I excused myself to the backyard to get some fresh air. The bridge girls laughed hysterically at the sight of me, just as Allen had hoped they would. Amy, as Elvira, slinked over and planted a wet kiss on my cheek. "What a sport," she said. Jackie and her daughter were dressed like a mama bear and her cub.

"We're getting ready to leave," she said. "Morning sickness. Well, all-day sickness, you know."

I squeezed her daughter, who felt like a little teddy bear. "Yeah, I don't feel so hot, either. Gretchen and Allen here yet?"

"You mean Sonny and Cher? They're cutting it up on the dance floor."

Amy handed me a purple frozen drink with an eyeball in it. "Only *Allen* is Cher."

I rolled my eyes. What that man wouldn't do for a trip to the Bahamas.

Jennifer and her son Max, dressed as a geisha and a little warrior, joined our table. Max had a plastic pumpkin full of candy and dumped it on the patio floor to pick out a sucker, the only sweet treat he was allowed. "How is childbirth class going?" she said as she patted my pumpkin.

"I've been learning to breathe. I can inhale to twenty counts now. When I started I could only go up to seven."

Jennifer nodded approvingly. "That'll get you through the tough contractions," she said.

Amy waved her hand through the air. "You going natural on us? I thought Jennifer was the only crazy one in the group."

Like everything else in pregnancy, there were decisions

to be made on how Emily would enter the world, too. Acupuncture, Bradley Method, Hypnobirthing, Demoral, Epidural, Doula, Caesarian, water birth. Our childbirth class was politically correct, going over all the choices, showing a few pain management exercises and tools and leaving the rest up to the couples. Jake claimed he wanted to coach, but this wasn't a football game and I wasn't sure I wanted him yelling at me from the sidelines. *Put some muscle into it, Montgomery! Show me what you got!* On the other hand, I didn't believe childbirth was a spectator sport, either.

I knew if my mother were alive, I'd probably want her there, even though she had instilled my fear of pain. She had kept a box of Band-Aids in her purse at all times and a first-aid kit in her glove box in case anything ever happened to me as a kid. One bloody knee sent her into hysterics. She took CPR, water-safety classes, and self-defense classes. As her guinea pig, my dad had found himself lying flat on his back on the floor when he least expected it.

Now that I was becoming a mother, I understood her protective nature, but wanted to avoid her paranoia. I craved calm. Calm birth, calm life.

"Pain is a state of mind," Jennifer said, unwrapping a Twix. "Rechannel your energy."

Amy cringed. "I tried going drug-free for about an hour. Then I felt like a boa constrictor was wrapped around my waist. Try breathing through *that*."

Jennifer shook her head and patted my arm. "Don't listen to her, Taylor. She didn't *practice*. Relaxation techniques can't be learned on the fly. If you want me to come over and help you, I will."

Amy, epidural. Jennifer, hynobirthing. Jackie, emergency C-section. Three very different birthing stories. I was making a mental note to ask Aunt Barb about my own birth when the sight of my husband in his ridiculous Charlie Brown shirt, bald cap, and big ears caught my attention through the window. From Dracula to Charlie

Brown. Maybe a man could change after all. I imagined Lorna was probably knocked out for his birth. *Wake me when he's all clean and ready for pictures.*

The wind picked up, blowing the paper lanterns that lined the patio and the black and orange party lights above our heads. A chill ran through me, causing goose bumps on my fleshy pumpkin. *She's cold,* I thought instinctively, and covered my belly with my jacket. Maternal instinct in action.

"I'm going in," I told the gang. I tried to stand, but my friends' faces blurred in circles around me, the party lights spinning above my head. The last thing I saw was a black cat, yellow eyes blinking, hissing at me from the bushes as my head hit the cold, hard pavement.

When I awoke, a man in drag stood over my bed. My eyes focused on my surroundings: mechanical bed, tubes in my arms, TV mounted on the wall, ugly nurse. "How you doin', babe?" a deep voice asked.

I squinted my eyes. "Allen? You scared the crap out of me. Where am I?"

"Hospital. Here I thought I would be the only one to pass out at the Halloween party."

I panicked and grabbed my belly, strapped with monitoring equipment. "Is she . . . ?"

"Your baby's fine. The doctor should be in any moment. Jake went outside for a bit. He's pretty shaken up. When I got here, he was crying."

I shook my head, then touched the large bandage on head. "Jake doesn't cry. He must've had too much to drink."

Allen took my hand. "You gave us quite the scare, Lucy. I rushed you over here in my car while Jake held you in the backseat. I've never seen him like this—white as a ghost."

I turned my head to watch the monitor and heard the rapid swooshing sounds of Emily's heartbeat. I inhaled a long breath and closed my eyes. "Is something wrong with me? Please tell me before Jake comes back in."

Allen removed his long black wig and sat on the edge of my bed. "I don't know for sure. Doctor said something about exhaustion. He asked me if you've been pushing yourself, experienced any anxiety lately."

I nodded. Of course it was my fault. But I only had eight weeks to get everything done, to put order to my chaotic life. I had to be ready.

The door swung open and Jake stood in the light, his face sad and pale, wringing his bald cap in his hands. Relief washed over him and he smiled. "You okay?"

I held out my hand for him. "Guess I've been taking this pregnancy thing like a sprint instead of a marathon. Didn't save up my energy for the final laps."

Allen excused himself and Jake took his place on the bed. He leaned over to kiss me and lay his head on my chest. "I don't know what . . ."

"I know," I whispered, and in that moment I felt we finally got each other. The vulnerability of love, of parenthood, of needing each other more than we ever realized.

Dr. Creighton cleared his throat, and we suddenly noticed he was standing at the foot of the bed. His hair was disheveled, with the outline of green paint around his jawline. "I think you did too much trick-or-treating," he said.

Jake and I sat up in the bed. "Don't tell me," I said. "Jolly Green Giant?"

The doctor rubbed his chin, wiping off paint he'd missed. "The Hulk. My family were all superheroes tonight at the charity costume ball."

Dr. Creighton even partied for charity. "Well, that's not too much of a stretch. Especially if you can use your powers to make me better."

The doctor walked to the right side of my bed and looked at me earnestly. "You're the only one who can do that, Taylor. Your blood pressure is a little high and you were dehydrated, so that's why we're giving you fluids. Have you been especially stressed out lately?"

"Uh, yeah," I said, starting to tear up. "We're getting ready to pitch Cover Girl on Monday, and we still don't have child care figured out, and my agency is probably going to merge soon and I'll be out of a job." My eyes stung.

Dr. Creighton grabbed my toes and gave them a little shake. "Here's my prescription then. Let's see how you take to bed rest for a few days, and I'll have you come in to see if that helps things."

My jaw dropped. "Bed rest? As in don't get out of bed *at all*? But that pitch is on Monday. Could I just sleep late and go to that and then go back to bed?"

Dr. Creighton looked at me compassionately. "Bed rest, all day, on your left side. To shake things up a little, you can lay on the couch, too. It's not so bad, Taylor. Read that novel you've been meaning to get to. Catch up on DVD rentals. Mandatory R and R."

I inhaled through my nose, twenty counts like an expert breather, and exhaled. The oxygen filled my lungs, making me feel better, my head cleared. I smiled. An excuse to lie around in bed all day to protect my baby and me? *No problem.*

CHAPTER 32

Wearing flannel pajamas and my mother's bunny slippers, I ate corn flakes and watched cartoons at 7 A.M. My friends told me my body was preparing for less sleep when the baby came. I could no longer sleep in as I had in my early days of pregnancy, and I woke up full of energy, eager to step into the November morning for a brisk walk. Then I remembered I was confined to bed. With pent-up mental zest, I called Allen and Jude on three-way to go over final notes for the pitch they would make later that morning. The successful Studio Baby launch had proved we knew how to reach women. I decided to put on a full face of Cover Girl makeup to be there in spirit with them. Besides, I didn't want to slug around like a zombie just because I was staying home.

Some time later, Aunt Barb came to make me lunch, and visit. "You still looking for a nanny, sugar?" She asked, after I'd eaten.

I sighed. "I have her on the hook, but I'm just not sure I want to reel her in. She's nice, young. Gorgeous, too. Mothers have enough to worry about without adding a hot nanny to the list."

"Oh, shoot. Jake wouldn't touch a nanny with a ten-foot pole."

I hadn't told her about his Close Encounter of the Kate Kind. I wished Aunt Barb was retired so she could watch Emily, but she was teaching third grade at the local elementary school. "You know someone I should talk to?"

Aunt Barb shifted in the chair, a smile on her face. "I may have the Poppins you've been looking for. I don't want to get your hopes up, but my neighbor is a widow, in her early sixties I'd guess, and she's looking to nanny. She's a retired pediatric nurse."

"What?" I nearly leapt off the couch. "A pediatric nurse? That's the jackpot of nannies! When can I talk to her? Would she come over here while I'm stuck to the sofa?"

Aunt Barb clapped her hands. "I knew you'd be pleased. But I have to warn you, she's pretty hot for her age."

"Very funny. You don't know what a relief that would be."

"I know how it's been weighing on you." She studied my face. "You look more and more like your mama," she said, rubbing her hand over the smooth leather of the armrest. Her eyes crinkled in memory.

"I think so, too," I said, touching the Honey Dew rouge on my cheek. "Do you think Mom and Dad can see us? That they know what's going on?" I had told Aunt Barb once that I didn't even believe in heaven, but I had to hold on to something, the hope that I'd one day see them again.

Aunt Barb pointed her finger up. "I believe they are wrapping their love around you every day, and you can do the same for them. I think your mother finally got the peace she always wanted and yes, I think she's overjoyed with your baby coming." Her eyes misted.

My heart ached. "Do you think Mom has forgiven her mother, then?"

Aunt Barb tilted her head, thinking it over. "I think when we get to heaven all is forgiven. I think my mother didn't have the mental health to know any better, and God would forgive her for stepping into the storm and so would your mother."

Forgiveness seemed impossible just months before. My anger was like an anchor. As I transitioned from one life I knew to the next, the weight seemed lighter.

That afternoon I dreamt I walked along a cobblestone path to a small white house with blue shutters, smoke rising up to the gray sky from the chimney. I wore a red sweater, too large for my frame, and wrapped it around my belly to warm us from the winter chill. When I stepped onto the porch, I heard the sound of women's voices rising and falling within.

A porch swing screeched and swayed in the wind. I raised my hand to knock on the door, then stopped. I waited another minute, straining my ears to hear the women. Gathering my courage, I rapped on the screen door. The voices stopped. The wood door creaked open, and a tiny woman with large brown eyes appeared before me. Her cheekbones were high and rosy, her mouth small and round. Familiar. Family. She didn't speak, but raised her hand to the glass on the screen door that separated us. A wave of recognition ran through me. Crazy Helen. No, not crazy. Just Helen. Grandma Helen.

She looked at my belly, and a smile crept onto her face. "That baby is special," she said through the door.

I no longer noticed the cold or the wind whipping at my hair. I looked past her into the room and saw three more women gathered around the fireplace, sitting in rocking chairs. A mix of legs and arms, but Helen blocked my view of their faces. I recognized my mother's ballerina legs, crossed at the ankles, bare feet tapping as she swayed in the rocker. "Mother," I breathed.

Helen opened the screen door and reached up to touch my face. "We were just talking about you," she said. "You're getting so close."

As I started to speak, I felt a sharp pain in my leg, and I awoke to find myself on the couch, the fan above on high speed. I curled my toes, my left side aching. I rubbed my leg and my calf muscle, disappointed a charley horse had spoiled my chance to talk to my mother. I ached to see her, even if it was only in a dream. I looked around the room and heard rustling in the kitchen.

"There you are," Jennifer said, wearing a baby blue yoga outfit and carrying Max, who squirmed to be let loose. "Your aunt let me in." When she let him down, he ran across the room, screaming in delight.

"Oh, the joys of mobility," I said, watching Max turn the corner, pumping his little arms and legs. "At least I've baby-proofed the house. Now I know why you always wanted to entertain at your house."

Jennifer didn't deny it. She sat next to me on the couch and handed me a gift bag. "Here are the book and tapes on hynobirthing we talked about and some things for acupressure. So much of the technique is imagery, and with your creative imagination, I honestly think you could pull it off."

The bag contained a simple black comb, a gel ice pack, a small wooden massager and a booklet on acupressure points. "To comb my hair before pictures?"

Jennifer took the comb from me and placed the teeth of the comb at the base of her fingers in her palm. She closed her fist. "See? It releases natural endorphins. Every time you feel a contraction, squeeze."

I laughed. "You're telling me a little old comb is going to kick the pain?"

"They say if you expect pain, you'll get pain. So think of it as energy moving the baby toward its goal," Jennifer said. "This will work along with your sleep breathing, your positive imagery—I personally chose hang gliding in Colorado—and acupressure points. But you'll need to practice a lot. You should've started this months ago, but for an overachiever like yourself I think you can catch up. And Jake or a doula can do the acupressure for you."

Jennifer was right. Expect pain, and you'll get it. That was the case in every area of life, wasn't it? As for Jake, at our childbirth class he had looked peaked watching the video of a live birth. Just to be safe, I would give Aunt Barb the role of back-up acupressurist. "No time like the present," I said, trying the comb trick. "As long as I can squeeze it into my oh-so-busy schedule of reading, watching marathons of *Baby Stories* on cable and power napping."

Jennifer looked at the mountain of magazines on the floor. "Boredom is out of the question," she told me as she got up to corral her precocious one-year-old.

Hours later, I whined into the phone to Allen, "I'm bored!"

"What happened to 'this will be the greatest thing since sliced bread'?"

"Oh, shut up. I've never been still this long in my life. My eyes are tired from being glued to the boob tube and reading, and everybody is too busy to talk to me on the phone."

"On that note, I have to get to a meeting," Allen said.

"No, you don't. Promise me first that you and Gretchen will come have dinner with us, picnic style in my living room. Aunt Barb packed my fridge, so there's plenty of food."

"You know I can't turn down your aunt's cooking," he said.

"Good. What's your meeting about?"

"Debriefing on the Cover Girl pitch. I don't think their execs had very good chemistry with Susan. She came off a little—"

"Cold? Arrogant? Bitchy? Well, it will be great if she gets the blame for once."

"They loved Jude, though. I've also got a little planning meeting for an upcoming baby bash."

"Oh, you shouldn't, really," I said, as I painted my toenails in alternating shades of orange, pink, and green. "Are you sure you know how to plan a party that doesn't involve alcohol and karaoke?"

Allen gasped. "Oh, ye of little faith. Return to your state of slugdom and leave the party planning to me. I'll tell Susan you said hello."

"Please do," I said sweetly. My cell phone beeped from

its place on the coffee table. I found it underneath a stack of magazines.

A text message from Jake in court. *I'm bored. U?*

I punched in my reply. *U kidding? Best time I've had lying down.*

A minute later, it beeped again. *Ouch. Keep it up and u won't get my famous hot fudge sundae 2nite.*

I smiled. *Fine. 2nd best then.*

Jake replied: *Good. U need sumthng?*

My spirits had lifted. *Strip-tez @ 6. DINR @ 8.*

☺ *Done. Over & out.*

After Jake had gained five sympathy pounds, he had hit the gym religiously, getting back the body he had when we dated in college. He had never stripped for me before, but it sounded like the sort of thing his ego would agree to.

I wiggled my rainbow toes and drummed my fingers on my belly. "What shall we do now, Emily? We've got two hours to kill before daddy comes home."

I plucked her journal from the pile of books on the carpet and turned to the bookmarked page and began to write.

Things I'll Never Do As a Mother

1. *Wear mommy jeans. (They flatten and widen your rump at the same time!)*
2. *Make your father carry a pastel diaper bag with a cartoon character on it.*
3. *Begin a lecture with, "When I was your age . . ."*
4. *Try to be cool by wearing the same style of clothes and listening to the same music as you do.*
5. *Lick my finger and use it to clean your face. We're humans, not cats.*
6. *Tell you to eat your asparagus. I hate asparagus!*
7. *Be a helicopter mom who hovers over your every move. I want you to feel confident in making your own decisions as you grow up.*
8. *Force you to take dance or cheerleading. If you got my coordination, you probably won't want to, anyway.*

Nor will Daddy force you into sports. I'll let you see what interests develop and we'll be your biggest cheerleaders.

I closed the journal as the timer in the kitchen sounded. My cue to watch more *Baby Stories.* I'd watched two dozen of them over the course of two days, and not one had been alike. After two drops of rewetting solution in each eye, I was ready to see what other mommies had in store for them.

Just as an Asian woman screaming in Japanese popped out her second healthy twin, Jake hollered from the kitchen. "Turn that off and get ready to be turned on, woman."

I nestled deeper into the couch, pulling the fleece blanket around my midsection as Marvin Gaye crooned from the speakers. Jake closed the blinds and placed a red dinner napkin over the lamp, filling the room with a soft red glow. Just as Marvin sang, "Let's get it on," Jake stood in the middle of the room, his back facing me, and slapped his bottom, then looked over his shoulder, a smoldering look on his face. He rotated his behind around and around, causing me to laugh out loud.

Jake spun around to face me, grabbed at his chest, and rubbed his hands all over it as if he were washing in the shower. He was as clumsy as a rejected Chippendale dancer, but he gave it his all. He inched toward me, beginning to unbutton his shirt at the top, licking his lips. He swung his shirt overhead and flung it at me, landing on my head. I hugged it to my bosom. His hips rocked back and forth like the pendulum on an old clock as he unbuttoned his pants, revealing his Batman boxers underneath.

"It's the Bat Signal!" I raised my hands to the air like a teenager at a rock concert.

He removed his pants and thrust his hips forward, jumping closer to me with each beat. His chest and legs were chalky white, his dress socks pulled up over his calves. After two failed attempts at lassoing my head with his dress pants, Jake gave up and used his hands to gently cup my face and pull me toward his manhood. I rubbed my hands over his tight buttocks as the song ended, replaced by a female shriek.

I pushed Jake's hips to the side to find Gretchen and Allen in the entryway, mouths agape. They turned their heads. "We'll just take a rain check," Allen said.

Jake scurried to put on his pants, while I rose to my feet, embarrassed. "No, it's not what you—"

"We're sorry, Taylor," Gretchen said as they left the room.

Bed rest or not, I wasn't about to let them leave. "No, stop!"

Allen suppressed laughter. "Really, honey. Even a preggo has needs."

"Yes, for comic relief. What you saw was a striptease, not fellatio!"

Allen doubled over laughing. "I've never heard you use that word."

"And I hope you'll never hear me use it again."

"It wasn't *that* funny," Jake hollered behind me.

Gretchen handed me a plate of brownies. "Well, we were still interrupting, and you could've—"

"No! I wasn't about to anything. I just lost track of the time. Jake was supposed to be home at six."

"So it's my fault," Jake said, standing next to me, his face flushed. His shirt was buttoned unevenly. "But hey, at least you caught the best part of the act."

"Were you going full monty on us?" Allen joked. "Seeing your bare white ass may have blinded me for a week." Allen shook his head at me. "I can't believe you got this guy to strip for you. The couch sloth wields much power."

I put my arm around Jake's waist. "What a preggo wants, a preggo gets."

CHAPTER 33

Dr. Creighton handed me the birthing plan worksheet at my thirty-six-week checkup. After a week of bed rest, I was given permission to rise from the cushions and enter the real world again. Just as I'd finally gotten the hang of doing nothing. I'd practiced hynobirthing techniques, imagining the colored clouds of calm surrounding me, lifting me up. Imagined my arm being lifted by a balloon. Imagined ocean waves creeping onto the shore and receding back again. I was a master breather. Jake had gotten into the act; he pinched my inner thigh while I breathed through the pain. After a few days, I had stopped slapping his hand away and before long I didn't feel it at all. My mind was right where it belonged. In my control.

"We're pretty flexible," the doctor said, going over the plan. "Music, videos, low lights, visitors. Did you decide on pain medication?"

"I think I'm going old school," I told him confidently. "Like my mother did and every generation before her. Why break the tradition now?"

Dr. Creighton frowned. "You sure? You've had a tough

time, both mentally and physically. Don't put any undue pressure on yourself to have a dream delivery."

"I'm long past idealized anything. What did your wife do?" I'm sure Ms. Perfect Ms. America had two pushes and out came her perfect babies, ribbons across their chests.

"She had epidurals both times," he said. "Low tolerance for pain."

Yes! At least I was trying. Dr. Creighton patted my knee. "Just know there's help if you need it."

"I can't believe there's only four weeks left." It seemed only yesterday that he broke the news of my pregnancy. How could eight months pass so quickly?

"You're considered full term next week, so it could happen at any time," he said. "Baby sounds good. You've gained well."

I snickered. Yeah, *real* well. A nice, round thirty pounds, but I'd grown to like the softness on my body, or at least to live with it. With the extra cushion, I felt more womanly than ever. I was sure my stretch marks looked like a map of Dallas covering my hips, bottom and thighs.

"So other people can be in the room?"

"If you'd like. Most women have their husbands in the room. He can stay at your head if he doesn't want to watch the actual birth," Dr. Creighton said.

Good point. That might ruin sex for him forever after. "It will just be Jake and my aunt. If I invited one girlfriend I'd have to invite them all."

"Let's see what Emily's been up to."

I laid back and Dr. Creighton checked my cervix while I clenched my teeth in pain. "Good," he said. "You're at a full one and fifty percent effaced." I knew from our class that meant I was starting to dilate. I would have to be at a ten and one hundred percent effaced—or thinned—before the baby could pass through. Dear Lord, my body was *actually* going through with it.

"You may want to go ahead and pack your bag and the

baby's bag," he told me. "Some women progress rapidly, others go beyond their due date."

I marveled that Emily would be a live human being. No longer a fantasy, the little girl in pink bows. The final countdown had begun. She would be real, and I would be her mother.

Nikki had left me two more messages, and I started thinking maybe Allen was right and she did want to hire me, or else pick my brain for employees I had to let go. I punched in her digits, and her receptionist patched me through to her cell phone, where I heard kids yelling in the background.

"Did I catch you at a bad time?" I asked.

"Oh, just a play date with my friends," she said. "Thanks for calling me back."

The lunch hour. You mean some people actually take that off to eat? My mommy friends wanted to have a play date once a month, but if I were still at Titan/Ace, it would have to be on a weekend.

"Listen, Taylor. I need a creative director immediately. I didn't call you sooner because I didn't think you'd want to work for a smaller agency, but I heard that Susan turned down your day care proposal and you might be merging, so I thought I'd try. Do I have a chance in Hades of getting you?"

I took a deep breath. "I'm open to anything at this point."

"Fabulous. How's next Tuesday? Carson, don't pull your sister's hair, baby," she yelled in my ear.

We agreed to meet at a popular bakery. If I didn't get a new job, at least I'd get a good pastry out of it. Two things I'd miss at Titan—the Studio Baby account and working with Allen. It was the account of a lifetime, and Allen made advertising bearable on the bad days.

When I finally got up, I went to my file cabinet, which was neatly disguised as paneling in the wall, and dug around for the non-compete and employment contracts I'd signed six years earlier. As legal documents go, they were fairly clear. I couldn't go after Ace's clients for ninety days after leaving unless a formal Request For Proposal was issued by the client.

The next day Susan pushed me one step closer to my decision to leave.

"Studio announced Anne Sims as their new president, and she is asking for a formal agency review. Six agencies, ours included, will vie for the business," she said, clearly angry. She hated losing more than she hated unstylish people and poor service at expensive restaurants. It didn't bode well to lose one of our biggest clients just after she'd inked the merger.

I remembered Hoffman telling me in Atlanta I was the only reason they were still with Ace. Had it just been an offhanded compliment? If I left Ace, did I have a chance of winning the account at another agency? *Did I really have the cajones to fight Susan for my favorite client?*

Since I didn't really do the whole slaving in the kitchen thing, Thanksgiving had always been on someone else's turf. Since we'd been married, we'd flown every year to either Houston or Austin, where Lorna's cook or Aunt Barb made a fabulous bird and I lounged for three days, kicking back with the guys, eating chips and downing brewskies while we watched football. With Emily's arrival just weeks away, flying was not an option, and I didn't want to suffer through such a long car trip.

Not going to Lorna and Bill's on our scheduled year caused a hysterical uproar in Houston. I could hear Lorna whining through the receiver. Jake did his best to calm her. "Mom, settle down. You know the doctor says no flying, and it's too close to the due date for driving that far. You'll just have to come here for once."

I sat at the kitchen table biting my nails. Not having my mother-in-law hate me was at the top of my list of things to accomplish in life. Jake was stern on the phone. "I know, Mom. It won't be the same. Lots of things won't be the same anymore. We won't be able to go skiing with you at Christmas, either. We're going to start a few traditions of our own around here."

I smiled, and Jake gave me a thumbs-up. I could practically hear the invisible umbilical cord between Dallas and Houston finally being cut. "Of course we'll invite you here," Jake said. "No, we may not get the bigger house like Amy's. Mom, it may be a shock to you, but many relatives sleep on sofas. Or, I could even buy an air mattress."

I had to wobble out of the room to laugh out loud at my husband's newfound bravery. And the thought of my in-laws sleeping on the floor was just more than I could take. Jake came up behind me and kissed my neck. I shook Emily up and down with my laughter. "An air mattress? Oh, no you didn't!"

"And you thought I was a mama's boy," he said.

"I could get into the whole new Montgomery tradition thing."

"Maybe you'll even cook a turkey before I turn gray."

"Ah, ah. Let's not get ahead of ourselves there, mister."

Jake grabbed me in his arms and lifted me up, much like a crane lifts a large mound of cement: very carefully. "Time to tuck my girls into bed," he said, his face turning crimson from the strain.

Jake rolled over in bed, slung his arm around my middle, and stroked my hair. "Are you crying?" He sat up and peered over me. I turned toward him, my face wet with tears.

"This will be our last Thanksgiving alone."

Jake wiped my cheeks. "That's right. Next year you can wake up to the sound of crying instead of the alarm clock," he teased.

"I guess we should enjoy the quiet then," I said, and nestled against Jake's chest. The still morning folded us into its tranquility. The clock ticked its rhythmic dance. The heater hummed, pushing the warm air through the vents. Cars roared down the street heading for their holiday destinations.

"Is something else bothering you?" He moved my hair out of my face.

"It would be so easy to take Nikki's offer, but I feel like I'm ready to be my own boss. Is that crazy? It's crazy, isn't it?"

"It sounds less crazy than working somewhere you're not happy. You know I'll support you, whatever decision you make."

My heart beat wildly. How did I ever have doubts about starting a family with this man?

"Would you like to shower first?" Jake offered.

"Let's make it a threesome."

"I can't think of a better way to start the day." Packing the phone booth was nothing compared to the feat of the gargantuan pregnant lady and her svelte husband maneuvering in a shower stall. As ridiculous as it sounds, it was sexy. Intimacy was sexier than sex itself.

Another gift had presented itself that Thanksgiving Day—the baby had lowered, leaving my stomach room to indulge in the feast. The downside was that my bladder got the squeeze, sending me to the bathroom every half hour or so; my increased ability to stuff myself with my aunt's marvelous cooking, however, justified the inconvenience of frequent bathroom trips.

Every holiday I fought with the old feelings of loneliness and grief that my parents were gone. Since my aunt and uncle had moved, I hoped I was stronger and could welcome the images of my parents and honor them. Obviously, I had a lot to be thankful for.

My nephew Sam stood in the doorway, holding a toy car and waving to me. I hadn't seen him since he was a newborn. His father Timmy appeared behind him and scooped him up into his arms. My middle cousin looked the same to me, a freckled blond with a crooked smile.

"Hey, Taylor," Timmy said as he opened the door. "Hey, Jake. Man, you're fit as a fiddle."

"I try," Jake said, and ruffled Sam's red hair. "Hey, pardner. You've got a cool car there."

"Car!" Sam hugged his plastic toy.

"He's so big now!" I shook his pudgy hand. Sam held out his hands and nearly leapt into my arms.

"Oh! Taylor doesn't have room for you, buddy," Timmy told him.

The rest of the family greeted us and hugging ensued. They were the huggiest bunch of people I'd ever met. Even the men had caught the hugging bug from Aunt Barb. My youngest cousin Michael had recently graduated from college and brought his fiancée, Sonya, whom my aunt had been treating like a beloved daughter-in-law for more than a year. Michael kissed me on the cheek. "You look beautiful," he said. "We can't wait to meet Emily."

"Thank you," I said. "Congratulations on your engagement."

Sonya kissed me, too. "We're moving to Dallas after we get married. We hope we're high on the baby-sitting list."

"Right after me!" Aunt Barb said. "I get first dibs."

"We're just glad you talked Mom into moving to Dallas," Timmy said. "We'd been working on her for months."

I looked at Aunt Barb quizzically.

She winked. "I decided the day you called me and told me you were expecting," she said.

"You decided right then?"

"You just cinched the deal, honey," she said. "Now let's go. I need all my girls in the kitchen."

Just as a mother would, Aunt Barb had moved for me, to be closer to all of her babies. In that house was the next generation of my family and old traditions started anew. The men gathered in the family room to watch football, and Jake bonded with them immediately. The women gossiped in the kitchen, cooking and planning for the future. For the first time since I could remember, I wanted my family, and all that it stood for. I wanted to share birthday parties and summer cookouts and Christmas mornings and lazy Sunday afternoons. I wanted to love them all and have them love me back.

December 1

Darling Emily,

Today is the first day of your birth month. Your mother is swollen and agitated, and anxious to meet you. I huff and puff getting in and out of my car and my walk has turned into a waddle. My sinuses are still stopped up. They call it pregnancy rhinitis and there's nothing I can take for it, but it's supposed to go away as soon as you are born. Swollen nose, swollen ankles, swollen fingers. I couldn't even wear my wedding ring this last month, but I've never been prouder to be married to your father.

After months of agonizing nanny searching, I've settled on a nice yet highly qualified woman named Mary Bright. She fits her name, warm and friendly and sweet. It will also be nice to say my mother's name every day—Mary. Mary Bright and Aunt Barb have made fast friends, and she'll know how to give you the best care because she was a nurse and adores babies. But I know taking care of you doesn't require a degree or thousands of hours working with babies, either. I know I'm going to take great care of you, and love you like no sitter could possibly love you.

Your daddy researched web cams so we can both watch you from our desktops at work. Technology these days! It even has twenty-times zoom capability. Can you believe it was your daddy's idea?

On the job front, the merger looks like it will happen before you arrive. Knowing my mean boss, she would do a round of layoffs just for the chance to play Scrooge. You know what? I'm not worried about my job anymore. My fear of not having enough money to give you a nice upbringing has dissipated. I'm even considering my own company. You've given me the strength to know anything is possible.

I don't know for sure what the future will bring, so I'm keeping our options open. Pregnant women have a right to change their minds.

Until next time,
Mommy

December made its presence known with a snowstorm and frigid temperatures on the night of our final childbirth class. Jake and I debated skipping the class. I figured most of the women in their last leg of pregnancy would choose to, but we decided to go, not so much for the hokey certificate of completion and more cookies I shouldn't eat, but because we were interested in the other couple's lives. The childbirth classes had turned out to be somewhat of a soap opera each week. *Tune in next week to find out . . .*

. . . did Pizza Boy get his promotion to district manager?

. . . did the Midget Lady win her litigation case against a large soft-drink company?

. . . did the Mexican Immigrants get citizenship?"

That night all the answers were revealed to us.

Pizza Boy did get his promotion. Extra breadsticks on the house!

Midget Lady won her case. They could buy a bigger house!

Mexican Immigrants did get citizenship! They brought little American flag cookies so we could celebrate with them.

Plus, Pizza Boy hosted a party for us, just as he had promised the first day of class. I'd been craving pepperoni all day!

Two couples, the real estate/Mary Kay couple and the farm couple, were missing, and Anita was late to class, as usual. No matter, we started eating without her. She bounded in several minutes later with a look of worry on her face.

"Hi, class," she said, not as singsong as usual. "I've got news about some of your classmates." We took our seats in the semicircle of chairs.

"First, the good news is Tom and Rhoda had their baby

this morning at five-forty A.M., and baby and mama are doing well." They were the farm couple.

The class cheered through pizza-stuffed mouths.

"Martha went into labor early. As you may remember, she wasn't due until January second, but she delivered Henry early this morning. He only weighs three pounds, and he is in the NICU. He had a lot of fluid on his lungs, but his chance of survival is good. They can do a lot for premature babies these days. I'm sure we'll all keep them in our prayers."

In the bathroom stall at the break, I found myself crying for Martha. The possibility of losing her child, of seeing his tiny body hooked up to IVs and an oxygen mask must be nearly unbearable. I found myself talking to God, a being I'd blamed for all of the tragedy in my life. In that moment of hysteria, I could only think of Him to turn to. "Please God," I prayed aloud. "Please protect Emily."

I could not know what it was like to lose a child, but I knew how heartbreaking just the thought of it was. I knew it could hurt even more than losing my parents. Emily was already my child, before I even saw her. The burden of mothers would always be that the love we had for our children would not always be enough.

CHAPTER 34

Pink balloons filled my office when I arrived at work the next day. Emily had dropped lower in my abdomen, causing a sharp pain to shoot through my legs every few minutes. At times it felt as if she were going to break through. Her time was near.

I'd considered calling in sick, but that day was my baby shower, which Allen and my creative staff—what was left of it—had slaved over the prior two weeks. I couldn't disappoint him or my other coworkers, who seemed genuinely interested in my pregnancy.

The snowstorm had passed, leaving a blanket of brilliant white snow on the ground. My mind went back to Henry. I asked Aunt Barb to light a candle for him at church and to pray for him to pull through.

Death happened. I could think there was a reason for it, a higher purpose. I could think there was something we're supposed to learn from it, that from all pain comes a clear understanding of life and human nature and our purpose on earth. *One day at a time*, Jake had said. That's all we had. I would control my days, my course through life, the impact I let things have on me. Death included. Life most of all.

The hum of my computer snapped my attention back to my day ahead. The first memo announced the merger of Ace and Titan with Jude as president and CEO and Susan as vice president and chief operating officer. The chief financial officer was Jude's business partner and best friend from college. The chief creative officer was still unnamed, and I figured the creative heads at Titan were probably fighting it out. The creative lead for the fourth-largest agency in the States with nearly half a billion dollars in annual billings—let them duke it out. Who needed the headache?

Susan had shared the news of the merger with us in our previous senior staff meeting and I acted surprised, as if I hadn't known it was coming. She assured us our positions were secure, but we knew we'd move down a notch in superiority. A couple of the VPs later told me they would consider leaving, but I knew better. They were part of something bigger, and it made them more profitable at the end of the day. With our profit-sharing plan, we would each be much richer, despite any demotions.

Allen brought in a steaming cup of coffee, decaffeinated with lots of sugar and cream. "You look like hell," he said. "I'm treating you to a massage and makeover from Paul."

"Allen, you really don't—"

"Yes I do, Taylor. You're a woman on the verge."

"I'm starting to believe it's just a part of parenthood."

Allen shook his head. "You need to relax. I don't know why you don't just take the next few weeks off."

I wanted so badly to tell him of my plans for leaving. I'd have to tell him before I told Susan. Besides, he topped my recruitment list. "I've still got to pull my weight around here," I said. "Don't even *think* about inserting a fat joke here. Besides, I'm saving up my vacation time to add more weeks to my maternity leave."

"Have it your way," Allen said. "And I'll take you to

Paul's studio at eleven-thirty. You'll be smashing for your baby shower."

I dug into the pile of paperwork on my desk and forced myself to get lost in the details of the creative. Was the headline strong enough? Was the picture captivating? Would customers even read the ad? Would they buy the product after reading the ad? I got so caught up in my work, I didn't hear Jude enter my office.

"That's why I like you," he said. "You're passionate about your work." He let himself in and sat in a chair opposite my desk, putting his feet up on the adjacent chair.

I tucked my pen behind my ear, the only way it wouldn't get lost in the stacks of papers on my desk. "I thought you left for Chicago. I'm sure your place is as caught up in the commotion of the merger as we are."

"I had some business to take care of here first." He took an envelope from his jacket pocket and held it in his hands.

I tried not to stare at his handsome suit or his Adam's apple that bounced when he spoke. He hadn't shaved that morning. "What's up?"

Jude smiled and leaned over my desk. I backed up. For a second I thought he was going to try to kiss me.

"I have a proposition for you."

The last thing I felt like doing was chatting up my new boss. Maybe it was a severance package. Could I possibly hope for three months paid?

"I'd like you to be our chief creative officer." He was serious.

I stared at him as if he hadn't stopped speaking. His mouth was closed, but I continued to look as if waiting for "Just kidding" to escape from his lips. "I think pregnancy has caused some hearing loss."

"I think you heard me loud and clear," he said. He took my stack of business cards from their stainless steel holder. "With the merger and all, you're going to need new business cards. May as well have a better title."

Besides being baffled, something didn't feel right. "This

wouldn't have anything to do with trying to keep the Studio account, would it?"

"I had breakfast with Anne today. She told me how much they like you. You could be the winning ticket to help us keep the account—especially if I make you creative chief. They're afraid they'll get lost in our bigger agency, but I don't think that would happen with you. She told me you gave them the idea for Studio Linens. They're going to launch in second quarter. That means their account could be worth fifty million dollars to us. I don't let go of money that easily."

"So I'm the Ace in the deck, so to speak." I might as well have fun with it. Going from being beaten down by Susan to begged for by Jude was quite a leap.

"I love the Studio account, but I'm not sure I'm interested in the position." I grabbed a handful of raisins from my bowl that previously held M&Ms. I still thought they looked like shriveled little bugs. What I wouldn't do for a healthy baby. Now I had the chance to be one of the most powerful creatives in the country.

He placed a piece of Titan letterhead on my desk. It had an awfully big number on it.

I gulped. The house in Amy's neighborhood was just a signature away. The live-in nanny. The new family-friendly Volvo. "You do realize I'm getting ready to have a baby. I'm taking off for at least eight weeks. Maybe longer."

Jude shrugged his shoulders. "Take ten weeks off. Just as long as you come back. Look, ask any of my employees, I'm a lot easier to work with than Susan. If you take this position you'd be working directly for me. Wouldn't it be nice to work for someone who gives you the respect you deserve?"

I twirled my pen in my fingers. Respect. The chance to work on national brands. No more insipid car dealer commercials. "What about Collins or Baker? I figured the position would go to one of your guys."

"You're one of my guys now, Taylor. Look, they both have

the experience, but they don't have the eye for the break-through creative that you do. You're a natural," Jude said.

"I . . . I don't know what to say . . ."

Jude handed me his two hundred dollar gold pen, want-ing my name on the dotted line. "I'll even give you a per-sonal assistant. Someone to run out and buy formula and diapers for you. Whatever you need."

I looked at the pen, glistening under the light, but I didn't take it. He put it back in his pocket and stood to leave. "I shouldn't go without hearing a yes in person," he said. "But I'll let you think it over. It would mean moving to Chicago, after all."

The massage table had a hole cut out in the middle where my belly went. My body hadn't relished a full-body mas-sage in more than a year, long before the punishing pretzel act of my pregnancy. My shoulders rounded from the weight of my bosom and my spine arched in resistance to the heavy front load. My hips languished in their support role cradling the baby. My legs were rickety old cranes, cracking with any sudden movement. My feet suffered worst of all, bearing the brunt of my new heft.

Paul's hands worked wonders on my tired, tense mus-cles. My body seemed to come back to me, bit by bit. As Paul massaged, the anxiety of the week, of my life, melted away. My mind was overtired from analyzing all that had been thrown my way. Baby Henry's premature birth. My promotion. Emily's arrival. I packed Emily's bags at two A.M. A strange, irrational part of me thought if her bags were packed nothing could happen to her.

Nearly lulled to sleep from Paul's magic on my swollen feet, I jumped when my cell phone rang. "Those aren't al-lowed in here," Paul said softly. I let it ring. I didn't want to have an answer for anything anyway. Let them figure it out on their own, I thought.

At the end of the session, a woman brought me a turkey sandwich on whole wheat with carrots and a chocolate mineral shake. I'd hoped they would let me stay in that

dark, quiet room forever, safe from the outside and its de-
mands. After Paul washed my hair, and washed away
more tension, my cell phone rang again. Paul "tsk-tsked,"
but I answered it anyway.

"Hi, honey," Jake said on the other end. "I've been trying to reach you all morning."

"I've been in meetings and now Allen is treating me to a
massage and makeover before the shower this afternoon."

"Allen beats me to the punch again. I wanted to invite
you to dinner tonight to celebrate," he said.

Had he heard about my promotion? Did he think I
should accept? "What are we celebrating, Jake?"

"Well, I didn't want to tell you until tonight, but
Maxwell is moving to New York City, so I've been offered
a senior partnership."

That was my Superman husband, leaping from junior to
senior partner in a single bound. In the nine months it
takes to make a baby. "Oh," I said, unenthusiastically.
"That's great, honey. Did you tell them anything?"

"No, you know how the game works. I thought we
could talk it over with a nice juicy steak," he said. He
knew I couldn't say no to a steak. He could talk me into
anything with a prime rib in front of me.

I couldn't tell him where I really wanted to go was
straight to bed, under the thick, warm comforter, where I
could be alone with Emily and away from everything. But
if I did that no one would see my new haircut or the warm
brown tones of eye shadow and soft coral blush and cocoa
lipstick on my face. As long as they couldn't see what was
going on inside that pretty little head of mine we'd be fine.

Forty multicolored seats sat in a semicircle around a glider
rocker for the Queen Poobah. My followers showered me
in a grand feast of fruit and cake and punch and more gifts
than I knew what to do with. Once again, I couldn't help
thinking we might need a bigger house for all of Emily's
things.

The accounting department gave us a deluxe stroller in a

feminine plaid print. Account services gave us a box full of diapers—three jumbo packs of each size, as well as five large packs of baby wipes. My creative department bought us a horse rocker and a handmade blanket with *Emily* stitched in it. Seeing her name on the blanket brought tears to my eyes, knowing that she would soon be swaddled in its warmth.

The Studio Inc. president sent a maple trunk filled with Studio Baby clothes from newborn through six months. I picked up the cotton outfits, which went from small winter clothes to larger summer clothes—four seasons of Emily to come.

Susan's gift was a digital video camera. The card read, "Treasure every moment, Taylor," which I was sure had been signed by her assistant. Allen and Gretchen, very much the couple of the moment, helped me take the gifts home and unpacked them for me. They giggled and kissed and acted like kids in love. I was so happy for them that I couldn't bother them with my problems. Besides, I owed it to Jake to talk with him first.

Just when I thought Jake and I had settled into a quieter future, we'd been thrown a curve ball. And another. The next several days passed in a blur. Besides more money, Jake's senior partnership meant higher-profile cases that could result in more international travel and longer hours at the office, despite having lawyers working for him. He had postponed his decision until the following week so we could think it over.

Jake had stopped socializing so often and working on the weekends. He rationalized he could give more of his work to junior partners or associates. He'd paid his dues, he thought. Some evenings, he brought his work home instead of doing it at his office. I enjoyed the warm glow of his office lamp, his body bent over legal documents, scribbling notes in a ledger. He was more present in my life. But I knew the promotion could change all that.

Jake was thrilled with my offer as well. Jude conceded that although he preferred I be based in Chicago, I could remain in Dallas, where Studio was headquartered anyway, and put together a crack team of creatives at our office. If Jake and I both took our offers, our household income would more than double. The old me with my dream house notebook stuffed with magazine clippings of the perfect bathroom and gourmet kitchen re-entered my mind. The lot we wanted hadn't sold yet. It could be built by summer, just in time for pool parties. We could get the summer condo at the lake, and take mini-vacations there every other weekend with Emily. Monetarily, anything we wished for could be ours.

Jake could get what he'd worked so hard for; I could be at the top of my game, strategizing creative campaigns for the largest companies in the world.

So why wasn't I satisfied?

MONTH NINE

Santa and the Stork

CHAPTER 35

Week 38: *Your baby weighs about 6½ pounds and is close to 21 inches long. This week, she sheds most of the downy coating that protects developing skin. The baby's lungs are now developed, and her body is fully formed and ready for birth.*

In those final weeks, I relished the hustle and bustle of the Christmas season. The more people, the easier I got lost in it. The more parties and merriment, the less time we had to think about the fork in the road and the future for our little family. Jude was pressuring me for a decision.

To take my mind off work, new obsessions filled my days. The curtains in the living room *had* to be replaced. Maybe Lorna was right, after all. The color was too drab for the room—I needed to brighten things up and it had to be done *immediately*. Not to mention the cleaning lady did a horrible job on the bathrooms. I'd just have to clean them myself, hands and knees and all! And Christmas shopping! I'd barely scraped the surface on gifts for our family and friends, and time was running out. I knew it wasn't just Christmas, though. I wanted our entire lives to be figured out before Emily came. Like a puzzle, every piece perfectly in place. Was it such an impossible dream?

Amy offered to be my personal shopper, but I was determined to do it myself, damn the crowds. As for the curtains, a quick trip to Bed and Bath Bonanza, and the perfect curtains caught my eye.

Emily bounced on my cervix with each excruciating step. I checked twice to make sure she hadn't broken through, since it felt as though her head were between my legs. I ignored the pain and pushed on, lured into each store by the fabulous Christmas lights and promises of holiday sales. Waddling from store to store like a mad duck on a mission, I checked off names with each swipe of the credit card. Like a pregnant shopper's heaven, sales associates promptly assisted me, fellow shoppers let me cut in line and chairs appeared out of nowhere for me to rest when needed. My days of special treatment were numbered. Or so I thought.

After a quick lunch of salad and Diet Coke and heartburn, I made it to the west wing of the mall to the Studio Baby display. In the window hung a promotional banner my team had created with a photo of a sleeping newborn and the copy I'd written: BRAND NEW BABY. BRAND NEW DAY.

Staring at the poster, my entire body relaxed, a huge weight lifted off of my shoulders. I had created the brand from scratch. I would fight for the business for *me*, not for Jude or Susan or anyone else. The bloated office and the fat paycheck didn't have the appeal it had just a year before, despite being able to move into my dream house.

No more burning the midnight oil just for the sake of making my work-crazed boss happy. No more weekend meetings just for the sake of looking busy. No more weekly travel. Besides, I wasn't the same Taylor Montgomery who'd entered the fast and frenzied world of advertising. In the last nine months I'd changed more than physically; inside I was a new woman, and she was a far better woman than I'd hoped for. I didn't need to belong to an agency of five hundred people to mean I was important.

Hadn't Studio Baby said just months before that I was the reason they were still with Ace? Why couldn't I? One husband. One baby. One account. One *big* baby account.

What I experienced standing there in the mall, with hundreds of people swishing past as I stared at that poster, was more than an epiphany. It was a high. A dreamer's high. An entrepreneur's high. A mother's high. Accordingly, my new company would be called Brand New Day.

Aunt Barb and Allen helped me put up the Christmas tree that afternoon. Until then I hadn't been in the Christmas spirit, nor had I even believed there was such a thing. The tree was small, as there wasn't much selection so close to Christmas, but it was perfect in my eyes. Plenty of lights and plenty of ornaments. The stained-glass angel I made in fourth grade. The wooden Santa I carved in seventh grade. The ceramic snowman I painted in ninth grade. The silver wedding bell Aunt Barb gave us the year we got married. The ornaments Jake and I had bought as souvenirs from vacations: the bronze Eiffel Tower from Paris, the red soldier from London, and the Hawaiian hula girl from Kauai. After the boxes were empty and the last sparkling red ball was hung, we stood back and admired the tree. I liked it better than the seven-foot trees we usually had each Christmas.

"We'll keep it up after Christmas so Em can see it." I hugged Aunt Barb.

"It reminds me of the Christmas trees you had growing up," she said.

"You forgot an ornament," Allen said, handing me a small pink box. I lifted the lid and inside lay a crystal ornament of a mother cradling her infant.

"I'm going to get weepy," I warned them. "I've been so worked up the last few days."

"Try the last nine months!" Allen said.

"You're nesting, dear," Aunt Barb said. "Perfectly normal."

"Alert the press!" Allen said. "Our Taylor is perfectly normal, after all."

Normal, I wasn't sure. Would a normal person turn down the job offer of a lifetime with a salary beyond her wildest dreams? Would a normal person give up a dream home and the chance for career fame? A normal person might not. But a mother would.

After Aunt Barb left for last-minute Christmas shopping, I told Allen about my new agency—the agency with no business plan, no clients, and only one prospect. A huge Request For Proposal that would require hours of no pay to get it done.

"I'll take it," Allen said, before I even offered him a position.

I bit my bottom lip. It was too much to ask, even of a best friend. To take a leap of faith with me, with no corporate safety net to catch us if we fell. "But there's a good chance they'll promote you to Dallas creative director after I resign."

"You're kidding me, right? I think I'd picket the place if you didn't hire me. There will be a place, right?"

"Eventually. Jake and I talked about some properties, but his ol' gal can't do much looking at this point. You know you'd be suckered into getting the place off the ground while I'm adjusting to mommyhood."

"I'd expect no less from me," he said. "Just let me wait until after the holidays. I'm expecting a damn good Christmas bonus after all the shit we've put up with this year. But I'll still help you get started on the side. Lord knows you've bailed me out when I needed you most."

"As far as salary—"

Allen held up his hand and shook his head. "Good thing I'm moving in with Gretchen—I won't have as many bills."

I hit Allen in the chest. "Get out! This is huge! You couldn't even stand having a roommate in college."

"My roommates never looked like Gretchen."

"Okay, then. Your first assignment as the creative director at Brand New Day is to not let me talk myself out of it.

I called Anne at Studio Baby and she agreed to let our company participate in the RFP."

"Wow. You have just secured your position as the Woman Susan Hates the Most. We'll be going toe-to-toe against Goliath."

"Allen, there's no one I'd rather throw rocks at giants with. I'm building this company on a wing and a prayer."

"You're forgetting talent, experience, creativity, looks . . . I could go on and on."

"Yeah, yeah. Put it in writing in the proposal, would you? And Merry Christmas, Allen. I mean it."

Later that afternoon, I sipped nonalcoholic bubbly and wrapped gifts in front of the fireplace while I waited for Jake to come home from the office. I tried not to think that it might be the last Christmas I could buy such expensive gifts. I'd grown up with much less. I could make do. The fire crackled, and I was at home and in love with my place in it. More importantly, I was at home in my skin. This chick was all right. Who needed more rooms and a swimming pool to mess with? Perry Como sang "Silent Night" and I cheerfully joined in chorus. Jake let me sing the whole song before he cleared his throat.

"You have such a great voice, Tay," he said, giving me a long hug. "I wish you'd sing more often."

"I have to feel like singing to sing," I said. "And today I feel like singing."

Jake handed me a small silver package with a matching silver bow. "It's early, but I'd like you to open it now."

I tore off the ribbon and opened the lid. Inside sat a platinum ring with three stones, the April, June, and December birthstones. "Our family ring," I said, tearing up. "It's beautiful, Jake." He slipped it on my finger. It sparkled against the lights of the Christmas tree.

He noticed the bookshelf behind me, with a row of pictures of my family I had set out earlier that day. He grabbed a frame of my parents and me in front of the tree at our last Christmas together. "You definitely got your mother's good looks," he said. "I wish I could've known them."

"Yeah, me too. They would've really liked you."

"And look at this," Jake said, admiring our Charlie Brown tree. "It's, uh, little, but in a funny kind of way—I like it."

"Your mom will hate it."

"Aw, c'mon, you know it's not the size that matters." Jake sat down and looked over the gifts strewn across the room. "Did you accept the job today?"

I took Jake's hand. "What do you think of the name Brand New Day?"

"I thought we'd decided on Emily," he teased.

"Jake!"

"I think it sounds great. You're gonna do it, huh?"

I loosened Jake's tie, longing to see him in his camel-colored cashmere turtleneck. I wanted to cuddle in front of the fire, to have my belly rubbed.

"I had a pretty interesting lunch myself," Jake said. "Talked to the senior partners. Told them I would only agree to be senior partner if I got only in-state cases. That I'd be working from home some. And not to expect to see me on Sundays, except for the occasional round of golf."

"They give you your walking papers?"

Jake laughed. "They looked as though I'd choked them. But they said they'd seriously consider it. Each partner opened up to what area they're most interested in. Even the old farts seem to be open to a little change in culture."

"Good for you!" I placed a red ribbon on Jake's head. "This is the only package I want for Christmas."

Jake kissed me, the taste of champagne on his lips. I licked my lips. "That stuff tastes better than mine. Have some senior partner bubbly, did we?"

"Little bit," he said. "Little bit."

"More, please." We kissed again and lay down on the metallic wrapping paper and ribbons. We undressed each other, warm from the roaring fire. My self-consciousness had long left me. I had mere days left to share my body with Emily.

After we made love, I slipped on Jake's cashmere sweater and we finished wrapping gifts. Emily moved, contorting my body. "That's not an easy thing to see," Jake said. "Was that an elbow?"

"Or a knee."

We placed the gifts under the tree and carried one for Emily up to her room. I wanted it to be there when we brought her home. It was a frame with three picture slots—the one on the left was Jake's mother holding him in the hospital, the one on the right was my mother holding me just after I was born, and the middle one would hold the first picture of me and my daughter. I placed it on her dresser.

Molly sat in Emily's crib along with a stuffed bear from Aunt Barb and a stuffed bunny from Lorna. I put a ribbon on Molly's red yarn hair. "You won't be the newest or the cutest," I told her. "But you'll be her favorite."

CHAPTER 36

Week 39: Your baby is ready to greet the world. At this point, the average full-term newborn—who is still building a layer of fat to help control body temperature after birth—weighs 7 to 7½ pounds. Your baby's organ systems are developed and in place. The lungs are the last to reach full maturity.

Laughter filled the halls of yet-to-be-renamed Ace Advertising. Somebody else's job, I thought cheerfully. I'd fondly refer to it as Tight Ass Advertising the rest of my days. I cleaned out my fabulously decorated office, my home away from home for six years. I felt worlds apart from my coworkers, who were getting stinking drunk at the Christmas party down the hall. Two years earlier I'd been promoted to vice president/creative director and moved from my smallish cubicle with the other artists and copywriters into my large office. I'd been eager, aggressive, and dedicated to my work and the firm. I could create a winning pitch in a day and a solid campaign in a matter of weeks. It was all that I was and all that I needed. The day my name had been put on the door had marked my greatest accomplishment, setting myself apart, moving up in the ranks of the advertising elite.

I would let the gold advertising medals and the numerous awards remain in the office for my successor to enjoy. I didn't need to take them home to know I was good at what I did. There would be more engraved plaques in my future.

"The party isn't the same without you," Allen said, a glass of wine in one hand and sparkling cider in the other.

"Thank you." I took the glass from him.

"What did Susan say when you told her?" Allen brushed the hair out of my face.

"You know, the usual well wishes: 'I told you so, you'll never make it on your own, I made you what you are.' I had the opportunity to praise her on what a great boss she's been, so I'd say we're even."

"Wish I could've been a fly on the wall. Just wait to see what I have in store for her. Even though this place has been a prison, you get used to the other guards and the inmates, you know? I'll miss my jail cell just a little bit."

"And people think ad execs don't have feelings."

Allen proposed a toast. "To Brand New Day."

"To better living and a better life," I said, and we clinked our glasses.

Allen and the other office musclemen were carrying boxes to my car when the phone rang. I was half-tempted not to answer it. Let someone else wrap up the loose ends. It was hard enough saying good-bye to everyone.

"Taylor speaking."

"I'd give anything for you to change your mind," Jude said on the other end.

"I appreciate that, Jude, but there's nothing you can do."

"How about a Mercedes as a company car? Four weeks of vacation?"

"I recall a certain unnamed advertising executive telling me friends and family were what were really important in life. And you know what? He was right."

"He still means it," Jude said. "Hopefully that guy gets as lucky as you someday."

"Oh, he will."

"Good luck with your new life, Taylor. I just hope you don't take it too hard when you don't get the Studio account."

"It's only business, Jude. Try to remember that in case you lose."

I had never been much for religion after my parents had died, but on Christmas Day, as I knelt in the pew for the first time in twelve years, it felt right. I nestled next to my husband, gazing upon the baby playing the Christ child in the manger, surrounded by Mary and Joseph and the Three Kings. I'd lived my life too long with a heavy heart.

Bringing a life into the world gave *me* renewed life, like breathing the air for the first time in over a decade. I looked at the world as a harmonious balance. For every tornado, there were sunny days. For every wreck, there were safe travels. For every child who died, there were children who prospered.

As the children of the congregation giggled and gathered to sing Christmas carols at the front of the church, I rested my eyes on a little girl with brown ringlets of curls, dressed in a crushed red velvet dress with white stockings and black Mary Janes. Someday that would be Emily up there, singing "Silent Night" as we proudly looked on. Jake made no mention of my change of heart. He only held my hand and shared our last Christmas alone.

Despite Aunt Barb's arguments, I insisted on hosting Christmas dinner. I did let Aunt Barb cook the turkey as I looked on, promising I would make it the next year. I'd never be a gourmet chef, but I'd be able to hold my own with an oven and a good cookbook. Lorna and Frank were skiing, but Jake's former nanny Maria joined us with one of her daughters, one last Christmas gift from me to Jake. Our guests admired Emily's nursery and even our little Christmas tree. The house was filled with warm sweaters cuddling close together and relaxed conversation and enough food to fill our stomachs until the New Year. The house wasn't our private modern love nest anymore. It was a baby-proofed family home to be shared with anyone who loved us. I was no longer afraid to let them in.

As for Jake, his days of strolling through the house buck-naked with the blinds up were officially a thing of the past.

The last hints of Christmas slowly disappeared, the red and green cookies eaten by an eager pregnant woman, the boxes and wrapping paper stuffed in the garbage bins, the thank-you notes stacked high on the dining room table. The world was prepping for the celebration of the New Year while I rested on the leather couch with my feet up and my fingers locked around the remote watching *The Brady Bunch* reruns.

"You coming to bed?" Jake said. "I thought I might crack one of those novels your family got me for Christmas."

I made room for him on the couch. "You're a lawyer, so they falsely assumed you were an intellectual."

"Hey, I read!"

"Law books don't count," I said. "Reading a novel might broaden your horizons."

"Broadening is my new thing," he said. "It's all about horizons." He kissed my bare knee and watched me.

"What?" I said. "Are you noticing my face is the size of a watermelon?"

"No. I'm just thinking that this was the best Christmas we've had. And we didn't even have to go anywhere."

"Imagine that. The Montgomerys as homebodies!"

"It ain't half bad. I kinda like this new family-friendly version of ourselves."

I took his hand and he heaved me to a standing position, and we met for an as-close-as-we-could-get hug. "This segment of the family could use some shut-eye," I said. We headed to our bedroom, passing the little teddy bear nightlight I couldn't resist turning on.

* * *

Sometime later I awoke in the night, as I had every night that month, for a trip to the bathroom. I leaned back on the toilet lid thinking of the dream I'd been having. My mind was fuzzy from sleep, but the images slowly came back to me. A long white hallway, dotted with red benches. My steps echoed as I walked down the hall, my pregnant belly ripe with readiness. A woman sat in the distance, her profile in shadows. As I approached her, she looked up at me and smiled. Mother. My breath suspended.

Her curly brown hair fell around her shoulders. Her bright blue eyes glistened as she spoke. "I've been waiting for this day," she said, lifting her hand to take mine. She squeezed my hand and her warmth spread through my body. "Every mother longs for the day she can watch her child share the mother love and pass it on."

"When did you get here?" I asked her, my voice small and shaking.

She placed her hand on my belly. "I've always been here. Always will be here."

The dream ended, but I was still leaking. "Honey," I said softly, then louder. "Honey!"

Jake stumbled into the bathroom in the pitch black, stubbing his toe. "Shit!" he said. "What, babe? Something wrong?"

I clicked on the bathroom light. "I just saw my mother. In my dream. And I'm still peeing. Only it's not pee. I'm no expert, but I think my water just broke."

Jake smiled a sleepy smile and scratched his head. "Great. I'll get the bags."

I used an ultra maxi pad and dressed in cotton sweats and caught a glimpse of myself in the mirror in the bathroom. I stood erect and admired my reflection, my swollen belly, stretched to the limit and full of baby, and I rubbed it adoringly. That would be the last day we would share this body. I wanted to stay as connected to her as I was at that moment.

Emily moved and more pressure shot to my cervix as another contraction sent me doubled over with another gush of amniotic fluid. Maybe it was time to get her out, after all. I awkwardly finished dressing, stuffing my swollen feet into my mother's red Keds and met Jake in the kitchen, where he had loaded himself down with the digital camera, diaper bag, my suitcase, and lastly, a granola bar.

"Stay right there. I'll put these in the car and be right back to get you," he said, rushing for the door. He opened the garage door, then turned back around. "God, you look beautiful."

Another contraction hit, feeling like someone took a handful of my skin and twisted and pulled it as hard as they could. Jake quickly returned and took a Polaroid picture of me, squinting and breathing through the pain. Beautiful—yeah, right.

The ten-minute ride to the hospital seemed to take forever. Contractions were three minutes apart. I could feel Emily moving down with each surge. I practiced my hypnobirthing, surrounding myself with a blue cloud as my anesthetic. I inhaled to twenty counts and exhaled slowly, the oxygen waking up my tired brain.

"Hurry, babe!" I clutched the door with one hand and Jake's thigh with the other, then remembered not to clench my muscles.

"That's good, baby!" Jake said.

It was then that I saw Jake for the man he had become in our six years of marriage, the man that he had become in the last nine months. My pregnancy had happened to Jake as much as it had happened to me. Just as I had, he went through the stages of denial, acceptance, confusion, and fear. And together we would experience the joy, the heartache, the bliss of parenthood. All along, I'd been fighting my desire for Jake to remain the man I had married and to mature into a loving father for our child at the same time. Our marriage was different because our lives were changing every minute, but it was stronger than it had been before.

Inside the hospital, Jake and I walked quickly to the elevator and took it to the third floor, where the birth center was located. At five A.M., the place was quiet, with only the shuffle of nurses and the buzz of machines in the air. A middle-aged nurse greeted us with a smile. I doubled over with a contraction.

"Looks like she's ready to go," the nurse chirped. I looked at her name badge. Mary, the name of my mother. Yes, she was with me.

"Your names, please?"

"Jacob and Taylor Montgomery," he told her, squeezing my hand as I breathed through gritted teeth.

"Right this way." Mary straightened me up and helped me to my room.

So this is it, I thought. *The room where my girl will enter the world.* The birthing suite was large and open, the bed topped with crisp white sheets and a taupe blanket, a floral recliner and couch against the wall. The faux wood floors glistened. Spacious, clean, homey.

Mary handed me my standard-issue gray gown and instructed me to change into it and get into bed. She promised she'd return to check for dilation. "How's the pain? Would you like some pain medication?"

I shook my head, my confidence building. "Pain isn't such a terrible thing." I hobbled to the bathroom to get changed before the next contraction hit. "I've worked through my share of pain. I'm sure I can handle this, too."

"No pain, no gain," Jake said.

"You don't get a say in this," I shouted at him through the bathroom door.

"I'm her acupressurist," Jake informed Mary. "Less important than the fact I'm the papa, apparently."

I emerged from the bathroom looking like an ashen hot-air balloon. Jake looked at me, his gaze soft and steady. "You're beautiful."

"Oh, hush," I told him, climbing onto the mechanical bed, but I appreciated his effort. I reached behind me to dim the lights. Relaxing jazz filled the room. Photos of my parents and Jake and me on our wedding day sat on the bedside table. Molly sat perched between the photos, ready for me to share any last-minute secrets. I wanted to give Molly a happy moment, to be able to tell Emily that Molly was there at her birth. I waited anxiously for the next contraction to start.

"We could try some of those kung fu exercises we learned in birthing class," Jake offered.

"You're not karate chopping me, Jake. Not yet." I sat back on the bed, my eyes closed, listening to the jazz, and waited and waited. Several minutes had passed and nothing. I lifted the gown to look at my belly. With each contraction and rush of amniotic fluid, my belly deflated. *I'll miss this*, I thought sadly.

"I'm here at your beck and call." Jake sat in the recliner next to the bed wearing a baseball cap, ready for the final game. "This is comfy."

"So glad *you're* comfortable, babe." I tried to adjust the bed into a semi-sitting position.

"Here, let me." Jake messed with the buttons, moving my legs upward and my back downwards.

"No! No!" I slapped his hand. "Let me do it. You boys just love fiddling with gadgets."

No position was comfortable since I constantly felt I was wetting myself. I finally shoved what amounted to a large diaper between my legs and clicked on the TV. "And don't even think about watching sports today," I said to Jake. My emotions were wild, like a radio picking up several signals at once. I was excited, anxious, sentimental, happy, agitated, elated—a mother's mixing bowl of drama.

Jake saluted me, zipped his lip, and picked up a *Sports Illustrated* he had brought.

Strong signal: agitation. "What did you bring for *me* to read?"

"Um . . . here's an *Entertainment Weekly*." He pulled it out of the bag and handed it to me.

Signal: excited. "I'm not in the mood to look at the beautiful people. I'm not going to tell Emily I was reading the fashion pages before she was delivered." I flopped the magazine onto the table. "Where's Aunt Barb? We should've picked her up. And the nurse?"

Mary appeared through the door carrying a clipboard with lots of paper on it. "Ooh, I love jazz. Doing better, Taylor?"

"Haven't had another contraction." The music began to irritate me. I didn't even like jazz.

"The hospital has a funny way of stopping women's labor." She handed Jake the clipboard. "Just a few papers I need you to fill out."

"Let's see where you are," Mary said, spreading my knees.

"Oh, God." Jake sprung up from the recliner as if it were aflame.

"You won't see anything," Mary assured him.

"Don't freak out on me now, Jake! This is nothing compared to what's to come."

Mary checked my cervix. "You're at a good three. But the baby's breech."

Signal: panic. "Breech! As in feet first? What do we do?"

"We usually have good success with turning the baby. A Caesarian would only be a last resort."

My body began to tense. I told myself to relax. *Last resort*, she said. *We can do this, Emily. You and I working together.* As if Emily understood my plea for progress, another contraction came on hard. I slammed a pillow to my face and screamed into it. Not something I had practiced in hypnobirthing. I silently scolded myself. Note to self: Screaming is the opposite of relaxing.

"Let's do our breathing exercises with her, Daddy," Mary told Jake.

Jake had always been competitive with me, but he couldn't come close to beating me at sleep breathing. The contractions became steadier, every five minutes apart. With my sturdy little black comb in place in my palm, we practiced a different acupressure point with each contraction—my shoulders, my lower back, my hips, and finally my feet. "That's it," I said as the contraction waned. "I'll take the foot/comb combo," I told Jake.

He peered over my belly from his seat at the foot of my bed, my feet still in his hands. "You want some fries with that?"

"Don't tempt me. I'll take a rain check on some cheese fries with ranch dressing."

Mary laughed and leaned over me on the bed; I was sure it was my mother I saw in her eyes, heard through her voice. "Look how far you've come," she said. "What a brave girl you are."

Dr. Creighton bounced into the room, too chipper for so early in the morning. "I hear you've got a stubborn girl on your hands."

I sighed. "First this, next pink hair and a pierced tongue."

Dr. Creighton worked my stomach like a baker kneading dough. He identified the baby parts, which wasn't hard with the loss of amniotic fluid. "She's sideways," he said with a grin. "You sure about no meds? Things are going to start heating up."

I opened my palm to show him my comb. "Magic comb. It's the latest technological rage. All plastic with ferocious teeth. Seems to be working."

"You're quite a woman, Taylor," the handsome doctor said. "If it goes well I'd like you to write about it in my next newsletter. Lots of women inquire about natural deliveries. You could be an inspiration."

Me? An inspiration? The woman who was afraid to hold a baby just nine months earlier? Well, now I couldn't let him or the other mommies down. Within minutes he had Emily facedown, and after another few contractions, she entered the birth canal.

For a change of pace, I eased out of the bed, the bulge of padding squishing between my legs. I made it three steps to the rocker, hoping I could rock through the contractions, still five minutes apart.

Jake pulled the cords at the window. The blinds swished open to reveal the sun peaking over the horizon, illuminating the snow.

"Hope the roads aren't icy today," I said. "I want people to come meet Emily."

"They'll come. Nothing can keep them away."

Stalled at the intersection of the Moment, in between contractions, Jake produced a labor massage ball Jennifer had loaned me. "Shall we mix it up a bit?"

"What do we have to lose?"

While he rolled the ball on my back, another contraction began, a slow burning from my back to the front of my stomach, as if my midsection had caught fire. I was sure the heat would melt that damn ball. Jake breathed with me, but the pain seemed to close my ears, and the only thing I could hear was my own heartbeat and the gush of oxygen into my mouth. I went to the ocean in my mind, standing on the beach with Jake, Emily in my arms. The waves came toward us, big beautiful white waves that swelled then crashed at our feet. Water came up past our ankles. The sand swirled at my feet, tickling them. Emily laughed and held her arm out toward the water as it receded back into the blue ocean.

I opened my eyes. "It worked!"

"This little ball?"

"No, not the ball! My ocean imagery. It worked. I didn't feel anything. Go back to my feet for the next one."

"Aye-aye, Captain."

I found my center: Molly sitting on the dresser across the room, her one eye steadily holding my gaze, her near smile forging me on. I remembered when I was six, just after my mother had let me take Molly down from her perch in my mother's closet. We couldn't afford a baby stroller like my friends at school had, so my dad got the TV box he'd been saving in case it went out before the warranty expired; the box I was told never to touch. On one flap he cut out the middle so I had handles. I pushed Molly around in her super deluxe Zenith TV box stroller for months. Molly had smiled at me as we slid across the carpet of our three-bedroom house, zig-zagged across the vinyl kitchen floor, her red yarn hair flapping against the box. Life with me had been quite a ride. I steadied my breathing. Anything was possible, including the life I wanted most for my family.

"Let's kick it up a notch." Jake grabbed a CD from the case I'd brought. It was Conway Twitty, my dad's favorite. I mentioned it to Jake in passing, on a walk the month before, and he bought it. I hadn't heard the songs in more than twenty years. "Care to two-step? We've got four minutes until your next contraction."

We two-stepped in large circles around the room, the three of us twirling together. Listening to the classic country music made me think of summer nights on the back patio, watching Dad and my mother dance under the stars. If the stars were aligned just right—my dad being home, my mother letting down her guard—I caught moments of intimacy.

Jake dipped me as the guitar strummed the final notes. With my head upside down, I saw Aunt Barb enter the room, made-up as if she were going to church, perfumed, hair-sprayed, and polished. "I see labor's no big whoop for the two of you," she sang, carrying cinnamon rolls I was forbidden to eat until after the delivery. I could smell the cinnamon across the room. Cruel, dear aunt.

"The contractions are stronger, but I'm getting used to it."

"Apparently so! If Jake needs a break, I can take over." She put her hands on her round hips. "I've been practicing acupressure on your uncle. Think I've got him hooked now." After assisting me back to bed, she wet a rag with ice cold water and slapped it on my forehead.

"Is my head sending smoke signals? Next, I'll ask you to cover me with snow like a kid on the beach. Might numb things a little," I said, thinking the idea may not be so ludicrous.

"Such a modern woman having babies like we used to! I never let the docs put me out. You know Grandma Bertha helped my mama birth her babies, right in our little house."

"The house that blew away?"

"That's right. And I was by your mama's side when you were born. So it's a legacy for us to stick together through this journey."

"I saw Mom. This morning when my water broke. She was waiting outside the delivery room. She spoke to me." I started choking up. "I hadn't heard her voice for so long."

Aunt Barb smoothed back my wet hair. "You know your mother couldn't miss out on such a special delivery."

"What was it like? When I was born?"

"Your mama thought it'd never end. Twenty-four hours she labored," Aunt Barb said. "We lived a block away from each other. She called me around midnight to tell me she was having contractions, so I hurried over. We walked and walked for hours it seemed. We almost burnt a hole in the carpet from all our pacing. Finally, around six in the morning, her water broke. By this time we were so tired we couldn't see straight. Your father slept through it and the alarm woke him at six, just in time to go to the hospital. She said, 'Barbie, if they say I can't have this baby now, you tell 'em to go to hell.' I'll never forget the look on your mama's face when they put you in her arms. Pure joy."

Tears streamed down my face.

CHAPTER 37

With my trio of helpers, the labor progressed with hand
squeezing, heavy breathing, and country crooning. More
Dixie Chicks. More Toby Keith. More Johnny Cash. I'd
heard that staying in an upright position could speed
things along, so we walked the halls of the maternity floor.
We paused long enough for me to see one new baby that
had recently joined the world, getting cleaned for his de-
but, before I doubled over in pain with another contraction. Even standing, I went back to the ocean, picking up
seashells with Emily, her little hand splashing in the water.
Waves coming in, receding.

When my contraction ended, I blinked back to the present. My friends stood in the waiting area watching me
with pained expressions. Amy, holding a sleeping Dylan,
shook her head. "You're insane," she said and then
switched to a cheerleader voice. "But you can do it!"

Jennifer, who from then on I'd refer to as my hypno-
buddy, gave me a thumbs up sign. "Blue cloud," I told her,
"with intermittent gusts of yellow." Allen stood biting his
nails, leaning on Gretchen for support. "Very ghetto," he

said, referring to my magic comb stuck in the top of my head. He was as nervous about the delivery as I was. I raised my hand as I passed them, like a boxer going up the ramp to get back into the ring. I imagined they chanted, "Taylor! Taylor! Taylor!" only I wanted a cooler name, so I switched it to "Meinhard," a German name, which meant strong and brave. I couldn't have done it without them. Or just maybe I could have. I was a whole lot stronger than I'd ever dreamed.

"You look possessed when you make that face, honey," Jake said after my contraction disappeared back into the ocean.

Aunt Barb explained. "See, she *is* possessed, Jake. She's possessed with bringing this baby into the universe, and it hurts like hell."

"It's actually fine," I told them as we reentered my birthing suite. That mind over matter stuff really worked as long as I kept convincing myself.

"I'll shut my mouth," he said, turning white. "I just don't feel so well, either."

"You're going to hyperventilate if you keep holding your breath every time she has a contraction, Jake," Aunt Barb told him.

"If you faint, I'll kill you," I said. "Is that possessed enough?"

Four hours into the labor I looked like I'd run a 10K marathon or gone ten rounds in the ring, but so far I was winning. I refused to be the victim, to give up control. Aunt Barb assured me there were no horns growing from my head. My lips were chapped from all the breathing, and I sucked ice chips to keep hydrated.

It was nearing eleven A.M. when Lorna, wearing a loud, expensive purple pantsuit, followed by Frank, made it to the hospital fresh off the slopes. "We haven't missed anything have we?" Lorna asked, air-kissing my aunt, then bending over to give me the same. I was too tired to laugh at her inane question.

"You look wonderful," she said to me, nearly touching

my sopping wet head of hair, then thinking better of it. Hugging Jake, she asked, "How are you holding up, son?"

As was typical, Jake got all the attention, even in my labor. "Good, Mom. Taylor's been super," he said through clenched teeth.

I playfully hit him in the arm. "At least I haven't kicked you out."

"Well, when I had—" Lorna started.

"That wasn't an invitation for you to go blabbing about your labor with Jake," Frank said. "We've all heard it a hundred times."

I thanked him with a smile.

"Can we buy you lunch, Jacob?" Lorna asked.

Jake turned to me. "Do you think you'll have her during the lunch hour?"

"Where's my Magic Eight-Ball when I need it?" I dug my fingernails into Jake's hand, grabbed my comb from my hair with the other, and placed it in my left palm.

"Time to leave," Mary said to my in-laws.

"Oh, dear," Lorna said. "Can't you give her a shot or something?"

"Out!" Jake said, and we battled stinging whips up and down the length of my body.

When I wasn't in the throes of a mind-boggling contraction, I stared at the baby monitor and listened to Emily's heartbeat. *Shoo. Shoo. Shoo. Shoo.* Beating quickly, rhythmically. I sucked an orange popsicle, and then a purple one.

My mind was cluttered with emotions as I grabbed Emily's journal for a final pre-birth entry, with shaky hands. What could I say in three minutes?

December 28th

Dearest Emily,
 I write to you from the bed on which you will be born. Okay, it's not as romantic as being born at home like my mom was, or underwater or in a taxi, but it's your one and

*only delivery, so it's special to me. Within the next hour,
I'll meet you for the first time. I can't wait to touch your
round cheeks, feel your skin, and kiss your little mouth.
I'm not sure I can be any more in love with you than I am
right now, but I'm told it'll grow each day. How can it
not? You'll reveal yourself to me bit by bit as time goes by.
I want to lay my eyes on you, the perfect mix of your father and me—our love in flesh form. I never thought I'd be
ready for this day, but here it is, and I am! My ears yearn
for your first cry. My body yearns for your warmth, skin
against skin, free from my womb yet connected by love. I
already miss you inside of me, your bulges and hiccups
and fullness. We can never be together like this again, but
I'll never forget it. Oh, God. CONTRACTION!*

MOM

As I slammed the journal shut and grabbed the sheets to
brace myself for the contraction, the afternoon sky filled the
room with its light. The contractions were harder, tighter. I
could no longer just close my eyes; I had to squeeze them
shut and concentrate more on my breathing. The ocean imagery stopped working. I began to see myself falling down
into the ocean from the pain, so I tried Jennifer's hang-
gliding idea, which seemed to work because the labor made
me extremely hot and the cool air flying off the Colorado
mountain was refreshing. I took in the scent of pine trees
and bubbling brooks and fresh flowers.

When I came out of it, I realized there were fresh flowers
in the room, though I hadn't heard the volunteer bring
them in. "You had a smile on your face," Jake said. "Can I
go there with you, too?"

I laid my hand on my belly, which was smaller due to
the loss of the amniotic fluid, and lower because Emily was
facedown, far into her journey. The flesh of my belly
had loosened, and I jiggled it and moved my hand over
what I thought to be Emily's rump. The door flung open
again—Mary, to check on me. If she didn't tell me it

was time, I was going to have my first serious talk with Emily.

"Mmm-hmm. It's time," she said, looking up at me with a grin.

My heart quickened. "Good answer!"

Jake looked up from his post next to my head. "Time! As in *that* time?"

"Yep. You're at a ten. Time to start pushing. I'll ready the room."

Within minutes, the room went from a cozy bedroom to a medical station. Mary pulled a white cloth off a metal table that held shiny equipment and utensils. A bright white light above my head beamed down on me like a spotlight on a stage. The baby cart was wheeled against the wall, ready for Emily. The nurse was calm and quick, moving effortlessly around the room, and then she concentrated on me. My legs were hoisted into stirrups. She instructed Jake to hold my right leg back when I pushed. Aunt Barb was assigned my left leg. Dr. Creighton arrived and confidently sat down in front of my spread legs.

"Where the hell have you been?" I teased. "The nurses and I did all the work!"

"That's the general idea," he said. "Let's do this, Taylor."

Mary concentrated on watching for contractions on the monitor, as if I couldn't feel them coming on like a roaring train coming down the track. "Now!" Mary said.

An incredible sensation of a cement block against my backbone, bearing down on my rectum took me by surprise. That was a baby? How was that ever going to get out?

Dr. Creighton instructed, "Raise up, Taylor, take a deep breath, head down, hold your breath, and push through your bottom."

Taking in a large breath, I put my chin to my neck, held my knees, and pushed with all my might, replacing what felt like a cement block with the imagery of Emily as I pushed her in a heavy cradle across the room. My face tightened from the exertion. My legs shook. Within me, I felt movement as Emily descended, and the pain turned into a raging fire in my loins that spread all over my body. I felt like I was inside the fire, and Aunt Barb handed me a cold, wet towel, which I used to cover my face. My body seemed to take over. The pushing began on its own. Emily was on her own timetable now. Strange grunting noises like the chants of an Aborigine tribe came from my lips. I'd lost control.

"I can't stop it!" I told them. Jennifer had warned me it felt as if you had to go to the bathroom and wouldn't make it in time. It's a BBM—Baby Bowel Movement. Baby moving over your bowels. Thankfully, I didn't let the feeling scare me, and I knew it was her head, her little body, ready to come out and say hello.

"That's okay, Taylor. Just keep pushing. Go with it," Dr. Creighton said. My drill sergeant Mary took charge again. "Push, push, push, push, push!" she sang, but I felt like Emily was doing all of the work, that my body had taken over my mind. The pressure was so intense I wondered if I was birthing quadruplets, all of them trying to escape at once.

I sucked in a breath and held it, pushed down using every muscle in my body for strength, and drove Emily further down into the birthing canal. With each round of contractions, Jake squeezed my hand and supported my neck. My head seemed to weigh a thousand pounds, my trunk at least a ton. After each push, Jake brushed my moist cheek with a kiss. "Good, honey," he said, over and over. "Thata girl," my aunt chimed.

"I see some baby hair," Dr. Creighton beamed over the sheet.

Exhausted, elated. Almost there. Almost here.

Mary patted my thigh. Another contraction and I pushed, grunting hard, "Nnnnnnnnn!" I imagined Emily leaving my body.

"Head's out. Hello there, Emily!" Dr. Creighton said as

he suctioned out her nose and mouth. "Want to see, Mama?"

I leaned up, peered over the sheet and saw her little head, the wet blackness of her hair, the red pouty mouth, and the tightly closed eyes, unsure of the light. Jake gazed at her and a whimper escaped his lips. I shared the same rush of surprise, of newness, of experiencing something so awesome and pure.

"Let's get her out, Taylor," the doctor said.

One last time, with eagerness, I pushed and felt Emily release from my body. She cried, her voice a trumpet announcing her arrival. She took deep breaths and filled her lungs with air. Her mouth quivered, her arms and legs thrashed—I imagined she was cold in her bright new surroundings. I observed her, a strange new being, but familiar. I ached for her. *My baby. My Emily.* Dr. Creighton wrapped her in a blanket and handed her to me. I touched her face to mine, the soft skin I had imagined, but it was more real, and she smelled of life, of blood. Her tiny tongue licked my face and her cries stopped.

"Hello, Emily. It's Mommy. It's Mommy." And her little dark eyes looked into mine and locked, and she knew. *I was her mother.* I kissed her softness over and over, not caring about the white film that still covered her face.

Jake kissed her, too, calling her, "My beauty. My beauty."

Aunt Barb cried heartily. "Thank you, Lord," she exclaimed. "She is *perfect!*" In turn, she kissed my forehead, then Emily's, then Jake's. Sniffling, she grabbed the video camera and captured our new family in a state of euphoria and discovery.

Jake cut the umbilical cord with two small snips and she was free from me. She was her own person, helpless in a new way. A small moan escaped me when they took her from my arms to clean her. Jake took the video camera and documented it. I couldn't take my eyes off her. I watched as they put the protective saline in her eyes and washed away the fluid she had lived in for nine months. They pricked her and she cried again. I called out to console her. "Mommy's right here, Emily. You're okay, sweetie." The voice that came from my throat was unfamiliar, gentle. It was soothing and real and maternal.

Emily calmed at the sound of my voice and her eyes darted around the room. Jake touched her tiny hand with his finger and she grasped it. "Nice grip, Em," he said.

"Seven pounds, nine ounces," Mary said, turning towards me. "Good size. And twenty-one inches!" She picked up the baby book and stamped Emily's footprints into the memory book. "Ready to breast-feed, Mom?"

A million butterflies had taken flight in my stomach. *Is this real? Did I do this? Is that baby really mine?*

Swaddled tightly, Emily was fresh and clean. I welcomed her back into my arms. I loosened her blanket and laid her warm body against mine in the position I'd learned in class. My breast was the same size as her little head. I laughed at the oddity of it. My nipple was not erect, but Emily opened her mouth and eagerly latched on. "Wow! She's like a little Hoover," I said.

Aunt Barb leaned in to get a better look. "Her jaw's moving correctly. I can't believe she got it right the first time!"

I marveled at Mother Nature, that my body knew what to do all along. I pressed my cheek against Emily's and heard the clicking sound that told me she was getting colostrum. Aunt Barb left the room to brag about Emily's achievement while Jake sat in the chair next to me, his arms resting over the railing, one hand on my head, the other on Emily's bare back. "I don't know why I ever doubted this," he said.

"I'm still scared," I said. "But it's the best scared I've ever been."

"We're a little family now," he said. "You were incredible. She's more than I ever imagined."

"She's got your ears." I pointed to the slight upturn of the lobe.

"That's right," he said, touching her ear. "And your toes." Her second toes were longer than the rest.

When I finished feeding her on both sides, Jake carried her out into the hall to meet her fans. Cheers rang out. I was drunk with joy at their reception. At the same time, a part of me wanted her back inside her warm cocoon where I could protect her. I put my hand on my empty abdomen, disoriented at our separation. We were no longer one.

A parade of visitors, friends, coworkers, and family streamed through all afternoon. They brought more gifts, more flowers, and cameras. I smiled and posed with Emily and cherished the brief moments I was alone with her before the next well-wishers arrived. I fed her every three hours and held her as she slept. I'd been in labor ten hours, but I was happy rather than exhausted. I watched Emily's jerky movements, her eyes open and close, the rise of her chest as she breathed. Every single moment was the most exhilarating thing I'd ever seen.

Amy brought a casserole, chocolate chip cookies, and more baby clothes for Aunt Barb to take to the house. "Welcome to Mommyville!" she said. "She's gorgeous." She cradled Emily in her arms. "It makes me ready for number three!"

"Goodness, girl. Hand me those rolls. I *am* starved. I feel like I haven't eaten in weeks." I grabbed one and tore it in half.

Allen and Gretchen visited later, carrying a plaid sack. "For when you're up in the middle of the night."

"You shouldn't have." I unpacked the contents: a bag of white cheddar popcorn, M&Ms and a DVD of *Rosemary's Baby*. "You *really* shouldn't have."

"What? It's the only baby movie I could find on such short notice. Besides, it's a *classic!*" Allen rubbed Emily's feathery hair. "See. No six-six-six."

"It's the thought that counts. How's life in the fast lane?"

"Hunky-dory. Translated, that means Susan's not back from vacation yet, so I plan on ditching work as much as possible until my official resignation on January second." Emily started to cry. Allen put his pinky finger in her mouth, which she immediately sucked.

"Allen! I have no idea where that finger has been."

Allen removed his finger. Emily's lip quivered and she began crying again. He held her out to me. "Dinner time? I get the hint. So *that's* what God made boobs for."

Jennifer and Jackie arrived next with their husbands and kids in tow. Jackie was already in maternity pants. "My body has no trouble remembering how to stretch," she said, rubbing at her slight pudge.

We toasted the mommies and drank sparkling apple cider until it was time to sleep. Or, for the rest of the world to sleep.

As for me, and probably hundreds of other mothers in the universe, I was up in the middle of the night with my baby. At two A.M. And four. And six. And eight. I slipped in and out of consciousness, but I wouldn't call it sleeping. My new nurse asked if she could take the baby to the nursery, but I wouldn't have it. I wanted to be by her side even if it meant I wasn't going to sleep the first day of her life. Jake offered to sleep on the pull-out couch, but I wanted one of us to be rested.

The most basic tasks turned into gargantuan feats. Sitting, walking, and yes, even going to the bathroom. My first potty break was a nightmare, quickly reminding me of the physical trauma my body had endured. I vaguely remembered Amy mentioning all the blood. She had told me I'd forget the pain, that mommy memory kicks in to erase negative memories of pregnancy and childbirth. Otherwise, we'd all have only one child.

To help quell the deep throbbing, I took prescription-strength Tylenol. I hobbled. I leaned on my hip with the support of a pillow. But when I gazed at Emily, every throb of pain was worth it. I would do it again just to have her here in my arms, in my life. Mommy memory was powerful medicine, indeed.

Jake and I held Emily as if we'd graduated magna cum laude in cradling. To be safe, we kept her wrapped up, so her little arms and legs and wobbly head were secure. I was no expert, but when I watched her watching me I couldn't help thinking she wasn't disappointed. That she knew what she was doing when she picked us to be her parents.

Chapter 38

The next day I woke up a mother. My first thought was not of food or water or the day ahead. It was my daughter— her food, her comfort, her every breath. As soon as my eyes shot open, I searched for her and found her sleeping peacefully on Jake's chest. "I've got to get a picture of that."

"She's an angel, isn't she?" Jake had showered and shaved at home. He was a handsome daddy. I had to give him that.

"Can you believe you're a father?"

"No. But I like it so far," he said. Emily made the cutest noises in her sleep. Jake took them to mean she liked him.

"Just wait 'til she's thirteen. I was a terror at that age."

"Well, she'll have a little brother or sister to pick on."

I raised an eyebrow. "She will, huh? My aching body heard you say that. Talk to me in a few years."

Before we knew it, our visitors had all come and gone and it was time to leave the hospital. The pediatrician signed Emily's release papers with a perfect bill of health. "She's got a hint of orneriness in her eyes, but that's about it," the doc said with a wink. "I'll see you in two weeks for a checkup. By then she should be back up to her birth weight."

When he left, I began to panic with thoughts only shared by a new mother. "What if my milk doesn't come in and she gets hungry? Or gets nipple confusion? Or doesn't get enough to eat?" I peered around the room, filled with flowers and pink bears and balloons. *Couldn't I stay just a little while longer?* I didn't want to leave the red button on the side of my bed that beckoned help at a moment's notice. The experts right outside the door. The twenty-four-hour supervision. The mommy helpers and body healers. *Could I do this alone?*

Then I looked at my center again, Molly, waiting to be packed up. I knew a little fear was normal, but I had it under control. I wouldn't be alone. We had our family now and I had Jake. Deep inside me, I sensed not only would I be a good mother; I would be a great one.

"Nurse Montgomery at your service, madam," Jake said. "You know Aunt Barb will be by every day to check on you. You're stuck with me for a whole week. I promise not to watch ESPN—much. I can *even* heat the oven for all those casseroles."

"We're going to be just fine." I nuzzled Emily's nose with mine. "Let's go home."

A homemade WELCOME HOME banner hung on the kitchen cabinets when we arrived at our house. Plates of food lined the counters. Jake carried Emily in her car seat, which was still much too big for her, despite the newborn headrest.

"This is your home," I whispered to her. I removed her from the car seat restraints and gave her a tour of the house, for which she kindly stayed awake. When I reached her nursery, Jake videotaped us entering the room. We introduced her to all of her things. I placed her in her crib, which seemed to swallow her. It had looked so small when we bought it. Would she really grow out of it someday? I wound her mobile. "It's a Small World" played, and within a minute, she was asleep in her new bed.

Jake and I bent over the crib to watch her. "I want to stay and listen to her breathe," I said.

"You can do that. Or you can get some much-needed sleep," Jake offered.

"Sleep is for wussies."

The phone started ringing. "Probably Mom wanting to know if we're settled in," Jake said. "And to schedule her first visit."

"Let's not answer it," I said. "Let's pretend the world is just us for a little while."

"Fine by me," Jake said. "What do you say Nurse Montgomery prepares one of the meals that mysteriously arrived from the natives, and we'll feast like kings?"

Emily stretched her little arms, her hands reaching just over the top of her tiny head. She squirmed and squealed before her face contorted into a cry.

"Hungry, baby girl?" I picked her up and snatched the Boppy pillow and swung it around my middle with one hand. Rocking together in the glider Jake had selected, I positioned her on one end of the nursing pillow. She rested against my chest while I unfastened the nursing bra with my other hand. Not the sexiest bra I'd ever owned, but definitely the most functional. My multitasking skills came in handy. I laid her down and her neck arched, her mouth open, searching for her meal. She latched on and my body tingled, my uterus contracted, and the prolactin kicked in, making me warm and sleepy. The last notes of the song played out as we rocked, drifting together into sleep.

Such was my new life, days drifting by, me not caring of the time or the world outside our walls. I was willingly living in a shell, a cocoon almost, my baby and I and the loving father and husband, who made sure I was nourished and rested enough to nourish and care for our baby. On the third morning my milk turned my breasts into stone monuments. They became so engorged I had to use the electric pump to alleviate the pain and express enough milk so Emily could latch on. I had enough to feed an entire village. On the fifth day the pain subsided and Emily drank enough to handle my supply.

New Year's Eve had usually meant lavish parties, drinking too much and dancing barefoot into the wee hours of the morning. It had been about getting dressed up and making love at three A.M. in a dark hotel room. But with our newborn, New Year's Eve was a private celebration, just the three of us, with shiny party hats and sparkling cider Jake had picked up at the drug store. Jake grilled steaks in the freezing cold and baked potatoes and tossed a salad. We ate crouched on the living room floor, our plates on the coffee table, bathed in candlelight. Emily lay sleeping in her bouncy seat, unaware that the year she was born had passed and a new one had arrived.

When Jake and I kissed at midnight, we kissed away the year we had survived together, which at one point I wasn't sure could happen. We kissed to our maturity, as individuals, surely, but moreover as partners. We celebrated life's changes and our ability to make room for them. Forgiving past grievances, moving on to better tomorrows.

On New Year's Day, Jake proposed we go for a drive to get some fresh air. The trees sparkled with melting icicles in the sunshine. We drove to a renovated business district with old brick warehouses that had been converted into business lofts. Jake pulled in front of a red-brick building with freshly painted windowsills. He turned off the engine.

"Why are we stopping?" I said, peering back at Emily sleeping.

"Come on. I want to show you something." He gently lifted Emily out of the car and pulled out a set of keys from his pocket, leading me toward the building. He opened the doors to a large interior with lots of open space, a cool winding metal staircase, and floor-to-ceiling windows on one wall.

Jake's voice echoed as he spoke. "Happy New Year, honey. If you like it, it's yours."

I surveyed my surroundings, putting together the space

in my head. My space. A large conference table in one corner, open workspace for employees in the middle, a creative brainstorming area to the left where circular couches and modern chairs could be occupied by real, live, paying clients. I raced up the stairs with Jake not far behind. Just the right size for a private workspace, big enough for a small table and chairs, a large desk, and chaise lounge to rest on with Emily. "With a little paint and some elbow grease I could have the coolest shop in town." I spun around, my excitement turned to worry. "How far from the house?"

"About fifteen minutes."

I calculated in my head. "So thirty minutes a day for travel time plus an eight-hour workday, times five days a week comes to forty-five hours a week away from Emily." I slapped my forehead. "God, that's too much. Even if it would've been sixty-plus at Tight A—you know."

Jake swung Emily gently at his side in her car seat. "I know you've been worried about being too far away from Emily. I have something to show you."

Back downstairs, Jake led me through the rear of the building to a large snow-covered backyard, a patio with a built-in grill, and plenty of room for a playground. Enough to appease the big kid Allen and the little munchkin. A stone path connected the building to a little white house with blue shudders, like the one from my dream. A quaint guesthouse. "What in the world?"

"The last owners built this house to be close to the business, and Amy had a heyday with it." Jake opened the door to reveal a cozy, fully-furnished living area and kitchen painted in calm pastels. Photos of our family lined one row of a bookcase and the rest was filled with children's books. I began to cry. Jake led me to the bedroom, converted into a playroom, where all of the things we didn't have room for in Emily's nursery had been neatly organized: a changing table, crib, and glider. Scenes from *Mary Poppins* adorned the walls. Mary floating from the sky with her umbrella. The carousel race. The dance on the chimney tops. And, of course, real kites hanging from the ceiling.

Jake looked at his watch. "Travel time approximately thirty seconds."

"I got Mary Poppins after all," I cried.

Emily opened her eyes and looked up at the brightly colored walls. I reached out and touched the soft downiness of her cheek. "Do you like it, baby girl?" I asked. I wrapped my arms around Jake. "It's perfect. Maybe I can pull this thing off after all."

"Are you kidding? Never get in the way of a mommy with a mission."

He was right. Mothering may be the hardest job in the world, but sheer determination and loads of love would see me through.

Jake pointed to the corner, to the tiny black camera lens on the shelf next to Winnie the Pooh. "Still got the Web cam, though. I can't let you have all the fun."

Jake seemed so proud of himself, so sure of our new place together.

We left Emily's private bungalow, marveling that every day would be Take My Daughter to Work Day. I looked back at the loft, where I could still express my creativity and have a rewarding career. It wouldn't be easy. But it wouldn't be half as much fun if it were.

Work was still two months away, in a future far away from my existence on Planet Baby, where my life was completely wrapped up in the tiny blessing that seemed so alien nine months before. For the first time I truly felt important, not self-important as I did at work, but important— no, *essential*—to someone else. Emily needed me for survival, and her helplessness made me love her in ways I never dreamed. I *wanted* to be needed for the first time in my life, and to give of myself was liberating. I was a mother in bloom. Bathing Emily, feeding her, singing, rocking. My triumphs were Emily's. A hearty burp, the day her umbilical cord fell off, holding up her head for several seconds at a time. The minor catastrophes— volcano poop that hit the door and walls, spraying breast milk, discovering the grime that lived in her chubby neck rolls. And the absurdness of parenthood—the lack of sleep, lack of showers, lack of non-baby conversation. And for Jake, the lack of sex. I did pleasure him one night about one A.M., but nodded off halfway into the act.

As Valentine's Day neared with its professions of love and goofy cards and warm sentiments, I relished a new kind of love. My mother and father had made me a handmade Valentine every year growing up. *Baby Love*, I wrote on the front of the folded pink heart made of construction paper. Inside the heart I placed a black and white photo of us, me placing a kiss on her cheek as she stared into the camera. I placed the card in her memory box alongside the pregnancy diary filled with my reservations and revelations. Now she'll know, I thought.

And with that I opened the pink leather journal where I wrote about new beginnings and our journey together. I went back and read my New Year's Resolutions with the subtitle:

Things I Will Most Likely Do As A Mother

1. *Make you wear your coat outside when you don't want to.*
2. *Cry at the drop of a hat at all your firsts—first crawl, first walk, first day of kindergarten, first time I see you with a baby of your own.*
3. *Worry that you will hate me, but stand my ground that I will know what's best for you.*
4. *Start lectures with, "When I was your age."*
5. *Stick my nose in your business. Even when you're fifty years old.*
6. *Not let you wear the cool but revealing clothes your friends wear.*
7. *Embarrass you to no end.*

I grabbed my pen and added: *Love you so much it hurts*.

"But the good kind," I told Emily, her eyes drooping in a near-sleep. I picked her up and carried her to my bedroom, exhausted. My mind raced with what the future would bring. I had a brand new life and a brand new attitude. I knew without a doubt that I would make it. As a wife, as a business owner, and most of all, as a mother.

With the moon big and bright in our window, Em and I nestled together in the flannel sheets of the king-size bed. She lay beside me, tucked in to my chest, her arms curled in, her head against my breast, her tiny feet pressed against my stomach. She suckled as I drifted into sleep. Just weeks before she had been inside of me, kicking me the same way. But on the outside, I could smell the scent of baby shampoo in her hair and feel her hot breaths. She had introduced me to a part of myself I didn't know existed. And I liked the new me.

Goodnight, sweet angel.

Q&A with Malena Lott

Q. *So the big question—have you been pregnant and did you draw on your own experiences to write this book?*

A. Yes, I've had three pregnancies and three healthy children, thank goodness. So I've spent five years of my life either pregnant or breast-feeding! All three of my pregnancies were very different. I was a little sicker with my boys (born first and third), but I was also seven years older for my third, so I think that (and keeping up with two children) may have had something to do with my extra fatigue. Although writers are supposed to be able to imagine anything, I don't believe I could've written this book had I not gone through the experience of pregnancy—highs and lows—myself. The first pregnancy is always special because it is truly a journey into the unknown and the first time you get to experience the miracle of childbirth. My food cravings when I was pregnant with my boys were all beef and salt (and I'm a former vegetarian), and with my daughter I craved sweet and sour. Couldn't drink enough cherry limeades when I was pregnant with her! I also drew on the pregnancies of my girlfriends. One of my friends had a lot longer bed rest than what Taylor goes through in the book.

Q. How much of the novel is autobiographical? What do you have in common with Taylor?

A. Fortunately for me, my husband and I have always had a close relationship and can talk about anything, even the tough stuff. I hit the jackpot when it comes to mates.

My first and third pregnancies were surprises, but we took the news better than my characters did. The funny thing is, when I got pregnant with my third, Owen, I thought, "now I know what Taylor felt like." Just as she wasn't sure she knew how to be a mother, I was concerned about mothering three kids. (So far so good.)

I based Taylor's grief over losing her parents on my own experience dealing with the death of my grandmother, who raised me. I was nineteen and cried myself to sleep at college nearly every night for months. Mother's Day is still a tough holiday for me.

Taylor and I also share an advertising career in common. As far as her proclivity for partying, Taylor has me beat hands down. I've always preferred a good book and movies to nights out on the town. But I can make a mean Ruby martini!

Q. This is your first novel. Why did you decide to write about pregnancy and the journey to motherhood?

A. My journey in getting this book from conception to delivery involved each of my children, while they were in utero! That alone speaks to the power babies have before they take their first breath. I conceived (pun intended) the idea while reading nonfiction pregnancy books when I was pregnant with Harrison, when I was 24 years old. I completed the outline during those nine months, and kept a diary to give to him someday. Then

I wrote the first draft when I was pregnant with Audrey two and a half years later, and polished the novel just after the birth of Owen. So the gestation of this novel was more than eight years! They say write about your passions and I am very passionate about motherhood. I love to write about relationships and growth, and pregnancy is a beautiful transformation story. Becoming a mother is a huge change physically, mentally and emotionally. Most people think about the physical pregnancy first, but for me, getting my head into the right place to become a mother was the bigger deal. And the flood of emotions and how all of your relationships change when you get pregnant and have a child is unlike anything else.

Q. *You touch on a lot of heavy issues for mothers in the book— career, child care, and the expectations women have about motherhood. How did you deal with those issues?*

A. Ah, yes. Supermom to the rescue, right? I was very concerned that I would not be a good enough mother. I had never been especially drawn to children, and the thought that another person's life depended on me for survival scared the heck out of me. I think each of those issues are very personal ones that each mother has to make for herself—not that she won't get a dozen opinions from others on both sides of the fence. I have tremendous respect for mothers. It is absolutely the hardest job in the world. I think judging mothers or trying to make women feel bad for having a career isn't fair. I remember when I was pregnant with my son—I had just been out of college for two years, mind you— and I wanted to continue to work after maternity leave. A colleague of mine (a male, go figure) asked me what my plans were for working. After I told him I had found a home day care for my son, he went on and on, self-righteous tone intact, about how his wife had an MBA, but she gave up her career for raising their son, and it made me want to cry on the spot. Later, my boss (also a male) pulled me aside and told me the guy was a jerk and not to listen to him; that his wife had worked after they had their son and to not worry about what other people think. I vowed I would never judge another woman for her decision. The choice is extremely difficult, but it is as individual as the pregnancy itself. My husband quit his job after the birth of our second child to work from home and care for our children. I made a higher salary and he genuinely wanted to do it. It was the best decision we ever made, even if it meant drastically cutting our household income.

Q. Taylor has a successful career in advertising. Why did you pick that profession for her?

A. When I wrote the book I worked in corporate marketing, but I had always dealt with ad agencies and thought that would be an interesting career. Having Taylor get a baby-oriented account when she is fearful of babies provided nice conflict. As a creative director, she was used to tapping into people's emotions to create campaigns, but she was closed off emotionally from herself and the ones she loved. She was forced to open up to create real intimacy with her husband and her baby. I ended up starting an ad agency of my own by the time I was working on my third draft, so I used my knowledge of the industry to bring her profession to life in the book.

Q. Do you believe the role of men as fathers has changed?

A. For the better! My father-in-law—not one to dole out compliments—recently told my husband that he was the best father he's ever seen. My generation (Gen Xers) is the first to have the expectation that the father will also share in changing diapers, feeding and watching the child, no questions asked. It will be incredible to see the bond fathers and children have as these children grow up. My husband spends more time with the children than I do because he stays home with them, which makes me jealous at times, but I know that I cannot do it all. I see a lot of women wanting to make their husbands think they don't know what they are doing when it comes to caring for children, which is sad. If given the chance, fathers can be very nurturing.

Q. *What in your view is the biggest misconception about pregnancy?*

A. I believe the biggest misconception is that it should be a rosy experience from start to finish, because moms-to-be are often disappointed that things don't go the way the fantasy has played out in their head. Unexpected pregnancy can really turn women's lives upside down. So many women tell me that they were in denial through most of their pregnancy because they weren't ready to accept the change. On the flip side, I think many expectant moms have an irrational fear that something terrible will go wrong even though there is only a small chance that miscarriage or a condition will occur. Access to the Internet means we can read about even the most bizarre cases and think that can happen to us. The misconception that women cannot handle the pain of childbirth is unfortunate, too. Expectant moms should be supported and educated instead of frightened about the delivery process.

Q. *Taylor chooses hypnobirthing to deliver her baby—what did you choose?*

A. Like most women, I was afraid of labor pains and was encouraged to get an epidural, so I didn't labor naturally for very long the first time around. Panic makes the pain worse, but no one had told me that. With my second labor, I had a terrible time with the epidural because the doctor couldn't get the needle in the right place. (After five painful tries, he did.) My back ended up looking like a pincushion. I was so afraid I couldn't have the baby without medication, because I had assumed I would get it. But with an epidural, you just sit around all day until the doctor says push, which can seem like heaven to some women, but it left me feeling disappointed. So the third time, I studied up and practiced hypnobirthing and I had a wonderful, natural delivery and felt great afterwards. The saying that women can do anything they put their minds to applies to bringing a child into the world, too.

Q. *What was your favorite part of pregnancy?*

A. The first time I felt my babies move is high on the list. It's that reality check that there really is a little person in there! Then actually seeing the baby move later in pregnancy is great entertainment. My favorite times were lying down in the bath and watching the baby roll from side to side. The delivery and first time I locked eyes with my children have to be the most magical experiences. I felt like my heart would explode.

READING GROUP
  DISCUSSION
  QUESTIONS

1. Taylor is shocked with the news that she is pregnant and waits a long time to tell anyone, even her husband. What does Taylor's experience tell us about surprise pregnancies? Is it fair to expect a woman to immediately bond with her unborn child? Should Taylor have told Jake sooner about her pregnancy? Why do women fear that people will treat them differently when they announce their pregnancy?

2. The issue of fear is dealt with throughout the book. Taylor is fearful about the pregnancy itself, her changing relationship with her husband, and whether or not she will be a good mother. Are expectant mothers' fears about pregnancy founded? How might women deal with the fear that something will go wrong? How does body image effect pregnancy? Is it society or mothers

who place such high expectations on motherhood and measuring up?

3. Pregnancy forces Taylor to grow up and to have an emotionally intimate relationship with her husband for the first time. How can a man be a part of a woman's pregnancy and journey to motherhood? Why do some men stray when their wives are pregnant? How can a couple reconnect and use pregnancy to get closer?

4. Being pregnant causes Taylor's grief over the death of her parents to resurface. Is it okay to be disappointed in our parents? Why do we idealize the role of parenthood? What can we learn from our own upbringing to become better parents ourselves?

5. Aunt Barb moves to Dallas to be closer to Taylor. How important is having a support network for women when they are pregnant? Can mothers' advice from past generations still resonate with young mothers today? The bridge girls also change during Taylor's pregnancy. How does the role of friendship change when one friend becomes a mother? Can relationships be maintained when each friend is at a different place in her life?

6. Taylor slowly brings out keepsakes from her life with her parents, including the rag doll Molly, photographs, and eventually her mother's shoes. Does keeping possessions of a lost loved one help us cope with death? Taylor dreams about the generations of women before her, and finally her mother speaks to her in her dream. Can people still have a relationship with a loved one after they have passed on? What can pregnancy dreams tell one about her state of mind?

7. Taylor goes on a roller coaster ride of emotions about the decision whether or not to work after she has Emily.

Have the expectations for women to stay home with their children changed in today's society? How can a woman deal with the guilt of working, whether she has chosen to do so or must work as a financial necessity? Her boss Susan is not supportive of her pregnancy and does not allow her to create a day care at the agency; are women who are not mothers generally supportive of working mothers? Do working mothers get unfair advantages that childless women at work don't get—such as getting to take off for appointments and missing work to take care of sick children and attend their children's functions?

8. Even though Taylor develops names as a part of her job, she and Jake take a long time to decide on the best name for their child. Does a name shape the future potential or personality of the child? Why do celebrities typically choose unusual names? Is naming a child after a parent or relative a good thing to do?

9. Taylor struggles to find a Mary Poppins-like figure to take care of Emily should she decide to continue working. With the high turnover of child care centers, are day cares equipped to provide the best care for babies and young children? Are mother's expectations too low or too high in finding a caregiver? Jake tells Taylor he wishes his mother had taken a more active role in his childhood instead of sharing much of it with his nanny. Is there a proper balance in the role of parents and the care giver? Is choosing a relative, such as a grandmother, to become the primary care giver a good idea? What conflicts could arise from that situation?

10. While Christmas shopping, Taylor decides to start her own small ad agency. Is it realistic for her to make such a big decision when she is so close to delivery and her emotions are so high? Can a mother balance owning a business and raising a family? Should she

have taken the chief creative officer job instead? Is having a nanny in the guest house behind her agency the best choice for her? Is it selfish for a mother to want to maintain a professional identity and personal interests outside of motherhood? Does a mother ever truly know if she is making the best decisions for herself and her family?

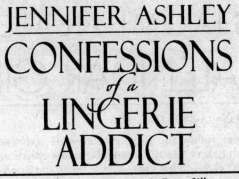

JENNIFER ASHLEY
CONFESSIONS
of a
LINGERIE
ADDICT

The fixation began on New Year's Day: Silky, expensive slips from New York and Italy. Camisoles and thongs from Beverly Hills. Before, Brenda Scott would have blushed to be caught dead in them. Now, she's ditched the shy and mousy persona that got her dumped by her rich and perfect fiancé, and she is sexy. Underneath her sensible clothes, Brenda is the woman she wants to be.

After all, why can't she be wild and crazy? Nick, the sexy stranger she met on New Year's, already seems to think she is. Of course, he didn't know the old Brenda. How long before Nick strips it all away and finds the truth beneath? And would that be a bad thing?

NAOMI NEALE
CALENDAR GIRL

Name: Nan Cloutier

Address: Follow the gang graffiti until you reach the decrepit bakery. See the rooms above that even a squatter wouldn't claim? That's my little Manhattan paradise.

Education: (Totally useless) Liberal Arts degree from an Ivy League university.

Employment History: Cheer Facilitator for Seasonal Staffers Inc. Responsible for spreading merriment and not throttling fellow employees or shoppers, as appropriate.

Career Goal: Is there a career track that will maybe, just maybe, help me attract the attention of the department store heir of my dreams?

No way. That's a full-time job in itself!

- -

reward *yourself* treat *yourself*

It's like getting **6 FREE ISSUES**

LOVE

EMOTION

INSPIRATION & HOPE

ROMANCE

PASSION

A MOMENT ON THE LIPS

PHYLLIS BOURNE WILLIAMS

Grant Price wants old classmate Melody Mason to work for his family's Boston investment company. Melody has retired from big business and is hiding. It is Grant's assignment to lure her back to the fast life. But when he arrives at her door, she doesn't look like the woman he remembers....

Melody has hidden herself away in rural Tennessee for a reason: she desperately needed a life change. So she has no intention of returning to a fast-paced lifestyle. Instead, she makes Grant an offer: stay, relax and find out what life is like without a hectic pace. Unfortunately, real life calls and Grant must return to Boston. Can Grant and Melody agree on what a good life truly means?
